THE WAR WITHIN

Visit us at www.boldstrokesbooks.com

By the Author

In Medias Res

Rum Spring

Lucky Loser

Month of Sundays

Murphy's Law

The War Within

THE WAR WITHIN

by

Yolanda Wallace

2014

THE WAR WITHIN
© 2014 By Yolanda Wallace. All Rights Reserved.

ISBN 13: 978-1-62639-074-4

This Trade Paperback Original Is Published By
Bold Strokes Books, Inc.
P.O. Box 249
Valley Falls, NY 12185

First Edition: July 2014

CREDITS
Editor: Cindy Cresap
Production Design: Susan Ramundo
Cover Design By Sheri (graphicartist2020@hotmail.com)

Acknowledgments

Most novels begin with a germ of an idea. This one actually began with a walk on the beach.

Jekyll Island offers miles of dog-friendly beaches that my partner, Dita, and I haunt each summer because our boxer, Joey, adores the water. During one of our visits, I turned to Dita and said, "Wouldn't it be great to set a novel here?"

I had already heard feedback from several readers who felt there was a decided lack of romance novels featuring older characters and I had heard from others who expressed a desire to see more tales of women in uniform. As the waves crashed around our feet (and paws), I began brainstorming a way to tackle both requests. Thus the idea for *The War Within* was born.

This novel might be the most challenging one I have ever written. Probably because it is my most ambitious. Four main characters, a timeline that spans more than forty-seven years, and love formed—or, in some cases, destroyed—by the crucible of war. What was I thinking? It wasn't an easy feat to pull off, but thanks to guidance from my editor, Cindy Cresap, and encouragement from Dita, I think I managed to make the pieces fit. The result is my most personally rewarding novel to date. I hope you like it, too.

My thanks, as always, to Rad and the rest of the BSB team for taking a chance on my initial submission and pushing me to dig a little deeper each time I put pen to paper.

Thank you, also, to the readers who continue to take the journey with me, not knowing where it might lead.

And, last but not least, thank you, Dita. I've said it before and I'll say it again: I wouldn't be here without you.

Dedication

To those who served. Thank you for your sacrifice.

PROLOGUE

Meredith Moser wasn't expecting the call. She and her granddaughter, Jordan, had spent every summer together since Jordan was four. Sixteen years of road trips, rental houses, bug bites, and sunburns. This was the year Meredith thought the streak would come to an end. This was the year Jordan would choose to spend the summer hanging out with her friends instead of being cooped up with her boring grandmother for three months. All the signs were there.

In addition to turning twenty-one, Jordan had recently finished her tumultuous junior year at Cal-Berkeley, where she seemed to be majoring in activism instead of marketing. Or were they one and the same? Either way, Jordan had chalked up so many arrests protesting one cause or another she would probably have a great deal of explaining to do the next time she sat down for a job interview. Meredith admired Jordan's passion, even if it sometimes felt misplaced.

When the call came, Meredith was glad she had been proven wrong. This was not the year her warm relationship with Jordan began to cool. This was not the year the little girl she had watched grow up became the woman who couldn't find room for her in her busy life. This was not the year her own life was turned upside down. Again.

"Hey, Gran," Jordan said. "Where are we heading this year?"

Meredith smiled as she held the phone to her ear. "You tell me. You've always been the one in charge of selecting the location. My only job is getting us there."

"Don't forget footing the bill. That's the most important part. Hold on. Let me find a map. Dad's got one around here somewhere, but it's so old Columbus probably drew it. Thank God for GPS, right?"

"A tool invented to give men yet another excuse not to stop and ask for directions."

Jordan laughed uproariously the way she had even before her pigtails had given way to a purple-streaked shag. Meredith heard her rummaging through drawers. She could picture the scene. Jordan, with the phone clamped between her shoulder and cheek, a line of concentration creasing her brow as she focused on the task that had captured her attention. Her earnest expression never changed whether she was building a sand castle when she was five or marching against the war in Iraq when she was eighteen. Now that the military had pulled out of the battle-scarred country, what would become Jordan's next *cause célèbre*? Meredith suspected she was looking for much more than a place to spend the next three months.

"Got it," Jordan said at last. Meredith heard paper rustle as Jordan unfolded the map. "Okay, here we go."

Each year, Jordan would spread a map of the United States, close her eyes, and point. Meredith would drive them from Wisconsin to whatever city Jordan's finger landed on. Jordan's selections had resulted in a lifetime of memories. Over the years, they had spent time cruising along Route 66, fishing for crawdads in Louisiana, swimming with dolphins in Hawaii, riding horses on a working ranch in Montana, and running from a hurricane bearing down on the Florida Panhandle.

"Where's your magic finger taking us this year?"

"Jekyll Island, Georgia. Do you know where that is?"

Meredith slowly drew in air through her nose as if to relieve the discomfort of a stitch in her side, but the pain she felt emanated from the center of her chest. "Yeah, I know."

She had resigned herself to one fate long ago. Now she had an opportunity to take a second chance on a future she had once thought impossible. With Jekyll Island as the end point for this year's trip, the journey would be more important than the destination.

Sandwiched between ritzier destinations in Hilton Head, South Carolina, and Amelia Island, Florida, Jekyll was almost an afterthought. It had been years since Meredith had been introduced to the tiny resort town on Georgia's coast. Yet she thought about it every day. A tranquil island she had never seen and a woman she thought she would never see again.

"Jekyll Island. How long a drive is that from here?"

Jordan's voice pulled Meredith out of the past, but only temporarily.

"About twenty hours."

"Let me drive. I bet I can make it there in half that time."

"I appreciate your enthusiasm, honey, but when we do arrive, I want to do it in one piece."

Meredith stared out at the pond in the backyard of her Racine, Wisconsin, home as she tried to stop her mind from wandering to a ravaged hotel room in the swirling cauldron of war-torn Vietnam. A decision she had made in that room had shaped the rest of her life. The decision had cost her dearly yet enriched her in so many other ways. Would she soon see the effect her choice had had on the woman she had left behind?

"See you soon, Gran."

"Yeah," Meredith said absently. "I'm looking forward to it."

PART ONE

THE JOURNEY

CHAPTER ONE

Jordan Gonzalez settled into a booth in the Wildcat Diner in Paducah, Kentucky, and reached for a menu. Her friends in Berkeley would be mortified by most of the dishes listed on the laminated paper, but half the fun of a road trip was gorging on food you'd never eat at home. The fare served at this greasy spoon definitely qualified.

"Good morning, ladies," the waitress said as she filled Grandma Meredith's heavy ceramic cup. The woman's drawl was as thick as the sludge that was supposed to be coffee.

Jordan took a pass on imbibing the viscous liquid, but Grandma Meredith happily acquiesced. Grandma Meredith could probably use the caffeine. She had tossed and turned all night in their cramped room in a hotel just off the interstate. This morning, she hadn't risen promptly at five to do an hour of yoga like she usually did. Instead, she had lounged around until a respectable but unheard of for her seven thirty. Then she had hit the shower while Jordan tried to find an outfit that wouldn't prove too upsetting for the denizens of Middle America.

Jordan knew better than to ask Grandma Meredith what was bothering her, though. Grandma Meredith was ex-military. When she felt like she was being interrogated, the only information she divulged was her name, rank, and serial number. Better to wait for her to open up on her own than to try to drag anything out of her. Jordan had three months to solve the mystery. No need to go chasing after red herrings on the second day.

The waitress—the name tag pinned to her ample bosom read Debbie—placed the steaming coffee carafe on a corner of the Formica-topped table and hovered a gnawed-on ballpoint pen over the order pad in her hands. Her bottle blond hair displayed a good three inches of dark brown roots. She had the raspy voice of a chain-smoking fifty-year-old, but Jordan was willing to bet she wasn't a day over twenty-five. She was cute in a backwoods kind of way. She looked a little like Cameron Diaz doing Method preparation for a movie role. "Do you know what you want, or do you need some more time to look over the menu?"

"Give us a few minutes, please, dear," Grandma Meredith said.

"Sure thing."

Jordan watched Debbie walk away in a swish of Day-Glo polyester.

Grandma Meredith chuckled as she peered at the selections on the laminated menu. "Brittany might have something to say about how you're looking at our waitress."

Jordan started at the mention of her girlfriend. If that's what she still was. The way they'd left off, it was hard to tell.

"Just because I'm not looking to buy anything doesn't mean I can't do a little window shopping."

"Brittany might see things differently. What's she doing this summer?"

"She and a friend were planning to drive up to Seattle to join the latest round of protests."

"I'm surprised you didn't go with her."

"I wasn't invited."

"Oh." Grandma Meredith looked as surprised as Jordan had felt when Brittany had announced her plans and Jordan realized they didn't include her. "When was the last time you talked to her?"

"The day I left California. I've left her a couple messages since then, but she hasn't called me back."

"She will."

"We'll see."

College was so much harder than she'd thought it would be. In high school, she had been the smartest student in all her classes. In

Berkeley, she was closer to the middle of the pack than the front. She wasn't used to being average. In her native Kenosha, her ever-changing appearance was considered borderline shocking. In Berkeley, her chameleonic look was par for the course. She didn't feel completely at ease in either city. Perhaps she could find a home in a third. If only for a little while. Three months in a new locale and a healthy dose of Grandma Meredith's tough love. Yeah. That was exactly what she needed to help her find her footing.

"Have you made up your minds?" Debbie asked when she returned to the table.

"I'll have an egg white omelet, two slices of wheat toast, a side of turkey bacon, and a glass of orange juice, please," Grandma Meredith said as she poured sugar in her coffee. The good stuff, not a lame blue-packeted substitute.

Jordan envied her metabolism. Grandma Meredith was pushing seventy, but she had the body, the energy, and the vitality of a woman thirty years younger. She should. She was on the go so much it was like she was still in the Army. When Jordan got to be her age, she hoped to have half her get-up-and-go and a fourth of her independence.

"What about you?" Debbie asked. "What'll you have?"

Jordan took another look at the menu. Lunch was hours away, but she wasn't in the mood for breakfast food. "Is it too early for a Hot Brown?"

The Hot Brown was an open-faced turkey sandwich covered in cheese sauce, topped with bacon, and broiled or baked to crispy perfection. Regional delicacy or a heart attack on a plate? Hard to tell. Either way, it looked too good to pass up.

"It's never too early for a Hot Brown." Debbie cast a hard glance at Jordan's T-shirt, which featured the iconic Change poster created for Barack Obama's first presidential campaign. "And it's not too late to change your politics."

Jordan's pulse began to race. Few things got her juices flowing like a good old-fashioned debate even if, as she suspected was the case here, she might be engaging in a battle of wits with an unarmed combatant.

"The last time I looked, my side won. If you seriously examine the alternatives, I think you'll find them sorely lacking in—"

Grandma Meredith cleared her throat. One eyebrow inched toward her close-cropped silver hair. On someone Jordan's age, Grandma Meredith's haircut would be considered gamine. On her, it was just cool. Heeding her warning look, Jordan changed course.

"I'll have a Hot Brown, a side of home fries, and a bottle of mineral water. And I like my politics just fine the way they are, thanks."

"Whatever." Debbie recorded her order, snatched the menu out of her hand, and walked away in a huff.

"Is it something I said?"

"It usually is," Grandma Meredith said with an indulgent smile. "You fought for the rights of the oppressed to express themselves without fear of reprisal. Why do you seem so surprised whenever I use mine?"

"You're forgetting I wasn't on the front lines. I patched up the unfortunate few who were." Based on the expression on her face, Grandma Meredith obviously wanted to say something else. She toyed with her napkin as she organized her thoughts. "It seems to me you could be a bit more discerning about choosing your battles. The wars you wage are either lost causes or moot points."

A rejoinder immediately came to mind, but Jordan didn't verbalize it. She had nothing to gain from comparing the figurative wars she fought to the literal one Grandma Meredith had contested. Nothing to gain and a whole lot to lose. Beginning with Grandma Meredith's hard-won respect.

She looked at her phone, hoping one of her friends had sent her a cheeky text or a funny e-mail she could share to ease the unexpected tension. No dice. Just another blog about the government stalemate in Washington and yet another picture of a same-sex military couple who were using the dissolution of Don't Ask, Don't Tell as an excuse to engage in some very active PDA while in uniform.

With no escape route, she tried to find common ground.

"I made a few phone calls before we left Wisconsin. I have three job interviews lined up for the day after we hit the island. If one of them pans out, I'll have a chance to earn some cash this summer so I can stop mooching off Mom and Dad every few months."

Last year, she'd worked as a lifeguard in San Diego. The year before that, she'd been a waitress in Seattle. That was after serving as a cage cleaner in a vet's office in Austin. Hands down, her least favorite job ever. This year, she'd learn to scoop ice cream, bag groceries, or man a tollbooth. Her final option was working as an unpaid intern for the weekly local newsletter handed out gratis to each visitor to the island. Given a choice, she'd rather ditch the paying gig in favor of on-the-job experience, but she wanted to feel like she was pulling her weight for once. Grandma Meredith always insisted she hold on to the money she made each summer, but why should she force her to pay all the bills if she didn't have to? Every little bit counted, right?

"What are you going to do this summer, Gran?"

While Jordan toiled at a temporary, usually low-paying gig each year, Grandma Meredith volunteered her services to any charity or non-profit that needed an extra set of hands.

"I haven't decided yet." Grandma Meredith sipped her coffee, a pensive look on her face. "This year, I think I'll play it by ear."

"That's new. You normally plan every day of your trip from start to finish. Sometimes every minute." Before Jordan could ask what had prompted the change, she noticed a man with thinning salt-and-pepper hair staring at their table. She leaned forward and lowered her voice to a conspiratorial whisper. "Don't look now, but the late-in-life Lothario across the room is looking at you like he's dying of thirst and you're the last drink of water for miles."

Grandma Meredith didn't bother to give the guy a first look, let alone a second. "I'm sure he'll find an oasis somewhere."

When the food arrived, Jordan took a picture of her sandwich with her phone and uploaded the photo to two of her favorite social media sites. "Papa George died when I was nine," she said, giving the molten cheese sauce time to cool so she wouldn't burn the roof of her mouth the first time she took a bite. "Twelve years is a long time to be alone. Don't you want to meet someone else?"

Grandma Meredith smeared honey on her toast. She looked outwardly calm, but something in her eyes hinted at inner turmoil. "I think we're all entitled to one great love, two if we're lucky. I've already met my quota."

Jordan's memories of Papa George were growing fuzzy but remained fond. She remembered how he used to dote on her and how he would spend hours making her laugh. She remembered him reading her bedtime stories and tucking her in at night. She remembered him making up funny songs while she, he, and Grandma Meredith skipped stones on the pond in their backyard. She remembered a man admired by all who knew him.

"Papa George is a pretty tough act to follow, and anyone you brought home to meet the family would have to earn my seal of approval before he'd be allowed to spend time with you." Jordan winked to let Grandma Meredith know she was only seventy-five percent serious. Okay, maybe eighty. "Take a chance. Put yourself out there. If you meet someone, great. If you don't, at least you had some fun along the way. That's always been my motto. Why don't you borrow it for a while?"

She took a breath as she tried to gauge Grandma Meredith's reaction to her words. Grandma Meredith's blank expression didn't give away what was going on behind her eyes. Jordan took an uncertain step forward.

"Papa George wouldn't want you to be alone."

"I'm not alone," Grandma Meredith said firmly. "I have bridge club, garden club, afternoons at the Y, and my volunteer work."

To Jordan's ears, those things sounded more like entries on a to-do list than the ingredients for a happy, well-rounded life. Something—a very big thing—was missing.

"I'm sure your volunteer work is fulfilling, but don't you want to be fulfilled in a way that's a lot more fun?"

She waggled her eyebrows to make sure Grandma Meredith got the joke. She could be so dense about sex Jordan often wondered if her mother was a product of Immaculate Conception.

Grandma Meredith demurely reached for her orange juice. "If you were younger, I'd wash your mouth out with soap."

"Why? You're the one who taught me to say whatever was on my mind."

"Correct me if I'm wrong, but I also taught you the value of running your thoughts through a filter before you give voice to them."

"That takes too long. Better to beg forgiveness than ask permission, I always say."

"Before or after the cops slap the cuffs on you?"

"Yeah, yeah." Grandma Meredith always gave her grief about her confrontations with those in power, but Jordan could tell she was proud of her for being willing to take a stand on issues others chose to avoid. "Before he died, I'd be willing to bet Papa George gave you permission to move on. Why don't you take it? I know he was the love of your life, but—"

Grandma Meredith's expression grew stern.

"Your grandfather was a good man and the best friend I've ever had, but he wasn't the love of my life."

Jordan couldn't believe what she had just heard. Her grandparents had the strongest marriage she had ever seen. When they were together, they were like school kids holding hands on the playground. Deliriously in love and with eyes only for each other. Had she misjudged what she had seen? "What do you mean? You two seemed so happy. Are you saying that wasn't the case?"

"We were happy. We had your mother and then we had you. I wouldn't trade the life we had for anything."

"But you didn't love him."

"That's where you're wrong. I loved him more than words can say."

Jordan picked up her fork and toyed with her food. Suddenly, she didn't feel like eating. She struggled to wrap her head around the idea that, as much as Grandma Meredith seemed to love Papa George, she might have loved someone else even more. "This is crazy." She dropped her fork in her plate with a clatter that made the people at the next table turn around to see what was the matter. "Does Mom know?"

Grandma Meredith shook her head decisively. "Your mother has always been eager to accept everything and everyone at face value. You never do. That's why I always knew you'd be the one who'd ask all the questions no one else has ever dared."

Grandma Meredith reached across the table and held her hand. Her touch was gentle yet firm. Grounding her, yet giving her wings to fly.

"Who is he?"

Grandma Meredith frowned in apparent confusion. "Who?"

"This guy you were so crazy about who wasn't Papa George. Do I know him?"

Grandma Meredith pulled away. "I don't want to talk about this anymore. I've already said too much as it is."

"Oh, come on, Gran. You give me an intriguing opening to a story, but you don't tell me the rest of it? You can't leave me hanging like that."

Grandma Meredith's eyes flashed. "This isn't a story. This isn't a mystery to unravel. This is my life we're talking about."

"I know," Jordan said gently. "I didn't mean to come off sounding flippant. I'm just...surprised." She placed a hand over Grandma Meredith's, reestablishing their connection. "But I want to understand. I really do."

"In that case, I'll ride shotgun. You drive." Grandma Meredith finished her coffee and placed twenty-five dollars on the table to cover the cost of the bill and the waitress's tip. Then she tossed Jordan the keys to her Escalade. "Because I've got a story to tell."

CHAPTER TWO

August 1, 1967
Saigon

First Lieutenant Meredith Chase climbed out of the belly of the transport plane and stepped onto the tarmac. The oppressive heat hit her like a slap to the face. She felt like she'd stuck her head in an oven that had been preheated to four hundred degrees. Only her whole body was broiling, not just her face. Sweat poured down her cheeks and slid down the back of her neck. What wasn't absorbed by her clothes pooled in the small of her back. She could feel semi-circles of dampness forming in the armpits of her Army-issue fatigues.

She tossed her heavy canvas rucksack over her shoulder, adjusted the angle of her helmet with the palm of her hand, and followed the other nurses as they headed toward a utilitarian gray metal building where their commanding officer and a small support team were waiting to process their paperwork.

As the parade of newcomers swept past them, male soldiers whistled and hooted to herald their arrival. Meredith's cheeks burned with embarrassment after one of them pulled his head out of the engine of the jeep he was tinkering on, looked her up and down, and said with a broad grin, "Welcome to BC, beautiful. I'd love to play doctor with you any time."

His fatigues were identical to hers, from the olive shirt and pants to the black combat boots. While she was neatly tucked and pressed, his rumpled shirt was unbuttoned, revealing a white undershirt that was practically transparent from perspiration. A thick pelt of curly hair covered his chest. A few damp tendrils peeked out of his grease-stained collar.

A thought entered her head with the certainty of fact.

That's the man I'm going to marry.

The mechanic could have been her twin. He was tall and blond with bright blue eyes and a dimpled smile. He looked like a college football hero accustomed to hearing a crowd's cheers on autumn Saturday afternoons instead of air raid sirens and shouts of, "Incoming!"

Meredith looked away, but not before registering the surname stitched on the right side of his shirt. Moser.

"It's better not to get too attached," the woman directly behind Meredith said. "It hurts too much to lose them once you get to know them."

Meredith turned to see who had spoken. Ah, yes. Robinson. The quiet one with the dark brown hair, green eyes, and broad shoulders who hadn't had much to say during the flight from Japan. She had been content to sit back and observe with a bemused smile on her face. Meredith had felt like she was passing judgment on everyone, deciding who would make it and who would wash out. Meredith wanted to know where on the spectrum Robinson thought she belonged—potential success story or abject failure?

"I take it this isn't your first tour." Meredith pitched her voice deeper in an effort to project an air of command. She hoped she sounded the part because she certainly didn't feel it. She felt like she was in over her head and she'd just stepped off the plane.

"As a matter of fact, this is my fourth." Robinson sounded like a world-weary veteran, which, Meredith supposed, she was. Even though they weren't on the front lines, they were at war, too. "I've been in the 'Nam off and on since '62."

Robinson took two long strides and drew even with her. Meredith knew Robinson's first name was Natalie, thanks to a quick round of introductions on the plane, but for some reason her surname felt like the more appropriate moniker. Robinson exuded leadership, even though she was, unlike Meredith, no more than a buck private.

Meredith's nursing degree and certification as a registered nurse meant she was awarded the rank of first lieutenant when she volunteered. Back in the world, Robinson must have been either a licensed practical nurse or an orderly. Otherwise, she would have been named an officer when she first volunteered. Five years later, though, her lowly ranking didn't make sense. With multiple tours under her belt, Robinson should have advanced to the rank of sergeant or corporal at the very least. Either something in her character or, more likely, something in her personnel file, had prevented her from moving up the chain.

Meredith didn't know why Robinson's superiors hadn't seen fit to grant her the promotion she seemed to deserve and she didn't care. Robinson was supposed to defer to her, but she had much more experience in this region. Even though they'd just met, Meredith would follow her anywhere.

"How old are you?" Meredith asked. She was twenty-three. Except for Doris, the middle-aged woman whose snores had serenaded them from the time their plane had taxied down the runway in Okinawa until it landed at base camp in Saigon, most of the other nurses appeared to be around the same age.

Robinson smiled and hooked a thumb in her waistband. She walked with the bow-legged, loose-limbed grace of a cowboy. Her stance only added to the impression. When she narrowed her eyes, she looked like a gunslinger sizing up her competition. "Don't you know better than to ask a woman how old she is or how much she weighs?"

Meredith had never experienced any qualms about answering either query. Then again, she had always been a little bit different from the girls she'd grown up with. Girls then; women now. Women with whom she still shared little in common except a place of origin.

"May I ask where you're from then?" She thought she detected a Southern accent when Robinson spoke but couldn't pinpoint which state was to blame.

Robinson smiled as if she found Meredith's discomfort amusing. "Jekyll Island, Georgia. You?"

"Omaha, Nebraska."

Robinson nodded. "Naturally."

"Why do you say that?"

"Nebraska's the Cornhusker State, isn't it?"

"Yeah, so?" Meredith couldn't follow her train of thought.

"You have hair the color of corn silk and eyes as blue as a Midwestern sky. Where else would you be from?"

When Robinson smiled again, Meredith felt the hair on the back of her neck stand on end. She'd never had a similar reaction to anyone before, let alone a woman. There was a name for people who had such feelings. A name she didn't answer to.

"You're going to roast in this heat, Nebraska. I hope you knew what you were getting into when you volunteered for this assignment."

Meredith laughed despite herself. "You sound like my mother."

Robinson raised a hand to the sky. "Heaven forbid." She looked at Meredith with a questioning but sympathetic frown. "Your mother doesn't approve of you being here?"

Meredith watched a Chinook helicopter come in for a landing. As the dual rotors slowed, soldiers rushed out and began unloading the cargo. Meredith swallowed hard as dozens of body bags were loaded in a fleet of ambulances and ferried to a building that must have housed either the morgue or graves registration. She dragged her eyes away from the unwelcome sight.

"In my mother's mind, it's okay for my brother to do his part and serve his country. I'm supposed to keep the home fires burning."

"In a few weeks, you might wish you'd listened to her." Robinson placed a steadying hand on her arm. "For what it's worth, I'm happy to have you here. Good nurses, like most things in Vietnam, are in short supply."

A lump formed in Meredith's throat. She'd been an Army nurse for two years. She'd seen more examples of man's inhumanity to man in those twenty-four months than she had in her entire life. She'd worked tirelessly and without complaint despite long hours and imperfect conditions. This was the first time someone had thanked her for her efforts. Robinson made her feel like her contributions mattered. Like *she* mattered.

"Thank you."

"Don't mention it. We're a small but hearty band. I'm glad I can welcome a new member. If you have any questions or simply need someone to talk to, let me know. I've been told I'm a pretty good listener."

"I'll keep that in mind."

When Robinson removed her hand, Meredith immediately longed for its return. She missed the comfort and sense of safety Robinson's touch had briefly provided.

The group entered a building marked Arrivals/Departures, which put Meredith more in mind of a pleasure cruise than a twelve-month stint in a war zone. Four ceiling fans whirred overhead, churning the still, stagnant air but providing little relief from the stultifying heat.

Meredith and the seven other nurses who had flown with her from Okinawa formed an orderly line parallel to the intake table, where a woman with a lieutenant colonel's silver oak leaves affixed to her uniform collar held court.

"At ease," the woman said, pushing her gunmetal gray chair away from the table. Her voice was filled with quiet command. It was a voice Meredith suspected was equally at home lavishing praise or giving blistering corrections. Her uniform was wrinkle-free, as if it and its owner had never seen a drop of sweat. Meredith would love to look that unruffled.

She and her companions dropped their duffels at their feet and folded their hands behind their backs as their CO slowly walked back and forth in front of them.

"I'm Lieutenant Colonel Billie Daniels. While you're in Saigon, you will be under my command."

Meredith thought her commanding officer would be a gray-haired veteran. Instead, Lt. Col. Daniels appeared to be only in her late twenties or early thirties—the space of time her mother often referred to as the uncertain age between immaturity and experience. Meredith hoped the LTC had more of the latter than the former.

Lt. Col. Daniels's dark hair was pulled back into a severe bun, which added to her intimidating appearance. Her eyes were like lasers. Every time she focused them in her direction, Meredith had to fight not to lower her own in deference.

"For the first month, you'll be working at one of the model hospitals we have established to help the locals provide quality medical care after the US no longer has a military presence in this country," Lt. Col. Daniels said. "Then you'll be randomly assigned to evacuation hospitals in Long Binh or Qui Nhon. You'll work the emergency room, triage area, and intensive care. Sometimes you'll see as few as ten patients per day. Other times you'll be inundated by over three hundred. When you work triage, your job will be to help the medics separate the expectant patients—those not anticipated to survive their wounds—from the ones who have a better chance of making it home."

"Permission to speak, ma'am?" a nervous-sounding voice asked from the end of the line.

Meredith knew the voice well. Lois Dunbar, its chatterbox owner, had talked everyone's ear off on the plane. Meredith knew much more than she cared to about her fellow first lieutenant's adventures with enlisted men from San Francisco to Hawaii to Japan. The ones in Vietnam, she supposed, were next on the list.

Lt. Col. Daniels stopped pacing in front of the line and turned to face Lois. "Permission granted."

"What happens to the expectants? Are they left to die?"

Meredith had the same question, but she hadn't dared interrupt the lieutenant colonel's speech to ask it. Lois was a braver woman than she was. Or more foolish.

"One thing we do not do in this man's army," Lt. Col. Daniels said with a flash of steel, "is abandon our own. You've sworn the same oath I have. Our mission is to save as many people as we can. If that means deciding against a six-hour surgery in a hopeless attempt to salvage a lost cause while we can save four other men in the same time, so be it. Expectants usually present with massive head trauma, multiple amputations, or other catastrophic injuries. We make them as comfortable as we can and someone on staff sits with them until they pass on. They are treated with the respect they deserve at all times and at no point are they ever left alone. Is that understood?"

"Ma'am. Yes, ma'am," Meredith and the rest of the nurses said in unison.

Meredith sneaked a peek at the end of the line. Lois looked so cowed she probably wouldn't speak even if asked.

Dare I to dream?

"If my calculations are correct, most of you have accumulated thirty days of leave," Lt. Col. Daniels said. "Time off can be taken any time as long as you have the days saved up and your absence doesn't conflict with staffing needs. Saigon offers its fair share of diversions. I'm sure each of you will be tempted to spend some time there when you're on leave. Even when you're out drinking with your friends, don't forget you're still at war. This entire country is a war zone. No area is safe, Saigon included. Vietcong sympathizers love targeting establishments where large crowds of American military personnel tend to gather. They place bombs in bars and strafe restaurants with machine gun fire from the backs of passing motorcycles. I want you to take every possible precaution. It won't guarantee your safety, but I'll sleep better at night knowing you didn't take any unnecessary risks. Never leave this base unaccompanied. Make sure you have someone with you at all times. And, above all, make sure someone always knows where you are. Is that understood?"

"Ma'am. Yes, ma'am."

"My aide, Private Flynn, will provide each of you with a work schedule and show you to your quarters." Lt. Col. Daniels pointed to a bespectacled young woman holding a clipboard. Flynn looked barely old enough to attend a sweet sixteen party, let alone enlist. "Settle in and get some rest. We have a long day tomorrow. Work shifts at the hospital are twelve hours on, followed by twelve hours off, seven days a week. Reveille is at 0500. For those of you on first shift, transport leaves at 0530 and your shift begins at 0600. If you're late once, you'll be put on KP for two weeks in addition to your regular duties. If you're late twice, it will result in the revocation of weekend leave for you and the rest of your unit for a month."

Meredith groaned inwardly. She knew how precious time off could be. If someone cost the unit time away from the base, she would instantly become a pariah in the barracks. Meredith didn't want to be that person. She resolved to get up and at 'em as soon as the first notes of reveille sounded instead of trying to grab a quick catnap while she waited for the crowd in the shower to thin out.

"I run a tight ship here, ladies," Lt. Col. Daniels said unnecessarily. Meredith could tell just by looking at her she wouldn't let any of them get off easy. "I expect each one of you to live up to the standards Uncle Sam and I set for you. Don't let me down."

After Flynn made sure all the i's were dotted and t's were crossed on everyone's paperwork, Meredith picked up her duffel and prepared to leave. She had first shift tomorrow. She planned to collapse on her bunk as soon as she had some chow.

"Robinson, Chase," Lt. Col. Daniels said. "Private Flynn will make sure your belongings are taken to your respective hooches and placed on your designated bunks. In the meantime, you're with me. I have an assignment for you."

Meredith tried and failed to meet Robinson's eye. She had an uneasy feeling the assignment would involve the body bags she had seen shortly after her plane had landed. Sure enough, Lt. Col. Daniels briskly led her and Robinson on the same route the ambulances had taken earlier.

"Private Robinson, it will be an honor to work with you again," Lt. Col. Daniels said on the way.

"The honor is mine, ma'am."

"Who did you piss off to get stuck with this gig? The last time I saw you, you were headed home."

For the first time, Robinson's implacable façade slipped the slightest bit.

"I was," she said with a shrug, "but I figured I'd be able to do more good here."

Lt. Col. Daniels flashed what Meredith suspected was a rare smile. "Silly me. I thought I had something to do with your decision to stay."

Robinson's cheeks colored. "I wanted to be where I was needed."

Lt. Col. Daniels patted her on the back. "Then you're definitely in the right place. We'll see what we can do to get you your stripes back."

"You don't have to put yourself out for me, ma'am."

"I'm not going to give them to you," Lt. Col. Daniels said. "You're going to earn them fair and square. Just like you did the first time." She turned to Meredith. "Chase, you're probably wondering why I chose you for this assignment."

The statement didn't seem to invite comment so Meredith remained silent.

"Your superiors have been raving about your ability to stay cool under even the most harrowing circumstances. I want to see if they're right. I want to know if you've got what it takes. And most of all, I want to know if you're half as good as your friend over here."

Lt. Col. Daniels's words felt like a challenge. An impromptu test Meredith hoped she wouldn't fail.

Lt. Col. Daniels led them to the morgue but didn't venture inside. She stopped with her back to the door. Meredith could hear the whirring of a generator and the rush of artificially cooled air. The pleasant thought of cooling off was tempered by the details of the assignment she and Robinson had been handpicked to carry out.

"Whether you're for the war or against it, please remember you're here to do your duty to the utmost of your ability. Through this door are the remains of some of the men our country has lost. It's our job to identify the bodies and determine the cause of death. The attendant on duty will assist and document, but it will be up to us to look in each body bag, locate the decedent's dog tag, and examine the wounds. In the real world, a doctor would perform this chore. In this one, the docs are too busy trying to save the living to concern themselves with the dead. That's where we come in. Are you ready?"

"Ma'am. Yes, ma'am," Robinson said with enough confidence for both of them.

Meredith followed Lt. Col. Daniels and Robinson inside the building. The refreshing blast of air conditioning was immediately overwhelmed by the smell of decomp.

"Here," Lt. Col. Daniels said, holding out an open jar of Vicks VapoRub. "This should help."

Following Robinson's lead, Meredith pulled on a pair of latex gloves and stuck a finger in the jar. She spread a thick line of the topical ointment under her nose. The pungent menthol fumes partially dispelled the odor of death.

Lt. Col. Daniels introduced them to the morgue attendant, a pale man with an air of almost preternatural calm. "Ladies, this is Private Elias Burke. He will record our findings, tag the bodies, and make them as presentable as possible for the flight home. Private Burke, First Lieutenant Meredith Chase and Private Natalie Robinson."

Burke drew himself to attention and snapped off a crisp salute. "I wish we could have met under less trying circumstances," he said after Meredith and Lt. Col. Daniels returned his greeting, "but it's a pleasure to meet you."

"Likewise."

Meredith eyed the zippered black body bags neatly laid out on the floor. Lt. Col. Daniels approached the closest. "I'll take the first to show you how it's done."

Her face was expressionless as she opened the bag. The body inside was of a man who appeared to be around thirty. His face was so serene he seemed to be sleeping, but the enormous hole in the center of his chest told the true story. His heart, lungs, most of his internal organs, and a large portion of his spine were missing. From his shoulders to his waist, only a small section of his ribcage remained.

"Mortar wound. Perhaps even a grenade," Lt. Col. Daniels said with clinical dispassion. "Cause of death, massive blood loss from significant internal injuries." As Burke wrote something on the first of a thick stack of paper tags in his hands, Lt. Col. Daniels located the dead man's metal dog tag and read off his name, rank, and serial number. Burke noted each on the tag and clipped the tag to the end of the body bag. Lt. Col. Daniels turned to make sure Meredith and Robinson knew what was expected of them. When she seemed satisfied that they did, she motioned to Robinson and said, "Okay, you're up next."

Robinson unzipped the next body bag. She didn't flinch as she revealed the man inside. "Shrapnel wound to the neck. Cause of death, ruptured jugular." She slid her finger into the jagged hole at the base of the man's neck and shoulder. "Some material still imbedded in the wound. Will need to be removed while the body is being prepped for shipment home." She read off the vital statistics on the man's dog tag, zipped the bag shut, and moved to the next body.

"No," Lt. Col. Daniels said. "It's Chase's turn."

Robinson looked over her shoulder. Her expression was skeptical. For a moment, Meredith thought she meant to disobey a direct order. Then, with a purposeful nod, she lowered her eyes and moved away.

Meredith's legs were leaden as she approached the body. She felt as ungainly as Frankenstein's monster. As if her limbs were not her own and she had no idea how to use them.

She tried to gather her thoughts as she reached for the zipper on the body bag. The black plastic material slowly moved up and down as if the person inside were breathing, but she knew that was only her mind playing tricks on her. No one came into this room alive and they definitely didn't make it out that way.

She kept her eyes focused on the floor as she slowly unzipped the bag. Only when she had gotten control of her breathing did she look up. She inhaled sharply but didn't cry out. In life, the soldier in the body bag had suffered a horrific injury. The indignities he had suffered after death nearly brought Meredith to tears.

"Tell me what you see, Chase," Lt. Col. Daniels said gently.

Half the man's head was missing. The right side was intact, but the left was completely gone. Hundreds of maggots filled the cavity. Meredith's stomach lurched and she tasted bile in her throat as she watched the plump creatures feed. The man's body had obviously lain unattended on the battlefield for quite some time before medics had been able to get to him. Flies had laid their eggs in his gaping wound. Now their offspring were feasting on what was left of his head.

"Chase?"

Meredith licked her dry lips and began to speak. "G-gunshot wound to the head. Most likely from an AK-47. Cause of death, catastrophic cranial trauma and massive blood loss."

Meredith's hands were shaking, but she tried to keep her voice steady. She could feel herself losing the battle with her nerves. Because she knew determining the cause of death was only one part of the task she had been assigned. Now she had to reach into the gore to find the man's dog tag so his family could know for certain their loved one had been killed in action and was no longer one of the missing or unidentified.

Meredith's stomach lurched again as she felt the maggots squirm against her gloved fingers. She bit her tongue to keep her breakfast down. The lumpy oatmeal and rubbery eggs she'd eaten in Okinawa had tasted bad enough the first time. She didn't want to try her luck on a second go-round.

"Good job, you two," Lt. Col. Daniels said after they had identified all the bodies. She discarded her gloves and washed her hands in a stainless steel sink. "I would tell you it gets easier, but nothing about this job is easy."

"Permission to be dismissed, ma'am?" Meredith asked after she finished washing up. She pressed her fingers against her temples to alleviate the pounding in her head brought on by the heat, the odor, and the mindlessness of war. "I-I could use some air."

Lt. Col. Daniels looked her up and down, appraising her as if she were a prize Guernsey competing for top honors at the state fair. Meredith didn't feel worthy of a blue ribbon. Not today. "Dismissed."

Meredith snapped off a salute and rushed to the door. Outside, she stood with her hands on her knees and took a deep gulp of fresh, unpolluted air.

"Are you okay?" Burke asked, sounding like a funeral home director attempting to comfort a bereaved family member. "Is there anything I can do?"

Meredith slowly straightened as she began to regain her composure. "No, I'm fine. Thank you for asking."

Burke walked away, most likely headed in search of an official authorized to sign off on the paperwork in his hands. Meredith stepped back inside, where Robinson and Lt. Col. Daniels were conversing in low tones. Their backs were to her so they didn't see or hear her approach. Meredith hesitated, uncertain whether she should stay or go. She didn't want to interrupt and she didn't mean to eavesdrop, but then she heard them mention her name.

"Chase impressed me today," Lt. Col. Daniels said. She sounded relaxed. As if she were playing catch-up with an old friend instead of having a conversation with a subordinate. Meredith wondered how long she and Robinson had been working together to reach that level of comfort.

"Did you know what was inside the third bag when you said you wanted her to have it?" Robinson asked.

"No, that was purely the luck of the draw." Lt. Col. Daniels took a long pull on her cigarette and exhaled a thick cloud of smoke. "She held herself together well. I've seen some who've tossed their cookies over a great deal less. You included."

Robinson pretended to take offense. "That was years ago. I've grown a cast iron stomach since then."

"Yeah, yeah." Lt. Col. Daniels extinguished her cigarette on the sole of her boot and draped a consoling arm over Robinson's shoulder. "Don't worry. You're still the best nurse I've ever worked with. Given time, though, Chase might take the title away from you."

"I think you're right. She seems to have the right stuff."

Meredith smiled at the compliments, but Lt. Col. Daniels's next question confused her.

"Is she one of us?"

Robinson seemed to have trouble with the question, if the time she took to respond was any indication. "I'm not sure," she said at length. "I don't think she knows yet."

CHAPTER THREE

"Your CO thought you were a lesbian?" Jordan asked. "Her gaydar must have been on the fritz."

"Why do you say that?"

"You were cooler than my parents were when I came out, but you're the straightest woman I've ever met." She frowned at the absurdity of the idea anyone would think otherwise. "On the Kinsey scale, you're probably a big fat zero. I, on the other hand, am a perfect six. A genuine, gold star lesbian. Did Robinson and Lt. Col. Daniels ever hook up? You make it sound like they were ex-lovers or something."

"I always thought they had a history, but in our day, you didn't talk about such things. We couldn't afford to be as open as people are now."

"Some still can't," Jordan said bitterly, thinking of all the members of the LGBT community who were still being discriminated against simply because of the way they lived their lives—and the people they had chosen to love. "What happened after you identified all the bodies?"

"We shipped them home and went to work," Grandma Meredith said matter-of-factly. "We started putting in shifts at the hospital, where we treated injuries that ranged from minor to mortal."

"What was the worst injury you ever saw?"

Grandma Meredith thought for a moment. Her eyes darted from side to side as if she was searching through a card catalog of memories. Then her eyelids slid shut as if the memory she had retrieved was too painful to be viewed for long.

"Sometime during the first month of my tour, we treated a soldier who had stepped on a land mine. Robert, his name was. Robert Laws. He asked us to call him Bobby." She shook her head, a sad smile on her face. "I remember it like it was yesterday. Robinson and I were on duty when he was brought in. He was wearing MAST trousers when they wheeled him into the ER."

"Mast what?"

"MAST trousers. They're a device you inflate to put pressure on the lower half of a patient's body to allow sufficient blood flow to the brain and heart to maintain viability. Despite the seriousness of his wounds, Bobby was awake and alert when he arrived. Logic said he should have been passed out from shock. I nearly fainted from the shock of seeing the condition he was in."

"Was it that bad?"

"He looked like a marionette whose strings had been cut. His right arm was twisted behind his head and his left heel was resting under his chin. His right leg was missing altogether. Without the MAST trousers, he would have bled out in the field. Instead, he was in the hospital cracking jokes and flirting with all the nurses. He took a particular shine to Robinson. As soon as he latched eyes on her, he pronounced himself head over heels in love."

"What did she do? Did she let him think he had a chance, or did she set him straight?"

Grandma Meredith's voice was as gentle as a spring rain. "He was dying. We all knew it. We couldn't call him an expectant because he was conscious and alert, but as soon as we deflated the MAST trousers, his blood pressure would drop and he'd bleed out in a matter of seconds. As I said, his right leg was missing. His left, as it turned out, had also been amputated by the force of the blast. The medic who had treated him in the field had placed it in the MAST trousers, hoping we'd be able to reattach it somehow. But, really, there was nothing we could do except wait for him to decide when he was ready to go. The doctors knew it, the nurses knew it, and so did he."

Jordan's heart ached as she began to mourn for a man she had never met.

"Robinson sat with him the entire time. She held his hand and listened to him talk. She listened to him tell stories about growing up in South Carolina and his adventures in Vietnam. The woman who warned me not to get too attached listened to every single tale Bobby told as if she had never heard anything so fascinating. She had never met him before, but she made him feel like they were lifelong friends. She made him feel like he mattered to someone, which, for a grunt too busy fighting off driving rain, leeches, and trench foot to see the big picture the brass loved to natter on about, was a very big thing." Grandma Meredith smiled in obvious admiration. "When he passed, she was right by his side. We had to pry his fingers from hers he was holding on so tight."

She looked down at her own hands as if they bore the marks Bobby had left behind on his way from this world to the next.

"That was the first time I ever saw her cry. Unfortunately, it wasn't the last."

Jordan could sense the bond that had once linked Grandma Meredith and Natalie Robinson to each other. She wondered what had driven them apart. Had the war come between them or something much more mundane?

Jordan flinched when her ringing cell phone shattered the silence. She reached into the console between their seats. "Sorry, Gran, I thought I'd turned off my phone."

"That's okay, dear. I could use a break anyway. There's a rest area coming up on your right."

Jordan glanced at the phone's display to see who was calling. Brittany. Finally. She checked the traffic with her side mirrors, turned on the blinker, and pressed the phone to her ear.

"Hey, Britt. Give me a second to pull over."

"Where are you?" Brittany asked, all breezy and casual as if nothing was wrong.

"Grandma Meredith and I just crossed the border between Tennessee and Georgia."

"Talk about Hicksville."

"Ah, it's not so bad. The rural areas remind me of home. Not nearly as many cows, but close enough."

"Like I said. Hicksville."

Brittany had a sarcastic sense of humor, but Jordan couldn't remember her turning the sarcasm on her with such venom. Brittany had changed—*they* had changed—and she didn't know how to fix it.

She pulled into a parking spot and shut off the engine. Grandma Meredith unbuckled her seat belt and got out of the car. Jordan didn't know if she really had to pee or if she was simply clearing out to give her some privacy.

"Back in a minute."

Jordan knew Grandma Meredith couldn't hear her, but she waited until she walked away before she asked, "What's going on, Britt?"

Brittany tried to laugh off her question. "You tell me. You called me, remember?"

"I called you almost a week ago."

"I've been busy."

"Doing what?"

"Packing up my apartment and preparing for the drive to Seattle. Now I'm here and semi-settled. I think I'm turning into a mushroom from all the rain, but the protestors' collective passion keeps me energized."

Jordan wished she could be there to experience the excitement for herself.

"Anyway," Brittany said as if she had more important things to do than work on their strained relationship, "I got back to you as soon as I could. How are things with you?"

"Confusing." Jordan ran her hands over the walnut steering wheel. The cool, smooth wood provided a soothing contrast to the heat building inside her. How could Brittany be so cavalier about something so serious? Didn't their relationship mean as much to Brittany as it did to her? "When my flight landed in Milwaukee, the first thing I saw when I checked my messages was a Facebook notification saying you had changed your relationship status from *In a Relationship* to *It's Complicated.*"

"And?" Brittany said warily.

"Are you breaking up with me?"

Brittany sucked in a breath as if she'd just been told there'd be a surprise exam on material she hadn't studied. "I changed my status because it *is* complicated."

"It seems pretty simple to me. I want to be with you and you said you felt the same way. What's complicated about that?"

"It just is." Brittany sighed. "I was hoping we could be civil about this."

"Civil about what?"

"We need to take a break."

Jordan's heart began to race. She had hoped she and Brittany would be able to talk things out, but the prospect seemed to be more of a long shot than a sure thing.

"We're going to spend the summer thousands of miles apart. I won't get to see you for three whole months. How much more of a break do you need?"

"A permanent one."

How had she known Brittany was going to say that?

"Why?"

"We moved too fast." Brittany sounded like she was scrambling for an answer. Something that sounded good without adequately addressing the question at hand. "I mean, how much do we really know about each other?"

"We've been sleeping together for seven months. We know every inch of each other."

"That isn't what I mean. Yes, the sex was great, and it was the one part of our relationship that seemed to capture most of your attention, but we were like cotton candy. All sugar and no substance. If you can't admit it, I will."

Jordan bit her lip to keep from crying. How could Brittany's opinion of their relationship be so different from hers?

"I know what you look like in various positions," Brittany said, "but I don't know what's going on inside your head. I always get the feeling you're telling me what you think I want to hear instead of what's really on your mind. Do you really believe the same things I do or are you simply parroting my ideas?"

"Social activism as a way to pick up chicks. Thanks for thinking so much of me."

"You know what I mean."

"Actually, no, I don't. Why don't you explain it for me?"

"You're not who I thought you were."

"Meaning?"

"When we first met, I was attracted to you because you seemed to have so much gravitas. I looked in your eyes and saw such depth of feeling. I wanted to explore those feelings with you. Once I got to know you, I realized your eyes aren't the mirrors to your soul. They're one-way, reflecting what the viewer sees instead of what you really feel. You're about as deep as a wading pool."

Brittany's words pierced Jordan's heart. She felt like a prized insect being pinned to a board and put on display. "Thanks for that." She stared into her lap as tears streamed down her cheeks.

"Like I said, I don't want to hurt you. I'm just being honest. You should try it sometime."

"Are you trying to say I've been lying to you?"

"Not exactly."

"What I asked you is kind of a yes or no question. 'Not exactly' isn't a valid response."

"Fine. You've been holding back. You shared your body with me, but not your mind or your soul. I don't get where you're coming from."

"I'm a fucking open book, Britt. Always have been, always will be."

"I beg to differ. You claim to be anti-war, but how can you be when you romanticize the role your grandparents played in Vietnam, one of the bloodiest, most misguided conflicts our country has had the misfortune of being involved in?"

"You met my grandmother once and my grandfather died long before I met you. If I embellished things a bit when I introduced you and Grandma Meredith, I did it because I wanted you to like each other. But let's get something straight. I love my grandparents and I am understandably proud of everything they've accomplished in their lives, but I didn't know any of their service history until Grandma Meredith and I began the trip down here."

"Yet I've lost track of the number of times I've heard you wax rhapsodic about the fact they met and fell in love while they were in the Army. Whenever you talk about them, you're as wrapped in the flag as they once were. I can practically hear you pledging allegiance to Uncle Sam and whistling 'Yankee Doodle Dandy.' You wear your grandfather's dog tags like they're some sort of fashion accessory when what they really are is a political statement. A statement of your true beliefs."

Jordan closed her eyes as she felt her life begin to spin out of control like a car that had just hit a patch of black ice. Family was important to her, but she would never allow them or anyone else to come before her principles. "You've said a lot of things during the course of this conversation, Brittany, but you're right about only one: you don't know me at all."

"And whose fault is that? Mine? Yours? Does it even matter at this point?"

"It does to me. I wish it did to you, too."

Jordan ended the call and let her tears fall. She had been misunderstood all her life. By friends, classmates, and strangers alike. People who took one look at her exterior and expected her to be something she wasn't. She'd thought Brittany was different. She'd thought Brittany could see her true self. How had she been so wrong?

"Grow up," she told herself as she knuckled away her tears. "You're twenty-one now. You're supposed to be an adult. Stop crying like a kid who has lost her favorite toy."

She took several deep, shaky breaths and tried to pull herself together as she watched Grandma Meredith talk with a group of older men crowded around a long black travel trailer with "The Wall" printed in big red letters on the side. Most of the men wore chaps or riding leathers. Their patch-covered vests made them look like a graying motorcycle gang. Grandma Meredith didn't seem to have anything in common with the ragtag group, but they were gabbing away as if they were old friends.

After a few minutes, Grandma Meredith shot a look in her direction. Her features creased into a frown. Turning back to the men, she pointed to the car, seemingly indicating she had to leave.

Jordan scrunched down in her seat after the men's heads swiveled in her direction. They probably couldn't see her very well through the tinted glass, but she didn't feel like being the center of attention. Theirs or anyone else's. She wanted to crawl into bed and pull the covers over her head until her life began to make sense again.

Grandma Meredith exchanged handshakes with the men and, in a few cases, heartfelt hugs. Then she began to walk back to the car with the sense of purpose she always displayed whenever she was on a mission.

Jordan sat bolt upright in her seat and took a quick peek in the rearview mirror to see if she looked like she'd been crying. Her eyes were red and starting to get puffy so she slapped on her sunglasses just before Grandma Meredith opened the door and climbed into the passenger's seat.

Jordan took another deep breath and mustered a smile, trying to look as if she didn't have a care in the world. She and Grandma Meredith talked about everything, but she wasn't ready to talk about the conversation she'd just had with Brittany. She didn't want her to feel partially responsible for the breakup. The fault lay with her and Brittany. No one else.

"Who were those guys?"

"They're with the Moving Wall," Grandma Meredith said. "The miniature version of the Vietnam Memorial that travels from place to place so vets who can't travel to DC can see it."

"Okay, but why were they hugging you?"

"I dug a bullet out of one's shoulder after the Tet Offensive. A couple of the other ones spent some time at the evac hospital when I was stationed in Long Binh."

"Small world, huh?" Jordan watched as the truck attached to the trailer slowly pulled out of its parking spot. The men she had seen Grandma Meredith conversing with escorted it on their motorcycles. Travelers all over the rest area watched the convoy make its way to the interstate, most doffing their hats and some pausing to salute. "Where are they headed now?"

"They'll be in Georgia most of the month. They're going to spend a week in the major cities like Atlanta, Augusta, and Savannah and a weekend here and there in smaller towns before they head down to Florida. After that, who knows?"

"Are you going to see it?"

"I might make a day trip when it reaches Savannah. We'll see."

Grandma Meredith's eyes dimmed with uncharacteristic sadness. Jordan had visited the actual memorial when her junior class had taken a field trip to Washington, DC, when she was in high school. Even though she hadn't taken part in the war herself, she had been incredibly moved by the sight of the hundreds of names etched into the stately granite wall—and how much the people behind those names meant to the visitors who came to see them. Papa George could have been one of those names. So could Grandma Meredith. Thankfully, both had made it through with relatively few scars to show for it.

Jordan started the car and reached for the gearshift. "Are you ready to hit the road?"

"Not yet." Grandma Meredith placed her hand over hers. "You seem upset. Did something happen with Brittany?"

Jordan felt the color drain from her face. "How did you know?"

Grandma Meredith smiled wanly. "I've been around the block a time or two. I recognize the signs. What happened?"

Jordan hunched over the steering wheel and picked at the walnut inlay with her thumbnail. "She broke up with me on the Internet, then called to make it official." She glanced at Grandma Meredith to gauge her reaction.

Grandma Meredith's eyes narrowed. She looked like a mama bear ready to fight off a threat to her cub. Jordan could have kissed her.

"Did she offer an explanation?" Grandma Meredith asked, giving her a consoling pat on the knee.

"More like excuses. For one thing, she thinks I'm shallow. Her exact quote was I'm 'as deep as a wading pool.'"

"She has a way with words, I'll give her that, but she could definitely learn some tact. A course in sensitivity might be beneficial as well."

Jordan felt her dark mood begin to brighten. "I knew I could count on you to be on my side. You don't think I'm shallow, do you?" When Grandma Meredith opened her mouth to respond, Jordan held up her hands to stop the flow of words before they could begin. "Don't. I've had enough constructive criticism for one day."

"I think you can take a little bit more."

"Do I have to?"

Jordan hadn't related Brittany's other reasons for leaving so she could spare Grandma Meredith's feelings. She wished Grandma Meredith would return the favor.

When Grandma Meredith turned to face her, Jordan could feel some of that tough love she'd thought she wanted coming on. "I'm not going to tell you to ignore what Brittany said because I think you needed to hear it. But hear this, too. What she said was based on her opinion. Opinions are like assholes. Everybody has one."

Jordan snorted laughter. She had never heard Grandma Meredith use any word stronger than fiddlesticks to express her displeasure.

She didn't know which was funnier, hearing Grandma Meredith utter an actual expletive or seeing the unabashed glee on her face when she did. She looked like a teenager sneaking a cigarette under the bleachers at recess. Like she was getting away with breaking the rules and having the time of her life in the process.

"Feel better?" Grandma Meredith asked.

Jordan conducted a brief personal inventory. "A bit, yeah. It's her loss, right?"

"You bet." Grandma Meredith cupped a hand against her cheek. "You have an old soul, honey. One day your heart will catch up. I know it will."

Jordan fanned her splayed fingers as she tried to hold a sudden rush of emotion at bay. "Stop before you make me start crying again. Besides, we're supposed to be talking about you." She put the car in reverse. "Are you ready to pick up where we left off?"

"Are you sure you want to hear more about my dull, boring life?"

"Dull and boring, my ass." Jordan pulled out of the parking lot and eased into the flow of traffic on the interstate. "I would call you GI Jane, but that makes me think of Demi Moore, which conjures up a completely different image altogether."

"The movie had its flaws—except for a few recent exceptions, most Hollywood war movies fail to get it right—but Demi did look powerful with a shaved head, didn't she?"

"That's one way of putting it. Super sexy is another." Jordan loved being able to talk openly with Grandma Meredith about her attraction to women without having to tone anything down for her audience. "Why can't I talk with my parents like this?"

"Have you tried?"

"Every time I do, Mom gets all flustered and doesn't know what to say. Dad just turns fifty shades of red and buries his nose in a book. To make it easier on them, I always change the subject to something safer and more innocuous."

"In their eyes, you're still their baby, and the last thing their baby should be doing is having sex. I was the same way when Diana started dating, and your grandfather was even worse. He nearly scared your poor father to death when Diana brought him home to meet us, but he and Frank ended up the best of friends."

"Guys are different. They can fight it out and forget about what made them start trading blows in the first place. Women don't usually start punching each other in the face like guys do, but they hold on to slights a lot longer. I doubt Mom will ever be as close to anyone I bring home as Dad was to Papa George. In fact, I'm half-convinced she thinks being a lesbian is a phase I'll grow out of like a bad haircut."

"Don't give up on your mother, honey. Be patient. She'll come around. One day, something will click and you'll see the light come on in her eyes. It takes some people longer to see that light than others. But when Diana does, you'll know it."

"How do you know?"

"Because that's what happened to me."

Jordan reflected on the story Grandma Meredith had told about her first day in Vietnam and the interesting bunch of characters she'd met after she arrived. Man. It had taken serious guts to do what they did. If the teaser was this action-packed, she couldn't imagine what the rest of the story would be like. She knew how it began and how it ended, but she had no idea what had happened in the middle. And she couldn't wait to find out.

Did that mean Brittany was right about her? No way. Being supportive of family members and being anti-war weren't mutually exclusive. Were they? She shook her head to clear her mind of a conflict she couldn't resolve.

"Do you think we'll run into Robinson this summer? You said she lived on Jekyll Island, right? She sounds fascinating. I'd love to meet her."

"She and I lost touch years ago. We didn't part on the best of terms. I don't know if she still lives in the same place. If she does, I doubt she would want to see me."

"If she is still rattling around the island, it would be cool if you two could kiss and make up."

"Yeah," Grandma Meredith said as she stared out the window. "That would be way cool."

CHAPTER FOUR

September 1, 1967
Saigon

Meredith looked out the rear of the truck as the transport vehicle headed back to post. A thick cloud of dust trailed in its wake. She squinted to see through the sandy filter as the sights and sounds of Vietnam flew past her vantage point.

Despite the spectacular views along the circuitous route between the base and town, she had found working in the hospital disappointing. She liked helping the locals become self-sufficient and she loved being able to ease the patients' suffering, but she had become frustrated by the fact that, aside from Lt. Col. Daniels, most of her superiors seemed more concerned with making sure everyone's uniforms were starched and pressed instead of guaranteeing the patients received the best possible care. The majority of the doctors on staff gloated about the cushy assignment they had received, while a relative few openly longed to be closer to the front lines where the real action was. Meredith just wanted to help, no matter her location. That was the reason she had signed up in the first place.

At the hospital, she had kept her head down and done her job as best she could, whether her patient was a local with a stomachache or a GI who had developed a raging infection after falling into a *punji* trap. The spikes in such traps were often deliberately contaminated to compound the misery of its victims and the medical personnel who searched, sometimes in vain, for the proper method to treat the infection.

Now that she had finished her final shift, she had forty-eight hours of leave. Two whole days of down time before she packed her bags and prepared to ship off to her next posting.

Long Binh was an evac hospital thirty-three clicks away. Based on the horror stories she had heard, it would be like leaving heaven for hell. The facilities were better than in Saigon, but the base was crowded, and the types of injuries she'd have to treat would be exponentially worse than the ones she had seen so far. Not to mention the Long Binh Jail also served as the primary incarceration center in Vietnam. For the past year, all of the Army's ne'er-do-wells and criminals had been housed in the stockade there. More were arriving every day. Meredith had heard the place was a powder keg waiting to blow. She hoped she'd be situated in another post before the explosion occurred. From the looks of things, though, no place in Vietnam was safe.

She held on to the metal support rail above her head as the deuce and a half, a two-and-a-half-ton transport truck, bounced over the pitted road. She braced herself each time the driver hit a pothole, preparing for the inevitable explosion. Just last week, a jeep filled with soldiers on leave had driven over a roadside bomb on the way back from one of the bars in town. Ambulances had been dispatched to the scene right away, but all four men were DOA by the time they reached the hospital. With the amount of damage inflicted, Elias had certainly had his work cut out for him making the bodies look presentable for their journey home.

What made a terrible situation even worse was the discovery that the explosive device had been crafted from material the US Army had unwittingly provided—dud bombs that had been scavenged by locals and fashioned into new weapons less obvious and more insidious than their previous incarnations. In Saigon, such attacks were rare. In country, they happened nearly every day. Meredith was headed in country.

She wondered how much time she would be able to spend away from base. How much time she would spend putting herself at risk.

She fingered the stainless steel dog tags dangling from the ball chain around her neck. Her name, Social Security number, blood type, and religion were stamped into the metal. If something happened to her, one of the dog tags would stay with her, the other would be collected and used to help treat her injuries or, if the unthinkable happened, identify her remains.

"I thought you were Protestant, not Catholic," Robinson said.

"I am. Why?"

Robinson pointed to her dog tags. "You're fondling those things like they're rosary beads."

"Nervous habit." Meredith tucked the tags inside her shirt and fastened her top button to keep them out of easy reach.

"Whatever works. Don't let me stop you."

Robinson leaned back in her seat as if reclining in an easy chair instead of being tossed to and fro by a driver who seemed more concerned with speed than safety. Meredith envied her ability to look at ease no matter how stressful the situation.

"Did you get posted to Long Binh?" she asked.

"I think everyone did." Robinson pushed herself out of her seat, stepped over the duffels piled in the aisle, and sat next to Meredith after one of the other nurses moved over to give her room. The various conversations going on around them continued without discernible pause. "The CO said Long Binh is going to serve as the US Army Republic of Vietnam HQ. Most of the USARV command and the units stationed in Saigon will be moved there if they haven't already."

The day the postings were announced, the other nurses had chatted about the assignment for hours. Meredith had been left not knowing what to believe. Was Long Binh a resort paradise filled with swimming pools, driving ranges, basketball courts, more restaurants and nightclubs than you could count, and an honest to God movie theater that played some of Hollywood's latest and greatest, or was it home to one of the busiest evac hospitals in Vietnam and a stockade teeming with angry prisoners? Robinson was the only person she knew who might know for sure.

"What's it like?"

"Everything you want it to be and then some. There's so much to do you never have to leave the base. If you want to party and have fun, Long Binh's the place. If you want to see all the horrors this war has to offer, Long Binh's the place for that, too."

"It sounds so big."

Meredith was overwhelmed not by the size of the base but by the realization she was inching closer to the front lines. Closer to danger. She didn't know how to give voice to her feelings, but she didn't have to. Robinson understood without her having to say a word. Robinson knew exactly what she was experiencing because she was experiencing it, too.

"Don't worry, Goldilocks." Robinson nudged Meredith's thigh with her knee. "If you get lost, I'll leave a trail of bread crumbs for you to follow."

Meredith felt the sense of calm that always washed over her when she knew she and Robinson would be working side-by-side. The most experienced nurses were assigned the night shift because enemy attacks were more likely to take place after the sun set. As a result, Meredith often found herself working from dusk to dawn. Some days, she saw more of Natalie Robinson than she did her own bed.

"It's good to know that no matter how bad things get, you and Lt. Col. Daniels will be there to talk me through it."

"The LTC's better at it than I am," Robinson said with an aw-shucks shrug.

"You're pretty good, too. Remember our first day here when the LTC asked us to go through those body bags?" Meredith shuddered at the memory. "I don't think I could have gotten through that day without you. And what you did for Bobby Laws? I've never seen anything like it. I never thanked you for either of those things, did I? Thank you for everything you've done for me since I've been here."

She squeezed Robinson's hand. Robinson returned the pressure for a second or two, but almost immediately drew her hand away.

"You don't have to thank me. What I did for Laws wasn't extraordinary but expected. As far as the first day is concerned, you would have done the same for me, if given a chance."

Meredith nearly laughed out loud. "When would I have the chance? You're the most stubborn person I've ever met. You won't let me or anyone else help you through the tough times. You always insist on doing it yourself."

"I don't like being dependent on anyone. I see patients who can't do anything for themselves, and the whole time I'm with them,

I keep thinking, 'I'm so glad that's not me.'" Robinson's eyes were downcast. As if she were ashamed of the admission. "But I suppose everyone needs someone sometime," she said softly.

Meredith was struck by the simplicity and the eloquence of Robinson's statement. For someone who didn't say much, she certainly had a way with words.

"Are you heading into town tonight?" Meredith asked.

She lived in the officers' quarters on base, Robinson in the tin-roofed hooch she shared with five other enlisted women. At the hospital, they shared the same locker room, shower, and break room. Despite their shared experiences and occasional forced intimacy, Robinson looked at her with what Meredith could only describe as mistrust. "Why do you ask?"

"George Moser asked me if I wanted to grab a beer with him. If you don't have any plans, perhaps you could tag along."

"In case you haven't heard, two's company and three's a crowd."

"You wouldn't be crowding in. There'll be eight of us. Four guys and four girls, including George and me. We're going to meet at Charlie's and head into town to see what kind of trouble we can get into. You should come with us. I could ask Lois to round up another guy to even things out. I'm sure the gang wouldn't mind if two more joined the party."

Robinson whispered something that sounded like, "But I would."

Meredith lowered her voice, too. "I don't blame you. Lois can be a handful. Most of her stories are variations on the same theme. If you've heard one, you've heard them all."

"She's looking for a man with medals on his chest and won't stop until she finds one." Robinson waved her hand dismissively. "I've learned to tune her out. Most of the time, she's nothing more than background noise. I'm just glad I don't have to live with her."

Meredith lowered her voice to a whisper. "I wish I could say the same."

Robinson's mouth twitched as if she were trying not to smile. Meredith wished she would allow herself the pleasure. Robinson never seemed to truly enjoy herself. Instead, she always acted as if she had been ordered to be on her best behavior, making it hard to get to know her.

"Are you sure you won't join us tonight?" A thought occurred to her. A possible explanation for Robinson's decided lack of enthusiasm for her plans for the evening. "You don't have a thing for Moser, do you? If you do, just say the word and I'll step aside. After all, you've known him a lot longer than I have. You saw him first."

"Relax, Goldilocks. I don't want to call dibs on George Moser. He's a nice guy, but he isn't my type."

"Are you looking for a man with medals on his chest, too?"

Robinson not only smiled. She laughed out loud. "Not hardly."

The finality of Robinson's tone made it seem like she thought their conversation had ended, but Meredith wasn't ready to drop the thread.

"I hate the idea of you spending the night alone when you spend so much of the day that way. When you aren't checking on patients or consulting with doctors, you're off in a corner by yourself nursing a cup of coffee or lying in your hooch reading a dime novel from the PX."

Robinson's gaze was steady and unblinking, her voice low and deliberate. "Have you been watching me?"

"No," Meredith said too quickly. The way Robinson was looking at her made her unsure of herself. She felt the need to explain herself much more than was probably necessary. "Well, yes. I worry about you. You need to let your hair down for a while. You seem so... intense all the time."

Robinson's eyes bore into hers, emphasizing her point. "Not all the time."

Meredith got a rare glimpse of the tenderness beneath Robinson's tough exterior. Usually only her patients were so fortunate.

"Is there anything I could say to convince you to change your mind about coming out with me? You could keep me company at Charlie's and help me entertain the boys while I wait for everyone to get ready. Lois is always the last one on the truck each morning. I'm sure tonight won't be any different. The first round's on me. What do you say?"

"I appreciate the offer, but I already have plans, thanks." Robinson rubbed her palms on her thighs. She rose to her feet as soon as the truck lurched to a stop. "Have fun tonight. I'll see you in Long Binh. Maybe I'll save a seat for you at the theater on movie night."

She grabbed her duffel and jumped out of the truck after the driver lowered the tailgate. Meredith tried to follow her, but Lois blocked her path.

"You didn't invite her to come with us tonight, did you?"

"Yes, I did."

Lois's eyes widened in surprise. "Why did you go and do that?"

"Did I do something wrong?"

Meredith nearly lost her balance when someone bumped into her from behind. She cleared a path as her heart began to race. Lois reminded her of a student the teacher had tasked with taking names when she had to leave the room. The rest of the students catered to her every whim to keep their names off the list. Had Meredith done everything she needed to do to remain in Lois's good graces or had Lois taken her name?

Lois patted the air with her hands in a placating gesture. "First tell me what she said. Is she coming with us or not?"

"No, she said she already had plans of her own."

"Good." Lois's relieved sigh blasted Meredith in the face like hot air from a rapidly deflating balloon.

"Why don't you want her to go to town with us?"

Lois looked around to see who might be listening, but they were the only ones left in the truck. Everyone else had cleared out.

"I served with women like her in San Francisco."

"What kind of women?"

Lois looked around again. The driver was filling the truck's gas tank, but he was too busy ogling a tight-skirted secretary from General Lewis's office to spare a thought for them.

"The kind of women you don't want to hang around with unless you're looking for a dishonorable discharge. The kind that usually gets weeded out after the men in white coats play Twenty Questions during the recruiting process."

Suddenly, the conversation Meredith had overheard on her first day in Saigon made sense.

"*Do you think she's one of us?*" Lt. Col. Daniels had asked.

"*I'm not sure,*" Robinson had replied. "*I don't think she knows yet.*"

Robinson and Lt. Col. Daniels were lesbians and they were wondering if she was, too. Meredith had met lesbians in the service before. Like Lois, she had always kept her distance from them out of fear someone would mistakenly point the finger at her and get her sent home to face a litany of questions for which she had no answer. This time, though, she wasn't so sure she could stay away. Or if she wanted to.

"I hear her…tendencies are the reason she lost her sergeant's stripes," Lois said.

"That can't be true. If the brass suspected she was that way, she would have been booted out, not bucked down."

Psychiatrists said homosexuals didn't make good soldiers, and the military had bought it hook, line, and sinker. Soldiers caught committing homosexual acts were charged with sodomy and purged from the ranks. Draftees were asked point-blank if they were homosexual. If they answered yes, they weren't allowed to enlist. Unless, of course, the country was at war like it was now and the military machine needed as many recruits as it could get its hands on.

Meredith wondered what would happen to Robinson, Lt. Col. Daniels, and the hundreds if not thousands of men and women like them after the tide of the war began to turn, and the number of personnel committed to fighting it began to decrease. Would they become victims of witch-hunts like so many of their predecessors had, or would they be allowed to continue performing the jobs they did so well?

"Robinson's the best nurse in our unit," Meredith said. "I've learned a great deal from her. So have you."

Lois pursed her pencil-thin lips. "How can you say that when she doesn't even have a degree? I'm an officer. She isn't. And won't be again, thanks to her predilections."

"Rank doesn't matter."

"I beg to differ. Rank is everything. You'd know that if you didn't have those stripes on your shoulders."

"Rank doesn't matter," Meredith said again, even though she had worked her ass off to earn her current position and hoped to rise even higher. "Knowledge does. Experience does. Robinson has both. I've learned more from her in a month than I did in years of nursing school. So have you. I think we both could learn a great deal more. I'm not going to stop being her friend simply because you think she might be different from you and me."

Lois folded her arms across her chest like a petulant child who wasn't getting her way. "Oh, she's different from me, all right, but I'm not so sure about you. Not after your spirited defense on behalf of your friend. Or should I say *girl*friend?"

Meredith felt her cheeks redden at the comment, which felt more like an accusation than a question. "Careful, Lois. That's how rumors get started. Don't go around saying I'm something I'm not."

"Prove me wrong and I won't have to. George Moser's getting blue balls waiting for you to show him the time of day. You should take pity on the poor man and offer him some relief. Otherwise, I might have to start sleeping with my eyes open so I can keep one of them on you and one on your *friend* Natalie Robinson."

After Lois turned and left, Meredith took her time gathering her things. The conversation with Lois had left her shaken. Would Lois go to the brass with her suspicions about Robinson or the baseless ones about her? She thought it best to stay on Lois's good side. But was keeping her good name reason enough to give in to Lois's demands? Perhaps not, but saving her career was. She hadn't come this far to be derailed by something that wasn't true. If she wanted to move up in the ranks, she needed to play by the rules with no hint of impropriety or scandal. She needed to stick close to George Moser and stay away from Natalie Robinson.

The situation made her feel dirty. After she took a long shower in the barracks, she slipped on a pair of modest heels and a sleeveless sheath she had picked up in Tokyo, grabbed her overnight bag, and headed to Charlie's.

The bar was run by a civilian contractor and was popular with enlisted men and officers alike, though most of the top brass preferred the exclusivity of the officers' club. Meredith had tried the OC a time or two, but it was too stuffy for her taste. The atmosphere at Charlie's was much more her speed. The food at Charlie's was better than the fare served up in the mess hall, even though it cost four times as much as it did back home. But the beer was cold, cheap, and plentiful.

When she walked in, Meredith spotted Robinson nursing one of those cold brews at the end of the bar. She thought about joining her, but Robinson had made it clear she wanted to be alone so she left her that way.

She waved to the owner, Charlie Miller, and took a seat at the other end of the bar. Charlie's wife, U'ilani, who worked as a waitress, ambled up to take her drink order. Charlie weighed probably a buck fifty soaking wet. U'ilani was easily twice his size. No wonder she acted as bouncer and he cowered behind the bar whenever one of the enlisted men had had one too many.

Charlie was from Texas and U'ilani was from Hawaii. Meredith didn't know where they'd met or how they had ended up in Vietnam. Both said it was a long story, but neither had offered to unspool the yarn.

"You look pretty tonight." U'ilani placed a mug of whatever was on tap in front of her. "You got a hot date?"

Meredith took a sip of her beer to swallow the bile that rose to her throat each time she thought about her conversation with Lois. "Something like that."

She glanced at the other end of the bar, where Robinson was chowing down on a burger and some Texas-sized fries. She was wearing sneakers, jeans, and a short-sleeved red silk blouse. She looked a lot more comfortable than Meredith did. She probably felt that way, too. Meredith's dress was shorter and more formfitting than she was accustomed to. She had too much skin and too many curves on display. She felt like she was playing dress-up, but she didn't know who she was dressing up for, George or Lois. She wished she could just be herself. She wished she could be with Robinson.

Where was she going tonight? What was she planning to do? Who did she intend to spend time with? Meredith wanted answers to all those questions and more.

She took another sip of her drink. She had been looking forward to going on leave for weeks. The thought of having a few laughs with George and the others had sounded like fun when he first proposed the trip in the mess hall two weeks ago. Now it was beginning to feel more like a chore. One she wasn't certain she wanted to perform.

George was probably harmless, but she didn't want to spend any more time with Lois than she had to. On the transport truck, Lois had exposed herself as a bigot. Meredith didn't want her to think she espoused her beliefs, but she couldn't afford to have her think she didn't.

Talk about a Catch-22.

"Would you like some food?" U'ilani asked.

Meredith tried not to eat more than a few bites during a date in case the guy she was with found her hearty appetite unappealing, but she was too hungry to go without. She pointed at Robinson's plate. "That looks good. I'll have what she's having. Except make mine well done." Robinson's burger was so rare it looked like it was still moving.

"You two keep eating like this and you'll look like me in a few years," U'ilani said with a loud belly laugh. The hem of her colorful muumuu swayed back and forth as she walked the length of the bar.

"You're beautiful just the way you are, U'ilani," Robinson said with a grin.

"Yeah, I bet you say that to all the girls." U'ilani pinned a hibiscus blossom behind Robinson's ear and chucked her under her chin before she handed the slip of paper containing Meredith's order to the cook, a young local in a pair of brown pants and a stained white T-shirt. "I need another Number Three, Tran. Burn this one."

"Yes, Mrs. Miller," Tran said in heavily-accented English. He grabbed a thick hamburger patty out of the refrigerator and tossed it on the grill. The resulting sizzle reminded Meredith of home. Of her father's famous backyard barbecues.

She didn't know where U'ilani and Charlie had found Tran, but he was fast and good. Her food was brought out in what felt like record time and it was prepared just the way she liked it.

"My compliments to the chef," she said when U'ilani came to check on her midway through her meal.

"I can't do that. Compliments would go to his head and he'd start asking for more money. Charlie and I would have to raise the prices to compensate, then you and all your friends would start complaining."

"Okay. Forget I said anything." Meredith swallowed another bite of her two-dollar meal. Back home, she could get a burger at

McDonald's for thirty-nine cents, fries for fifteen. But that was in the real world, and the real world was thousands of miles away. Besides, this was her last weekend in Saigon. Who knew what awaited her in Long Binh? "I hope I get food like this where I'm going."

"You should. Tran has a cousin who works in one of the restaurants on post. He'll take care of you until you come back home where you belong."

Saigon was nothing like home, but Meredith would rather be here than anywhere else. She looked around Charlie's. It was close to 1900 hours and the place was starting to fill. George and the others would probably turn up soon. Robinson deserved to know Lois had it in for her so she could take the necessary precautions. If she wanted to drop a word in Robinson's ear about the situation, she needed to do it now. She finished her meal, tossed her napkin in her empty plate, and grabbed her mug as she prepared to head to the other end of the bar.

"Going somewhere?" George asked. He spun her in a circle as a sudden blast of doo-wop erupted from the jukebox. His Hawaiian print shirt was even more colorful than U'ilani's dress. Blue, yellow, and red birds of paradise flocked over a black background. His tan chinos and brown loafers looked tame in comparison.

Meredith held up her nearly empty mug. "I was getting a refill."

"Here. Let me." As he took the mug out of her hands, she smelled the competing aromas of cologne, aftershave, and hair pomade. "Same again, Charlie. Times two this time."

"You got it." Charlie poured two drafts and set the frosted mugs on the counter. "Here you go, big spender."

George took a seat next to Robinson. "You want one, Nat?" he asked, indicating the beer.

"No thanks, George. I was just about to head out."

Meredith had never heard anyone call Robinson "Nat" before. She tried to imagine herself saying it but couldn't manage the feat. There was still too much distance between them for her to utilize a name that felt so familiar.

George spun around on his bar stool. "You're not coming with us?"

"Not tonight."

"Maybe next time, huh?"

"Maybe." Robinson drained the rest of her beer.

"Have one on me before you hit the road," Meredith said, trying to prolong their encounter.

"Thanks, but I don't have the time." Robinson left a bill on the bar for a tip. "Have fun this weekend. I'll see you later."

Meredith watched her leave, wishing she knew where she was going and wishing even harder that she could go with her. What did Robinson do when she didn't have to worry about who might be watching? Meredith longed to find out but doubted she'd ever get the chance.

"Nat's a tough nut to crack, but you couldn't ask for a more loyal friend," George said.

Meredith drew herself out of her reverie. "How long have you known each other?"

"I met her during my first tour. That was—gosh—three years ago."

"So you know each other well?"

"I'm tempted to say yes, but how well do you really get to know someone over here?" George rested his elbows on the bar and gave her the once-over. "You look beautiful, by the way, though I probably should have said so much earlier in the conversation."

"Probably." Meredith felt herself start to relax. She didn't know what George's expectations were for the evening, but at least he didn't seem to be in a hurry to get to the point where she had to decide whether the night would end in ignominy or a blaze of glory. "Tell me about yourself."

"Me?" He took a sip of his beer and wiped foam off his upper lip with the back of his hand. "There isn't much to tell. I'm from Wisconsin. Racine, to be exact. I'm the oldest of three kids. My brother's a sophomore in high school and my sister is beginning her freshman year at the university in Madison. I joined the Army right out of high school because I thought it was my chance to see the world. I never thought I'd get stuck in the same part of it for the foreseeable future."

"Have you seen any action?"

He was quiet for so long Meredith regretted asking the question.

"Yeah, I've spent some time in the bush," he said at last. "The way things are going, I'm sure I'll be back there before too long. A buddy of mine said the Vietcong have two hundred miles of tunnels underground. They're so well-stocked the VC could live in them for months without poking their heads up for air. Someone's got to roust them out or else we might look up one day and find ourselves surrounded. If we aren't already." He took a long drink out of his rapidly emptying mug. "Given a choice, I'd rather stay here and work on cars. It reminds me of being back home, tinkering on my jalopy in my parents' garage."

Meredith remembered how happy he had looked the first time she had seen him, covered in grease and surrounded by spare parts.

"What kind of car do you have?"

He smiled at the change in subject. "A 1957 Cadillac Eldorado. I named her Caroline after a girl I used to be sweet on once. The Cadillac company makes the best cars on the road. They look good, they're dependable, and they never let you down. Caroline's temperamental because she's getting on in years, but she's my baby. Someday, I'm going to have six more just like her. One for each day of the week."

"Won't that make Caroline jealous?"

"No, because she's my first. She's always going to be special."

"I assume we're still talking about the car."

George rubbed the back of his neck, which had turned the same shade of red as his cheeks. Meredith found his boyish enthusiasm and gentle ways hopelessly endearing. The night had just begun, but he was already a refreshing change from the grabby guys who asked a few questions to be polite then spent the rest of the night trying to get from first base to home plate as quickly as possible.

"Enough about me," he said. "Tell me about you."

"What is there to know that I haven't told you already?"

Whenever they shared a table for meals—which they'd done a handful of times in the mess hall and two or three times at Charlie's— he asked her so many questions she felt like she was a defendant on the witness stand and he was the prosecutor trying to prove her guilt.

"You've told me about your parents, your sisters, and practically every person you've met in your life, but you haven't told me anything about the person I want to know about the most: you. Tell me about you, Meredith. Who are you, and how did you trade a spot in the church choir in Omaha, Nebraska, for a bar stool in Vietnam?"

His question should have been easy, but for some reason, Meredith found it difficult.

"I could try to paint myself in the best possible light, but that wouldn't be honest, and I don't want to lie to you, George."

"Uh oh," he said with what she hoped was mock horror. "Here comes the old brush-off. Should I order something stronger than beer?" He raised his hand as if to beckon U'ilani.

"Only if you want to."

His smile faded and he dropped his hand. "I'm sorry. I didn't mean to hurt your feelings. I was only making fun." He looked genuinely contrite. Genuine. The word suited him much more than the garish shirt he must have borrowed from a hoochmate. "Tell me. What were you going to say?"

"The truth is, I don't know who I am. I guess I'm what you call a work in progress. I know what I want to be, but I don't want to be defined solely by a title. Nurse. Wife. Mother. I want to be all those things, but I don't want any of them to make me stop being Meredith."

She felt like she was babbling so she forced herself to stop. Otherwise, her insecurities might send him running for the hills before they made it through their first date.

"Does that make sense?" she asked, hoping he could tie her jumbled thoughts together without having to exert too much mental effort.

"It makes perfect sense. You want to be happy."

In one short sentence, he had perfectly summed up what she had been struggling to explain for years.

"How can something that sounds so simple be so hard to achieve?"

"Because sometimes other people's versions of happiness and ours are two very different things. That's when you have to say, 'Screw them,' and live for yourself, not someone else." She was about to compliment him on his insight when he said, "Nat taught me that."

He placed a hand in the small of her back. She didn't shy away from his touch the way she usually did when someone tried to get close. She felt more comfortable in his company than in any other man's, but did comfort equate to attraction? Could it lead to love? When she looked at him, she didn't feel the tingling hands or butterflies in her stomach other women described when they talked about the men they were dating. She wanted to feel the spark of mutual attraction. She wanted to know what it was like to fall in love. Could George Moser show her?

"Here come the others," he said with a nod toward the door. "Are you ready?"

She felt a heavy weight settle on her shoulders. "As ready as I'll ever be."

She looked behind her and saw the rest of the group approaching them. Lois and a burly MP named Steve Johansson led the way. Steve's neck was wider than both of Meredith's thighs put together. His biceps were the size of canned hams. Two other couples trailed in his sizeable wake.

The sense of dread Meredith had felt earlier returned in spades when Lois said chirpily, "You two look cozy. Where's the nearest hotel room when you need one, huh?"

Steve squeezed Lois's butt like it was a loaf of bread he was checking for freshness. "Don't worry, baby. We'll get there soon enough. Just you wait and see." Lois squealed and slapped his hand, which only made him bolder. He pulled her body close to his and humped her like an animal in heat. "Stick with me and I'll show you the time of your life."

"From what I've heard, more like the fastest thirty seconds," George said under his breath. Meredith covered her mouth with her hand to hide her smile.

Hector Ortiz, a fellow MP, tried to cool Steve's jets before they revved out of control. "Save some for later, okay, buddy?"

"What's the matter, Ortiz? Are you afraid I'll make you look small in front of your girl?"

Hector playfully punched Steve's meaty shoulder. "I've seen what you're working with, you dumb Swede. There's no way in hell you could ever make me look small."

"Take that back, Ortiz."

Steve grabbed Hector and wrapped him in a headlock. Hector's face quickly turned tomato red after Steve locked his hands together and tightened his hold. Hector struggled to loosen Steve's grip. Just when Meredith thought he was close to passing out, he finally managed to slip free. He ducked under Steve's arm and twisted it behind his back in some kind of submission hold. Steve rose up on his tiptoes like he was trying to fly away from the pain.

"Who's the big man now, Johansson?" Hector asked, reaching around to slap Steve's cheek.

One of the nurses sighed dramatically. "Is it just me or does anyone else find it odd that whenever soldiers get together, all they do is compare the size of their penises? They can be talking about cigars, rifles, or Louisville Sluggers, but the real subject is what's dangling between their legs."

"Take it from me," another nurse said. "Neither of these guys has much to brag about."

Lois fixed Alice Poythress, the last nurse who had spoken, with a hard look. "How would you know?"

Alice drew herself up to her full 5'2" height. "How do you think?"

While Steve and Hector threw jabs that were becoming less and less playful, Lois stared at Alice as if she wanted to pull her hair out. Meredith expected a full-blown melee to break out any second.

Stepping in to play peacemaker, George placed himself between the tiring warriors. Steve and Hector continued to jab at each other, but George easily dodged their blows with quick feints of his head and shoulders. He circled, bobbed, and weaved like a seasoned pro.

"Keep it up and you guys will have to arrest yourselves for disturbing the peace," U'ilani said. She slapped the barrel of a baseball bat against her palm to let them know she didn't intend to let them go on much longer.

Steve and Hector punched themselves out a few seconds later. Hector shook his arms to alleviate the pain from the buildup of lactic acid in his muscles. Steve's broad chest heaved as he tried to catch his breath. His mouth worked like a fish out of water as he tucked in his shirt, a white Oxford so tight Meredith was surprised it hadn't burst at the seams during the scuffle.

"At least I'll do my time with a smile on my face. Right, baby?" He goosed Lois in the ribs, which produced a squeal so loud it made

Meredith's eardrums vibrate. He chased her out the door like a Neanderthal looking for a mate to drag back to his cave.

Meredith could practically smell the testosterone in the air.

If this is what I have to look forward to, this is going to be a long evening.

She wasn't wrong. The night seemed to drag on endlessly as Lois and Steve necked their way through one bar after another. Lois was apparently more impressed by Steve's pugilistic display than Meredith had been. Meredith wanted to spend hours walking the crowded streets taking in all Saigon had to offer—the flashing neon signs, the colorful vendors, the heavily made-up women on nearly every corner promising "good boom-boom for good price"—but the rest of the group seemed more interested in getting drunk. George was the only exception. He seemed as excited about exploring the city as she did.

"Next time," she whispered in his ear as they trailed behind the others to yet another bar, "let's make it just the two of us, okay?"

"You'd like to go out again?"

"You don't?"

"Of course I do," he said eagerly, "but with Steve and Hector going toe-to-toe in Charlie's, and Steve being Steve everywhere he goes, I wouldn't blame you if you didn't want anything more to do with the male of the species."

She put her hand in the crook of his elbow. "You're different from the other members of your tribe."

"Thanks. I think."

He swung her overnight bag like a beat officer twirling his nightstick. Good thing she didn't have anything fragile stashed inside.

When they arrived in town, the others had been so afraid they might miss out on something they had decided to head straight to the bars instead of finding hotel rooms. Meredith wished she had spoken out against the idea. She felt silly. They must have looked like a band of hoboes as they prowled the city with their belongings in their hands.

As they walked up the bustling main thoroughfare, she spotted a familiar figure heading toward a quiet side street. "Hey, there's Robinson."

As Robinson neared the corner, she took an almost furtive glance behind her. She was alone, in direct defiance of Lt. Col. Daniels's command not to go into the city unaccompanied. Meredith lifted her arm to beckon for her to join them, but Robinson kept walking. Before Meredith could call her name, George grabbed her and spun her around in another impromptu dance move. He finished with a flourish, dipping her so low she feared he'd drop her on the sidewalk.

"What are you doing?" she spluttered in shock as she dangled inches above the ground.

George gave her a hard look and shook his head almost imperceptibly. Taking the hint, she zipped her lip and waited for him to explain his actions. She smoothed her dress with her hands after he abruptly jerked her upright.

"Guys, Meredith and I are going to take off." He wrapped his arm around her waist and pulled her close. "It's time to check into one of those hotel rooms Steve has been bragging about all night. You've got my motor running, man."

"Atta boy, Moser," Steve said, his words slurred as he leaned heavily on Lois's shoulder.

Lois struggled to remain upright under Steve's weight. "I want a full report when we get back to base, Meredith, and don't skimp on the details."

"I'll make sure she has plenty to tell you," George said with a lecherous wink.

"What's gotten into you?" Meredith asked in a fierce whisper after she and George moved out of everyone's earshot.

"I was trying to protect your reputation."

"By sullying it? Everyone thinks you and I are about to find a cheap hotel room and have sex."

"I had to do it. I didn't want you to call out to Nat."

"Not you, too." She pried his arm from around her waist. "I thought you said she was your friend."

"She is. That's why I was trying to protect her."

"Why do you feel the need to protect her from me?"

"Not from you. From Lois and the others."

"What do you mean?"

"Nat was headed to Suzy's Bar, a place that's off-limits to all military personnel. If she gets caught there or is simply seen going inside, it would be the end of her Army career."

"Where's the harm? It's just a bar."

"It's not just *any* bar. We don't have any bars like it in Racine, and I doubt you have any in Omaha, either."

"What kind of bar is it?"

"Suzy's caters to a certain clientele." He chose his words carefully. "People…like Nat."

"Oh." She hadn't known such places existed. What were they like? Were they really so different from any of the other bars she had been to? She bet Suzy's was like no other place in the country. Maybe even the world. She longed to pay it a visit but knew such a thing could never happen. Not tonight. Not ever. "So you've heard the rumors about Robinson?"

"They aren't rumors."

As she had earlier that day, Meredith feared for Robinson's future. And her safety. Since George was friends with several MPs, Meredith wondered if he had reported the information to them and it was just a matter of time before the net closed in. She doubted it. He sounded sure of himself but not judgmental.

"I meant it when I said Nat's my friend. Friends keep each other's secrets. She's a good person and she's always been good to me. I don't care what she does or who she does it with." He gave her a moment for his words to sink in, then he jerked his chin over her head, drawing her attention to the building directly behind her. The sign above the entrance read Lotus Blossom Hotel. A pink flower made of neon lights glowed from the roof several stories up. *Vacancy* flashed in the flower's petals. "Is this place okay?"

Meredith's heart sank. "Are you asking me to have sex with you so you'll continue to keep Robinson's secret?"

"Of course not," he said with a flash of indignation. "I want to spend the night with you, Meredith, but not tonight and definitely not here." He punctuated the comment with a sweet smile. "I did three months in country a while back, which means I qualified for a week of R&R. When my orders finally come through, I was hoping you could take a couple days' leave and join me. I was hoping we could use the time to get better acquainted. Nothing has to happen then, either, unless you want it to."

Meredith imagined seeing the wonders Japan, Taiwan, Singapore, the Philippines, Thailand, Hong Kong, or Malaysia had to offer, but she wondered what price she would have to pay for the privilege.

"Don't answer me now," he said hastily. "Just tell me you'll think it over."

"I will."

He shoved his hands in his pockets, suddenly shy. "I chose this place because it's all I can afford. I was planning on getting two rooms. One for you and one for me. I won't get one for us until you ask me to, okay?"

Meredith felt something stir inside her. Like a dormant fire slowly sputtering to life.

"Okay."

George held the door open for her, and they went inside. When the small, sweaty man behind the counter asked if they wanted to rent a room for the night or for the hour, Meredith looked away in embarrassment.

"We'll take two rooms. For the night." George paid the bill and accepted two keys. He dropped one key in her upraised palm and pocketed the other. Then he walked her to her room, a single on the third floor. "I'll be right across the hall if you need me."

He turned to leave, but she placed a hand on his arm so he'd linger a few moments longer.

"I had a wonderful time tonight."

"So did I." His face lit up as if he had been expecting bad news and had received the opposite. "Would you like to do it again sometime?"

She had already said so once, but he apparently needed confirmation. "Yes, I would."

"Perhaps we could talk about it over breakfast. I know a place nearby that isn't half bad. We could meet downstairs in the lobby tomorrow morning around eight."

"That would be lovely."

She tried to think of the proper way to say good night. A kiss felt like too much, a handshake not enough. She stood on her tiptoes and gave him a peck on the cheek. His beard stubble felt like sandpaper beneath her lips.

"Thank you for a wonderful evening."

"You're welcome." He held a hand against the side of his face as if he had been burned. "I'll see you in the morning."

"Good night, George."

He waited in the hall as she unlocked the door and turned on the flickering fluorescent overhead light. Only after she was safely inside with the security chain in place did he finally leave his post. She watched through the peephole as he stood staring at her door with a goofy smile on his face, then turned and entered his own room.

Her room was small and nondescript. A scuffed linoleum rug covered the floor. Its black and white diamond pattern led the way to the small bathroom, which contained a toilet, a cracked sink, and a claw-foot bathtub. A twin bed had been placed in the center of the room. A lime green chenille spread with a raised pink lotus design covered the bed. She tested the mattress with her hand. A bit firmer than she might have liked, but not too bad.

A black Bakelite table lamp and matching clock sat on the nightstand. An emerald and gold upholstered chair was angled toward the window, where gray metal blinds had been drawn to allow natural and artificial light to stream inside.

Meredith tossed her purse on the bed and dropped her small overnight bag on the floor. She had brought sleepwear and a change of clothes, but she wished she had thought to bring an extra pair of shoes. Her feet were killing her.

She kicked off her accursed heels, crossed the tiny room, and peered through the blinds. Car horns honked and bicycle bells chimed incessantly as groups of locals, sailors, and soldiers weaved their way in and out of traffic. The flow had seemed chaotic from street level. From her new vantage point, it looked almost balletic.

She raised the blinds and opened the window to get closer to the action. The clock read well past midnight, but she didn't feel like sleeping. She wanted to rejoin the throng three floors below. She wasn't supposed to do so without an escort, but she didn't plan on venturing far. Maybe a block or two. No farther than the end of the street at most. Then she'd come back here to this cramped room and settle in for the rest of the night.

What was the worst that could happen?

❖

Meredith clutched her purse with both hands as she slowly made her way up the street. Her heart broke a little each time she passed a child in ragged clothes or an adult with a missing limb and a pair of makeshift crutches. People young and old followed her with their eyes, their arms outstretched and their voices plaintive as they begged for spare change. Earlier, George had shielded her from this reality by placing himself on one side and an MP on the other while she and the other women walked between them in a makeshift safe zone. Now she was seeing the terrible toll the war was taking on the people the US military was trying to save. Time would tell if their efforts were worth the price being exacted.

Reason told her to turn around and retreat to her hotel, but she had thrown reason out the window the instant she had sneaked out of her room and crept down the hall with her shoes in her hand so she wouldn't wake George. She suspected he would feel compelled to accompany her, but she didn't think he would be made to feel welcome where she was going. She didn't know if she would, either.

She slowed as she reached the end of the block. She cautiously turned left at the corner. The bar George had spoken about earlier loomed ahead. A discreet sign above the door read Suzy's. Underneath the name of the bar were the words Members Only. Unlike the other nightclubs in the area, Suzy's didn't feature large windows and open doors that invited passersby to peer inside. The front door was closed and appeared to be locked, though Meredith could hear music and laughter coming from inside.

"Okay," she whispered to herself. "You've had your fun. Now you can go back to your room."

But her feet refused to obey.

Drawing closer, she watched as a woman approached from the opposite direction. The woman was tall with short, slicked-back hair. She was wearing jeans and a plain white T-shirt. With her small breasts and freckled face, she could have passed for a boy, but her small hands and slightly rounded hips gave her away. She smiled as she met Meredith's gaze. "Going my way?" she asked in a thick Australian accent.

Meredith looked around to see if she saw anyone she knew. The coast was clear. Lois and the others were long gone and George was safely tucked into bed at the Lotus Blossom. Meredith squared her shoulders. "Yes, I am."

The woman grinned. "This must be my lucky night." She offered her arm. Meredith took it, thankful for the company. "I'm Kerry. And you are?"

Meredith froze, uncertain whether she should give her real name or concoct an alias. She decided against lying. What was the point? She was visiting Suzy's just this once to satisfy her curiosity. Nothing more. After tonight, she didn't plan on setting foot inside the place again. What harm could it do if she told someone who she was? "I'm Meredith."

"I'm pleased to meet you, Meredith. I'll make sure my subsequent questions aren't nearly as hard to answer as my first," Kerry said with a cheeky smile.

She rapped on the door five times in a rhythm that must have been code. A few seconds later, a panel in the door slid open and a pair of suspicious brown eyes filled the hole. Kerry said something in Vietnamese and the panel slid closed with a bang. Meredith heard a series of locks click. Then the door opened. Muted yellow light spilled onto the sidewalk. Meredith smelled cigarettes, sweat, beer, and perfume. The aroma could have been overpowering, but for some reason, she found it intoxicating.

"After you," Kerry said.

All conversations seemed to cease the instant Meredith stepped across the threshold. She felt eyes crawling over her body, sizing her up and staring her down. She had never felt so out of place. All around her, women were being openly affectionate with each other. Kissing, dancing, holding hands. She had danced with her female friends in high school when the boys were too scared to give it a try, but those spins around the floor of the school gymnasium were nothing like what she was seeing now. She had danced with her friends to pass the time. These women seemed to be trying to make time stand still. She backed away, feeling like an intruder.

"I should go."

"Why?" Kerry urged her forward. "You just got here."

"I don't even know why I came."

Robinson materialized out of the shadows. "I think you were hoping I'd buy you a drink," she said as she walked through a haze of cigarette smoke. She was wearing the same clothes Meredith had seen her sporting in Charlie's, but they looked different on her now. *She* looked different, though Meredith couldn't figure out why.

"You two know each other?" Kerry asked after she greeted Robinson with a kiss on the lips followed by a warm hug.

"You could say that," Robinson said.

"I should have known. You always end up with the most beautiful women." Kerry replaced her look of disappointment with a sunny smile. Then she took Meredith's hand and kissed it. "It was nice meeting you, Mer. If you ever get tired of the good old US of A, don't hesitate to take a trip Down Under. Good night, Robbie."

She and Robinson exchanged nods that seemed to speak volumes—to them, anyway. Meredith had no idea what message they were attempting to impart to each other.

Kerry paid a quick visit to the bartender, then headed to a table on the far side of the room, where Lt. Col. Daniels was sitting with a buxom blonde perched on her lap and a skeptical look on her face.

Meredith turned back to Robinson. "Kerry's fun. I like her."

"She likes you, too. Then again, she always falls for the new girls."

"Thank you for the compliment, but I wouldn't call myself a regular." Robinson's unblinking stare was unnerving. Meredith wanted to show she wasn't affected by her or the unfamiliar environment. "How about that drink?" she asked with all the bravado she could muster. She took a step toward the bar, but Robinson didn't move.

"The beer's warm and the drinks are watered down."

"Then why do you come?"

"Because I can be myself here."

"And I can't?"

Robinson scowled. "You don't belong here, Meredith."

"Lt. Col. Daniels seems to think so. Isn't that what the two of you were speculating last month?"

Some of the wind seemed to go out of Robinson's sails. "You heard us?"

"Loud and clear. You haven't been as circumspect as you thought." Robinson's face went pale beneath her tan. Meredith rushed to attempt to allay her fears. "I haven't said anything, but Lois is starting to spread rumors about you."

"That's nothing new."

"Aren't you afraid what she might do?"

"If I live my life in fear, I'm not really living, am I?" Robinson looked at her as if daring her to disagree.

"Is there a problem here?"

Lt. Col. Daniels's voice in her ear made Meredith jump. "Ma'am. No, ma'am," she said, barely resisting the urge to salute.

"I'm happy to hear that." Lt. Col. Daniels glanced from Meredith to Robinson and back again. "I'm glad you came, Meredith."

"Thank you, ma'am."

"Relax, lieutenant. In here, it's just Billie."

"Yes, ma'am."

Lt. Col. Daniels squeezed Meredith's elbow the way she always did when she tried to instill confidence in one of her charges. She released her grip and turned to Robinson. "Are you okay, Nat?"

"Yeah, Billie, I'm just peachy."

Lt. Col. Daniels flashed one of her rare smiles. "In that case, enjoy your evening." She returned to her date, who had begun to pout in her absence.

"Shall we get a table?" Robinson asked. "I'm sure your dogs are barking after walking around all night in those shoes."

Yet again, Meredith marveled at how well Robinson seemed to know her. "I can't keep anything a secret from you, can I?"

"Nope. So I'd advise you not to try." Robinson ordered two beers from the bartender, and placed the mugs on a vacant table near the small dance floor.

Meredith took a sip of her beer and tried not to make a face when it turned out to be as warm as Robinson had warned her it would be.

"How was your date?" Robinson asked.

"Lois talked a blue streak, and Steve and his friends had way too much to drink, but George was nice. We made plans to go out again sometime."

"I see." Robinson watched two women hold each other close as they swayed to the music. Meredith had worked with both women briefly in Okinawa, but she had no idea they were romantically involved. Both had mentioned having boyfriends back home and had the pictures to prove it. Why should she have doubted them? How many other women did she know who had told similar stories that weren't true? She tore her eyes away from the pair when Robinson asked, "Why did George let you wander the streets alone?"

"He didn't. I mean, he doesn't know I'm gone. I sneaked out of the hotel without telling him I was leaving."

"Hotel?" Robinson frowned. "I knew the two of you were getting close, but I didn't know you were together."

"Like I told you back at base, tonight's our first date. We're not sharing a room or anything. He's across the hall from me."

"Oh." Robinson's posture seemed to relax the slightest bit. She always sat and stood so ramrod straight, it was hard to tell.

"I spotted you on the street while the group was deciding which bar to hit next. I tried to say hello, but George stopped me because you were on your way here, and he didn't want anyone to see you. He told them we were going to check into a hotel room, but he simply wanted to get away from everyone so he could have a chance to explain. Everyone will assume he and I slept together tonight, but he hasn't laid a finger on me."

"Yet." Robinson folded her arms on the table. Meredith had never noticed how large her hands were. Her own looked dainty in comparison. "Where are you staying?"

Meredith ceased her examination of Robinson's short, blunt nails and long, tapered fingers. "The Lotus Blossom."

"At least he chose a place that's out of the way. Most of the guys in our unit end up in the Regency at the end of the night so everyone knows exactly where they are and exactly what they're up to. There's no need to brag about your conquests when your friends can practically watch you in the act."

Meredith had seen the dilapidated hotel while she and the others were walking around. The structure was located within stumbling distance of the most popular bar in town. A steady stream of GIs and civilians were beating a path to its doors.

"What did George want to explain?" Robinson asked. "Why he and I have a bad habit of being attracted to the same women?" She took another sip of her beer. Meredith waited her out, waiting for her to explain what she meant. "He used to have a huge crush on Kerry because she gets as excited about cars as he does."

"He didn't mention her, but he said the rumors about you are true."

"They are true." Robinson reached for the book of matches resting on the table. The name of the bar was printed on the back of the matchbook, right above the strike stripe. On the front was an illustration of a woman in a top hat and tails. The woman was beautiful and handsome at the same time. She reminded Meredith of someone she knew. She reminded her of Robinson.

"How did George find out about you?"

Robinson lit a match and watched it burn. "I told him."

Meredith was taken aback. She thought Robinson's sexuality was a secret. Apparently, the secret was an open one. She watched the dancing flame edge perilously close to the tips of Robinson's fingers. "Have you told anyone else on base? Besides the LTC, of course."

"No." Robinson tossed the match into an ashtray, where the flame winked out and died, leaving a thin trail of smoke behind. "I'm crazy, but I ain't stupid." Her Southern drawl grew thicker as the night wore on.

"If someone found out, I'm sure the LTC would do everything in her power to protect you."

"She couldn't protect me without exposing herself. I wouldn't ask her to put herself at risk to save my sorry ass." Robinson pocketed the book of matches. Meredith had never seen her smoke, but she could easily imagine her gallantly lighting a cigarette for a woman who did.

Meredith watched as Lt. Col. Daniels and the blonde climbed a flight of stairs in the back of the bar.

"There are rooms upstairs for people who want to be alone," Robinson said without waiting for Meredith to ask for an explanation.

"Oh." Meredith's heart raced as she imagined Lt. Col. Daniels and the blonde getting to know each other better. Emboldened by her surroundings, she asked, "How does it feel when a woman touches you? Kisses you? Does it feel like when a man does it?"

"I wouldn't know."

"You haven't been with a woman?"

"No," Robinson said with a laugh. "I haven't been with a man."

"So you're a virgin?"

"Not by a long shot. Are you?"

"No."

"What was his name?"

Meredith's thoughts turned to high school once more. "Tommy Coughlin. We did it in the backseat of his car after a sock hop during senior year."

"Did you enjoy it?"

"I guess."

"I'll take that as a no." Robinson leaned forward in her seat as if she wanted to make sure Meredith didn't miss a word of what she was about to say. "When a woman kisses you, she makes your toes curl. When she touches you, she sets your skin on fire. And when she makes you come, your body explodes."

Meredith swallowed hard, rendered speechless by the force of Robinson's words and the images they evoked.

"Did Tommy Coughlin make you feel like that?"

Meredith leaned back in her chair to give herself more room. Robinson felt too close. Physically and emotionally. She needed distance, but Robinson wasn't giving it to her.

"Did he?"

Tommy's hands had been clammy, he had kissed like he read the instructions in a how-to manual, and the whole desultory experience had lasted less than two minutes. Meredith had been left wondering what all the fuss was about. Would it be better with George, or was she destined to go through life feeling vaguely unfulfilled? Looking into Robinson's eyes, she found her voice.

"Let's just say I like your story better."

"So do I."

Robinson glanced toward the stairs, where another couple was disappearing into the darkness.

"Do you have a room up there?" Meredith asked.

"I didn't come here tonight looking for sex. I came here so I could stop hiding for a while."

"I can't imagine you hiding from anyone or anything. I admire that about you."

Robinson shifted in her seat. She looked slightly uncomfortable. As if she weren't used to receiving compliments.

"Perhaps hiding is too strong a word," Robinson said. "I come here when I want to feel like I'm part of a group, not segregated from one."

"I know what you mean."

"Do you?" Robinson raised her eyebrows, her expression a mixture of doubt and what looked like hope.

"Yes, I do."

Meredith had felt segregated earlier tonight. She still did. She didn't belong with Lois and her friends. She didn't belong here. Perhaps she didn't belong anywhere.

She remembered something George had said before they left the base. He had said he joined the Army hoping to see the world and had gotten stuck in one part of it. She didn't want to get stuck. She didn't want to spend her life spinning her wheels. Perhaps Robinson could help her find traction. Whenever Robinson looked at her, though, she felt anything but sure-footed. She felt like she had been cast adrift in a powerful and unpredictable tide.

Robinson was looking at her now. Waiting for her to answer a question yet to be asked. A question she didn't know how to pose, let alone respond to.

"Which hotel are you in?" she asked in an effort to end the lingering silence.

"None. I'm staying with a friend."

"Is she here?" Meredith looked around the room. "I'd love to meet her."

Robinson cocked her head. "Why?"

"I want to see what kind of woman you find attractive."

"It seems to me you want to see a lot of things tonight." Robinson's expression was inscrutable, but the look in her eyes left little to the imagination. "Huynh isn't that kind of friend. And you're the kind of woman I find attractive. But I think you already know that, don't you?"

She reached under the table and slid her hand down the back of Meredith's calf. Meredith gasped at her touch. She tried to pull away, but Robinson tightened her grip.

"Relax. I know you want this."

She lifted Meredith's legs, draped them across her lap, and slipped off her shoes, the infernal pumps Meredith wished she had left on the shelf. Then she began to massage Meredith's sore feet.

"Does that feel good?"

Meredith closed her eyes and slumped in her chair as she finally felt herself begin to relax. She sighed in contentment as Robinson's fingers kneaded all the right spots. "I'll give you five hours to stop what you're doing."

"There's a reason lesbians always wear sensible shoes. So we don't experience this kind of torture."

Meredith smiled as her head lolled against the back of her chair. "Score one for your side."

Robinson stiffened when the door opened, but her tension dissipated when the new arrivals revealed themselves to be two local women who were obviously a couple instead of a group of MPs on a raid. Robinson said she could be herself here, but how could she possibly enjoy herself when she couldn't stop jumping at everything that moved? She was like an animal being hunted. She was the prey and everyone outside this room was a predator. How could she possibly hope to triumph over such impossible odds?

At least Robinson wasn't fighting this particular battle alone. Meredith could feel everyone's anxiety grow with each new arrival and wane when the newcomer turned out to be a friend instead of a foe. She felt the group paranoia begin to seep into her as well. She suddenly remembered where she was. And who she was with. If someone saw her here, how would she explain her presence? Would anyone believe she was just visiting?

She couldn't get over the irony of the situation. The military would give her a medal if she killed an enemy combatant, disown her if she was caught simply having a drink in a bar filled with women who preferred the company of other women. She didn't make the rules, but she had agreed to live by them. She abruptly straightened, pulling her legs out of Robinson's lap.

"Thank you for the massage."

"Would you like to dance?" Robinson asked.

Meredith slipped her feet back into her shoes and looked at her wordlessly. If she said yes, would she be agreeing to a simple dance or something much more complex? She didn't have time for complications.

"I should go."

Robinson downed the rest of her beer and pushed her chair away from their circular table. She held out her hand as a wistful country song began to play and the dance floor began to fill. "Come on. It's Patsy Cline. They play Patsy Cline in Nebraska, don't they?"

Meredith listened to the opening strains of one of the late singer's signature ballads. She felt as crazy as the lovelorn woman Patsy was pretending to be. Only she wasn't pretending. Or was she?

She took Robinson's hand and followed her to the dance floor. Robinson made space for them in the crowd of couples and turned to face her. When Meredith put her hands in position, Robinson chuckled softly.

"This isn't Nebraska, Goldilocks. I think you'd better let me lead."

She placed one of Meredith's hands on her shoulder and gripped the other in hers. Then she placed her other hand in the small of Meredith's back. Their bodies were almost close enough to touch.

Meredith felt an odd sensation low in her belly. A strange combination of tension, curiosity, and excitement. She liked it.

As Robinson guided her in slow circles, Meredith could feel her strength. When Robinson pulled her closer, she could feel her heat. She didn't think twice when the urge came to rest her head on Robinson's shoulder. Instead of fighting it, she succumbed.

She listened to Robinson sing the song's lyrics in an alto that was nearly as rich as Patsy's. She watched the women around her whisper declarations of love as they slowly twirled in the dark. She felt her thundering heart begin to slow. And she wondered if she had finally found a home. Was this where she belonged? In this place with this woman, now and forever?

The lights flashed twice in quick succession and Robinson cursed under her breath. "Shit."

"What's happening?" Meredith asked as scores of women began to rush for the nearest exit.

Robinson released her. "It's a raid. That signal means the police are at the door. Probably a few MPs, too."

"The military doesn't have jurisdiction here, does it?"

"It doesn't matter. If they catch us here, we're dead. We have to leave without them seeing us. Quick. This way."

Robinson pushed Meredith toward the back of the bar as people began to pound on the front door as if they meant to break it down. The doorman leaned against it like a human barricade. He was a big man, but Meredith doubted he could hold out for long.

She struggled to remain upright so she could avoid being trampled by the panicked women surrounding her. Military women whose careers could be ruined by the merest hint of scandal. Tonight, she was one of those women. Robinson's hands on her waist provided much-needed support.

"What about Lt. Col. Daniels?" she asked, trying to spot her in the sea of worried faces.

Robinson looked over her shoulder. The path to the stairs that led to the second floor was blocked. "She's gotten out of worse scrapes than this before. She'll be fine."

Meredith chose to believe her, even though Robinson didn't sound convinced. She didn't have time for doubts.

She followed the crowd to the back door. She had nearly reached it when Robinson pulled her toward what looked like a storeroom. Boxes of liquor and crates of wine were stacked everywhere.

"They'll be waiting at the front door and the rear exit," Robinson whispered, "but I doubt they have the place completely surrounded." She quickly closed the storeroom door as a wave of men wielding batons rushed through the main entrance.

"What do we do now?" Meredith asked.

"We go out the window."

Robinson moved several cases of whiskey out of the way and slowly raised the window. Meredith held her breath when the small aperture's metal frame squealed in protest, but the sound apparently wasn't loud enough to alert anyone to their hiding place because she didn't hear any booted feet running in their direction. She could hear voices shouting commands in the bar and on the street, but none in the narrow passageway between Suzy's and the building next door.

"I'll go first to make sure it's safe," Robinson said.

"And if it isn't?"

"I'll distract them long enough for you to get away."

"Wait. Don't sacrifice yourself for me."

Meredith tried to stop her, but Robinson scooted through the window and dropped down the other side before she could. Robinson looked left and right, then reached for Meredith. "Your turn."

"Is it safe?"

"As safe as it's ever going to be."

Meredith shimmied through the window and, putting her trust in Robinson, followed her through the alley.

"Go slow," Robinson said. "We don't want anyone to see us coming."

Robinson needn't have been so cautious.

A crowd of curious onlookers had gathered in front of Suzy's. Their attention was focused on the front door as several women were herded out of the bar and loaded into the back of a waiting police van. Meredith couldn't bear to look as the crowd pointed and stared at the women as if they were exhibits in a zoo. She had very nearly been one of those women. She had been spared the pain of public embarrassment, but how many others had not been as fortunate? How many would be paraded across the base on Monday and shipped home to unforgiving families? She didn't want to fall victim to the same fate.

She and Robinson skirted the crowd and slowly edged away. They walked as casually as possible, trying not to draw attention. Meredith kept waiting for someone to tap on her shoulder, slap a pair of handcuffs on her wrists, and haul her off to the stockade, but the tap never came. When she and Robinson reached the main street, she nearly fainted in relief.

"Does this happen every week?" she asked after several people brushed past her to get a closer look at the action in front of Suzy's.

"Every couple of months, the police and the MPs bust in and arrest enough people to give the crowd a show. They harass the rest and let them go with a warning not to come back. The next few weeks, attendance drops. Only the locals show up. Everyone else drifts back in over time, and the process eventually repeats itself."

"Have you ever been arrested?"

"No, I've been lucky so far, but there's always a first time." Robinson gently pulled her away from the spectacle. "Come on. I'll walk you back to your hotel."

"You don't have to do that."

"Yes, I do. You're here because of me. I'm not going to let anything happen to you."

The stubborn look on Robinson's face told Meredith it would be pointless for her to argue. She fell in step beside her as she escorted her through the city streets. If possible, the traffic was even more snarled than before.

"When will you find out what happened to everyone?" she asked. She hadn't seen Kerry or Lt. Col. Daniels in police custody or in the crowd out front. Hopefully, they had managed to escape or find a good place to hide until the excitement died down.

"Kerry will let me know. Either she'll write me a letter or she'll come to see me the next time she visits the base."

"How did you two meet?"

"Through Huynh." Robinson looked over her shoulder to make sure they weren't being followed. "Kerry works for the Red Cross. When Huynh's son Hoang was sick, she couldn't get any of the local hospitals to treat him because his father's a black American GI and having a mixed race child is taboo here."

The military discouraged relationships between soldiers and locals. Such relationships frequently occurred despite those efforts, occasionally producing children who couldn't find places in the society in which they were born. Robinson had intimated she wasn't sleeping with Huynh, and Meredith doubted the woman was an enemy agent, but Robinson's friendship with her could cause trouble for her before all was said and done.

"Huynh turned to the Red Cross out of desperation. She stood in front of a support vehicle and beat on the hood until the driver opened the door. Kerry took her in and told the driver to head to the closest Red Cross field station, which happened to be located on my base. I was on duty when they showed up. They were quite a motley crew—a sick baby, a worried mother, and three panicked aid workers. Huynh was yelling in Vietnamese, Kerry was tossing out Australian slang, and Hoang was screaming at the top of his lungs. I finally managed to piece their stories together and figure out what was wrong. I examined Hoang, discovered he had what I suspected was a perforated bowel, and got him prepped for surgery. It was touch and go for a while, but Hoang's a fighter. He pulled through with no complications. Huynh thinks Kerry and I saved her son's life."

"You did save his life. If left untreated, his condition could have been fatal."

Robinson shrugged. "Anyone with medical training could have diagnosed him."

"But not everyone with medical training cared enough to treat him. You did."

Robinson didn't accept this latest compliment any better than she had the earlier one. She quickly changed the subject to deflect attention away from herself, a tactic Meredith noticed she used quite often.

"Huynh couldn't afford to give me money, and I wouldn't have dared ask for any. As payment, she offered me a place to stay whenever I'm in Saigon."

"But Vietnamese civilian areas are off-limits."

"So is the place we just left. That doesn't leave me with many options, does it?"

Meredith slowed her pace. Her hotel was only a few blocks away now, and there were so many questions she hadn't yet asked. She decided to begin with the most important. "Are you and Kerry still together?"

"No. We never were, really. We had a few laughs to ease the tension after a life-and-death situation, but we were never an item. It was fun while it lasted, and we'll always be friends, but we could never make it as a couple."

Meredith couldn't believe Robinson made her relationship with Kerry sound so cut-and-dried.

"Don't you want to fall in love?"

"Of course I do, but I'd rather wait until I'm Stateside full-time before it happens. It's stressful enough worrying about myself out here. It would be even worse worrying about someone else." She looked at Meredith out of the corner of her eye. "You'll see what I mean if George gets transferred to the front lines."

"He and I are just friends."

"For now." The muscles in Robinson's jaw crawled as she clenched her teeth. "I've seen the way he looks at you. He's already smitten."

"What about me? Don't I get a say?"

Robinson stopped in front of the Lotus Blossom when they reached the end of their journey. "Whether you choose to claim your destiny or allow someone else to decide your fate is entirely up to you, Meredith. But I need you to do me a favor." She sighed as if she was reluctant to say what was about to come next. "Thank you for visiting the way I live, but please don't come back unless you intend to stay. It's too dangerous. For you and for me."

Meredith felt as if the ground on which she was standing had suddenly shifted. She fought to maintain her stability. "I would never intentionally do anything to put you at risk. If you want me to stay away from you—"

"It's not about what I want, Meredith. It's about you. I know what I want, but I don't think you do. Not yet, anyway. When you figure it out, you know where to find me."

"Robinson—"

Meredith didn't know what she intended to say, but she didn't get the chance to find out.

A massive explosion rocked the street. The sound was like the end of the world. A heavy, percussive boom, quickly followed by shattering glass and ear-piercing screams.

Robinson threw Meredith on the sidewalk and covered her body with her own as rubble rained down on them.

Meredith heard moans of pain and cries for help. In the distance, sirens began to wail. The odd *ooh-ah*, *ooh-ah* sound she couldn't quite get used to.

Robinson raised her head and brushed Meredith's hair out of her eyes. "Are you okay?"

"I'm fine." Meredith's ears were ringing. She shook her head in a vain attempt to clear it. She closed her eyes when a wave of dizziness hit her so hard she thought she was about to lose the hamburger and fries Tran had worked so hard to make.

"Are you sure?" When Meredith opened her eyes, Robinson's face was a mask of concern. Blood ran freely from a cut on her forehead.

"Yes, I'm okay, but you're hurt." Meredith pushed Robinson off her and scrambled to her feet. She peered at the cut just above Robinson's left eyebrow. "I think you need stitches."

"It's just a scratch." Robinson swiped at the blood and wiped her hand on her jeans. "Get inside where it's safe." She pushed Meredith toward the lobby of her hotel and took off running. Toward the smoke and flames not away from them.

"Where are you going?" Meredith shouted at her retreating form.

"To help the injured."

Meredith kicked off her shoes and fell in behind her.

"Where are *you* going?" Robinson asked.

"To help you."

To her credit, Robinson didn't try to stop her. Meredith could be stubborn, too. Together, they raced toward the burning ruins of the Regency Hotel.

"You're barefoot," Robinson said, pointing at the debris-strewn ground. "Watch out for the shattered glass."

Broken bodies littered the sidewalk. Some were in flames, others were already burned beyond recognition. Meredith gagged on the sickly sweet smell of charred flesh. She told herself to remember her training so she wouldn't begin screaming hysterically like the unfortunate woman whose dress had melted into her skin.

Robinson sat the woman down and told her not to move until the ambulances arrived. She bent and pressed her fingers against the neck of a man who had been impaled by a three-foot-long piece of steel.

"No pulse."

Meredith was so overwhelmed by the amount of devastation and the number of casualties she didn't know where to focus her energy. Her head was still fuzzy, making it hard to concentrate. She turned to Robinson for guidance. "What do you want me to do?"

"Help me triage according to the normal protocols. If they're ambulatory and coherent, corral them next to that bike stand. Put the most critical cases here in the street so the medics can get to them first."

"Got it."

Meredith began to sort through the victims, praying she wouldn't come across anyone she knew. Her prayers weren't answered.

Her heart lurched when she found Alice's seemingly lifeless body under a pile of debris. Both her legs were broken, the left one bent at an impossible angle. The grisly compound fracture was the least of her worries, however.

Meredith dropped to her knees, ignoring the pain as shards of glass dug into her skin. She felt a faint pulse at the base of Alice's throat, none at all in her extremities. Blood streamed from a wound in her side. Meredith needed something to staunch the flood or Alice would exsanguinate before help arrived. She looked around for a towel or strip of cloth. Anything she could use to put pressure on the gaping hole.

"Here. Use this."

Meredith turned at the sound of a familiar voice. George stood behind her, offering his shirt. She pressed the gift against Alice's side. The colorful cotton cloth quickly turned dark red.

"Is she going to make it?" George asked.

"I don't know yet."

George squatted next to her. "When I heard the explosion and discovered you weren't in your room, I knew I'd find you here. Both of you."

He looked over at Robinson, who was performing an emergency tracheotomy on a man whose airway had been crushed by falling concrete. Nurses were allowed to perform simple procedures. A tracheotomy wasn't one of them. Under the circumstances, Meredith doubted anyone would hold it against her. Robinson was up to her elbows in blood, but her patient appeared to be breathing through the tiny tube she had inserted in his throat.

"You're in danger here," George said. "There could be other bombs."

"What do you want us to do," Robinson asked plaintively, "leave these people here to die?"

"Of course not."

"Then stop bitching and lend us a hand."

George pushed himself to his feet. "Tell me what to do."

The first ambulance showed up ten long minutes later. The police soon followed. Robinson finally backed off when MPs and local police began to cordon off the area.

"Good job," Lt. Col. Daniels said. Meredith had been so busy tending to the injured she hadn't noticed the LTC in the crowd. She almost cried when she saw her standing on the sidewalk safe and sound instead of rotting in a jail cell. "Even though you're off duty, I plan on recommending each of you for a service medal."

"Thank you, ma'am."

Meredith felt like she was part of the smallest, most ragtag unit in the Army. She, George, and Robinson were covered in blood. Some of it was theirs; most belonged to the victims they had tried to help. By Meredith's estimation, they had saved more than fifty people. Unfortunately, they might end up losing at least twice that number to the senseless act of violence that had ripped through the heart of the city.

"Get cleaned up," Lt. Col. Daniels said. "And get someplace safe. If you can find one."

"Ma'am. Yes, ma'am."

Meredith and Robinson looked at each other but didn't speak. What were you supposed to say at a time like this? For a night like this one, there were no words. Tears filled Meredith's eyes, clouding her vision. Why were her emotions so close to the surface? Because of what she had just seen or because of what she was starting to feel?

"I think it's time we officially called it an evening." George swept Meredith into his arms. The soles of her feet stung from dozens of cuts. When she looked at the ground, she could track her movements by the bloody footprints she had left behind. "Are you coming with us, Nat?"

"Please do," Meredith said. "I want to take a look at that cut."

Robinson absently touched her forehead, then let her hand drop. "I'll be fine. You're worse off than I am." She bent and examined the soles of Meredith's feet. Her expression said she didn't like what she saw. "Your feet are shredded and you have glass imbedded in the wounds. Do you have tweezers, George?"

"In my shaving kit back at the hotel."

"Give me your kit. We need to do some minor surgery."

"We? What do you mean we?"

George looked squeamish. Meredith flinched when he tightened his grip on her legs. Now that her adrenaline had stopped pumping, the pain had started to set in. Her feet and knees felt like they were on fire.

"Calm down. You won't have to do anything more serious than carrying her upstairs and holding her hand. Can you manage that?"

George nodded fervently. "Yeah, I think so."

"Then let's go."

With Robinson leading the way, George took Meredith to their hotel and carried her up all three flights of stairs to her room. He waited in the hall while Robinson helped her prepare to take a bath so she could disinfect the cuts. Robinson peeled off her bloodstained dress and helped her into the tub. Meredith sighed when she lowered her body into the warm water.

Robinson pointed to the other room. "I'll be out here if you need me."

When Meredith finished bathing and pulled the stopper in the tub, she saw streaks of pink spiraling down the drain. Her blood mixed with the water.

"Okay in there?" Robinson asked from the other side of the bathroom door.

"Yeah," Meredith said shakily. "I'm fine."

She dried herself off with a towel, pulled herself out of the tub, and sat on the closed lid of the toilet. After she pulled her nightgown over her head, she inspected her ruined dress. Tonight she'd worn it for the first and last time. She tossed the dress in the trash so she could begin to put the night behind her.

"Ready?" Robinson asked.

"Ready."

After Robinson opened the door, George came inside and carried Meredith to the bed. Robinson turned the chair toward her and inspected her cuts like a jeweler examining a diamond for flaws. "They're not as deep as I thought, but you're going to have a hard time wearing shoes for a while."

Meredith hissed in pain when Robinson used the tweezers to pull bits of glass from her knees and the soles of her feet. George offered his hand. Meredith clamped on to it like a lifeline. A connection was being forged in this room. A bond she didn't think would ever break. She clenched her teeth as Robinson probed her wounds. "Someone tell me a story."

"Like once upon a time and all that?" George asked.

Meredith flinched as Robinson retrieved another shard of glass. She didn't know how much more she could take without crying, but she didn't want her tears to be seen as a sign of weakness. "I don't care. Just tell me something to take my mind off this."

George shrugged helplessly. "I don't know any fairy tales. There are some limericks I could recite, but they aren't fit for mixed company."

"Or any other kind, for that matter," Robinson said.

"Can you do better?" George asked with a hint of challenge in his voice.

"I couldn't do much worse."

"Prove it then."

"All right," Robinson said thoughtfully as if she were searching her memory banks for a story that was most appropriate to the situation. "When we were little, my brother and I used to go barefoot all summer long. Our parents insisted we wear shoes to church each week so our fellow congregants wouldn't think we were too poor to afford them. As soon as services were over, though, off they went. We wanted to feel the sand between our toes and the ocean on our skin. Shoes just got in the way."

Meredith could practically smell the salt air. "I didn't know you had a brother. Where's he serving?"

"Paul got drafted, but he failed his physical. He hurt his foot one summer when I was twelve and he had just turned ten. Our uncle Raiford had a wind chime on his front porch. Every time we went to visit him, Paul liked to jump up and hit the chime with his hand to make it tinkle. This particular year, Uncle Raiford was having some work done on the porch. The contractor he had hired was good at what he did, but he didn't like to clean up after himself. He had left some old boards lying around. After Paul jumped up and hit the chime, he landed on a rusty nail. He said it didn't hurt, but he started crying when he couldn't pull it out."

"What happened?" Meredith asked, forgetting about the pain in her own feet.

"I went and got Uncle Raiford, who removed the nail and fired the contractor. Aunt Celia put a penny and a piece of fatback on Paul's foot because everyone knows that's how to keep someone from getting tetanus."

"Is that why Paul was marked 4F?"

"No, the nail cracked a bone in his foot. The bone didn't heal properly. He didn't realize it at the time and it didn't stop him from playing football all through high school and college, but the Army docs didn't think his foot would be able to hold up to all the miles of marching he'd be subjected to."

Meredith looked at her own feet. Were her wounds severe enough to send her home or would she be able to continue her mission?

"Welcome to the war, Meredith," Robinson said after she dropped the last piece of glass into the trash. "You're a veteran now." She tore a towel into strips and used them as bandages. "My job's done. Take care of her, okay, George? I need to check on Huynh and Hoang."

Meredith fought back tears as she reached for Robinson's hand. "Stay with me. I don't want you going back out there tonight. It's too dangerous."

Robinson looked down at their clasped hands as if she wasn't used to being anyone's cause of concern. She gave Meredith's hand a quick squeeze and let go. "Don't worry about me. I'll be fine." She rose from her chair. "Can I count on you to keep her safe, George?"

"I won't let her out of my sight again. That's a promise."

"Thanks, buddy. I owe you one." Robinson turned and waded into the crowd of frightened guests milling around in the hall. Meredith watched her swim against the current until she faded from view.

George turned back the covers. "Let's get you to bed. For real this time."

Meredith wearily laid her head on the pillow as George covered her with the sheet and bedspread.

"You got lucky," he said. "You could have been killed tonight."

"But I wasn't."

"Even so, I plan on sleeping in the hall tonight so you can't sneak out again. If you want to play Florence Nightingale one more time, you'll have to climb out the window. Unless you grow a pair of wings, I doubt you'll be up to the challenge."

"Don't worry." Meredith's eyes began to close of their own accord. "I'm too tired to leave this bed."

His voice softened as he backed off the hard line he had taken. "We can explore Saigon some other time. I'm taking you back to the base in the morning."

Meredith forced her eyes open. "No, you aren't. Robinson has the right idea. We can't turn tail and run because of what happened tonight. Tomorrow, you're going to take me shopping so I can buy a new dress."

"You're as crazy as she is," he said with a shake of his head. "Get a good night's sleep. I'll see you in the morning."

He pressed a kiss to her forehead and returned to his room. After he left, Meredith tried to give in to her overwhelming exhaustion.

Every time she closed her eyes, her mind filled with visions of George and Robinson searching for survivors of the blast. Vivid images of them treating the living, consoling the dying, and paying respect to the dead.

She thought she'd be seeing a lot more of the affable man from Wisconsin. As she listened to the continuing sounds of chaos outside her window, however, she feared she might never see the willful woman from Georgia again.

Chapter Five

Jordan felt like she was watching a war movie in which her grandmother had a starring role. When she was younger, she used to beg Grandma Meredith and Papa George to tell her stories about their adventures in the Army, but each had always found an excuse not to grant her request. Now Grandma Meredith was breaking the silence once and for all. The experiences she had undergone were worse than Jordan had ever imagined. How had she managed to return home without suffering any of the physical or mental injuries that had plagued so many of her fellow veterans? Nights like the one she had just described would have haunted Jordan for the rest of her life.

"Geez, Gran, you could have been killed."

"You sound like your grandfather."

"But it's true." Jordan took her eyes off the road long enough to sneak a peek at Grandma Meredith's face. She looked so unruffled the story she had just told could have happened to someone else. "You could have died that night, and you sound so calm about it."

Grandma Meredith looked down at her hands, which were primly folded in her lap. "I had my moments."

"When?"

Grandma Meredith sighed deeply. She seemed almost ashamed to admit she was human, complete with all the requisite frailties and faults.

"I was in denial for days after the incident. I told myself I would be fine as long as I didn't allow myself to feel the pain. I would be fine as long as I could remain numb and didn't think about what happened. Alice was in dire shape, and those two nurses I'd served with in Okinawa were dishonorably discharged after news of their arrest became public knowledge. I didn't see them get escorted off the base, but Lois couldn't wait to tell me all about it. Two of our colleagues' lives were ruined by someone's prejudice, and she was practically gloating. It could have so easily been me being paraded around in handcuffs and locked in the back of a police van, but I couldn't afford to empathize with them. I had to keep going. To keep moving. To pretend that night never happened. That it didn't mean as much as it did."

Grandma Meredith paused as if she had said too much, but she didn't remain quiet for long.

"Reality hit me after I was transferred to Long Binh. I ended up in the infirmary because of the injuries to my feet, and all I could do when I was in there was think. As I lay in bed day after day, I started getting more and more depressed. When Natalie came to see me, I burst into tears the second she walked in the room."

Jordan found it interesting Grandma Meredith alternated between referring to her former friend by her first and last names as if she couldn't figure out if they were supposed to be close or estranged. They had obviously grown close at some point. Close enough to share a dance and, perhaps, a great deal more. What had happened to drive them apart, Grandma Meredith's feelings for Papa George or Robinson's feelings for her?

"When I saw her," Grandma Meredith said, "I finally realized how close both of us had come to dying. If we had walked a little slower, we might have been in front of the Regency when the bomb went off. And if the building had collapsed while we were trying to save the people trapped inside, we would have been the ones in need of rescue. When the MPs burst through the door at Suzy's, Natalie didn't hesitate before she went out that window. She was willing to put her career on the line in order to save mine. I'll never forget that."

"I like this Robinson chick more and more with each passing mile. She's a real badass. Both of you are heroes. You know that, right?"

"I didn't take charge that night. I followed someone else's lead. If anyone's a hero, Natalie Robinson is. I'm not."

Jordan should have known Grandma Meredith would play the modesty card. She always downgraded her achievements, no matter how large or small. But this one? This one was huge.

"Did Alice pull through?"

"Yes, thank goodness. She was shipped home as soon as she was well enough to travel. She had to undergo several surgeries and many, many months of rehab, but she was eventually able to get back on her feet. We've kept in touch over the years. She sends me a Christmas card each year, along with pictures of her grandkids and a family newsletter detailing the high points of the year. I return the favor, but her newsletter's always a good bit longer than mine."

"I'll try to give you more to write about this year."

Jordan didn't often regret being an only child. When she was a kid, her parents had spoiled her to no end and bought her everything she wanted. As she grew older, however, she found it increasingly difficult to be the sole focus of their attention. When she screwed up, she had no one to blame but herself, which made her parents' disappointment even more painful to deal with. Each time one of them gave her a classic "How could you" look, she longed for a brother or sister with whom she could commiserate.

"Are you still in contact with the other women you served with?" she asked.

"Most of them, yes."

"Why did you and Robinson lose touch?" Jordan couldn't imagine severing ties with someone who obviously meant so much.

"When I got back to the States, I followed the war's progress for a while, but life eventually got in the way. Your mother came along, and you know how needy she can be."

"Tell me about it. And if you say, 'Like mother, like daughter,' I'll smack you."

"My lips are sealed."

"I hope not. I'm enjoying hearing about your adventures in Vietnam." Jordan turned on the windshield wipers as she drove into a rain shower that had seemingly sprung up out of nowhere. "Looking at the map, Jekyll Island doesn't seem very big. Robinson shouldn't be too hard to find. Where did she used to live?"

"Her family had a house on the south end of the island, but I don't know if she or it is still there."

"You haven't Googled her or looked her up on Facebook?"

Grandma Meredith pursed her lips. "People of my generation prefer the phone book to Facebook."

"I will drag you into the twenty-first century if it kills me. Did you find a listing for her in your obsolete resource?"

"The number I had for her is disconnected and her new one is unpublished."

"Amateur. Give me five minutes on a computer with a good WiFi connection and I'll find her for you." Jordan glanced at a sign that said Jekyll Island was seventy miles away. So close. One more hour and they'd be there. She couldn't wait for the interminable drive from Wisconsin to end, but she wanted Grandma Meredith's story to go on forever. "Robinson really had the hots for you, didn't she?"

"I wouldn't put it that way."

"How else would you put it? Would you prefer if I said she had feelings for you instead? Same difference. She flat out told you she was attracted to you and she gave you a foot massage when you wore the wrong shoes on your date with Papa George. A foot massage. Do you know what an intimate gesture that is?"

"You forget I used to give sponge baths to complete strangers."

"True that. If the stranger was hot enough, I'd whip out my little sponge and a bar of soap in a heartbeat. Feet are different, though. Feet are icky. I can barely bring myself to touch my own. As for someone else's, forget about it."

"Then I guess you aren't planning on changing your major to podiatry any time soon."

"Ha, ha."

Jordan had changed her major three times before she finally declared what she hoped would be the one that stuck. She still had a chance to graduate on time, but senior year wasn't going to be pretty. Perhaps she should forget about working this summer. She needed to have some fun before she spent the next nine months stuck in class all day and studying in the library at night. She could use the money, but she could use a few good laughs, too. If she was lucky, maybe she, like Grandma Meredith, would have a night to remember forty years after the fact.

"Man, I wish I could have seen the look on Robinson's face when you walked in Suzy's all big and bad like you owned the place. Talk about jaw-dropping."

The first time she had ventured into a gay bar, she had been intimidated by people who were so much more comfortable with themselves than she was at the time. By the end of the night, however, she had been overwhelmed by the acceptance of strangers who had been so willing to welcome her as one of their own.

"My entrance was hardly worthy of accolades. You've been watching too many romantic comedies."

"No, I haven't. I've been listening to yours. Though I guess it's less of a romance than an epic drama with moments of comic relief. What's it like to star in your own version of *From Here to Eternity*?"

"Not as fun as it sounds. I didn't see Montgomery Clift or Burt Lancaster running around anywhere."

"Forget them. Give me Deborah Kerr or Donna Reed instead."

They shared a laugh, but the sound quickly died in Jordan's throat. She rubbed her chest with the heel of her hand. The more distance she put between herself and Brittany, the more her heart ached. A girl she cared about and thought she loved had dumped her with an explanation that had provided more questions than answers.

She tried to tell herself she was upset now simply because the hottest chick on campus was no longer in her bed, but the attempt at levity made her think Brittany's crack about her being shallow might be more accurate than she cared to admit.

She was not her family. Yes, Grandma Meredith and Papa George had served, but she had no desire to follow their lead. Yet she couldn't deny she loved hearing Grandma Meredith recount her experiences during the war. Did that make her a hypocrite? Did it mean Brittany was right? Was she running away from who she was by pretending to be someone she wasn't? Was she a lemming mindlessly following the herd, or was she acting of her own free will?

She felt like Grandma Meredith when she was laid up in the infirmary. All she could do was think. And she didn't like the places her mind was going.

She regarded her reflection in the rearview mirror. There was only one way out of the funk she was in, and it didn't involve reading a self-help book or wallowing in self-pity. She needed to replace one hot chick with another. If she found a willing beach bunny to pass the time this summer, all her problems would be solved. Or at least temporarily forgotten.

If she had to choose between forgetting and facing the facts, she'd choose forgetting every time.

Chapter Six

September 29, 1967
Long Binh Post

Robinson slipped into the back of the theater near the end of a Bugs Bunny cartoon. Meredith spotted her while Bugs was complaining about making yet another wrong turn at Albuquerque. The movie was about to start, and the theater was filling up fast. Seats were at a premium. Standing alone in the semi-darkness while everyone else huddled with friends, Robinson scanned the crowded room for a place to sit.

Meredith watched Robinson take on her current mission the way she did the ones that were much more serious—with her usual intensity. Her jaw was set, her posture was perfect, and her eyes were so bright they were like a twin set of spotlights shining in the dark.

Robinson's eyes were like napalm. Meredith felt like her skin was on fire every time Robinson turned those eyes in her direction. She had never felt anything like it. She wanted to embrace it. She wanted to run away from it. Instead, she had chosen to ignore it. How much longer could she go on pretending Robinson was nothing more than a colleague and trusted friend?

"Shove over." Lois nudged Meredith with her hip, trying to get her to take up as much space as possible. "I don't want her sitting next to us."

Meredith's first instinct was to comply with Lois's request, but she resisted. She and Robinson had been on separate shifts for weeks. They had seen each other only a handful of times since they'd arrived in Long Binh, and hadn't spent any real time together since she'd been released from the infirmary. Meredith had missed her. She hadn't realized how much until now.

She whistled sharply to get Robinson's attention. Robinson's head whipped around as if an alarm had sounded and she needed to get to the air strip to offload wounded soldiers from an incoming chopper. Meredith made room on the narrow wooden bench and waved her over. Robinson nodded and began to walk toward her.

Lois elbowed her in the ribs. "What are you doing?" she asked in a fierce whisper.

"George has guard duty tonight and you're going to sneak out to meet Steve in the armory as soon as the movie starts. I don't want to sit by myself for two hours like a knot on a log if I don't have to."

"But what will people say if they see us fraternizing with her?"

"Who's going to say anything? The only person doing any talking is you."

Lois looked at her, examining her face. Then her own face twisted into a mask of contempt. "I don't know what George sees in you." Lois bolted out of her seat and looked down at her. "You don't want to cross me, Meredith." Her tone was ominous. So were her words. "I could make life very difficult for you and your girlfriend." She brushed past. When she reached the aisle, she gave Robinson a wide berth. "You can have my seat," she said icily. "I was just leaving." She turned to give Meredith a pointed look before she stalked up the aisle.

Robinson squeezed into the space Lois had vacated. "Is she off to get nekkid with Steve in their love nest in the armory?" she asked, her accent thicker than ever.

"How did you know about them getting naked?"

Robinson smiled at her as if she were a child who had just made an adorable mistake. "Get it right, Goldilocks. When you're naked, you don't have any clothes on. When you're nekkid, you don't have any clothes on and you're up to something. Those two are definitely up to something."

"Yes, but how did you know? Lois hasn't told anyone what she and Steve are up to except the women in our hooch. We can't afford to keep secrets from each other because we've all had to cover for each other from time to time."

"Did you tell her where you were the night the Regency was bombed in Saigon?"

"Of course not."

"Then you obviously know how to keep a secret. You should tell Lois to try harder to keep hers. This base is like a small town where everyone knows everyone else's business. Gossip travels fast."

"Point taken," Meredith said.

Lois hadn't had anything derogatory to say about her for a while now, but Meredith hadn't given her a reason. She and George had been officially a couple since their adventurous first date in Saigon. They hadn't shared more than a few chaste kisses since that night, but unless you were willing to settle for any hovel with a flat surface and a door that locked, it was hard to find a place or a time to get romantic.

"Lois and Steve are going at it like rabbits," Robinson said. "If she doesn't end up pregnant before the end of her tour, I'll eat my hat."

"Maybe Steve is shooting blanks. Have you considered that?"

"I try to consider him as little as possible, but I don't think he can say the same about me."

Meredith heard a trace of bitterness in Robinson's voice.

"What do you mean?"

Robinson looked around the room, silently reminding her they were surrounded by hundreds of people. "I'll tell you later." Even though they were whispering, at least a dozen people were close enough to hear what they were saying.

Meredith replayed parts of their conversation in her head to see if either of them had said anything incriminating. She felt privileged to be one of the few people aware of Robinson's secret. The trust Robinson had placed in her felt one-sided, however. Robinson had allowed her to be privy to something she kept hidden from most of the world, but she hadn't returned the favor. How could she when parts of her remained a mystery even to herself? She had never been fond of self-examination—for the past few years, she had always been too busy earning her nursing degree or putting it to use—but being around Robinson made her want to find responses to all the questions she had left unanswered. To give voice to the ones she had left unasked.

"Do you want to go for a swim after this is over?" she asked. The average temperature in South Vietnam was eighty degrees year-round, which made the pool a popular destination. She wanted to cool off, even if relief would only prove temporary. And, most of all, she wanted to spend some time with Robinson away from prying eyes and eager ears.

Robinson gripped the bench with both hands and stared at her feet as if she needed to weigh her decision carefully. Meredith could almost hear her thoughts. How would it look if she and Meredith went away together? Would anyone notice? If they did, what would they say?

Meredith wished she didn't care what other people thought, but she couldn't afford not to. She had joined the Army to escape the bonds of her provincial hometown. When she returned—if she returned—she wanted it to be on her own terms. A dishonorable discharge didn't fit into her plans. Neither did her friendship with Natalie Robinson. But plans, like a woman's mind, were meant to be changed.

"What do you say?" she asked after Robinson didn't provide an immediate answer to her question.

Several long seconds later, Robinson finally looked up. "I've already seen tonight's movie, and it's hot as hell tonight." Meredith felt her skin prickle when Robinson fixed her gaze upon her. She felt cold and hot at the same time. She shivered at the odd sensation. "Why don't we go now?"

It was Friday night. Saigon was so far away it was nothing but a pleasant memory. Most of the off-duty personnel were divided between the theater and the on-base nightclubs. The pool complex would be crowded tomorrow with people participating in and watching a friendly competition between the fastest male and female swimmers on post. Organizers had spent all afternoon placing lane dividers in the pool and hanging bunting all around the complex. Tonight, though, the place was probably deserted.

Meredith looked at the movie screen. The opening credits for *It's a Mad, Mad, Mad, Mad World* had just begun to roll. The four-year-old comedy featured a cast of thousands who produced nearly as many laughs during their madcap search for a cache of missing money. Meredith had seen the film before, too, but she had been looking forward to seeing it again. After the crazy two months she'd had, she desperately needed to laugh. But she and Robinson had never had occasion to be alone, and the thought of spending some quiet time with her proved irresistible.

"It's a date."

They left the theater and returned to the living area, where they retrieved their swimsuits from their respective hooches. They met up outside the tent Robinson shared with five other nurses and walked toward the building where the indoor pool was housed.

"Tell me about you and Steve," Meredith said. "You made it seem like he has it in for you."

Robinson shrugged as if it wasn't a big deal, but her expression said otherwise.

"He made a play for me once and I turned him down. I think I bruised his fragile male ego when I did, because he's been on my case ever since. At first, it was stupid stuff like you'd expect to see from an elementary school bully. Since he's been dating Lois, he's gotten worse. I don't know what she's put in his ear about me, but every time our paths cross, he glares at me like I kicked his dog. Other times, he points at his watch and says, 'Tick tock.' I suppose that's his way of saying my time is coming. If I were a betting woman, I'd wager he had something to do with the raid at Suzy's the night you and I were there. He knew I was going to be in town. He probably tipped off the police, hoping I'd get caught and hit with an eventual dishonorable discharge."

Meredith slowly nodded as the missing pieces of a challenging puzzle fell into place. "When I saw him the next day, he said he'd heard we had a close call the night before. I thought he was talking about the bombing at the Regency. Maybe he was talking about the raid at Suzy's instead."

"Did he know you were there?"

"No one does."

"Do you wish you hadn't gone?"

"No, I'm glad I did. I had a delightful time with you that night. You're a wonderful dancer."

The words felt funny until she saw how good they made Robinson feel.

"Why haven't you been back? Kerry keeps asking about you," Robinson said hurriedly as if to make it clear her question wasn't prompted by her own ulterior motives but someone else's. "I think she has a bit of a crush."

"You asked me not to come back. You said I didn't belong there, remember?"

"Perhaps I was wrong," Robinson said with a wistful smile. "It wouldn't be the first time." She shoved her hands in her pockets as if she didn't know what to do with them. "Did you tell George you went to the bar?"

"No, and I feel like I'm keeping something from him. I want to tell him because I don't want there to be secrets between us, but I don't know if he'd understand why I went after you that night."

"Why did you come looking for me?"

"Because I wanted to be with you." Meredith almost whispered the words. It was the first time she had ever said them out loud. She still wasn't sure what they meant. Weeks after the fact, nothing about that night made sense. She doubted it ever would.

Robinson chuckled. "Yeah, I doubt your boyfriend would understand you wanting to be with someone else."

Meredith swung her leg behind her and tapped Robinson on the butt with the side of her boot. Laughing, Robinson returned the favor and darted out of reach before Meredith could retaliate. Meredith ran after her, enjoying feeling like a kid again. The trip back in time proved all too brief. Robinson quickly grew serious when two people Meredith didn't know drew near. Meredith felt the same anxiety emanating from her she had sensed that night in Suzy's. Robinson couldn't afford to let down her guard, even in an area that was supposed to be considered safe.

"When Steve and I talked," Meredith said after the couple passed by without incident, "he smiled at me like a card shark with an ace up his sleeve."

Robinson nodded, seeming to agree with her assessment. "All I know is, I trust him about as far as I can throw him."

"I'm beginning to feel the same way about Lois."

"With friends like her," Robinson said under her breath, "who needs enemies?"

"Have you been hiding from her and Steve? Is that why I haven't seen much of you lately?"

Robinson's eyebrows knitted as her features formed into a fierce scowl. "My daddy taught me not to run from anything. He told me to stand my ground and fight for what I wanted, no matter the size of the competition."

Meredith heard the edge that had crept into Robinson's voice. She felt the heat of her rising fury.

"Lois can run her mouth all she wants. I'm not afraid of her, Steve Johansson, or anything they might try to do to me." She took a breath. "I haven't been around much because I've been trying to help Brenda Washington get settled in."

"Do I know her?"

"You should. She's the nurse all the brothers have been fighting over. The one who looks like she should be trading lines with Sidney Poitier instead of emptying bedpans."

Meredith hadn't spent much time with any of the nurses outside her unit. Their faces and names ran together in her mind.

"Have you been seeing her?"

"Yes."

Meredith felt the unexpected sting of jealousy.

"But not in the way you think. She got posted here the same time you and I did. She went swimming her first day and someone made a crack about draining the pool so he could scrape the tar out of it. She tried not to show it, but I could tell she was hurt by what happened. I wanted to make sure the assholes who said what they did hadn't broken her spirit."

The Army had been integrated for years, but Meredith hadn't failed to notice most of the varied ethnic groups that comprised its ranks tended to stick together. Leave it to Robinson, in many ways an outsider herself, to cross the color lines.

"You should have said something. I would be happy to help."

"No need. She's fine now. She recently started seeing a guy in Alpha Company. She doesn't need me anymore. I could use your help with something else, though."

"Those are words I never thought I'd hear cross your lips."

"Am I that bad?"

"If I hear 'I got it' or 'I can do it myself' come out of your mouth one more time, I'll scream." They shared a laugh that felt ten times more real to Meredith than the ones any movie could have produced. "Seriously. What do you need me to do?"

"We're coming under fire back home from protestors who think the military is made up of a bunch of baby killers. USARV thinks we could use some good publicity. A few of us are heading out on a sortie this Sunday to provide medical care to some of the people in the surrounding villages. We're going to slap on some Band-Aids and hand out a few lollipops. Basic PR stuff. Nothing too taxing. Right now, the team is composed of me, Lt. Col. Daniels, four medics, another nurse, a war correspondent from the *Washington Post*, and eight infantrymen tasked with guarding our safety. We're going to take a chopper out and drop in on five or six villages. The LTC's going to be in command of the mission. Women aren't often put in charge of male soldiers, so I want to make sure nothing goes wrong. If the mission goes sideways, I want to make sure no one can try to pin the blame on her."

"Is that where I come in? I don't see how I could make a difference."

"You could make all the difference in the world. You were incredible in Saigon at the Regency bombing. You stayed calm and kept your head despite your own injuries. You already had my respect, but I think you earned the guys' admiration that night. That's the kind of person I want on the chopper with us. We've got two nurses—three, if you count the LTC—but we could use one more. I can't think of anyone I'd rather have by my side than you. If the LTC can push the updated orders through in time, would you like to come?"

Meredith thought about the beggars she'd seen in Saigon. The innocent people who had lost everything after wayward bombs destroyed their homes. The ones trapped in a vise between the Western military and the Vietcong. Theirs were the real faces of war. They needed her help just as much as if not more than the soldiers did.

"If you need extra incentive, the LTC is authorized to grant each person who participates three days of in-country R&R at Vũng Tàu. And the best part is, it won't count against our thirty days of annual leave."

In-country R&R, brief reprieves spent along the South Vietnamese coast, were normally granted solely to men who had earned Soldier of the Month or similar accolades for their service on the front lines. To bestow women with such an honor was unheard of, which meant either the Army was hard up for good publicity or someone in HQ thought the mission would be hairy. Both were probably true, one more so than the other.

"R&R sounds good," Meredith said," but I don't need a reward to coerce me into doing the right thing. I'd love to help."

"Good." Robinson looked sheepish. "Because I already told Billie you said yes."

"You stinker." Meredith smacked her on the arm. "What would you have done if I'd said no?"

"If I thought you'd turn me down, I never would have asked you the question."

"Isn't that stacking the deck?"

"I prefer to call it hedging my bets."

Robinson smiled like a mischievous child. Meredith liked catching a rare glimpse of the playful side of her personality. All too often, Robinson kept her at a distance. Except for one night in Saigon when they had ventured much too close. After that night, she had fled to the safety of George's arms. What would happen if she left their embrace?

In the changing room, she and Robinson peeled off their sweat-dampened olive drab uniforms. She told herself to avert her eyes like she did when she and the other nurses changed into or out of their scrubs, but when Robinson unhooked her bra and slipped off her white cotton panties, she couldn't turn away. Their frames were different, but their bodies were the same. Smooth muscles formed from months of basic training and years of strenuous work. Hands roughened from constant washing and exposure to disinfectants. Feet calloused from long hours spent making rounds in sick wards with precious little opportunity to sit for more than five minutes at a time.

How could they be so different when so many things about them were so similar?

After they had swum several laps, Meredith draped her arms across a lane divider. "When did you know?"

Robinson joined her in the middle of the pool. "When did I know what?" she asked, swimming in place.

Out of habit or self-preservation, Meredith looked to see who might be listening. But they were safe here. No one else was around. She was finally free to ask the one question she had never dared.

"When did you know you preferred women to men?"

The words felt foreign on her tongue. Like a language she was learning to speak but hadn't mastered.

Robinson moved closer. She assumed a position identical to Meredith's but on the opposite side of the divider. Her elbow was just inches away, erasing the vast distance that had once gaped between them.

"I struggled in school when I was a kid because I hated to read. I'm the kind of person who would rather do something than read about it. When I was ten years old, one of my teachers gave me a dog-eared copy of a Nancy Drew book for my birthday. *The Secret of the Old Clock*, it was called. I remember being disappointed at first. I felt like you do when you unwrap a Christmas gift and find out you've received underwear and socks instead of the toy you'd asked for. When I saw the beautiful girl on the cover, I felt something stir inside me."

Robinson's accent grew thicker as she grew more comfortable with her subject. Her gentle drawl made Meredith long for a porch swing and a glass of iced tea. Her warm voice provided a stark contrast to the cold water. Her eyes had lost their patented intensity. Her gruff exterior had disappeared. The hard planes of her face had softened. The woman inside the soldier had finally risen to the surface. Meredith had never seen her look so striking.

They had known each other for months, but Meredith felt as if they were meeting for the first time. "You're lovely," she wanted to whisper, but she settled for, "Tell me more."

Robinson chuckled as if recalling a fond memory. "I ran home, locked myself in my room, and read the whole book before Mama got supper on the table. When I discovered it was part of a series, I had to have all the other books, too. I saved my allowance each week and bought a book each time I had enough money in reserve." Robinson rested her head on her folded arms. The faraway look in her eyes held Meredith spellbound. "Nancy's best friend in the early books was Helen Corning. I used to imagine I was Helen riding around in Nancy's roadster helping her solve mysteries. Then the writers stuck

Helen in a corner somewhere, Nancy fell in love with Ned Dickerson, and I was heartbroken on two counts. Years later, I met a woman who made me realize I didn't have to imagine the life I wanted. I could live it. That's what I've been doing ever since. Living my life the way I want to live it, not how somebody else thinks I should. Someday, if I'm lucky, I'll find someone to share my life with."

"What kind of person are you looking for?"

"Someone like you." Robinson's gaze was unblinking. "A woman who is as smart as she is beautiful, and as tough as she is tender. A woman who isn't afraid to follow, but also knows how to lead."

Goosebumps formed on Meredith's skin as she remembered following Robinson's lead on the dance floor at Suzy's. When everything she had believed about herself at that point had been revealed to be a lie. She trembled from the realization.

"Are you cold?" In fact, Meredith had never felt so warm, inside or out. Robinson briskly rubbed her arms, raising her body temperature but clouding her thoughts. "To tell you the truth, I've had enough exercise for one day. I don't know who was worse today, the doctors or the patients, but all of them drove me to distraction. We can get out if you want. We still have time to see the rest of the movie if there are any seats left."

"I don't care about the movie. I want to stay right here with you." Robinson's eyes darkened as Meredith swam closer. "I want to kiss you. Will you let me?"

❖

October 1, 1967
Xom Que

In the mess hall two days later, Meredith ate in silence while she listened to George list all the reasons why she shouldn't be boarding a chopper bound for Xom An Loc in less than an hour. After stops in Đồng Xoài, Ap Bau Bang, Tân Uyên, and Xom Que, she and the rest of the team would return to base several hours later. If, that is, they didn't run into resistance along the way.

"It's too dangerous," George said. "I'm not letting you go."

"Orders are orders. I can't disobey them any more than you can."

He sighed in obvious frustration. "You might not care whether you live or die, Meredith, but I do. I'm not going to sit here and let you put your life at risk without putting up a fight."

"I'm putting my life at risk simply sitting here having chow. Haven't you heard what happened at Charlie's last night?"

George looked off into the distance. "Yeah, I heard."

Details were still filtering in, but the news wasn't good. Last night, an explosion had leveled Charlie's. Dozens were hurt, nine were killed, including Charlie, U'ilani, and the person believed to have planted the bomb—Tran. The Millers' chef and trusted friend had turned out to be an agent for the VC.

"Tran's cousin Phat was stopped outside the gate this morning. Steve said Phat had enough C4 strapped to his body to blow up this whole base."

"See? It doesn't matter where I go, George. As long as we're in this country wearing these uniforms, the war will always find us."

"That doesn't mean you have to go out looking for it."

"I appreciate your concern, but there's no need for you to be so overprotective."

"Overprotective? I'm not trying to protect you. I'm trying to save you. The Fifth Cavalry tangled with the VC in Ap Bau Bang less than seven months ago. They killed over two hundred of the enemy and took three as prisoners, but there could be more in the area. The place is a known Communist stronghold and you want to go in there unarmed. I know you'll have a protection detail, but eight men aren't enough. You need a whole regiment."

"The brass planned this mission. If Lt. Col. Daniels thought the op was too dangerous, I doubt she would have agreed to it."

George stabbed a piece of mystery meat with his fork. "Your Lt. Col. Daniels is so intent on proving a woman can do everything a man can, she can't think straight."

"You don't think women are capable of being good soldiers?"

"I think everything has its limits. I believe women can do anything they set their minds to, but they don't belong on the front lines. No one does."

His hands were balled into tightly clenched fists. As part of the motor pool, he had spent more time on various bases around the country than he had on patrol. At moments like these, he seemed to question the role Uncle Sam had assigned him in this tragic play. Should he be content to ride out the war in relative safety shuttling dignitaries back and forth, or should he fight for an assignment in-country?

Meredith doubted he would be comfortable in either locale—and she suspected his uncertainty was the main reason he was upset about her participation in today's mission. She had no doubts about her role in the war, but he seemed consumed by doubts about his.

"Orders are orders, but you had a choice," he said softly. "You didn't have to volunteer for this mission."

"I know, but I wanted to."

"Are you sure? I mean really sure? I want to know if you're boarding the chopper today because you want to or because Nat asked you to."

Meredith didn't respond. Not because she didn't want to, but because she didn't know how.

"Tell the truth. Nat put the idea in your head, didn't she?"

"She told me about it, but she didn't talk me into it, if that's what you're asking. No one can convince me to do something I don't want to do, you included. I'm going because I want to."

Meredith glanced across the room. Robinson was sitting with Helen Cummings, the *Post* reporter who would be accompanying them today. The room was crowded, but their table was otherwise empty. As if no one wanted to be quoted saying something on or off the record.

Helen was wearing brown cargo pants, an open-collared shirt, and a tan safari jacket. A brown fedora placed at a rakish angle sat atop a shock of lustrous dark hair. Each of her many pockets bulged, stuffed with pens, notepads, extra rolls of film for the bulky camera dangling from her neck, and spare cassettes for the tape recorder resting next to her untouched breakfast tray. She reminded Meredith of Martha Gellhorn, the glamorous war correspondent, journalist, and travel writer whose tumultuous relationship with Ernest Hemingway had attracted even more attention than her award-winning work.

Helen and Robinson sat on opposite sides of the table. Helen leaned forward to capture Robinson's every word with her tape recorder. An open notebook lay within easy reach. She said something that made Robinson smile, something Meredith noted was happening with increasing frequency during the course of their meal.

She thought she was the only one who could make Robinson smile like that, but Helen was proving her wrong. She shoveled her food into her mouth without tasting it. George regained her attention by gently stroking her hand.

"Sometimes I think you want to be with her more than you want to be with me."

The words rang in her head as she took temperatures in Xom An Loc, disinfected elephant grass cuts in Đồng Xoài, and looked over her shoulder in Ap Bau Bang.

Did George's words hold an element of truth? How could they? With him, she was comfortable. She knew exactly where she stood. She was sure of who she was and what was expected of her. With Robinson, nothing was certain. So why did she keep going back for more?

As the chopper prepared to land in Xom Que, the last stop on the trip, she thought back to Friday night when she had thoroughly embarrassed herself.

Robinson's eyes had darkened when Meredith moved closer to her. When Meredith had said she wanted to kiss her, her expression had followed suit. She had released her grip on Meredith's arms and slowly backed away. The distance between them had been less than a foot, but it had felt like more than a mile.

"What's wrong?" Meredith's voice had sounded small and childlike, even to her own ears. "Don't you want to kiss me?"

"No."

Meredith had felt almost crushing disappointment. "But I thought—"

"That it would be easy? That you'd ask me, I'd say yes, and you'd get to pat yourself on the back for taking a chance? You want to kiss me because you're curious about how it would feel. You want to kiss me because, for you, it's a game you think you're not supposed to be playing. For me, this isn't a game. I don't *want* to kiss you,

Meredith. I *need* to. Sometimes I need to kiss you even more than I need to breathe."

The yearning in Robinson's eyes had been so great Meredith had wanted to turn away, but Robinson's penetrating gaze had held her fast.

"Knowing you don't feel the same way hurts. Being around you hurts."

"Is that why I haven't seen much of you since Saigon? Have you been avoiding me?"

Meredith had desperately wanted her to say no. She abhorred the idea she might be causing her pain, but Robinson's response had only confirmed her suspicions. Given voice to her fears.

"I asked Lt. Col. Daniels to change my shifts."

Tears had welled in Meredith's eyes. "Because of me?"

"For the good of the unit. I can't do my job when I'm around you."

"That isn't true. We make a great team. We worked so well together in the aftermath of the Regency bombing Lt. Col. Daniels wanted to give us medals afterward."

"That was before."

"Before what?"

"Before I started wishing I was the one who got to stay with you that night instead of George."

Meredith's stomach flipped as the chopper pilot banked sharply and located a spot in an open field to set the bird down. The infantrymen spilled out of the opening at the back of the helicopter as soon as the exit ramp touched the ground, their M-16s cocked and ready. Meredith watched from the top of the ramp as they scanned the area.

"Clear!" the squad leader said.

Lt. Col. Daniels led the rest of the team off the helicopter. "Keep your head down!" she yelled as Meredith disembarked.

Meredith was tired and hungry. She had been too upset to finish her breakfast and she'd already burned off the C-rations she'd eaten for lunch. In her weakened state, the wind from the chopper's whirling rotors nearly blew her off her feet. She clutched her dwindling cache of medical supplies as she ran in a crouch.

She looked back after she heard a thud, followed by a yowl of pain. Helen had tripped on something in the thick underbrush and gone down. Her helmet askew, she sat rubbing her right ankle.

Meredith turned to help her, but Robinson waved her away. "I'll take care of her. Get to cover."

"You asked for my help. Why won't you let me give it to you?"

Before Robinson could reply, squad leader James Meadows grabbed Meredith's arm and urged her forward. "Come on, Lieutenant. Let's dee-dee."

Meredith had been exposed to the slang term a time or two, but had never heard it defined. Assuming Sgt. Meadows wanted her to pick up the pace, she followed him and the rest of the infantrymen to the thicket of trees that surrounded the tiny village. She prayed they weren't running headlong into an ambush. The group had been lucky so far, even in Ap Bau Bang, but luck eventually ran out. She didn't have a weapon and had been given only rudimentary firearms training after she volunteered. If they encountered hostiles, how was she supposed to defend herself—by throwing a roll of gauze at them? She doubted that defense would prove particularly effective.

"Your ankle doesn't feel broken," she heard Robinson say, "but your mobility will be hampered. I want you to stay in the chopper until we get back from the village. I'll take a closer look then."

"There's no fucking way I'm missing out on this story," Helen said. "The pilots can babysit the plane. I'm going with you."

"But—"

"No buts. I'm going with you and that's final."

Meredith looked back. Robinson was sitting on her haunches, a look of grudging admiration on her face. "It's been fifty forevers since I've met someone as stubborn as you."

"You should look in the mirror more often."

"Shut up and hold on to me."

Meredith heard more amusement than anger in Robinson's words. When she took another look over her shoulder, Robinson was helping Helen to her feet.

Helen put an arm around Robinson's shoulders and leaned against her for support as they made halting progress. They quickly established a rhythm and began to pick up speed.

Meredith churned her rubbery legs as fast as she could. She could hear Robinson and Helen crashing through the underbrush. Finally, they reached the trees. The chopper remained on the ground, but with the exit ramp elevated, Meredith felt cut off. She wondered if the ground troops felt the same sense of disconnectedness when they bedded down in enemy territory each night.

Lt. Col. Daniels placed a finger against her lips, signaling for silence. Everyone stood as still as statues. No one spoke. Meredith listened for movement in the jungle, but all she could hear was the pounding of her heart and the rush of air in and out of her burning lungs.

"Move out," Lt. Col. Daniels said quietly a few minutes later. "Last stop. Let's make it a good one."

Sgt. Meadows and three of his men led the advance. Four more brought up the rear. They were less than two miles from base. Less than two miles from being home free. So why couldn't Meredith shake the feeling they were on the verge of impending disaster? Meadows seemed to sense something similar.

"This doesn't smell right to me, ma'am," he said to Lt. Col. Daniels after they reached the village. "Something's missing."

When Meredith looked around, she saw the same things she had seen in the other villages: locals struggling to maintain their way of life while a war went on around them.

A small garden filled with green, leafy vegetables was being tended by a wizened woman wielding a carved wooden hoe. A few feet away, four goats bleated in a makeshift pen that looked ready to fall apart if a strong breeze blew through. Women of all ages stood in the open doorways of grass-roofed huts, curious but shy children hanging on to their legs as if they were security blankets.

"There are no men here," Lt. Col. Daniels said.

"Bingo." Sergeant Meadows turned his head and spat a line of tobacco juice on the ground. A few scattered droplets clung to his lower lip. The rest dribbled down his chin, but he didn't bother to wipe them away. He adjusted his rifle, shoving the butt under his arm and pointing the muzzle at the ground. "Either someone planned a big fishing trip and didn't invite me, or this place is full of sympathizers. Either way, I suggest we do what we came here for and do it in a hurry so we can dee-dee back to post."

"I agree," Lt. Col. Daniels said. "Chase, help Robinson assess our visitor. If she can't walk under her own steam, take one of the infantrymen and get her back on the chopper ASAP. Krug and I will assist the medics."

"Yes, ma'am."

Meredith handed her bag of supplies to Dolores Krug, a tough-as-nails fifteen-year nursing vet who was on her fourth tour. Dolores didn't have the greatest bedside manner but was the most experienced member of their unit. Today, a level head would come in handier than a warm heart.

While Dolores and Lt. Col. Daniels introduced themselves to the hesitant villagers, Meredith joined Robinson and Helen at the edge of the village. Robinson was trying to examine Helen's ankle, but Helen was so busy taking pictures she wouldn't sit still.

"What do you need?" Meredith asked.

"I need you to hold her down long enough for me to determine if we're dealing with a break or simply a bad sprain."

"There's no need to resort to violence, ladies." Helen set her camera down and leaned against the base of a wax apple tree. Overripe pieces of the pink, pear-shaped fruit littered the ground. Meredith brushed some of them aside so she could kneel next to Robinson and Helen. "Do all nurses have as much responsibility as the ones in your outfit seem to?" Helen asked as Robinson began to examine her in earnest.

"It depends on where you're stationed." Robinson ran her hands up Helen's ankle. Meredith could see the worn black leather of Helen's boot beginning to bulge. By the time they got back to base, they might have to cut the boot to get it off. "On some bases, nurses are allowed to perform simple procedures like digging out shrapnel or closing up after surgery because the medics are so busy running to the next casualty. On other bases, the docs don't let you do anything except hand them a scalpel when they ask for it."

"You certainly look better than any of the doctors I've seen thus far. Or maybe I'm just a sucker for a woman in uniform."

Helen's voice was designed to be heard above the din in busy newsrooms and crowded bars. It easily carried to the infantryman who stood less than twenty feet away. He turned and eyed them up and down. Then, shifting his rifle from one shoulder to another, he walked away and said something to two of his companions. The three of them looked over and laughed none too politely.

"Ouch!" Helen flinched and hissed in pain after Robinson exerted pressure on her ankle. "I was about to compliment you on your gentle touch. Now I'm glad I didn't."

"Your ankle isn't broken, but you'll need to stay off it for a while."

"Perish the thought. I'm supposed to fly to Da Nang in a few days. There's no way I'm missing out on such a plum assignment. Give me some aspirin and a cane and I'll be fine. Though a little TLC wouldn't hurt. When will you take R&R you earned from this trip? Perhaps I could meet you in Vũng Tàu when you're there."

Robinson cut her eyes at the trio of infantrymen staring in their direction. "Nothing's been decided yet, ma'am."

"Ma'am? Why must you be so formal? Are you the shy, retiring type, or are my charms simply lost on you?"

"I don't know what you mean, ma'am."

How could a woman so intelligent be so ignorant of the way things were? Meredith cleared her throat and indicated the men standing guard. Helen followed her gaze. A look of recognition crossed her face, quickly followed by one of resignation.

"Oh, I get it." Helen picked up her camera and snapped a picture of Lt. Col. Daniels surrounded by smiling children. "It's unfortunate you two are unable to be open about who you are."

"But I'm not—"

Robinson quieted her with a look mixed with equal parts anger and disappointment. Meredith felt disappointed, too. In herself. Why had she been so quick to try to correct Helen's assumption about her?

"Times are changing. It's a different world out there."

Robinson opened a bottle of aspirin and shook out two pills. "You're not in the world right now, ma'am. You're in the 'Nam."

Helen swallowed the aspirin with a sip of water from Robinson's canteen. Then she scribbled something in her notepad. "That's a good line. I may have to use it in a story. Are you sure you don't want to sit down for an in-depth interview?"

Robinson offered her hand and pulled Helen to her feet. "What could I possibly have to say that would interest your readers?"

"Plenty. I've got an hour's worth of tape in my pocket and I have enough in here for a week's worth of copy."

Helen held up the notepad. A neat round hole appeared in the center of it as if by magic. Shreds of paper floated to the ground like flakes of snow, a rare sight this far from the mountain regions. Meredith watched the flakes fall, suddenly realizing this year would be the first time in a long time she wouldn't have a white Christmas. Helen seemed just as hypnotized. Robinson broke both of them out of their respective trances.

"Gunfire! Get down!"

Meredith dove for cover. Robinson and Helen joined her in the trees. Helen lay on her belly like a soldier in the trenches, her camera pointed at the action. Her fingers worked the shutter and film advance lever so fast Meredith doubted she took time to focus on what she was shooting.

Robinson wrapped her arms around her helmet, brought her knees up to her chest, and curled up tight, making herself as small a target as possible. Meredith mirrored her position and squeezed her eyes shut.

In her mind, she could see George shaking his head in disapproval and hear him saying, "I told you so." In reality, what she heard was the steady pop of gunfire and the clamor of competing voices. Lt. Col. Daniels and Sgt. Meadows barked orders, though their commands seemed to be at odds. Sgt. Meadows was telling his men to return fire while Lt. Col. Daniels was telling them not to shoot because women and children were in the line of fire. On the other side of the village, male Vietnamese voices were yelling something Meredith couldn't understand. Chaos reigned.

Throughout it all, Meredith could hear the constant clicking of Helen's camera as she snapped picture after picture. Meredith thought of Dickey Chappelle, the female photojournalist who had been killed two years before while on patrol with a Marine platoon on a search and destroy mission south of Chu Lai. Chappelle was the first female reporter in history to be killed in action. Meredith wondered if Helen was about to be the second.

Meredith forced herself to open her eyes. Men dressed in black were swarming out of the jungle on the other side of the village. The muzzles of their AK-47s flashed and bucked as they fired round after round. She had heard about these men. They weren't the uniformed, professional soldiers who launched well-planned offensives at the front lines. These were local guerillas, teenagers given minimal amounts of training after being pressured or shamed into joining the Vietcong.

"We're outnumbered!" Lt. Col. Daniels yelled above the noise of the firefight. "We can't win this one. Let's get out of here with as little collateral damage as possible." She gave the signal to retreat.

Sgt. Meadows ordered his men to lay down cover fire while the medical personnel ran toward the jungle.

"Damn!" Helen sounded so distressed Meredith thought she had been shot. Meredith was trying to see where she had been hit when Helen held up her camera and said, "I'm out of film."

"You can change rolls when you get back to the chopper," Robinson said. "Can you walk?"

Helen tried to put weight on her injured ankle. She fell to her knees before she managed to take two steps. Robinson moved toward her.

"Meredith, help me do a fireman's carry. I'll take the left side. You get the right."

Meredith quickly moved into position. Helen wrapped her arms around their shoulders while they reached under her legs and locked their arms together.

"Ready?" Robinson asked. "On three. One, two, three."

Meredith used all her remaining strength to help lift Helen off the ground and carry her through the jungle. She ducked each time she heard a bullet fly past her head, hoping the next one wouldn't find its mark. She wanted to stop when they reached the clearing, too tired to go on and too scared to run out into the open.

"Almost there," Robinson said. "You can do it."

The adrenaline surge provided by Robinson's gentle encouragement gave Meredith the burst of energy she needed to make the final push. She half-walked, half-ran as they carried Helen to the waiting helicopter.

"Where's the rest of your crew?" the copilot asked as they climbed onboard. "We need to get off the ground now."

"They're on the way," Robinson said. "About two minutes back."

"From the sounds of that firefight, we don't have two minutes."

Meredith peered out one of the windows. The gunfire was getting closer. The jungle moved as if it had come to life. Then Lt. Col. Daniels burst into the clearing. Sgt. Meadows and his men were right behind her.

Meredith counted heads, starting with the people still on the ground and ending with the ones already on board. "Eighteen." Everyone had made it out of the village and, miracle of miracles, no one seemed to be hurt.

Then Lt. Col. Daniels went down.

"Billie!"

Robinson leaned forward, straining to help but unable to do so from afar. Meredith grabbed her and held on to make sure she didn't bolt out of the chopper and try to rescue Lt. Col. Daniels on her own. Meredith held her breath as the LTC writhed on the ground in obvious pain.

"Look," Robinson said. "She's getting up."

Lt. Col. Daniels staggered to her feet favoring her left arm. A patch of red had bloomed on her shoulder and was beginning to spread. She moved toward the helicopter. The faster she ran, the bigger the patch began to grow. Meredith hoped the bullet hadn't hit an artery or she could bleed out before they made it back to base. If they made it back to base.

Lt. Col. Daniels and the infantrymen were a few feet from the chopper when their pursuers appeared at the edge of the jungle.

"Hurry up!" the pilot yelled. "We need to get airborne before they get set up."

Meredith looked at the enemy soldiers. Two were on their knees. They lifted rocket launchers to their shoulders and took aim. Defenseless, all she could do was pray their weapons wouldn't find their mark.

Robinson pulled Lt. Col. Daniels up the ramp. The LTC collapsed as soon as she was onboard. Robinson draped her across her lap and cradled her head in her arms. Robinson's eyes were wide, but showed no signs of panic when they settled on Meredith's. Meredith felt the connection that had formed between them. No matter what happened during the next few minutes or over the course of the war, they would be bound by the events of this day for the rest of their lives.

"Now's the time for you to do that thing you do," Robinson said after the ramp lifted and the chopper slowly—too slowly—began to rise into the air.

Meredith reached inside her shirt and pulled out her dog tags. She fingered the engraved metal as if each letter were a rosary bead.

She heard a whoosh as the first rocket flew into the air. She braced herself for impact. She prepared to die.

As she comforted herself with thoughts of walking down the aisle in a flowing white dress and carrying, bearing, and holding a child, the rocket passed less than a foot in front of the chopper's nose. The second just missed the front rotor. The copilot called out each near miss. The chopper's engine whined as the pilot gunned the throttle.

"Okay," the copilot said with an audible sigh of relief, "we're out of range."

Meredith's body sagged as all the tension she had built up since the Vietcong appeared suddenly left her muscles. She felt simultaneously drained and exhilarated. Coming so close to death had made her appreciate life. She had so much to be thankful for, starting with the brave people on the chopper with her and ending with a wonderful man who was anxiously awaiting her return.

"Show of hands," Lt. Col. Daniels said weakly. "How many of you could use a change of underwear right now?"

The men laughed, accepting her as one of their own. Meredith crawled over to her to take a look at the bullet hole in her shoulder.

"Where the hell did the VC come from?" Lt. Col. Daniels asked after the laughter died down.

"Tunnels under the village," Sgt. Meadows said. "I spotted the entrance to one of them just before all hell broke loose."

"Does Command know about this?"

"They will as soon as you get back to base and debrief General Westmoreland."

With Lt. Col. Daniels wounded, Meredith had expected Sgt. Meadows to break the chain of command in an attempt to earn brownie points with high command. He was obviously a man of honor instead of ambition.

"How's the wing?" he asked.

Lt. Col. Daniels peered at her bleeding shoulder as Meredith examined her wound. "It's a through and through." She raised her head to get a better view. "I'll end up with a nasty scar—two of them, in fact—but I'll live."

"Looks like you got your ticket punched." Meadows sounded almost envious. "You're going to make it home before I do."

Lt. Col. Daniels shook her head. "I've got too much to do here to even think about going home. A couple stitches and I'll be fine. Right, Chase?"

"You'll need more than a couple stitches. More like a couple dozen."

Lt. Col. Daniels shrugged. "Six of one, half a dozen of the other."

Robinson passed Meredith a pair of scissors from her first aid kit. Meredith cut away Lt. Col. Daniels's sleeve. Then she disinfected the wound and packed the hole to stop the bleeding. She wrapped the wound tight and secured the bandage with medical tape.

After she finished tending to Lt. Col. Daniels, she found a seat and tried to come to terms with what had just happened. She examined the sea of faces surrounding her. Everyone talked and laughed easily, bonded by the traumatic experience they had just shared. Was this how it was for men in the bush? Was this how lifelong friendships were formed? If so, Meredith thought she had forged several today.

Helen, who had changed film when she boarded the helicopter, quickly exhausted another roll. "How does it feel to complete your first mission?" she asked, reloading yet again.

Meredith couldn't put what she was feeling into words. She had never felt such camaraderie. She was honored to be able to serve alongside these men and women. She was so proud to be part of this group—and even prouder to have Lt. Col. Daniels as her commanding officer. Was there no limit to what she or any woman could do?

"I'm just glad it's over," she said, but it felt more like the beginning than the end.

CHAPTER SEVEN

W hy the beginning?" Jordan asked.
"You might say it sounds strange, but that was the day I realized how much I cared for…everyone. I thought I was going to lose Natalie. I thought George was going to lose me. For me, that was the day everything changed."

"You fell in love with Papa George while bullets were whizzing over your head?"

"Nothing that dramatic. My feelings for him began to shift in a more romantic direction after Saigon. In Xom Que, I was too busy trying to stay alive than fall in love. Over breakfast that morning, I could tell how much George cared about me. As I lay in the jungle a few hours later praying not to die, I regretted not sharing my feelings with him and everyone else I cared about. I regretted not saying, 'I love you,' when I had the chance."

"Well, you weren't exactly the touchy-feeling type back then, Gran." Grandma Meredith winced as if her words had struck a sensitive spot. Jordan pretended not to see it. "But at least you're making up for it now. I've always heard there were no atheists in foxholes. I didn't know they were overrun with romantics, too."

"There's no faster way to get in touch with your feelings than to come face-to-face with your own mortality. When I was curled up in the dirt trying not to get caught in the crossfire, all I wanted was for the people I loved to know how much they meant to me. I wanted to get out of that jungle and tell them so."

"And you did."

"And I did."

Grandma Meredith seemed even more surprised by her story of survival than Jordan was. Jordan tapped the brakes, slowing to five miles per hour above the posted speed limit. She usually drove at least ten miles over the designated limit when she was on the interstate, but she wanted Grandma Meredith to finish her story before they got to Jekyll Island. If she dropped the thread now, she might not pick it up again when they arrived. She'd be more concerned with unpacking the car, shopping for groceries, and getting settled into the house she had rented for the summer. Even now, she was digging out the long list of instructions the homeowner had sent her. Those things were important, but Jordan wanted to know what had happened during the rest of her tour. It had taken her this long to detail two months and there were another ten to go.

The needle on the gas gauge hovered over the quarter-tank line. Jordan decided to fill up sooner rather than later. She moved into the right lane, took the next exit, and tried to find the cheapest prices. A BP station was closest, but she hadn't stopped at one since the company's negligence contributed to the oil spill that had devastated the Gulf Coast. She pulled into an acceptable station, parked next to an available pump, and shut off the engine. She unbuckled her seat belt but didn't get out of the car.

At the rate they were going, the summer would end before Grandma Meredith's story did. Not that Jordan was complaining. She had discovered so many things about Grandma Meredith she never knew—and so much more she had never suspected.

She wasn't surprised Grandma Meredith had experienced brushes with death—she had been in the middle of a war, after all— but she had no clue she'd had a brief flirtation with another woman. She might have to adjust Grandma Meredith's Kinsey score. That zero was starting to look a little wobbly.

Jordan marveled at how well her grandparents' unconventional love story had turned out. Then she reminded herself what Grandma Meredith had said when they began this leg of their trip. As much as she had loved Papa George, she had loved someone else even more.

Had Grandma Meredith's attraction to Natalie Robinson been more than fleeting? Was she the one Grandma Meredith had cared for all this time?

Nah. Couldn't be. She would have told me before now. I know she would.

Jordan got out of the car, started the pump, and stuck her head in the open driver's side window while the gas flowed into the tank.

"Did you and Papa George get to go on R&R together?"

"No. His orders and mine came through at the same time and we ended up in different cities. He went to Bangkok and I went to Vũng Tàu."

"I was hoping Lt. Col. Daniels was able to arrange a romantic getaway for you."

Grandma Meredith frowned as if an unpleasant memory had just resurfaced. "The LTC was something of a miracle worker, but there were some things even she couldn't fix."

❖

December 15, 1967
Vũng Tàu

Each time she was called to Lt. Col. Daniels's office, Meredith felt like a recalcitrant high school student who had been summoned to see the principal. At least she had company this time. Robinson was by her side as she stood at attention in front of Lt. Col. Daniels's paperwork-strewn desk. Flynn sat nearby taking notes. The woman probably slept with a clipboard in her hands.

"At ease."

As Meredith and Robinson relaxed their stiff postures, Lt. Col. Daniels leaned back in her chair. The sling she had worn for nearly a month was gone, though she still favored her left shoulder from time to time.

"I want to go over the ground rules before you head out. Vũng Tàu is known as Sin City for a reason. There are over a hundred bars in the area. Most of them are named for American towns and landmarks to make us feel at home. In the bars and on the street, anything can be had for the right price. As long as none of the local laws are broken, the military tends to look the other way. You'll probably run into some of the Allied troops on the beach or in town. Aussie and Kiwi forces are headquartered nearby, as well as several of our Army and Navy support units. You might see some off-duty VC as well. Rumor has it their forces take R&R there, too. Unconfirmed reports say the line of barbed wire stretching from the jungle to the water line on the northern end of the beach was put in place to separate the VC from the Allies. Be careful, no matter where you are. The VC might not be your only enemies this weekend. Some of the men you'll come across haven't seen a woman in months. When their money runs out, they might be tempted to take from you—by force, if necessary—what the 'beach girls' won't give them without the correct fee. Look out for each other. If you leave your hotel for any reason, make sure you don't do it alone."

"Ma'am. Yes, ma'am."

"There are a few nurses stationed at the base hospital in Vũng Tàu," Lt. Col. Daniels said, "but R&R on the base itself is limited to servicemen. Thanks to Uncle Sam, a room has been reserved for each of you in the Majestic, a hotel near the beach. You should have a perfect vantage point to see some rather interesting sights. And that's putting it mildly."

Meredith didn't care about the random couplings of horny GIs. She was more interested in crisp cotton sheets, a real bed instead of a bunk she could never get truly comfortable on no matter how exhausted she was, and all the sea air she could draw into her lungs.

"Every deuce and a half we have here in Long Binh is either spoken for or out of commission, so a flight crew will chopper you to Vũng Tàu and back. I'm sure the pilots and gunners will thank you profusely for the respite. A trip to Vũng Tàu is a reward that doesn't come down the pike very often."

Meredith wasn't looking forward to boarding a helicopter again after the bullet-riddled flight out of Xom Que, but she preferred a short, relatively smooth chopper ride to the longer, bumpier one she would have had to endure in the back of an uncomfortable transport truck. By the time they arrived, her bottom would have been so tender she probably wouldn't have been able to sit for a week.

"After you land, someone from the motor pool will drive you to your hotel. You'll be given a stipend for meals and incidentals, but you'll be on your own while you're there."

Flynn handed Meredith and Robinson an envelope filled with cash. Meredith could almost taste the freedom. Three whole days of peace and quiet. Three days without reveille or roll call. Three days of living without having to worry about the dying. And three days of trying to figure out where she and Robinson stood.

Robinson had been much more relaxed the last month or so, and she was smiling a lot more in general. She seemed, for lack of a better word, happy. Meredith wanted to know what had happened to change her attitude, but they hadn't had a chance to talk—*really* talk—since Xom Que. Meredith wanted to talk to her about that day—and the night in the pool. Because she couldn't get either out of her mind.

"If you miss your transport and fail to return to base as expected, you will be considered AWOL and you will be brought up on charges. Enjoy your time off, but don't do anything stupid. That means no overnight visitors in your rooms, no embarrassing incidents in town, and no vanishing acts when your leave is up. Don't make me come looking for you, ladies. Because when I find you—and I will find you—you'll wish I hadn't. Do I make myself clear?"

"Ma'am. Yes, ma'am."

Lt. Col. Daniels's expression, so hard one moment, quickly softened. "I wish I was going with you, but someone's got to do the work around here." She scooted closer to her desk and shuffled a pile of paperwork into a neat stack. "Dismissed."

Meredith and Robinson saluted, picked up their duffels, and walked out.

"Transport doesn't leave for another thirty minutes," Robinson said. "I'm going to head back to my hooch to wait for mail call."

"I'll go with you. The only mail I ever get is twice-monthly letters from my mother. I enjoy the updates from home, but I could do without the constant prodding for me to reconsider my decision and come home. The only way I can return to the States before the end of my tour is if I was wounded or pregnant. One I hope will never happen, the other not for a few more years."

"I'm sure George would make a good father."

"You think so?" Meredith's enthusiasm more than made up for Robinson's decided lack of it. "I'll have plenty of time to find out after the war's over."

"If the war ever ends. The conflict has been dragging on for years with no resolution in sight. I doubt anything happens to change that any time soon."

Meredith felt confident she and George would eventually be reunited if the war managed to separate them, but she wasn't so sure about her and Robinson. She feared the end of her tour would mark the end of their friendship as well.

When her hitch was up, she planned to return home, get a job in a civilian hospital or doctor's office, and settle down. Robinson would most likely reenlist as she'd already done three times before. Unless Meredith's plans changed by next summer, she and Robinson would be reduced to pen pals.

Meredith hoped they'd stay in touch after the war ended, but exchanging letters didn't seem like enough. How could a few words on a page capture the essence of someone as complex and confounding as Natalie Robinson? Only the real thing would do. And the real thing would be thousands of miles away. Meredith already felt the pain of their parting and they hadn't even said good-bye.

She had been in Vietnam since August. She had seen more in those four months than she had in her previous twenty-three years. Bodies broken, mangled, and burned beyond recognition. She had become a nurse so she could help those in need, but as the casualty count continued to rise, she couldn't tell if her efforts were making a difference.

How could she stay and witness another year of horror? But how could she go and leave the men and women she served with to fight the battle without her? She didn't want to leave the people she loved behind. Robinson, George, Lt. Col. Daniels, the men and women in her unit. She loved them all. One more than the rest. One she thought about constantly. Couldn't imagine ever being without. Yet the possibility—the very real possibility—existed that they would soon part.

She shook her head to clear her thoughts. The future was too uncertain and the present was no sure thing. For now, nothing else mattered except the next three days.

"Have you ever been to Vũng Tàu?" she asked.

"No. This is my first trip."

Meredith felt as if she and Robinson were finally on equal footing, a plateau she had been trying to reach since the day they met. Why had it taken so long for them to reach common ground? Now that they were here, Meredith didn't want to waste the opportunity to deepen their friendship. This weekend was their best chance. And perhaps their only one.

"Maybe we can explore the city together. I hear the governor of Indochina built a mansion there that's a sight to behold."

Robinson gave her a sidelong glance. "You do know this isn't a sightseeing trip, don't you?"

Meredith blushed at her transparent eagerness. "I know."

"Good. Because I hope you aren't expecting me to play tour guide. R&R means rest and relaxation, not ramble and roam. For most of this trip, the only sights I'm planning on seeing are the insides of my eyelids."

Meredith couldn't help feeling deflated. Each time she tried to get closer, Robinson pushed her away. She was tempted to ask her why she wouldn't let her in, but she thought she knew the answer. She was already in too deep.

What was it Robinson had said that fateful night in the pool? *I don't want to kiss you, Meredith. I* need *to. Sometimes I need to kiss you even more than I need to breathe.*

She had never desired anyone as much as Robinson seemed to desire her. When she looked at George, she felt a warm, rosy glow. When Robinson looked at her, she felt an all-consuming fire. A fire that now seemed to be extinguished. She missed its heat.

When they entered Robinson's hooch, Lois was standing at the foot of Robinson's bed. She was holding an envelope with colorful Vietnamese stamps affixed to the front. The envelope's flap hung open. Lois gripped the letter inside. She froze when she saw Robinson walk toward her. "I—I thought you were gone."

"Sorry to disappoint you, Lieutenant. Unless you've been assigned different housing, you don't have reason to be here."

"I was looking for Dolores. The truck's waiting."

"She's probably already on it, which is where you should be."

"Fine. I won't stay where I'm not wanted."

Lois hid the letter behind her back and made to leave, but Robinson dropped her duffel on the floor and blocked her path. "Not so fast. Return my property before you go."

"Like I said, I thought you had already left." Lois stuffed the letter inside the envelope, and shoved both into Robinson's outstretched hand. "I was going to hang on to that for you while you were gone."

Robinson slid the envelope into the back pocket of her jeans. "Then you decided to read it instead?"

"The way you sound, I didn't know if you could read," Lois said, mocking Robinson's thick Southern drawl. "I was trying to do you a favor."

Robinson moved toward Lois, her body language as menacing as the look on her face. "One thing I don't need is a favor from you."

"I'll remember that the next time you decide you want to change shifts." Lois skipped past Robinson and darted out of reach. "Have a good time in Vũng Tàu. Don't do anything I wouldn't do. And, Meredith," she said, pirouetting in the aisle between the evenly-spaced bunks, "try not to worry about what George will be getting into while he's in Bangkok. From what I hear, it's anything goes over there, and you know boys will be boys. Hopefully, the only souvenir he brings back is the kind that doesn't require shots."

She snickered as she headed out the door. Robinson looked like she wanted to chase after her to get one more word in, but she managed to hold her ground.

"Are you ready to go?"

"Past it."

Robinson grabbed her duffel and slung it over her shoulder. Meredith followed her out the door. As they walked across the base, Robinson pulled the envelope from her pocket, unfolded the letter inside, and began to read. A smile immediately creased her face.

"Good news from home?" Meredith asked.

"What?" Robinson looked up as if she had forgotten Meredith was with her.

"Is that a letter from your family?"

"No." Robinson quickly folded the letter, returned it to its envelope, and shoved both into the recesses of her duffel. "From someone I didn't expect to be hearing from so soon."

Meredith waited for Robinson to elaborate but wasn't surprised when an explanation didn't prove to be forthcoming.

"Have you had any tough cases lately?" she asked when the silence began to drag on. "I haven't seen anything more serious than a bad incidence of trench foot the last few days, but quiet spells don't usually last very long."

"I hope you're wrong about this one."

"So do I. I've had all the action I can take for the foreseeable future."

"I hope you're wrong about that, too." Robinson looked as if she was trying to be matter-of-fact, but her studied nonchalance appeared rehearsed. "Kerry stopped by the other day. She has some time off and she wants to meet up when we get to Vũng Tàu. She's been there a ton of times and knows all the most popular places, as well as the out-of-the-way ones. If you want a tour guide, she'd make a better one than I would. Are you interested?"

Meredith wanted to see the city, but she wanted to see it with Robinson. This trip was their reward. Why couldn't they enjoy its spoils together? Instead, Robinson seemed to be trying to pawn her off on Kerry so she could be free to do her own thing.

"Do you plan on spending all three days catching up on your beauty sleep?" she asked.

"I'm going to spend them making up for lost time, that's for sure."

They showed their orders to the men on duty in the makeshift terminal and were escorted to the airfield. Meredith swallowed hard as she neared the idling helicopter. In her dreams, she could still hear the bullets bouncing off the fuselage as she and the others tried desperately to escape the advancing VC soldiers in Xom Que. She hoped history wasn't about to repeat itself. This time, the shooters could have better aim.

Robinson seemed to sense her trepidation. She offered her hand after they were buckled into their seats. Meredith gripped it as hard as she could.

"First-time flyer?" the pilot asked with a wry smile. "Don't worry. I haven't lost a passenger yet."

"There's always a first time."

Robinson tightened her grip. "Today isn't going to be that day."

Looking into her eyes, Meredith felt the same way she did when she looked into George's. Safe. Protected. But there was something more. An undercurrent she felt but couldn't name. What was it about Robinson that continually threw her off her stride? And why did being off-balance feel so good? Scary, but exciting, too. Kind of like she had always imagined falling in love would feel.

It wasn't that way with George, she thought as she stared out the open door. He made it so easy to love him. Everyone he met ended up crazy about him, herself included. Why did Robinson have to make it so hard to care about her? With her, everything was a challenge. Even a task as simple as trying to be her friend often seemed monumental. Meredith had to endure the whispers of people like Lois, who were so willing to denigrate what they didn't understand. Each time Lois made some snide comment about Robinson, Meredith asked herself why something that was supposed to be wrong felt so right.

She awakened from her reverie when she felt Robinson's body press against hers. Robinson's body was the perfect combination of hard and soft. Hard muscles accentuated by soft curves.

Too hard. Too soft. Just right. I guess I deserve the nickname she gave me. I really am Goldilocks.

"Look." Robinson pointed at the view past one gunner's head. "There's your mansion."

Meredith peered out the open door. Below them, a stately mansion dominated the landscape.

"It looks like something out of a fairy tale."

On one side, mountains large and small rose into the sky. On another, the South China Sea lapped against a curving white sand beach. In between, houses, hotels, and restaurants fought for dominion. The hotels appeared to be winning.

"I think that's Nui Nho." Robinson pointed to the small mountain at the southern end of town, then to a larger one on the other end. "So that must be Nui Lon."

Meredith's eyes drifted from the mountains down to the beach as the pilot descended to give them a closer look. The sand and sea were filled with sunbathers and swimmers. A steady stream of sun-baked, crew-cut men with women on their arms headed to a series of small huts lining the beach.

"Those must be the beach girls Lt. Col. Daniels was talking about."

The copilot chuckled knowingly. "This is Vũng Tàu, ladies. If you know how to negotiate, ten bucks goes a long way."

"So does a case of the clap."

Meredith didn't fail to see the hungry look on Robinson's face as she watched the soldiers enter the huts to spend some private time with the girls of their choice. In another time and another place, would she be allowed to join the parade without drawing unwanted attention?

After the chopper landed at the base, a GI from the motor pool led Meredith and Robinson to a jeep and drove them at breakneck speed to their hotel. Meredith was so grateful to arrive in one piece she nearly knelt and kissed the ground like a visiting pope.

The first thing she did after they checked in was head up to her room so she could check out the view from her balcony. She threw open the heavy blackout curtains and stepped onto the terrace, a wide rectangular space with enough room for a patio table and two lounge chairs.

Her room faced the beach, which seemed even more crowded than it had during their brief flyover. Hopefully, there was some available space around the pool because she certainly didn't see any near the water.

She sighed deeply as a warm ocean breeze kissed her skin.

"Is being here worth the price you had to pay?"

Meredith looked to her left. Robinson was standing on her own balcony, a dreamy smile on her face. Meredith had never seen her look more at ease. She looked like the weight of the world had been lifted from her shoulders. Funny how much a change in location could change someone's outlook. It had certainly changed hers.

"I thought I was going to die that day in Xom Que," she said.

"So did I."

"Is that the closest brush you've had?"

"During my first tour, a mortar landed near the OR while we were in the middle of surgery. A nurse and two medics were critically injured. I ended up with a broken wrist. One of the medics died at the scene. The nurse and the other medic survived but couldn't remain on active duty. My CO stuck me behind a desk until I healed up. Those were the longest six weeks of my life. I'd rather dodge bullets than shuffle papers any day."

"I don't know what frightens me most," Meredith said, "getting hurt or seeing someone I care about wounded." It felt so good to talk with someone about her fears without worrying if the listener considered her weak or unfit for duty.

"That's a tough one, but it explains why George ripped me a new asshole when we got back to base after the dustup in Xom Que. If I had known the mission would end up going sideways, I never would have asked you to come."

Robinson looked so remorseful Meredith longed to console her, but there was a four-foot gap between them, not to mention a seven-story drop to the ground.

"If I had to do it over again knowing beforehand how everything would turn out, I'd still say yes."

"Really?"

Meredith couldn't tell if Robinson looked touched or dubious. She gripped the railing, wishing she could bridge the distance between them. "I trust you, Natalie. There isn't anything you could ask me that I wouldn't do."

"Are you sure?"

"I'm positive."

Robinson gifted her with a warm smile. "If I asked you to keep calling me Natalie, do you think you could manage it?"

Meredith had been telling herself for months she wanted them to be closer. Now that the opportunity was finally presenting itself, she felt herself shy away. "I could try."

"If it doesn't feel right, you don't have to keep doing it. But I love the way you say my name, Meredith. Say it again." Meredith saw what looked like desire wash over Natalie's features. "Say my name."

Before Meredith could grant her request, someone knocked on Natalie's door.

"I think your tour guide's here," Natalie said as the mask she usually wore slid back into place.

"Wait."

Meredith no longer wanted to go sightseeing. She wanted to explore what had just passed between them. But Robinson—Natalie—left the balcony and entered her room. Soon Meredith heard the door open, followed by the sound of Kerry's cheerful voice offering an effusive greeting.

Kerry bounced onto the balcony like a kangaroo, one of her country's most famous native creatures. She was wearing tennis shoes, khaki shorts, and a short-sleeved white button down shirt over a black tank top. "I hear you want to see Vũng Tàu."

"I thought I did. Now I'm not so sure."

"This could be the only time you're in town. You might as well make the most of it. Do you want an all-day tour or something more down and dirty? I know which one I'd prefer, but I'll leave it up to you."

"I wouldn't want to impose."

"Nonsense. Squiring a beautiful woman around town is hardly an imposition. Are you ready? If we leave now, we can hit the main tourist areas, bend our elbows for an hour or two in one of the local bars, and be back here in time for dinner."

Kerry slid a pair of dark sunglasses over her eyes. Her almost manic energy was such a contrast to Natalie's laid-back demeanor Meredith was having trouble adjusting.

"Sounds like you have a full day planned."

Kerry shrugged. "You're only going to be here for three days. I figured we'd get the sightseeing out of the way first, then spend the rest of our time lounging around the pool or on the beach. When I say 'we,' I mean me and you because I doubt our friend here will come up for air long enough to leave her room."

Natalie frowned as if Kerry had said something she shouldn't.

"Oops. Sorry, mate."

Natalie rebuked Kerry with a look before turning to Meredith. "Go. Have fun. You can tell me all about it on the way back to Long Binh. That way, you'll have something to take your mind off the flight."

Today, holding Natalie's hand had been all the distraction she had needed.

"Sounds like a benediction to me." Kerry rubbed her hands together in anticipation. "Enjoy your afternoon, Robbie. We can compare notes later. Shall we, Mer?"

Meredith met Kerry in the hall and they left the hotel on foot. During their walking tour of the city, Kerry introduced her to several sights that were jaw-dropping in their unparalleled beauty but left Meredith strangely unmoved.

"I thought you wanted to do this," Kerry said as they sat nursing their drinks in a crowded downtown bar. The airmen at the table across from them were taking turns singing bawdy pub songs. The lyrics grew more risqué after each round of drinks delivered by the mini-skirted waitress. Meredith doubted some of the acts the men sang about were physically possible, let alone pleasurable.

"I did. I mean I do."

"Just not with me."

Meredith trailed a finger along the curve of her half-empty bottle of Coke but didn't respond.

"I told Robbie this was a bad idea, but her head's so high in the clouds she can't think straight at the moment." Kerry pushed her mug of beer aside and rested her arms on the table. "You're really into her, aren't you?"

"Why would you think that?"

Meredith wondered if she looked as shocked as she felt. No one had ever asked her a question like that before. Because they had never dared or because the answer was obvious to everyone but her?

"I'm—"

She tried to form a response to Kerry's question that wouldn't make her seem defensive. She wanted to let Kerry know she was seeing someone—a man—without trumpeting her heterosexuality.

"I'm dating George Moser. Didn't Natalie tell you?"

"Yeah, she told me. George is a good bloke. He's fair dinkum, even though he is a Yank. And a man," Kerry added with a grin. "Robbie's seeing someone, too, but I haven't made up my mind yet if I believe either of you are serious."

"Natalie's dating someone?" Meredith couldn't believe what she had just heard. But if Natalie had someone in her life, it could account for the positive upswing in her mood. She was falling in love. "Who is she seeing? For how long?"

Kerry checked her watch. "I'd say about three hours, give or take. They've been writing back and forth for months like a couple of lovesick schoolgirls, but they haven't seen each other face-to-face since the whole thing started."

"Do I know her?"

It had to be someone who could move about the country without raising suspicion and whose correspondence with Natalie wouldn't draw the attention of anyone in the mail room. She could think of only two people who fit both categories. One was Kerry. The other was Helen Cummings.

"Is Natalie seeing Helen?" Kerry looked momentarily stunned. "She is, isn't she?"

"I've already opened my big mouth once. I'm not going to comment any further on the subject." Cradling her mug of beer, Kerry leaned back in her chair. "Besides, you should be having this conversation with Robbie, not with me."

Meredith felt a knot form in the pit of her stomach. Her initial suspicions about Natalie and Helen had apparently been confirmed. When Helen visited Long Binh two months ago, she had piqued Natalie's interest and, perhaps, captured her heart.

Meredith didn't know how she was supposed to feel. She wanted to share Natalie's happiness, but she could sense only her own unease. Conflicting emotions warred within her.

She wanted to know why Natalie hadn't said anything about her liaison with Helen. She had been open about her relationship with George. The least Natalie could have done was return the favor. Did Natalie think she wouldn't be supportive? Did she think she wouldn't understand? Or was she trying to spare her feelings?

"If you have feelings for her," Kerry said, lowering her voice until it was barely audible, "I suggest you tell her sooner rather than later. Who knows? You might already be too late. Helen's had two months to lay groundwork while you've been trying to make up your mind about who you want to be with."

Meredith shivered involuntarily. Fear made her feel cold despite the hot sun beating down on her face and arms. She was afraid of losing Natalie's friendship. Afraid of losing her love. Had fear cost her the kind of happiness she had always dreamed about but hadn't been able to attain?

She examined her heart as she stared into the depths of her drink. She allowed the emotions she had tried to suppress have their way. She needed to be honest. With Natalie and with herself. She wasn't happy for Natalie because she was jealous of Helen. She wanted to be the woman Natalie was seeing. She wanted to be the one Natalie held in her arms. The one who captured her attention. The one with whom she shared her hopes and dreams. She wanted all these things, but none of them were possible unless she gave up the life she knew for one she had never imagined for herself.

The sound of rotors chopping the air drowned out the sounds of the singing airmen and the rock music blaring from the tinny handheld radio dangling from a metal chain around a tipsy sailor's neck. When the men craned their necks upward, Meredith followed suit. She spotted four helicopters flying in a tight, controlled pattern. Her heart sank when she saw a large red cross on a white background painted on each of the birds' noses, identifying them as medical evac vehicles.

Each chopper probably contained at least three wounded men. More if their conditions weren't critical. Either way, the base hospital was about to receive several new patients.

The men grew quiet, undoubtedly placing themselves in their injured comrades' shoes. One tossed a half-eaten hamburger at the passed-out sailor, who came to with a jerk.

"What's going on?"

"Wake up and turn that shit off." The burger tosser pointed to the sky. "Those are our guys up there. Show some respect."

The sailor twisted the radio's power button, bringing the latest anti-Vietnam protest song from Country Joe and the Fish to an abrupt end. The only sounds that remained were produced by the heavy traffic on the street and in the sky.

Meredith watched the helicopters continue their slow, almost stately progress. She hoped there were enough nurses on duty at the base to handle the incoming onslaught. In Long Binh, they were occasionally forced to grab anyone they could find to sit with the expectants so the nurses could be free to assist in the treatment of patients with better prognoses. Nurses were accustomed to the carnage they saw every day. Personnel conscripted from other parts of the base weren't. She feared some might end up with lingering emotional trauma. Were others about to become similarly afflicted?

Kerry touched her arm. "You're on R&R, Mer. Take a load off. Let someone else handle this one."

"I can't put the war behind me when the opposing sides are fighting just a few miles away." She looked up at the mountains and hills that were keeping her from seeing the struggle firsthand. "How did you know what I was thinking?"

"You and Robbie get a distinctive look in your eye when you think about work. It's as if a light goes on. Your face—your whole body—changes. You look like you could conquer the world or heal everyone in it, probably at the same time. I consider myself lucky to have met you both."

"I feel the same way about you and Natalie. I think it's fair to say I've never met anyone quite like either of you."

"Lesbians, you mean?" Kerry asked with a smile. She mouthed the word some seemed to find offensive.

"No. Women who aren't afraid to stand up for what they believe in, no matter how many people might stand in opposition."

"Is that what I was doing?" Kerry downed the rest of her beer. "I thought I was living my life and having a few laughs along the way."

Meredith remembered a similar statement Natalie had made a few months earlier. *If I live my life in fear, I'm not really living, am I?*

"You and Natalie are certainly cut from the same cloth."

"Two peas in pod. Isn't that what you Yanks say?" Kerry glanced at the GIs, who were becoming increasingly agitated. A few were muttering something about rounding up as many VC as they could find and showing them what was good for them. Kerry tossed a few bills on the table to cover the cost of their drinks and the waitress's tip. "I think my fellow pea will have my arse if I don't get you back to your hotel ASAP. It's about to get wild out here." She signaled for a cab, finally managing to flag one down after several unsuccessful attempts. "Are you all right?" she asked as the driver headed for the Majestic. "You seem quiet."

"I feel like I should be doing something besides sitting here twiddling my thumbs."

"I know you want to go to the base, but you can't. You've got orders. You're supposed to be on R&R, not volunteering for extra duty. I doubt the guards at the gate would let you in, despite your good intentions."

"Men are fighting and dying all across this country. Their bravery makes me feel like a coward."

"Cowards don't go into the bush armed with nothing more than a bag of tongue depressors. You aren't a coward, Mer. You're a hero."

Meredith couldn't bring herself to speak the words that might lower Kerry's high opinion of her. Heroes weren't afraid to tell the people they loved how they felt about them. Heroes overcame their fears; they didn't give in to them. She was no hero.

After the cab dropped her off at her hotel, Meredith rode the elevator to her floor and stared at Natalie's closed door, wondering what was happening on the other side. She wanted to let Natalie know she had made it back safely, but she didn't dare interrupt. She didn't want to catch Natalie in the act—or see the look of soul-deep satisfaction the act had surely produced.

She entered her own room and, after a forgettable room service dinner she barely touched, fell into a fitful sleep. She was serenaded—tormented, really—by the sounds of voices and laughter coming from Natalie's room. She was awakened by much different sounds. The sounds of heavy fists pounding on a door. She sat up in bed and squinted against the bright light steaming through a crack in the curtains she had neglected to completely close.

"Tick tock, Robinson. Your time has finally come."

The voice, though muffled, was instantly recognizable. It was Steve Johansson's voice. But what the hell was he doing here in Vũng Tàu at—she peered at the clock next to the bed. Seven in the morning?

"Open up, Robinson. It's time to face the music."

Suddenly, Meredith knew exactly why Steve was here. He was hoping to witness what she hadn't wanted to see: Natalie and Helen in a compromising position.

She climbed out of bed, threw on her robe, and opened her door. Steve and three MPs were standing in the hall. Their crisp uniforms smelled of starch and authority.

"Ah, Meredith," Steve said with a reptilian smile. "You're just in time for the show. You can watch while I arrest your friend."

Meredith tightened the belt of her robe. She didn't want to watch, but she couldn't turn away.

Steve banged on Natalie's door again. "Last chance, Robinson. If you don't open this door, we'll let ourselves in and the hotel will stick you for the cost of the repairs. You've got three seconds. One. Two."

Natalie opened the door and leaned against the jamb. "I thought I'd save you the trouble of trying to guess what comes after two."

Meredith admired her feistiness, but doubted provoking Steve was the wisest option to take under the circumstances. He was clearly determined to make the task he had been assigned as miserable as possible for her. Making him angry would only increase her despair—and his obvious delight.

"You know why we're here, so step aside and let us do our job."

Natalie folded her arms defiantly. "Not until you tell me what you hope to find."

Meredith thought Natalie was stalling for time so Helen could escape out the window—until she remembered they were seven stories up and Helen had nowhere to go. Stalling wouldn't solve the situation, only delay its inevitable outcome.

"Do you really want me to spell it out in front of so many witnesses?" Steve indicated the hotel guests who had begun to poke their heads out of their rooms to see what was going on. "We've received reports you've been fraternizing with a female civilian in direct violation of Army policy against such relationships."

"I didn't know the Army had a policy against civilians."

The onlookers laughed and Steve's face turned bright red. He trembled with barely-controlled fury. Yet Natalie seemed to be enjoying herself. Her military career was about to end in humiliating fashion and she was smiling about it? Steve had the ammunition he had sought for months. He had Natalie, he had Helen, and if he searched the room, he'd find the love letter in Natalie's duffel. He had finally won, yet Natalie was acting like the victor.

Meredith felt like she was missing something. She moved closer, but one of the MPs held out an arm, warning her to stay back.

"I'm trying to be civil, Robinson," Steve said. "Tell your visitor to come out here so we can get this over with."

Natalie finally stepped aside. "Feel free to look, but I don't think you'll find what you're looking for."

"I'll be the judge of that."

Steve and one of his fellow MPs rushed into the room. The other two remained in the hall with Natalie to make sure she didn't make a run for it. Each held her by the arm as if she were already under arrest.

Meredith wondered if she should call someone. Lt. Col. Daniels was the first person she thought of, but the LTC was both too far away and too low on the chain of command to stop what had already been set in motion.

Meredith heard the tinkle of glass breaking, followed by a series of bangs, crashes, and thuds. Helen seemed to be putting up quite a struggle. Several minutes later, however, Steve came out of the room empty-handed.

"Where is she?"

"Where is who?"

"The woman who left these behind." Steve brandished an overflowing ashtray. "You don't smoke." He held up a lipstick-smeared cigarette butt. "And this isn't your shade."

"I didn't take you for an expert on women's cosmetics."

Meredith whirled when she heard Helen's distinctive voice. Unlike Natalie, who was still in her nightgown, Helen was fully dressed. She was wearing her usual uniform. Cargo pants, safari jacket, and an open-collared shirt. Her trademark fedora was firmly in place. She held a cup of coffee in one hand and an omnipresent cigarette in the other. She blew out a trail of smoke and extinguished her cigarette in the ashtray Steve was holding.

"Thank you. Private Johnson, is it?"

"It's Johansson. Sgt. Johansson." Steve turned to show her the stripes on his uniform sleeve.

Helen bowed slightly. "I stand corrected."

"Are you Helen Cummings?" he asked.

"I am."

He held up the ashtray. "Are these your cigarettes?"

"They are."

Steve looked smug as he pointed at Natalie. "And do you know this woman?"

"You know I do. Otherwise, you wouldn't have asked the question. This exercise is proving quite tiresome, Sergeant. Shall we skip to the point so Private Robinson can get dressed and we can conclude the interview we began yesterday?"

"Interview?"

"My dear boy." Helen patted Steve's cheek. "If you know who I am, you must also know what I do for a living." She flashed her press credentials. "My readers are very interested in this war and the men and women who are fighting it. Private Robinson is one of those women, and you are preventing me from procuring the information I need to tell her story to the masses. Or would you prefer I told a different story? One about how certain members of our proud military would rather go after one of their own than the enemy."

She raised her camera and snapped a few quick shots. The MPs covered their faces with one hand and their names with the other. Then they began to scatter like cockroaches after a light comes on.

"We're out of here, Sarge," one of them said. "Tell your girlfriend to get better intel next time."

Lois. Meredith wasn't surprised to hear she'd had a hand in this.

Even though he had obviously lost the latest battle in his and Natalie's never-ending war, Steve refused to accept defeat. "Tick tock, Robinson." He shoved the ashtray into her gut, but she didn't even flinch.

"Check your watch, Johansson, because I think it might be broken."

Steve walked away like a schoolyard bully who had finally had the tables turned on him, but Meredith knew he'd be back. He would keep coming until he finally had his way. As long as he was around, Natalie would never be safe.

"I owe you one," Natalie said after Steve had left and the guests had returned to their rooms.

"What you owe me," Helen said, "is an interview. Get dressed. I'll meet you by the pool in twenty minutes."

Natalie peeked into her room. "You'd better make it an hour. Johansson left me a mess to clean up."

"Leave it for the maid. It'll give her something else to do besides scrubbing cum stains out of the sheets." Helen reached into her jacket and pulled out a stack of letters tied together with a piece of twine. The letters were identical to the one Meredith had seen earlier. The one Lois had intercepted and tried to use against its recipient. "Do you want these back?"

"Why don't you hold on to them for a while? I'll get them back from you when the war's over."

"Whenever that is." Helen returned the letters to their hiding place. "See you in twenty minutes."

"Sixty."

"Who's counting?"

"Thank you, Helen."

Helen patted the letters in her pocket as if to assure herself they were still there. "It was not only a pleasure, but an honor." Her normally booming voice was uncharacteristically quiet. "See you downstairs."

After Helen left, Meredith felt like all the air had been sucked out of the room. She and Natalie were caught in a vacuum. She struggled to breathe.

"Did Kerry show you a good time yesterday?" Natalie asked.

Meredith followed her into her room and closed the door. "I almost lost you just now and you want to talk about sightseeing?" She picked up a pillow that had found its way to the floor. When she tossed the pillow on the bed, she took note of the rumpled sheets. Had they been that way before Steve searched the room or after? Had Natalie and Helen made them that way or had Steve taken out his fury on everything he could find because of the one thing he couldn't?

Natalie stooped to pick up an overturned chair. "Let's go over the list of possible subjects. Would you like to talk about the fact that Johansson is trying to get me tossed out of the Army, and someone else who's supposed to be on my side is all too happy to help him?

Would you like to talk about the battle less than ten clicks from here that resulted in scores of wounded and fifteen KIA yesterday?"

Meredith could still see the helicopters flying overhead. See the faces of the men as they watched them pass.

"Would you like to talk about the bombing that cost two of my best friends their lives?"

Meredith thought of Charlie and U'ilani. Their happiness had inspired her to seek it for herself. Now they were gone.

"Or would you rather talk about the fact that I had a brave, beautiful, and incredibly sexy woman in my bed yesterday and nothing happened because all I could think about was you?"

"You didn't sleep with her?"

"How could I when the woman I really wanted was right next door? Do you have any idea how much I love you, Meredith?" Natalie's question sounded like a wail of despair. "You couldn't possibly. Because if you did, you wouldn't have to ask me what I want to talk about."

"I'm sorry. I didn't mean to—"

Meredith reached for her, but Natalie pulled away.

"Has George asked you to marry him yet?"

Meredith was thrown by the sudden conversational shift. "What? No."

"He will."

"How do you know?"

"He told me so."

"George and I have talked about marriage as a possibility, but nothing in this world is certain. Did he tell you he wanted to marry me?"

"He wanted to be sure I wouldn't stand in his way. And I won't. Because, in the end, he and I want the same thing—for you to be happy. As much as I want to, I can't make you happy, Meredith. Not because I'm not capable, but because you won't let me show you how much we could accomplish together. What we've done here is a fraction of what we could do if we set our minds and our hearts to it, but you're too afraid of what everyone would think to allow yourself the happiness you deserve. The happiness you want to have, not what you're expected to settle for."

Meredith didn't have a rebuttal for Natalie's argument because everything Natalie had said was true. She had always wanted to know how it felt to fall in love. The moment she realized she already knew was also the moment she realized how it felt to watch the one she loved slip through her fingers.

She looked around at the ruined room.

"How can you do this? There's no place to run. No place to hide. No place that's safe for you to be who you are. How can you live like this?"

"Because, for me, there is no other way."

Meredith wished the decision was as easy as Natalie made it sound. Natalie made her feel things she had never felt before, but when she thought about what her family and friends would say if she admitted to being attracted to a woman—

Not just attracted. In love. She was in love with Natalie Robinson. If they knew—if they even suspected—her life would never be the same.

"I want to be with you," she said, "but I can't. I just can't."

"I know." Natalie dropped her head. "But that doesn't make it any easier to hear." She replaced the drawers in the dresser and began to pick up the clothes that had been dumped out of them. Meredith knelt to help her. "When we get back to Long Binh, I intend to ask Lt. Col. Daniels for a transfer."

The news was unexpected, but Meredith felt relief instead of surprise. She was disappointed by her reaction. Natalie was walking away. And she was letting her do it because she was too afraid to ask her to stay.

Their hands brushed as they reached for the same blouse in the pile of clothes on the floor. Neither let go. The small piece of cloth was the only thing that still bound them together. As soon as they released their grip, the last tenuous tie between them would be severed. Forever.

Meredith trailed her finger across the back of Natalie's hand.

"Where will you go?" she asked, unable to look Natalie in the eye. She knew she'd burst into tears if she even tried.

"Wherever they send me."

Meredith forced herself to look up. To look into eyes filled with disappointment and pain. Eyes that undoubtedly matched her own. "What will you say when the LTC asks why you want to leave?"

"I'm sure I won't have to *say* anything. She'll know." The tears Meredith had tried to hold back began to fall. Natalie cupped her hand against Meredith's cheek, her voice as gentle as her touch. "Be happy, Meredith. And tell George if he ever hurts you, he'll have me to deal with."

Meredith laughed through her tears. She tried to talk but failed, unable to say the words she longed to say. Unable to tell Natalie she couldn't possibly be happy without her. Unable to tell her she loved her, too.

So she did the only thing she could. She kissed her. She kissed her with all her heart. She kissed her with all her soul. She kissed her good-bye.

CHAPTER EIGHT

Jordan couldn't move. She and Grandma Meredith had been parked in front of a modest ranch house on Jekyll Island's North Beachview Drive for a good thirty minutes, but neither had bothered to get out of the car. The neighbors probably thought they were crazy. Not the first impression she had hoped to make, but she didn't give a shit. Everything she had ever assumed about Grandma Meredith and Papa George—everything she thought she had known about love—had been proven false. She needed a minute to wrap her head around those realizations, the summer neighbors' first impressions be damned.

"You chose Papa George because it was easier to be with him than to be with a woman?"

"I chose him because I loved him and wanted a family."

"You chose him because you were too scared to be yourself."

"Perhaps."

Jordan gripped her cell phone like a kid squeezing a security blanket. She needed reassurance, but she didn't know how to find it or where to look. Who was she supposed to call when the person who always talked her down from the ledge was the one responsible for putting her there this time?

"Papa George might have been your second choice, but he made you happy. Didn't he?"

Grandma Meredith gripped her hand. "I was happy with him, yes, but something was missing."

Jordan knew exactly how she felt. She hadn't felt whole until she came to terms with her feelings for other girls. She and Grandma

Meredith were tight. How could she not have known Grandma Meredith had gone through similar struggles?

"Papa George knew how Natalie felt about you, but did he know how you felt about her?"

"He mentioned it once or twice in Vietnam, trying, I suppose, to see where he stood or to force me to be honest with myself. I either denied it or changed the subject because I wasn't ready to admit Natalie's feelings for me were mutual. Once George and I returned Stateside, my love for her wasn't something we talked about. It was the proverbial elephant in the room meant to be discussed only in hushed tones or raised voices. We didn't do either. I made my choice, George supported my decision, and we made a life together. I lived the life I chose to live. The one I had always imagined."

"But not the one you wanted. That's why you were so supportive when I came out to you. Because you didn't want me to make the same mistake you did."

A flash of anger sparked in Grandma Meredith's eyes. "Marrying George wasn't a mistake. Having a family wasn't a mistake. The only mistake I made was not being honest with myself or the people I loved."

Jordan's head spun the way it always did when she tried to cram in too much information all at once. "I assume Mom doesn't know."

Grandma Meredith shrugged helplessly. "I've always wanted to tell her, but I didn't know how. I didn't want her to feel like having her—having a family—was something I felt obligated to do instead of something I truly wanted."

Grandma Meredith always seemed so confident. So sure of herself. Jordan had never seen her look so uncertain. She wanted to comfort her, just as Grandma Meredith had done for her when she had made her own hesitant declaration about her sexuality, but she felt too betrayed to make the effort. The life she had known was a lie and she wasn't ready to face her new reality. She turned to take a closer look at the woman she'd thought she knew.

"My life, though fulfilling, is incomplete. Seeing Natalie again would provide closure to a chapter that's been left unfinished for far too long. Will you help me find her?" Grandma Meredith wiped away tears. She had reached the crossroads of a journey nearly seventy years in the making and the effort was clearly wearing on her.

"I can tell how much the idea of seeing Natalie again means to you, but have you considered the consequences? What if she doesn't want to be found? What happens if you look for her and she's not here? Or what if you do find her and she says she hasn't forgiven you for choosing to have a life with Papa George instead of one with her? A lot could go wrong when you start messing with the past, Gran. If this doesn't turn out the way you want it to, are you prepared to handle the disappointment?"

"I've been preparing myself for this moment for forty-seven years. I'm ready for anything that happens."

"If you find her, what will you say?"

"I have no idea. I hadn't planned on trying to find her, but there has to be a reason we ended up in her hometown this year. You might call it dumb luck, but I call it destiny. Whatever I say to her when I see her again has to come from the heart. Of course I'm hoping she feels the same way she did the last time we spoke, but if she doesn't—if she has a lifetime of resentment she can't get past—I'll understand. I just want her to see I'm not the scared little girl she once knew. I want to introduce her to the woman I've become."

"I don't get it. Your first kiss was your last kiss and you haven't seen each other since you were in your twenties. How can you say you're still in love with her after all this time?"

Grandma Meredith spoke with quiet conviction. "Because I am."

"I hate to play devil's advocate, Gran, but what if it's too late? What if she and Helen hooked up after the war or she made a life with someone new? You chose to be with someone else. What if she did, too?"

Grandma Meredith looked off into the distance as if she hadn't considered the possibility that the alleged love of her life had moved on without her.

"I'll cross that bridge when I come to it."

When Grandma Meredith looked back, Jordan saw a familiar determination in her eyes. She hoped the bridge Grandma Meredith so desperately wanted to cross hadn't already been burned.

PART TWO

THE DESTINATION

CHAPTER NINE

Meredith pedaled her bicycle along a picturesque shaded pathway. She slowed as she neared the fire station, wary an emergency vehicle might dart into traffic after suddenly being called into service. A warm breeze redolent of pine, oak, and Spanish moss swept across her sweat-dampened skin. She was dressed in sneakers, spandex leggings, and a Green Bay Packers T-shirt, but the oppressive humidity made the outfit feel like cold-weather gear instead of workout wear. A wide sun visor and oversized sunglasses protected her head and face from the blazing sun.

She and Jordan had been in town a little over two weeks. Plenty of time for her to familiarize herself with most of the major attractions on tiny Jekyll Island but not enough time for her to locate Natalie.

The residents were friendly enough when Meredith introduced herself and said she would be living in town for the summer, but they clammed up as soon as she asked if they knew Natalie Robinson or could help locate her. Meredith wasn't surprised by the wall of silence. She knew from experience denizens of small towns could be protective of their own and standoffish with strangers, but she was determined to continue her search, with or without help. She had come too far to give up now.

She pedaled toward the Jekyll Island Museum, then circled back and stopped in front of the Georgia Sea Turtle Center. The ruins of the Horton House, an almost three-hundred-year-old remnant of Georgia's British colonial period, were supposed to be around here somewhere. Frances Turtledove, who lived next door to the rental house Meredith was staying in, had told her the Horton House was a sight not to be missed. She hadn't told her, though, it would be so hard to find.

Meredith and Frances chatted every morning while Frances tended to her garden and Meredith cooled down from her yoga workout. Frances's gardening skills were impressive, but her sense of direction left much to be desired.

Meredith unfurled a map of the island, draped it across the large basket affixed to the bicycle's handlebars, and tried to locate her current position. That explained it. She was in the wrong spot. She was on Stable Road. The Horton House was on Riverview Drive, several streets over.

"Looks like I did it again."

She and George used to joke that no road trip was complete without at least two wrong turns. She had already made one, which meant she had one to spare.

She looked up when she heard a vehicle approach. A Ford Bronco slowly made its way down the street, the driver in no apparent hurry to get where she was going. The driver raised her hand in greeting. Meredith lifted hers in kind, but she froze as soon as she got a better look at the driver's face. The woman looked just like Natalie. Or how she had always imagined Natalie would look if she ever saw her again. The sharp angles of her face had been softened by time, and her once-brown hair was sprinkled with a liberal dose of gray, but her eyes had the same intensity.

"No, it couldn't be."

As the Bronco drove past, Meredith's mind tried to convince her the woman's resemblance to Natalie Robinson was a product of wishful thinking. But her heart knew otherwise.

Natalie was here, after all. Now what? Meredith couldn't catch up to the Bronco on her bike, but there was no telling how long it would be before their paths crossed again. After nearly a lifetime apart, would this one brief encounter be the only reunion they were allowed to experience?

Meredith reached inside her T-shirt, pulled out her dog tags, and ran her fingers over them as if the raised letters and numbers were a set of rosary beads. She had made the gesture countless times. In times of mortal danger and in moments of quiet reflection. She made it again now, seeking comfort during a moment of uncertainty.

Then Natalie hit the brakes, spun the wheel, and turned the car around. She pulled up beside Meredith and lowered the passenger's side window. "Are you looking for something?"

"As a matter of fact," Meredith said, staring into the face of the woman she had last seen when her age and waist size were roughly the same number, "I was looking for you."

❖

"Dude, this is a handicapped spot," Jordan said as Hayden switched off her car. The BMW had an out-of-state license plate, a custom paint job, and a set of four-thousand-dollar rims, but no handicapped parking decal. "You can't park here."

"I'm not planning to set up camp. I want to put the beer on ice before we hit the beach so it will still be cold when we get there. If the space is empty, that means our downstairs neighbor isn't home. If we hurry, we'll be gone before she shows up. Come on. It will only take a sec."

Jordan had met Hayden and her friend Willow on her fourth day in town. She had been walking on the beach when Hayden's barely-there swimsuit and banging bod caught her eye. Hayden had responded with the inevitable, "Do you see something you like?" but she had looked so good lying there in next to nothing, Jordan had been able to overlook the lameness of the line.

They had been hanging out ever since, having the sort of mindless fun Jordan thought she needed after Brittany kicked her to the curb and Grandma Meredith's confession threw her into a tailspin. But somewhere along the line, being with Hayden had stopped being fun. Some of the things she and Willow said gave Jordan pause. Jordan couldn't tell if they meant what they said or if they really sucked at trying to be funny. But they were trust fund babies from Charleston, South Carolina, and she was a small-town girl from Kenosha, Wisconsin. Perhaps something got lost in translation.

While Willow grabbed the case of beer they had bought from the package shop a few miles away, Hayden snagged the bag containing margarita salt, limes, and a bottle of tequila. "I think we have time for a quick round of body shots. Are you game, Jordan?"

"Yeah, sure. It's five o'clock somewhere."

Jordan climbed out of the backseat of the convertible as Hayden and Willow headed for the stairs that led to their second-floor condo. In the unit below theirs, a large German shepherd pushed his face between the blinds in the front window and started barking his head off. The deep-throated sound was beyond intimidating.

"Who's he?" Jordan waved at the shepherd, who stopped barking and scraped a paw against the window as if he were waving back.

"He belongs to Tatum, our downstairs neighbor," Hayden said with a dramatic eye roll. "He's a sweetheart, but she's a raging bitch."

"Wouldn't you be if you were stuck in a wheelchair for the rest of your life?" Willow asked.

Jordan jogged to catch up to them. "Is she sick or did she have some sort of accident?"

"Neither. She was in the military and she was shot while she was stationed in Afghanistan. Or maybe it was Pakistan." Hayden shrugged. "One of the 'stans. I can't remember which. The location doesn't matter. The result is still the same, right?"

"Too bad," Willow said. "My cousin, Riley, works with her at the Remember When Inn, the place near the beach that features rooms decorated like the sets from classic TV shows. Riley's the day manager and Tatum works nights. Riley's bumping uglies with the owner, though, so Tatum usually ends up getting stuck with all the work. Riley said she used to be hot."

"She's still cute," Hayden said as she unlocked the condo door, "but who's got time to play nursemaid all day?"

"Not me. That's for sure." Willow placed the beer on the counter with a sigh of relief. "What about you, Jordan? Could you date someone with a disability?"

"I don't know. I've never thought about it, but I like to think I would be dating the person, not the disability."

"And have people staring at you everywhere you went?" Hayden wrinkled her nose in distaste. "That's very PC of you. Fortunately, I'm un-PC enough for both of us."

A point she was making all too clear. Jordan didn't know what she was looking for this summer, but Hayden wasn't it. She grabbed her oversized hemp beach bag and draped it over her shoulder. "I've got to go."

"What about body shots?" Hayden asked with a lascivious grin. "I was looking forward to licking tequila off your skin."

"Some other time." The prospect of casual sex didn't hold the appeal it had ten days earlier. The problems she had hoped to forget about were still at the forefront of her mind and they didn't appear to be going anywhere any time soon. She needed to stop avoiding her issues and start dealing with them or she'd end the summer as mixed up as she started it. "I'll see you around."

"Dude, I think you just got dumped," Willow said as Jordan headed for the door.

"She'll be back."

Jordan closed the door behind her. "Not in this lifetime."

By the time she reached the sidewalk, she felt as if a burden had been lifted, though a heavier one remained. Her reaction to Grandma Meredith's revelation surprised her. Disappointed her, too. She wished she could be happy Grandma Meredith had finally come to terms with her feelings for Natalie and buried her uncertainty about her sexuality, but what about her feelings for Papa George? Had she truly loved him or had she settled for a life with him just so she could accomplish her goal of starting a family like she was ticking off items on a to-do list? Jordan hated to think of Papa George as anyone's Plan B. He deserved better than that. He deserved more.

Jordan began walking across the parking lot. The blacktop was so hot, the soles of her sandals were sticking to the pavement. She fanned the hem of her Make Love Not War T-shirt to produce a breeze, but it only made the hot air hotter. She gave up on trying to cool down when she saw a woman in a wheelchair heading toward her.

The woman had a ripped upper body—the well-defined muscles in her biceps, triceps, and forearms rippled each time she spun the wheels of her chair—but her withered legs seemed to swim inside her gray sweatpants, which, in this heat, were apparently worn for camouflage instead of comfort. She had a canvas grocery bag on her lap and a gym bag draped across the back of her wheelchair. Her T-shirt read, Marine Corps Veteran.

Jordan figured the woman must be Tatum, the downstairs neighbor Hayden and Willow had told her about. Willow's cousin had said Tatum used to be hot. Jordan had news for her. Tatum still was.

Tatum's medium-length brown hair was pulled back into a ponytail, from which a few sweat-dampened tendrils had escaped. Her hazel eyes were intense and focused. With her military background, that was no surprise. Neither was her ramrod straight posture. She looked like she was standing at attention even though she was sitting down.

Her eyes searched Jordan's questioningly. Uncertainly. As if she were waiting for Jordan to say the wrong thing so she could pick a fight. Apparently, the raging bitch part of Hayden's description wasn't too far off. Jordan tried to think of a comment that could be considered innocuous instead of incendiary.

"Your dog's cute."

Jordan grinned after her statement provoked a brief smile.

"Thanks, but he prefers to be called handsome."

Tatum continued on her way and Jordan on hers. Jordan jumped out of the way when Hayden's BMW, traveling several miles above the posted speed limit, came barreling around a curve. She made it through the close encounter unscathed, but Tatum wasn't quite as fortunate.

Jordan looked back when she heard a crash and the sound of glass breaking. The instant she saw the telltale yellow spill slowly spreading across the black pavement, she knew Tatum's newly purchased jar of orange juice had shattered.

"Sorry," Hayden called out in a singsong voice.

"No screwdrivers for you two tonight," Willow added, laughing as if she found the situation hilarious.

"Assholes," Jordan said under her breath, mentally kicking herself for wasting almost two weeks of her life on people who obviously weren't worth two minutes of her time.

Tatum seemed intent on trying to maintain her dignity as she gathered her scattered belongings. Her reusable shopping bag was within easy reach, but the canvas material was soaking wet and filled with shards of broken glass. She placed the bag on her lap and set her sights on a fallen tomato. Though the tomato had remained intact, it had come to rest tantalizingly out of her grasp. Her dog was barking in her condo's front window again, obviously anxious to lend her a helping hand. He scratched the double-paned window with one large paw.

"Coming, boy," Tatum said with a grunt as she leaned over the side of her chair. She stretched as far as she could but couldn't reach the elusive tomato. As her frustration grew, so did the amount of profanity that spewed from her full lips. She made one more desperate grab for the tomato but came up short yet again.

"Let me help you with that."

Jordan jogged over to her, picked up the tomato, wiped dirt and debris off the bruised skin, and presented it to Tatum as if it were a gift instead of a possession. "Not quite as good as new, but there you are."

Tatum took the proffered tomato and tossed it in the wet bag soaking her lap. A dark spot had already formed in the crotch of her sweatpants, making her look like she had pissed herself. She released the wheelchair's brakes and began to wheel away. "Thanks, but I don't need any help."

"You don't want help from anyone or just from me?"

Tatum turned to look at her, her eyes flashing fire. "I don't need your help or your pity. If you hurry, you might be able to catch up with your friends."

"They're not my friends."

"You could have fooled me. You've been partying with them every day for the past two weeks. You seemed pretty friendly then."

"Yeah, well, things change." Jordan didn't want to be baited into an argument, despite Tatum's apparent intentions to do just that. She took a deep breath to gain control of her temper before it slipped free of its reins. "Why don't we start over? My name's Jordan. I'm in town for the summer. My grandmother and I came down from Wisconsin to sample some of your vaunted Southern hospitality."

"I'm Tatum." She gave Jordan's hand a quick shake and jerked her chin toward the spot where she, Hayden, and Willow had nearly collided. "Those two don't look like anyone's grandmother."

"No," Jordan said with a laugh, "they don't."

"Are they from Wisconsin, too?"

"No, I met them shortly after Grandma Meredith and I arrived. I was hoping to land a job for the summer, but none of my interviews panned out. I was hanging around the beach one day feeling sorry for myself and my lack of prospects when I hooked up with Hayden and Willow. That sounds awful. I mean, I didn't hook up with both of them. Just Hayden. We've been kicking it for a week or so, but—" She forced herself to stop talking. "I'm rambling, aren't I?" She shifted her weight from one foot to the other, betraying her anxiety. "I always ramble when I get nervous."

"Why do I make you nervous?"

Jordan shrugged, ignoring the unexpected tug of attraction she felt when Tatum turned her intense gaze squarely on her. "I don't know. You just do." She reached for the canvas bag on Tatum's lap but didn't close her fingers around the straps in case Tatum lashed out with a few more choice words. "Are you sure I can't help you with that? You're going to cut yourself if you aren't careful."

Tatum looked at her lap, where bright red drops had begun to mix with the dark gray stain. "To tell the truth, I think I already have."

"I'll take this." Jordan grabbed the grocery bag and held it at arm's length. Orange juice seeped from the saturated material. "Let's get you inside so you can get cleaned up." She began to walk toward Tatum's condo. "That one's yours, right?"

"You don't take no for an answer, do you?"

Jordan grinned. "Not if I can help it."

Tatum hurried to catch up, then wheeled past her. "Careful," she said as she slipped the key into the lock. "As soon as I open this door, all hell's going to break loose."

Heeding the warning, Jordan took a step back. Tatum pushed the door open and spread her arms as her German shepherd vaulted into her lap. He covered her face with doggie kisses and wagged his tail as if he hadn't seen her in days when, in actuality, it had probably only been a few hours.

"See?" Tatum said between laps of the dog's big, pink tongue. "I told you he was vicious."

"I can tell."

Tatum patted the shepherd's haunches and pointed to the ground. "Lincoln, down."

The dog obediently jumped off Tatum's lap and stood next to her chair. Cocking his head, he leaned toward Jordan and tentatively sniffed the back of her hand before giving it an enthusiastic lick.

"I think he likes you," Tatum said as Jordan's entire hand practically disappeared into the dog's mouth.

"I doubt it's me. It's probably the orange juice." Jordan dried her hand on the back of her shorts and scratched Lincoln between his ears. He closed his eyes as one of his hind legs thumped against the walkway in canine bliss.

"Definitely not the orange juice. Come on inside."

Jordan crossed the threshold and took in the condo at a glance. "Nice place. Did you just move in?"

"No." Tatum wheeled into the living room and tossed her keys on the coffee table. "I've lived here for a little over two years."

"Oh."

"As you can probably tell, I'm not big on feng shui."

Jordan took another look around. The place was a blank slate devoid of personality. In the small living room, a brown loveseat and matching armchair were angled toward a flat-screen TV. The open kitchen a few feet away featured the standard appliances, but the battered microwave obviously received more use than the stove. No paintings or photographs adorned the beige walls. The only accessory of any kind was a hideous ceramic sea turtle on the coffee table.

"Someone gave me that as a going away present when I joined the Marines," Tatum said. "During down times when there wasn't anything to do except count grains of sand, my buddies in the Corps took turns painting the turtle's shell. Some of the paint jobs were so bad a kindergartener could have done better; others were pretty impressive. Not like it mattered. After a few beers, no one could tell the difference anyway." She reached for the grocery bag. "Thanks for your help, but I can take it from here if there's someplace you need to be."

"I've got all summer. What's a few more minutes?" Jordan headed to the kitchen and set the grocery bag in the sink. She began to pull pieces of broken glass out of the bag and toss them in the trash. "Go get cleaned up. And don't forget to disinfect those cuts."

Tatum watched her unpack the bag, obviously torn between whether she should stay and supervise or trust a complete stranger to have free rein in her kitchen.

"Go," Jordan said. "I've got this."

"Keep this up and I might have to hire you as a maid."

"Don't say that too loud or I might ask you about salary, benefits, and performance bonuses. I am on the lookout for a job, you know."

"Permanently, or just for the summer?"

"Just for the summer. I want to finish my senior year before I lock down something long-term. If you hear of anything, let me know."

"I don't know if Willow or Hayden told you, but I work at one of the hotels in town. Summer is our high season and we're especially packed this year. I could use an extra person to help deal with the influx of guests. If you're serious about wanting a job, stop by sometime and fill out an application."

"Cool. Tell me when and where."

"The Remember When Inn tomorrow afternoon around one. I'll let HR know you're coming. The owner, Bud Norman, has final say on all hiring decisions. He drops by every day after lunch. He'll take a look at your application, ask you a few questions, and show you around the property."

"So I'm brown-nosing the wrong person?"

"You don't have to stop on my account, but I'll let Bud know to expect you."

"I'll be there. Thanks."

"Don't thank me now. You haven't gotten the job yet."

"Details," Jordan said with a wink.

Tatum wheeled to the bedroom and pushed the door almost closed. "Stay."

Lincoln stationed himself outside the door and lay with his head on his paws, his eyebrows arched in anticipation.

"Where are you going to school?" Tatum asked through the partially open door.

Jordan raised her voice so Tatum could hear her in the other room. "Berkeley."

"Really? That's a great school."

Jordan heard a grunt of effort and assumed Tatum was transferring in and out of her chair in order to exchange her wet sweatpants for something dry. "You don't have to sound so surprised."

"Sorry. I didn't mean to."

Tatum's voice sounded farther away. Like she'd left the bedroom to go into the bathroom. Jordan hoped she remembered to put antiseptic on the wounds in her legs. The cuts were plentiful but, hopefully, they weren't very deep.

"Do you need some help?"

"No, I got it," Tatum said. "I'm almost done."

Jordan opened the refrigerator and began to put away the groceries. She felt almost domestic. Was this how it felt to be married? Too bad this was probably as close as she would ever come to finding out.

When Tatum came out of the bedroom, Lincoln scrambled to his feet and trotted to the front door. He grabbed his leash with his mouth and turned to look at Tatum.

Jordan dried her hands on a dish towel. She had put away all the groceries, washed the canvas bag, and left it on the Formica-topped counter to dry. "Looks like someone's ready to go for a walk."

Lincoln dropped his leash and barked once in agreement.

"It'll have to be a short one. I have to come back, take a shower, and get ready for work."

Jordan tossed the dish towel on the counter and reached for her carryall. "Do you mind if I go with you? Lincoln reminds me of my girlfriend's—" She stopped and corrected herself. "My *ex*-girlfriend's dog. They look so much alike they could be litter mates."

"What was her name?"

"Who, the dog or my ex?"

"Take your pick."

"My ex's name was Brittany. Her dog's name was Blue, but I called her Yellow because she was afraid of everything that moved."

Tatum laughed. "No wonder Brittany's your *ex*-girlfriend."

"You know, that's the first time I've seen you smile for more than two seconds at a time. You should do it more often. It looks good on you."

"I'll get right to work on that."

Tatum's bone-dry sense of humor reminded Jordan of Papa George. She figured it must be a military thing.

Tatum waved Jordan over. "Come on if you're coming."

Tatum clipped Lincoln's leash to his collar and opened the door. He nearly pulled her arm out of its socket as he dashed outside. Jordan walked beside them as Lincoln explored the shaded complex, stopping to smell every tree, plant, bush, and blade of grass that came within ten feet of him.

"How long have you had him?"

"About eighteen months. My aunt bought him for me. My doctors suggested I seek counseling after I was injured, but I'm not much of a talker. My aunt decided Lincoln was the next best thing. He and I are still getting to know each other."

"That's surprising. I would have sworn you'd known each other all your lives."

Jordan could have said the same thing about herself and Tatum. How was it possible to feel so comfortable with someone she barely knew?

"Are you in the military?" Tatum asked, pointing to the dog tags dangling around Jordan's neck.

"Oh, God, no. I prefer to fight my battles with words instead of a gun. These are my grandfather's. My grandmother gave them to me after he died. Prostate cancer. Probably brought on by all the Agent Orange he was sprayed with when he was in the bush. I wear these tags when I want to feel close to him." She curled her fingers around the worn metal tags. "Papa George died when I was a kid, but, this summer, I feel like I've lost him all over again."

"How long was he in Vietnam?"

"A little over six years. My grandmother was stationed there, too. Not as long, but she got into some serious scrapes during the twelve months she was there."

"My aunt served, too. Listening to her stories prompted me to join the NROTC when I was in high school and to enlist when I graduated. My father hated the stories for the same reason I loved them: they made me want to follow in my aunt's footsteps."

"Do you regret enlisting, considering what happened to you?"

"Not for a second. Where was your grandmother stationed?"

"All over. Saigon, Long Binh, Hanoi."

"When?"

"From 1967 to 1968. When her tour ended, she thought about extending, but she and my grandfather decided to get married instead. They came home and started a family. My mother was born nine months after the wedding, so it isn't hard to figure out what they did on their honeymoon. Given what she told me during the trip down here, I wonder if she was thinking of someone else the entire time."

"What do you mean?"

"My grandmother said she's always had feelings for someone else. Someone she met during the war."

"She was in love with another man?"

Jordan shook her head. "Another woman."

Jordan expected Tatum to have some kind of reaction to the response, but Tatum didn't even flinch.

"What's your grandmother's name?"

"Meredith. Meredith Moser now. Back then, she was Meredith Chase."

Tatum switched Lincoln's lead from one hand to the other and wiped her palm on the front of her fresh pair of sweatpants. "Was she a nurse during the war?"

"Yes. How did you know?"

Jordan wondered if Grandma Meredith and Tatum's aunt had served together during the war, but Tatum's reply quickly put her theory to rest.

"Lucky guess. Most female service members back then were either nurses or secretaries. I had a fifty-fifty shot."

"True. Grandma Meredith and I ended up here by accident, but she believes it's fate. The woman she had feelings for used to live here, but I'm not sure she still does. Grandma Meredith has been looking for a couple of weeks, but she hasn't been able to find her. I tried for a while, but I didn't get very far."

Not to mention her heart hadn't been in it.

"You are in Dixie, you know. Locals aren't very forthcoming with Yankees."

"So I've noticed. I've tried to convince Grandma Meredith too much time has passed, but she has her heart set on making things right."

"Did they end things on bad terms?"

"To put it mildly."

"What was the woman's name?"

"Natalie Robinson. Do you know her?"

It was a long shot, but Jordan felt obligated to make the effort. She had made Grandma Meredith a promise, after all. Tatum answered the question with one Jordan had been asking herself for weeks.

"Why is your grandmother looking for someone she hasn't seen in more than forty years?"

"It's a long story," Jordan said softly. "I could try to tell it, but I don't quite understand it myself." She changed the subject for her own peace of mind. "Where did you serve?"

"Afghanistan. Kandahar and the surrounding regions."

Jordan was relieved Tatum didn't say Iraq. The conflict there had been reviled both at home and abroad. Still was, even though it was technically supposed to be over. The war in Afghanistan was equally tough for Jordan to swallow but was slightly more palatable. "Is that where you were…wounded?"

Tatum nodded.

"What did you do in Kandahar? Were you there before or after women were allowed in combat? I assume after."

"No, before. I was there when women could serve only in limited roles. We could fly choppers and jets during combat missions, but we couldn't go on sorties with ground troops."

Jordan wondered if Grandma Meredith's sortie counted as an official mission. If so, she was one-up on Tatum. "Were you a pilot?"

"I wish. I would have loved to have gotten in on the action. I was a translator."

"You speak Arabic?"

"Now who seems surprised?" Lincoln raised his leg to pee against a tree, but after the half-dozen other pit stops that had preceded this one, he seemed to have run out of juice. Tatum tugged his leash and directed him back toward the condo. "I studied Spanish in high school, but one of my teachers said I'd make more use of Arabic.

He gave me an hour of lessons after school every day for four years. His foresight paid off. When I graduated and completed compulsory training, Uncle Sam put me on a plane to the Middle East. I acted as an interpreter during interrogations and transcribed captured intel."

Jordan didn't understand how Tatum could have received such a catastrophic injury if she had spent her entire military career stuck behind a desk. "If you weren't on the front lines, how did you end up in the line of fire?"

"My team and I were following a lead on a suspected terrorist hideout when we drove into an ambush and snipers began using our Humvee for target practice. All the members of my team were wounded, but my injuries were the most severe."

"Where were you hit?"

"I took three bullets, one each to my shoulder, spine, and upper thigh."

Tatum pointed out each spot. Jordan looked at her, trying to imagine the scars hidden under her clothes. Were they more superficial than the scars on Tatum's soul or just as deep?

"How long were you over there?"

"Some might say too long."

"What do you say?"

"Not long enough. I wanted to be there when the job was done. I still do."

Jordan couldn't decide if Tatum was brave or foolhardy. "Once a soldier, always a soldier?"

"Ask your grandmother. She'll tell you. Most civilians—even ones from military families—don't understand how it is. A war doesn't end after one side declares victory or both sides sign peace treaties. It keeps going as long as the combatants draw breath. As long as the memories remain fresh. For me, memories are my constant companions."

Jordan flashed back to some of the stories Grandma Meredith had told her during the drive from Wisconsin. "Are they memories or nightmares?"

"Sometimes, it feels like they're one and the same."

Jordan knew the feeling.

When they returned to Tatum's condo, Lincoln stood panting in front of the door.

"I'd better get going," Tatum said, "or I'm going to be late for work."

"Oh, okay." Jordan felt deflated. She wasn't ready for her time with Tatum to come to an end, but she understood why it had to. "I'll get out of your hair so you can get ready."

"Would you like a lift to the beach? I drive a hand-controlled Mustang, not a fully loaded Beemer, but it gets me where I want to go."

"I'm sure it does. Thanks for the offer, but it's a beautiful day. I think I'll walk. Thanks for the tip on the job, too. I'll be sure to check it out." She held out her hand. "It was nice meeting you, Tatum. Do your friends call you Tater Tot?"

"Among other things."

Tatum smiled again. This time for much longer than two seconds.

Instead of spending the day on the beach, Jordan wanted to spend it hearing about Tatum's adventures in Afghanistan and the challenges she faced after she lost the use of her legs. But unlike Jordan, who had no obligations for the next three months, Tatum had real world responsibilities she needed to attend to, and Jordan didn't want to keep her from them.

"Maybe I'll see you around, Tater."

"Maybe."

Jordan turned toward the beach. A summer that was shaping up to be nothing like any of the others she and Grandma Meredith had spent had just gotten even more interesting. Very interesting indeed.

CHAPTER TEN

W ell, you found me," Natalie said. "Now what?"

Meredith hesitated. She didn't know what step she should take next. She had dreamed of this moment for years, but she hadn't imagined how it would play out. A plan, a strategy, or any sort of guidance would have come in handy.

"How about I buy you a cup of coffee?"

"I'm not big on drinking coffee in the middle of the day. Make it tea and you've got a deal."

Natalie climbed out of the Bronco and tossed Meredith's bicycle in the back. When Natalie closed the SUV's rear door, Meredith stepped forward to give her a long-overdue hug. Evidently, the pain from their parting was still too fresh, even after all these years, because Natalie neatly sidestepped the attempted embrace. She opened the driver's side door and slid behind the wheel. "Where to?"

"I'm in your hands." After she settled into the passenger's seat, Meredith removed her visor and sunglasses and placed both in her lap. She could tell she had a case of hat hair but hoped it wasn't too bad.

"A friend of mine, Beverly Simmons, owns a little café not too far from here. We may be able to sneak in and out before the dinner rush arrives."

"Sounds perfect." Meredith sat back and openly stared at Natalie, taking her in. She shook her head in wonder. "When I left Vietnam, I never thought I'd see you again."

"And now you're here."

"Now I'm here. You look—"

Natalie held up one hand in protest. "If you tell me I look exactly the same now as I did in 1967, I'm going to put you out of this car without bothering to pull over first."

Meredith chuckled. Natalie's appearance had changed, but her personality had certainly remained the same. "There are so many things I want to say. I don't know where to begin."

"Why don't we start with the obvious? What are you doing here?"

"That's an easy one. My granddaughter and I vacation together every summer. We pick a city at random and spend three months exploring the area. This year, we ended up here."

"You and George had children? How many?"

"Just one. A daughter. Diana. She's married to a wonderful man. His name's Francisco Gonzalez, but everyone has always called him Frank. He and Diana met while they were in college at the University of Wisconsin. He was an exchange student from Bogota, and she volunteered to help him deal with the culture shock. He must have made the adjustment because they've been married for twenty-five years. They have one child, my granddaughter, Jordan."

"How old is your granddaughter?"

"Twenty-one. She just finished her junior year at Cal-Berkeley. She's having a bit of a rough go of it at the moment. Her girlfriend broke up with her a few weeks ago and she didn't see it coming."

Natalie arched an eyebrow at the reference to Jordan's girlfriend, but she didn't make an editorial comment.

"Jordan was hoping to find a job this summer, but she hasn't been able to land anything yet."

"Is she still looking for work?"

"She says she is, but I think she's enjoying being twenty-one more than she is being gainfully employed."

"I envy her. When I was that age, I was a wide-eyed new recruit setting foot in Vietnam for the first time. My job wasn't to discover how much alcohol I could drink in one sitting. My job was to stay alive."

"I'm grateful Jordan made the trip at all. I thought she'd spend this summer in California with her friends, but I guess she hasn't tired of me yet."

"Did George make the trip with you?"

Meredith's spirits flagged. She hated telling people who didn't know about George. Each time she had to tell someone he had passed on, it felt like she was losing him all over again.

"Only in spirit. He died several years ago. I've been on my own since then."

"I'm sorry to hear that. George was a good man."

"Yes, he was. The best. I miss him dearly. As he said at the end, we had a good run."

"I'm glad to hear that. What I mean is, I'm glad you made the right choice for your life. You got everything you always wanted."

Natalie's voice was tinged with both satisfaction and regret.

"What about you?" Meredith asked. "Did you get what you wanted?"

Natalie smiled wanly. "In a way."

"What did you do when you came home from the war? Did you stay in nursing or did you move on to something else?"

"Nursing is in my blood. I couldn't give it up. I still can't. I worked at a hospital in Savannah for almost forty years. I tried to retire when I reached the appropriate age, but retirement didn't take. I'd seen too many of my friends retire and kick the bucket shortly after because they didn't have anything to do. I was determined not to have that happen to me. A few years ago, I started working at the Peaceful Manor, a nursing home on St. Simons Island. I drive over every other day to take care of the residents, some of whom are younger than I am. It doesn't pay much, but it keeps me busy."

Meredith wanted to ask her about her personal life, but she didn't want to pry. Now that a love once lost had finally been found, there would be plenty of time for questions later. They couldn't make up for forty-seven years in one day.

Natalie pulled into the gravel-lined parking lot of the Bread and Butter Café and found a space near the entrance. When they went inside, Beverly Simmons greeted her with a warm hug.

"As I live and breathe. If it isn't Natalie Robinson. I haven't seen you in ages."

Beverly seemed to be the type of woman who lived life at full volume, but Natalie's reply to the enthusiastic greeting was typically low-key.

"It has been a while."

"Are you coming to the potluck tomorrow night?" Beverly asked. "I know you'd rather gouge out your eyes with a dull, rusty spoon than spend two hours dodging unwanted advances from the gaggle of helmet-haired women who treat our monthly get-togethers like speed dating night at a singles bar catering to senior citizens, but everyone would love to see you. If you do come, make sure you bring your famous chicken and dumplings. They are simply to die for. Who's your friend?"

"Beverly Simmons, Meredith Moser. Meredith and I served together in Vietnam."

Beverly's painted-on eyebrows arched. "Ah, a veteran. Welcome to the Bread and Butter, Meredith." She wrapped her arms around Meredith as if they were old friends instead of new acquaintances. "In my place," she said, holding Meredith at arm's length, "all active or former military members receive a ten percent discount every day except Veterans Day and the Fourth of July. Those days, you get to eat for free. Consider it my way of saying thanks for all the sacrifices you made on my behalf. If you served with Nat, you must know Billie. Did you come to pay her a visit before her condition worsens?"

"What do you mean?"

Meredith felt a sense of foreboding she hadn't experienced since George's oncologist took her aside and told her there was nothing more he could do.

Beverly grew pale. "You didn't know that—"

"No, she didn't," Natalie said sternly.

Beverly covered her mouth with her hand. "Leave it to me to let the cat out of the bag." She shot Natalie an apologetic look as she wrung her hands in the hem of her apron. "Let me get you two a table so you can talk. What'll you have?" she asked after she showed them to a booth in the back of the small rectangular building.

"I was going to order a glass of sweet tea," Natalie said, "but I think I could use something stronger. Bring me a gin and tonic."

"Make that two."

"Oh, me and my big mouth." Beverly patted Meredith's arm. "I'm so sorry I said anything. I'll be right back."

"What's going on?" Meredith asked. "The general's ill?"

Billie Daniels, the woman she and Natalie used to affectionately call LTC, had become a three-star general before she retired after thirty-five years of service.

"She has Alzheimer's."

"No." Meredith's heart sank. An Alzheimer's diagnosis wasn't as frightening as cancer, but it was just as fatal and its effects just as debilitating. "What stage?"

"Five, though she's starting to verge on six." Natalie ticked off Billie's symptoms on her fingers. "She has noticeable gaps in her memory, her thinking isn't as clear as it once was, and she's sometimes confused about time and place. She can still care for herself for now, but I don't know how long that will be the case."

She didn't have to remind Meredith there was no stage after six. After six came death. Release from suffering for the afflicted, but the continuation of it for the loved ones left behind.

"Is she living with you?"

"No. She's a resident in the nursing home where I work. She moved into the Peaceful Manor as a preventive measure. She's been there about two years now."

"Was that decision hers or yours?"

"It was mutual. She realized she wasn't as sharp as she once was, and I wanted to have a hand in her care, so the Peaceful Manor seemed like the best solution."

George had had in-home hospice care for the last few weeks of his life. He had been adamant about being able to die in his own bed surrounded by family instead of strangers.

"The Peaceful Manor. If you tell me where it is, I'll pay Billie a visit tomorrow."

"I think she'd love that." Natalie wrote the name and address of the nursing home on a napkin and slid it across the table. "You were one of her favorites."

"No, I think that honor belonged solely to you." Meredith folded the napkin and zipped it inside her fanny pack. She took a sip of her drink after Beverly set the glasses on the table. She was thankful Beverly had gone heavy on the gin and light on the tonic. "Does Billie have family nearby?"

"We are each other's family. She has relatives in Savannah, but they're Bible thumpers who have issues with her being a lesbian and haven't spoken to her in several years. I'm hoping they'll come around before she reaches the end so they can have a chance to make amends. Once she's gone, it will be too late for them to take back the things they've said."

Meredith nodded soberly. "Late-stage patients are often soothed by objects from their past. Old photos, favorite foods, or perfumes and lotions with a familiar scent. Does she have a book she finds particularly meaningful? Perhaps I could read to her."

"She has always been especially fond of *To Kill a Mockingbird*. I read portions of it to her on my days off. I keep a copy in my car. You can borrow it if you like."

Meredith took another sip of her drink. "Are you two together?" she asked, the gin loosening her tongue. "When I told Jordan about our time in Vietnam, she thought you and the general were involved. Are you?"

"We were at one time." Natalie stirred her drink with the thin red straw leaning against the side of her sweating highball glass. "Remember when I told you I once met a woman who made me realize how life could be?"

Meredith smiled at the memory. That was the night she had asked Natalie if she could kiss her.

"Billie was that woman."

Meredith wasn't surprised to hear Jordan's suspicions confirmed. Natalie and Billie had always been close. Now she knew why.

"How did you meet? In the service?"

"No, before then. She came to speak at my high school when I was a senior. She looked so beautiful in her uniform, I sat in the auditorium feeling like a bobbysoxer swooning over Frank Sinatra. I approached her after the presentation, we started talking, and she invited me out for a soda. We became friends and, eventually, lovers. After I enlisted and wound up being assigned to her unit, the romantic side of our relationship ended, but we never stopped being friends." She stared into the depths of her drink. "She's meant so much to me for so long. Losing her is going to be tough to take."

Meredith reached across the table and covered Natalie's hand with her own. "I am so sorry, Natalie."

Natalie allowed herself to be comforted by Meredith's touch for only a moment before she pulled away. Meredith had hoped Natalie would be able to forgive and forget everything that had gone before. It seemed forgiveness was the easy part. It was forgetting that was going to be hard.

"Where are you staying while you're in town?"

"I rented a house not too far from here. The owners' last name is Campbell."

"Erma and Aaron. I was wondering where they disappeared to this summer. They must be at their son's place in Alabama. He has a beach house in Gulf Shores."

"Since everyone here seems to know everyone else's business, why wouldn't anyone tell me yours?"

"What do you mean?"

"I've been looking for you since the day Jordan and I arrived, but no one claimed to know anything about you."

"I'm not surprised. That's the way things are around here. But I am surprised no one said anything to me about you. On the other hand, I tend to keep to myself. I go to work and I come home. That's about it. I don't get out much."

"Except to attend potlucks thrown by talkative restaurant owners?"

"I'm not sure I'm going tomorrow night."

Natalie rubbed the back of her neck as if she was having a hard time adjusting to seeing Meredith here in her world. Meredith couldn't blame her. The last time they'd sat down like this felt like a lifetime ago.

"Don't you want to?"

"I haven't made up my mind yet."

"I'll go with you if you need moral support."

Natalie nearly choked on her drink. "Are you asking me for a date?"

Meredith let out a nervous laugh. "Only if you say yes. Jordan texted me a little while ago. She's going to head to the outlet mall in Brunswick bright and early tomorrow morning to find the perfect power suit for a job interview she has scheduled for tomorrow afternoon. That means I'll be on my own most of the day. I could make a green bean casserole to complement your chicken and dumplings. A potluck sounds like an ideal way to introduce myself to people in town so they won't think I'm some crazy Yankee who asks too many questions."

"I'm afraid it might be too late for that. You don't need to go to a potluck to introduce yourself. If you've been asking as many questions as you say you have, believe me, everyone already knows who you are." Natalie leaned back in her chair. "What do you really want, Meredith?"

"You." Meredith reached for her hand again. "What I want is you."

❖

Jordan knew something was up as soon as Grandma Meredith walked into the house. She had been riding her bike for hours, but she seemed more excited than exhausted. Her face was glowing and she couldn't keep still.

"How was your day, honey?" Grandma Meredith asked after she pulled off her visor and sunglasses and ran a hand over her close-cropped hair.

The question seemed more cursory than curious. Jordan had planned to tell her about jettisoning Hayden and Willow this morning and meeting Tatum shortly after, but her news would have to wait. Putting her research on the Remember When Inn on hold, she closed her laptop, folded her legs underneath her on the couch, and focused on Grandma Meredith's smiling face.

"What's going on?"

After she grabbed a bottle of water from the kitchen, Grandma Meredith sat in the armchair opposite her and took a breath as if she needed a moment to gather her thoughts. "I found her."

"You what?" Jordan didn't have to ask who. Judging by the look on Grandma Meredith's face, her impossible dream of finding Natalie Robinson had come true. Jordan's news of making a potential new friend felt inconsequential in comparison. "How? Where?"

"I guess you could say it was a happy accident. I took a wrong turn while I was trying to find the Horton House and ended up on the wrong road. While I was trying to figure things about, Natalie drove right past me. I knew it was her as soon as we locked eyes, but she said she didn't recognize me until she looked in her side mirror and saw me rubbing my dog tags."

"Then what happened?"

"She turned her car around and I treated her to a drink at a cute little restaurant one of her friends owns. It's called the Bread and Butter Café, and the pastry case up front is filled with the most decadent desserts imaginable. Red velvet cupcakes, dirt cake, Mississippi mud pie—"

"Save the restaurant review for later, Gran. Stick to the script. Did Natalie forgive you for choosing Papa George over her or not?"

Grandma Meredith's smile faded. "We didn't get that far. After I told her you and I would be in town for a while, she asked if George was with us. I had to tell her he had passed on."

"Oh, bummer." Jordan remembered how painful it had been to perform the same chore whenever she used to run into family friends or distant relatives who didn't know. She not only had to deal with her grief but theirs as well. Not to mention their embarrassment over committing such an awkward social faux pas. "How does she look?"

Grandma Meredith's smile returned. "The same. Older, but the same."

"What did you talk about?" After forty-seven years, they had a great deal to catch up on, which explained why Grandma Meredith had been gone for so long.

"She told me about her job and—"

"Wait. She's still working? What is she, like, seventy-two?"

"Seventy-three. At our age, we may shave a few pounds off our weight, but we make sure to claim every single year we've been allotted."

Jordan remembered when the standard retirement age was sixty-five, but the number seemed to get higher and higher every year. With her luck, she wouldn't be able to stop working until she was a hundred. "What does she do?"

"She works at a nursing home in St. Simons three days a week plus the occasional weekend if she needs to cover for someone who has the day off."

"Isn't that awkward, taking care of people who are the same age as she is?"

"I'm sure it is, but she seems to enjoy it. She did tell me, though, that one of the residents is someone I know. Billie's living there now."

"Your former CO? She's here, too?"

"Yes." Grandma Meredith's voice cracked as if she were near tears.

"What's wrong?"

"Billie isn't doing very well. Natalie says she has Alzheimer's."

Jordan had hoped the brave, daring woman from Grandma Meredith's stories had found a happy ending somewhere far away from the perils of battle and the frustrations of bureaucratic red tape. "The way you described her, I thought she'd live forever. How long does she have?"

"A few months. Maybe a year. I'm going to see her tomorrow. I want to spend as much time with her as I can while I'm here. I pray she remembers me. If she doesn't—"

"She will." Billie and Grandma Meredith had gone through so many harrowing experiences together. Jordan knew Grandma Meredith would be devastated if Billie didn't remember any of them—or her. "Take the car. I don't have to go shopping for new clothes. I can pull together an outfit from the ones I brought with me. They didn't bring me luck on the last round of interviews, but maybe this time will be different."

"You don't have to change your plans. Natalie said she would drive me. Like most Alzheimer's patients, Billie doesn't react well to change. Natalie wants to be there in case something goes wrong."

"Is she being protective of Billie's feelings or yours?"

"Both, I imagine. You were right, by the way. Natalie and Billie used to be an item."

"I knew it. My gaydar is never wrong."

"Are you sure about that?"

Jordan's excitement over having her suspicions about Natalie and Billie confirmed dimmed as soon as she remembered how blindsided she had been by Grandma Meredith's revelation about herself. "Okay, almost never. So what happens next? Are you going to see Natalie again? Outside of the nursing home, I mean."

Grandma Meredith blushed. "I kind of invited myself to dinner."

Jordan almost didn't recognize this newer, bolder version of her grandmother. "Where? At her place?"

"Not quite. Her friends have a potluck at each other's houses each month. This month, the owner of the café we went to today is hosting. Natalie wasn't planning on going, but I twisted her arm. Which reminds me. I need to check the pantry to see if I have everything I need to make green bean casserole. Will you be okay on your own for dinner tomorrow night?"

"Don't worry about me. I'll scrounge up something while you're out on your date."

"It's not a date."

"Food. Conversation. Spending time with the woman you love. Sounds like a date to me."

Jordan had never imagined a scenario where she would spend the night at home alone while Grandma Meredith and her girlfriend painted the town red. But this was her new reality, whether she wanted to face it or not.

"Good luck tomorrow," Grandma Meredith said.

"Same to you. But if you get lucky, please don't tell me. I love you, Gran, but there are some stories I don't need to hear."

CHAPTER ELEVEN

The halls of the Peaceful Manor smelled and felt as antiseptic as the many hospital wards Meredith had worked in or visited over the years. The forced cheerfulness of the pastel colors and artificial flowers in the dormitory-style building made her almost unbearably sad. Being here reminded her of her own mortality. The last time she'd seen Billie, they were both young and vital. Now Meredith was a widow and Billie was dying from an insidious disease slowly robbing her of both her memory and the dynamic life force that had helped Meredith survive her tour in Vietnam. Meredith regretted losing touch with her. She and Billie—and she and Natalie—had lost so many years they couldn't get back. Now it was too late. Perhaps it was too late for her and Natalie, too.

Natalie had been cordial to her but not especially warm. Meredith tried to see the situation from Natalie's perspective. If someone had broken her heart and showed up forty-seven years later asking for another chance, how willing would she be to grant the request? Not very. And not without a lot of convincing. Meredith intended to spend the next three months, if not the rest of her life, pleading her case. She might not be successful, but at least she could say she tried.

But first she had to prepare herself to see Billie. Not as she used to be. As she was now.

"Are you ready?" Natalie asked gently as they stood outside room sixteen.

Meredith clutched the worn paperback copy of *To Kill a Mockingbird* Natalie had let her borrow. "I think so."

"Let me go in first. I can tell right away if she's having a good day or not. If she's up for visitors, I'll tell her you're here and let you know when you can come in."

"Okay."

Meredith felt as nervous as she had on her first day in Vietnam. When Billie had ordered her and Natalie to identify the remains of the soldiers zipped inside a neat row of body bags. This was another trial by fire. One Meredith wished she didn't have to face.

"Billie?"

Natalie knocked on the door, slowly pushed it open, and stepped inside. She left the door slightly ajar. Through the small opening, Meredith heard the murmur of voices. Natalie's still-rich alto, followed by a voice that had once been powerful enough to rattle the rafters overhead but now sounded paper thin.

"I brought someone to see you," Natalie said. "Do you feel up for a little company?"

"Friend or foe?" Billie asked.

Natalie chuckled. "Friend. An old one. Meredith?"

Meredith took a deep breath, let it out slowly, and walked into the room. Mementos of Billie's long and distinguished career lined the walls and filled nearly every available surface. Photos of her in and out of uniform. Local magazine and newspaper articles chronicling her achievements. Velvet boxes containing colorful medals trumpeting her bravery. Meredith wondered how many of the accolades Billie remembered and how many she had forgotten.

"Meredith? Meredith Chase?"

Meredith felt her shoulders sag with relief. The frail woman in the bed was a shell of her former self, but for today at least, her eyes were bright and her mind was as sharp as ever.

"It's Meredith Moser now, ma'am."

"So you and George Moser got married after all."

"Yes, ma'am."

"Relax, lieutenant. In here, it's just Billie."

Meredith remembered Billie telling her the exact same thing one night in Suzy's Bar. Billie winked as if she remembered it, too. She opened her arms for a hug. Meredith happily obliged, feeling sharp bones and a thin layer of skin where strong muscles used to be.

"It's good to see you, Billie."

"You, too, Meredith." Her grip on Meredith's hands was surprisingly strong. "What brings you to Georgia? Or need I ask?" Her eyes drifted toward Natalie, who had taken a seat on the far side of the room. Close enough to be of use if called upon but far enough away so she wouldn't infringe on their conversation.

"Actually, my granddaughter did."

"Is she here, too?" Billie looked around expectantly.

"She's on vacation with me, but she didn't make the trip today."

"You should bring her by sometime. I would love to meet her. If she's anything like her grandmother, she must be something special."

Meredith teared up, not only at the compliment but at the realization of the beautiful, intelligent, and honorable young woman Jordan had become. "She certainly is."

Billie threw back the covers, a thick down comforter and flannel sheets. The temperatures outside were oppressive. Inside, the air conditioning felt like it was on full blast. "Hand me my housecoat, Natalie. Let's go to the courtyard so we can sit in the sun and get out of this icebox for a while."

As Natalie helped Billie dress, Meredith grabbed a spare wheelchair from the hall. Meredith pushed Billie outside as Natalie led the way to a grassy courtyard lined with wooden benches.

"That one looks good."

Natalie pointed to a bench located under the sprawling branches of a towering oak tree. The vantage point offered a nice mixture of sun and shade.

Meredith placed Billie's chair near the bench and took a seat beside her. They talked for hours, reminiscing about times both good and bad. When Billie's energy started to wane, Natalie announced it was time to put an end to the reunion.

"Why so soon?" Meredith asked.

"Billie needs her rest. When she gets fatigued, she's more likely to have periods of confusion. The periods are growing more and more extended, so I'd like to avoid the next one as long as I can."

"I understand. I'm disappointed, but I understand."

Billie had nodded off, her chin resting on her chest. When she woke, would she remember Meredith had been to see her?

"I'll see you later, Billie," Meredith said after she and Natalie helped Billie back to her room.

"It was good to see you, Meredith. I'm so glad you came." Billie gripped Meredith's hand and reached for Natalie's. After Natalie moved closer to the bed, Billie held both their hands in hers. Held them hard as if she wanted to bestow some of her fading strength upon them while she still could. Her voice retained little of its former air of command, but her words had lost none of their power. "None of us are promised tomorrow. You two have missed years of yesterdays. Make the most of today." Her eyes were filled with longing, as if she realized days like today would soon become the exception rather than the rule. Like she wanted to live each moment as if she might never see its like again. "That's an order." She settled back on the bed and quickly fell asleep as if the effort to get her point across had exhausted her.

Meredith looked at Natalie as the sound of Billie's gentle snores began to fill the room. Were they supposed to pick up where they left off, or start anew? At the moment, both options seemed like more than Meredith could manage.

"Are you ready to go?"

"Yes," Meredith said. "Please take me home."

❖

Jordan pulled at the cuffs of her new suit as she sat across from Bud Norman, the owner of the Remember When Inn. She tried to keep her eyes focused on his face instead of his god-awful comb-over that put Donald Trump's to shame. Each time he gave his hair a pat, she was surprised his fingers didn't come away coated with boot black shoe polish. The dye job perfectly matched his red and black outfit and the tons of University of Georgia memorabilia in his office. Jordan tried to remember some Georgia Bulldog trivia, but she had been raised in the Big 10 instead of the Southeastern Conference. She could talk about the Wisconsin-Minnesota rivalry all day. Georgia-Florida? Not so much.

"You have a varied background," Bud said, looking over her résumé. "I like a person who can do a little bit of everything. Let's pretend for a second you already have the marketing degree you're studying for. What kind of ideas do you have about getting this place some much-needed publicity?"

Jordan mentally reviewed the research she had conducted the day before in order to be prepared for questions like this one.

"First of all, I would take the inn's general concept a step further. To go along with the themed rooms, the employees could dress as characters from some of the classic shows you feature."

"Tatum, my night manager, suggested the same thing once, but I told her the idea was too cheesy. If I remember correctly, my exact phrase was, 'If I follow your suggestion, we'd all have Kraft sharp cheddar stamped on our foreheads.'" Before Jordan could kick herself for coming up with an idea that had already been floated and discarded, Bud chuckled conspiratorially. "The idea was a good one. I just didn't want to pay for the extra uniforms."

"What if you passed on the expense to the employees? You could provide the additional uniforms for a discounted price and account for the employees' share of the cost by way of payroll deduction."

Bud scribbled a note in the margin of her job application. "I like that idea. What else do you have?"

"The Beach Music Festival is a big draw every summer, isn't it?"

"The biggest we have. I can't dance a lick, but I've attended the festival almost every year since I was a kid."

According to Jordan's research, the Beach Music Festival was the largest of its kind on the Georgia coast. Each August, thousands of beach music fans flocked to the island to shag dance to the sounds of their favorite bands. One of the websites she had found featured dancing couples spinning, twisting, and twirling through the sand like their two bodies shared the same mind.

"You could make a bid to become the host hotel for the musical acts on the bill or become one of the main sponsors of the event itself. If you placed a winning bid, you could become known as the island's premier destination hotel and you'd make money hand over fist."

Bud made another note. Jordan thought she was making a good impression, but she had thought the same thing after her other interviews, too. Hopefully, the results of this one would be different.

Bud stood, signaling the question-and-answer session had come to an end.

"I'll have my day manager check your references while I take you on a tour of the property. If everything checks out and we decide to hire you, how soon could you start?"

That was promising.

"How does tomorrow sound?"

Bud laughed, making his bulbous belly bob up and down like a Southern Santa Claus. "It sounds like we'd be lucky to have you on board."

Jordan hoped he wasn't simply paying her lip service, but she'd find out one way or the other as soon as someone called to tell her she'd gotten the job or let her know she'd been passed over. She owed Tatum a debt of gratitude for setting up the interview. And if she managed to get the job, she'd owe her a lot more than that.

❖

Meredith put on sandals, a pair of crisp white linen pants, and a cream-colored linen shirt with a subtle floral print. After she gelled her hair into gentle spikes, she began to apply her makeup. Not too much. Just enough to camouflage a few of the fine lines that seemed to grow deeper each year.

She felt like she was getting ready for prom night. If Natalie showed up wearing a tuxedo, it would complete the mental images dancing in her head. Images of brightly colored taffeta dresses, ill-fitting flannel and wool suits, crudely executed papier-mâché decorations, and fondly remembered songs from yesteryear. When Natalie rang the doorbell, however, she was wearing jeans, boots, and a Western-style shirt.

"You look dashing." Meredith fingered one of the pearl inlaid snaps on Natalie's shirt front.

"And you look beautiful."

"Thank you." Meredith touched her hand to her hair, feeling more like a schoolgirl than a senior citizen.

"You're welcome." Natalie's voice cracked like a teenage boy on his first date. She cleared her throat in an attempt to mask her apparent nervousness. "Shall we go?"

Meredith held up one hand. "In a minute. I'd like to introduce you to my granddaughter first."

Natalie followed Meredith into the house. Jordan lay on the couch in the living room, one eye on the Jodie Foster movie flickering across the TV screen and the other on Natalie. Her T-shirt was emblazoned with a political statement that skirted the fine line between wit and vulgarity. Meredith sometimes longed for the days when clothes were meant to be worn for what they were instead of functioning as editorial columns or miniature billboards, but the ever-changing array of slogans emblazoned across Jordan's chest often served as indicators to her mood. Today's meant proceed with caution.

Meredith stood behind Jordan and placed her hands on her shoulders. "Natalie, this is Jordan. Jordan, this is—"

"Let me guess." Jordan muted the movie and swung her long legs off the couch. "You must be the infamous Natalie Robinson. I've been hearing about you for two weeks and several hundred miles." She looked Natalie up and down. "Are you really as much of a badass as Grandma Meredith makes you out to be?"

"Probably not. But for the sake of argument, let's say I am." Jordan didn't laugh or even crack a smile at Natalie's attempt at humor. "Tough audience," Natalie said under her breath. She resorted to flattery as she tried to find firmer conversational footing. "My niece said you were beautiful, but I'm afraid she didn't do you justice."

"Your niece?" Jordan cocked her head. "I don't think I've met her."

"Sure you have. Tatum Robinson. You met her yesterday outside her condo. You helped her with her groceries after she dropped her shopping bag in the parking lot."

"Tatum's your niece?" The look of recognition on Jordan's face quickly turned into one of disapproval. "When I asked her about you, she acted like she didn't know who you were."

"Tatum has always been a bit standoffish with strangers. Her father—my brother—claims she inherited the trait from me. He's probably right. It runs in the family, though Paul appears to be immune. I doubt she was trying to mislead you. She was probably being protective."

"I think I'm the one who needs protecting."

Jordan wrapped her arms around a throw pillow and hugged it to her chest. Meredith sat next to her and pressed a kiss to her temple before draping an arm around her shoulders.

"I know this is a lot to take in. I've given you a great deal to process these past few weeks, and I may be asking too much of you."

"You think?" Jordan gripped the pillow tighter and stared down at her bare feet. Her toenails were painted black, an appropriate color choice, given her steadily darkening mood.

"But I hope you realize my love for your grandfather hasn't diminished despite the revelations I've made. Neither has my love for you. I'm the same person I was before we began this journey, Jordan. Nothing has changed."

"You're wrong, Gran. Everything has." Jordan gripped the dog tags hanging around her neck and rubbed them with her thumb, a move Meredith found hauntingly familiar. "How can you tell me you loved Papa George in one breath and say you love her in another?"

Meredith glanced at Natalie to judge the effect Jordan's words had on her, but Natalie's face didn't betray what was going on behind her eyes. Meredith's shoulders slumped as she absorbed Jordan's pain. "I know how close you were to George and how close you still feel. I'm not asking you to love him any less or to end your allegiance to him."

"Good. Because that isn't going to happen."

"I didn't expect it to."

Jordan looked at Natalie. When she spoke, she sounded like George used to each time he met one of Diana's dates.

"I want to like you. I do. Grandma Meredith made you sound like a wonderful person and I'm sure you are, but I hope you realize you have some big shoes to fill."

"It's just dinner, honey," Meredith said.

"It's not just dinner, Gran. It's the beginning you've been looking for. Make it count, okay?"

"I'll try."

Meredith went to the kitchen to fetch the green bean casserole.

"Have a good night," Jordan said as Natalie and Meredith made their way to the car. "I'll leave the light on for you."

Jordan's initial reaction to meeting Natalie had knocked some of the wind out of Meredith's sails and put an all-too-real spin on things. This was no fairy tale with the requisite crowd-pleasing happy ending. There were too many raw, unresolved emotions in the way—Jordan's, Natalie's, and hers.

In the Bronco, she sat with the green bean casserole carefully balanced on her lap. A thick potholder protected her legs from the heat of the foil-covered aluminum pan as Natalie began to make the short drive from the Campbells' house.

"I'm sorry," Meredith said. "I had no idea Jordan would react that way, though I guess I should have expected it. She's very protective of her grandfather's memory."

"No apologies necessary. With George Moser's genes in her body, I wouldn't expect any less. I would like to know, though, why she seems to think I'm here to take George's place in your life. What exactly did you tell her about Vietnam?"

"I told her about the challenges we faced as soon as we stepped off the plane from Okinawa. I told her about the camaraderie I felt working side-by-side with you at the model hospital in Saigon. I told her about dancing with you at Suzy's one minute and searching through the rubble of the Regency Hotel for the bodies of our friends the next. I told her about fearing for my life during the shootout in Xom Que. I told her about wanting to kiss you one night in a pool in Long Binh. And I told her about saying good-bye to you in a hotel room in Vũng Tàu."

"I remember all those things. The series of quiet moments and life-altering events that made my penultimate tour of Vietnam the hardest by far. I remember holding you in my arms and wishing I never had to let you go. I remember fighting my growing feelings for you, knowing they would never be returned. I remember longing for a future I doubted I would ever have. And I remember being treated to a glimpse of that future, only to watch it disappear. When we were in Vũng Tàu, you said you wanted to be with me but you couldn't."

Meredith remembered saying the words—and seeing the hurt on Natalie's face as she heard them.

"I moved on from that moment, but I never truly recovered. I haven't completely opened my heart to anyone since that day, a preventive measure, I suppose, to safeguard against additional despair. Sometimes, I wonder if I did the right thing or if I've failed to live up to the standards I once set for myself."

"You once said, 'If I live my life in fear, I'm not really living, am I?'"

"Those words were uttered by a headstrong, cocksure kid with more bravado than brains. I've grown older, but I don't know if I've grown wiser. A wise woman wouldn't be in the position I'm in now. A wise woman, when given a chance to revisit past mistakes, would have kept driving."

Meredith remembered the despair she'd felt when Natalie drove past her on Stable Road and the hope she'd felt when Natalie hit the brakes and turned around.

"I told Jordan something else, too," Meredith said, turning to face her. "I told her about loving George but being in love with you. I loved you, Natalie, but I wasn't ready to admit what I really wanted. Who I really was."

"And you are now?" Natalie pulled to a stop in front of Beverly and Mary's house. "Why should I believe you're ready now? Why should I believe that this time your actions will match your words? Why should I believe you won't run away again as soon as the summer ends?"

"Because this time, instead of running, I'm ready to make a stand."

❖

Jordan couldn't believe Tatum had lied to her. Jordan had asked her point-blank if she knew Natalie Robinson and Tatum had said nothing. Not only did she know her, she was related to her, a fact she had conveniently neglected to mention. Jordan was tired of being lied to—and of not knowing who she could trust.

When the phone rang, she started not to answer. She forced herself to reach for it in case it might be good news. She could certainly use some of that.

"Hello?"

"Hey, it's me. Tatum."

Hearing Tatum's voice in her ear stunned Jordan into silence. She didn't know whether to tell her off or listen to what she had to say. She allowed her temper to make the decision, a move she might live to regret but seemed too good to pass up.

"I'm glad you called. Does the name Natalie Robinson ring a bell with you? It should. She is your aunt, after all."

Tatum paused. "About that."

"Don't bother."

"You're not going to give me a chance to explain?"

"If you ask me, you already had your chance. And you blew it."

"Wait a second. When we ran into each other, I didn't know you from Eve. Did you actually expect me to share personal information with someone I'd just met just because you looked good in a pair of booty shorts and you helped me pick up some spilled groceries? Sorry. I'm not that trusting and I doubt you are, either. I can tell how protective you are of your grandmother. You would have done the same thing if you were in my position. I'm sorry your grandmother kept part of her personal life secret from you, but it's not the end of the world. You're still several calamities short of a country song, Jordan. If your truck breaks down or your dog dies, I'll put in a call to Nashville for you. In the meantime, suck it up."

Jordan was taken aback by Tatum's bluntness. "You really are a Marine, aren't you?"

"Did you think my fancy wheels were just for show?"

The tense situation might not have called for it, but Jordan laughed nevertheless. Tatum was even better at dishing out tough love than Grandma Meredith.

"Sorry. I already apologized to one Robinson tonight. I might as well add another to the list."

"Aunt Natalie was at your place tonight?"

"Yeah, she and Grandma Meredith are out on a date."

"Are you okay with that?"

Jordan thought about how happy Grandma Meredith had looked when she saw Natalie standing on her doorstep. "I'm getting there. I can see how much Grandma Meredith loves her. Hearing about it is one thing. Seeing it is another."

Grandma Meredith had said people were entitled to one great love in their lives, two if they were lucky. When Papa George died, Grandma Meredith had lost one love. Now she had been lucky enough to find the second. How could Jordan possibly stand in her way?

"I doubt you called to listen to me unload on you. What can I do for you, Tatum?"

"I'm calling to thank you for the five-hundred-dollar referral bonus I'll earn if you decide to take the job."

Jordan's breath caught. "I got it?"

"The position's yours if you want it. Bud said he already discussed the starting salary with you. Is that right?"

"Yes."

The salary wasn't the greatest, but it was competitive for the market and, since it was only a temporary position, Jordan couldn't complain too loudly about how much—or how little—she'd be getting paid to do it.

"Would you like some time to think it over and get back to me with your response? If so, you can call me, Riley, or anyone in HR."

"No, that won't be necessary," Jordan said quickly. She didn't want to give Tatum the chance to change her mind. "I accept."

"In that case, welcome aboard. It says here you're available to start tomorrow. I'll order you a uniform tonight. We use a local outfitter, so the order should arrive in one to two business days. Until it does, the dress code for you will be business casual. When you arrive tomorrow afternoon, Riley will provide you with a name tag, a new employee packet, and a user ID and password for the automated time clock. As I'm sure Bud informed you during your interview, your shifts will vary according to work load. We'll start you off on the two-to-eleven shift so you can get a feel for both the afternoon and evening operations. Riley will be in charge of your training."

Willow had said Riley's position with the inn was little more than set decoration because of her relationship with the owner. Tatum was the one who did most of the actual work. Jordan wished Tatum would be the one showing her the ropes. How much could she learn from someone whose only discernible talent appeared to be her ability to suck a golf ball through a garden hose?

"She should be able to answer any job-related questions you may have," Tatum said. "In the meantime, do you have any questions for me?"

"Just one. How's Lincoln?"

Tatum's laugh was low-pitched and unbelievably sexy.

"Hold on. Let me check." After a brief pause, Tatum said, "He says he's fine, but he wants to know when you plan to take him for another walk."

Tatum was calling from the hotel, which meant Lincoln was in her office with her. Did he provide protection during the overnight hours of her shift or did she simply enjoy his company?

"I don't know what his schedule looks like this week, but tell him we could give it a try next weekend if he doesn't have to work."

"Hold on." Another pause. "He says he's looking forward to it."

"So am I," Jordan said, though she couldn't decide who she was looking forward to seeing more, Lincoln or his master. "Thank you for the opportunity, Tatum."

"No need to thank me. You earned it."

Jordan ended the call and covered her face with a throw pillow as she let out a delirious scream. After two weeks of gloom, things were finally looking up.

❖

Natalie trailed her fingers over the Bronco's pockmarked metal hood as she walked around the front of the car to open the passenger's side door. She pulled the door open and held out her hand. Meredith accepted the offer of help. Feeling Natalie's hand in hers made her feel young again. Fortunately, the callowness of youth had been tempered by years of experience.

"I wish we could go somewhere and find a quiet place to talk." Meredith continued to hold Natalie's hand long after she needed its support. It was contact she sought instead. A chance to reestablish the connection they had once had. "But your friends are waiting for you to make an appearance."

Natalie glanced toward the house. Beverly, Mary, and their guests were standing with their faces pressed against the living room window, not bothering to hide their blatant efforts to spy on her and Natalie.

"I never expected my private life to be the object of anyone's fascination," Natalie said, "but in a small town like this one, uncovering fresh gossip is the most popular spectator sport. Nosy old biddies."

Chuckling, Meredith finally let go of Natalie's hand and gave her shoulder a quick squeeze. "If they annoyed you as much as you pretend they do, I doubt you would have accepted Beverly's invitation to join them for dinner or still consider them your friends."

Natalie reached into the backseat for her pot of food and slammed the car door shut with her elbow. Meredith accompanied her up the azalea-lined walkway. Eight potted begonias led up to the painted concrete steps to the front door.

"I've known most of the women in this house longer than I've known some members of my own family." Natalie climbed the steps as an overfed domestic gray did figure eights through her legs. "They may get on my nerves from time to time, but I know they'll always be there for me when I need them and there's something to be said for that."

"I feel the same way about the members of my bridge club. We may talk about each other when someone's back is turned, but if anyone else tried to disparage a member of the group, she'd have a fight on her hands."

Natalie's lips curled into a smile. "I feel like I'm falling. Not hard and fast like before but gentle and slow as if in a dream. This time, maybe I'll find a softer place to land."

Meredith felt Natalie's previous iciness toward her begin to thaw. "Here's hoping."

Beverly opened the heavy oak front door before Natalie or Meredith came close to ringing the bell. In full hostess mode, she was wearing a flowing caftan worthy of a '40s-era movie star. All she needed was a spiral staircase to walk down, a cut crystal highball glass to wave around, and the witty words of a talented screenwriter to spout.

"Now that you two are here, the real fun can begin. Come in and stop standing on my doorstep like you don't have a pot to piss in or a window to throw it out of."

Beverly pressed a cheek to Natalie's in a semblance of a hello kiss. After Beverly treated Meredith to the same greeting, Natalie and Meredith stepped into the foyer. A few women were talking quietly in the living room. From the looks of it, the rest had escaped to the backyard, where Tiki torches burning mosquito-repellent citronella wicks bathed the area in a festive glow.

"Natalie." Beverly waved a bejeweled hand as she led them into the living room. "You know how this works. The rest of the food's spread out in the dining room. Find a place to set your dishes down and introduce Meredith to everyone while I fix you two a couple of drinks. Gin and tonic, right?" She stepped behind a fully stocked bar that took up most of one wall. "Well, go on. I'll have your drinks ready before you know it and meet you out back. Now off with you."

In the formal dining room, Meredith placed her casserole between a bowl of potato salad and a platter filled with sausage balls. "I'm guessing Beverly's partner doesn't talk much."

Natalie nudged a hash brown casserole closer to a plate of cheese straws to make room on the table for her chicken and dumplings. "Mary learned a long time ago the only word she needs to know how to say is yes. Because as we say in the South, if Mama ain't happy, nobody's happy."

Meredith laughed long and loud. "Unlike most of the expressions I've heard since I've been here, I don't have to be a local to understand that one."

"No, but like most things, it certainly helps. Are you ready to meet everyone, or would you prefer to have some liquid courage first? It isn't too late to back out, you know."

Meredith took Natalie's arm. "It seems to me," she said, wrapping both hands around it, "you're more nervous about tonight than I am. What gives?"

"According to you, you've been asking a lot of people a lot of questions the past few weeks but didn't get any answers. Now it's their turn to question you. Except in their case, I don't think they'll allow you to plead the Fifth."

"Are you afraid of what they'll ask or what I might say?"

"Both."

Natalie opened the sliding glass door that led to the backyard. Women ranging in age from forty to eighty sat in weathered Adirondack chairs haphazardly arranged on the broken-tile patio or on the lush green grass covering the large lot.

Mary rose to greet them, then pointed out two available chairs. After Natalie and Meredith were seated, she led everyone through a round of introductions.

"Don't worry, Meredith," Mary said after the last woman had taken her turn. "There will be a quiz later, but I'll give you a chance to earn extra credit to improve your overall grade."

Meredith laughed dutifully at the retired teacher's variation on an old joke. "I'm almost afraid to ask, but what would I have to do?"

Mary sat back in her chair as Beverly settled into her lap. She patted Beverly's leg possessively. "Thanks to Sherlock Holmes here, we've managed to deduce a few things about you. You and Natalie met during the war. She was interested; you weren't. You did one tour, came home, got married, and started a family. Nat stayed and continued to fight the good fight. Am I right so far?"

Meredith took a sip of the drink Beverly had given her after she'd made her way onto the patio. "So far."

"Since you're attending our little soirée tonight," Mary continued, "I'm assuming your interest in Nat has taken a turn from the platonic to the Sapphic. I have only one question for you. Have you ever been with a woman before?"

Natalie shifted in her seat as her friends circled Meredith like a school of sharks zeroing in on dinner. "You don't have to answer that."

"I know," Meredith said. "I want to."

Except she wasn't sure she wanted to give the answer in this environment. The question should have been Natalie's to ask, and the answer should be Natalie's to hear. Natalie's alone.

Natalie downed half her drink in one swallow and retreated into the darkness, ceding the spotlight to Meredith.

Meredith set her glass on the wide arm of her chair and leaned forward in the sharply angled seat. "Yes, I have been with a woman before."

"When? Who?"

The questions might have been on the tip of Natalie's tongue, but they hadn't spilled from her lips. They had come from someone seated to her right.

"Last year. Enough time had passed after George—my husband—died that my friends felt comfortable enough to ask me if I was ready to start dating again. The idea of returning to the fray at my age held very little appeal to me, and I told them so. I've loved two people in my life. One was gone and the other I thought was equally lost."

She saw more than one set of eyes turn in Natalie's direction.

"I went to visit my granddaughter before the start of her junior year at Berkeley. I spent a weekend touring the campus and meeting her friends. On a whim, I decided to make a side trip to San Francisco before I returned home. I had made several friends in the area when I was stationed there before the war and I sought out one who had decided to make it her home when she got out of the Army. When I called her up, she invited me to her house for dinner. We split a couple of bottles of wine and reminisced about old times. Then we brought each other up to date on everything that had happened in our lives since we completed our respective tours of duty. She and her partner ran a small screen printing business for several years before they sold it to a mid-sized corporation and retired off the proceeds. She said she and her partner had broken up since then but were still on friendly terms. They met once a month to have what she called 'ex sex.'"

Meredith had never heard the term prior to the night in question, but a few women laughed in apparent recognition.

"I told her I couldn't imagine sex without love. I couldn't imagine sleeping with someone without my emotions getting involved, especially old ones. She said it was easier than I might think. The wine must have made me adventurous because I put my glass down, walked over to where she was sitting, took her hands in mine, and said, 'Show me.'"

"Did she?" Beverly asked.

Meredith grinned. "Several times."

The femmes clapped and the butches whistled to show their admiration. Meredith felt like the belle of the ball.

Beverly stood and held up her hands to get everyone's attention. "The only thing left to say after a story like that is, 'Dinner is served.'"

Everyone headed to the dining room and filled their plates. Dinner was informal, so they ate balancing their plates on their laps or their upraised palms. By the end of the night, Meredith felt like part of the family.

"When is the next get-together?" she asked as she hugged Beverly good-bye. "I have a pork tenderloin recipe I've been meaning to try if you don't mind me experimenting on you."

"Not at all. Nat will give you the details. Won't you?" Beverly opened her arms for a hug. Natalie leaned in to give her a peck on the cheek, but Beverly latched on and wouldn't let go. "I'm so happy for you," Beverly said in a stage whisper. "Until Meredith came back into your life, Mary and I thought you were waiting for Billie to die before you allowed yourself to live."

Meredith flinched at the reminder of Billie's imminent passing. She didn't know what to say to refute Beverly's statement. By appearing at the potluck together, she and Natalie had been branded a couple. The designation was far from official, but Natalie seemed increasingly amenable to the idea of making it a reality.

"Same time next month?" Natalie asked as she walked Meredith to the car.

"I can't wait."

CHAPTER TWELVE

Even though she had plenty of company, working the night shift made Jordan nervous. She had seen too many grainy surveillance videos of late-night holdups not to feel a bit of trepidation every time someone walked through the automatic door.

She double-clicked an icon on her computer desktop. Four viewing panels appeared on the screen, filled with live feeds from the Remember When Inn's security monitoring system. She took herself on a virtual tour of the property, starting with the grounds and ending with the hallways, lobby, and common areas. She looked for signs of unusual activity, but was greeted by the same old-same old—guests frolicking in the pool, lounging in the late afternoon sun, pumping quarters into the vending machines, filling coolers with ice despite the posted warning that such activity was prohibited, and puttering along on rented bikes or souped-up golf carts.

"That takes care of that."

With the security check out of the way, she closed the program and plastered on a smile as she prepared to check in a late-arriving guest. After she completed the transaction and handed over the guest's key card with what she hoped was the right amount of good cheer, Larry Nixon beamed like a proud father. Larry had been with the Remember When for nearly fifteen years, and Riley had asked him to give her some hands-on training.

"Nice job," he said.

"I had a good teacher."

Their training sessions had gone well. Larry was knowledgeable about the job and willing to share everything he had learned. He wasn't willing to hang around after his shift was over, however. Jordan took a quick glance at the clock on the opposite wall. A few minutes before seven. Almost time for Larry's shift to end. At the top of the hour, not a minute before or a minute after, he'd clock out and head home. Then she'd be left to man the desk alone.

The walkie-talkie on Larry's worn leather belt crackled, and Tatum's voice carried through the speaker. "Larry, come see me before you leave."

Larry unclipped the walkie-talkie and thumbed the microphone. "You got it, boss."

"Ooh, somebody's in trouble."

Larry placed the walkie-talkie next to Jordan's workstation. "She probably wants an update on your progress. Do you want me to lie or tell the truth?"

"Whatever gets me a raise."

Jordan had expected her addition to the team to be met with friction from some members of the staff—it had taken her several weeks to earn her co-workers' trust at some of her previous jobs—but the staff of the Remember When had welcomed her with open arms. She was still getting used to some of the quirks in the reservation system, but Larry had worked at the hotel longer than anyone else, and he occasionally had problems with the system, too.

Jordan straightened her name tag when a pair of guests with three preteen kids in tow approached the front desk. As Jordan checked them in, the parents asked her for her opinion of the water park that dominated the landscape on the south side of the island.

"The slides are awesome. One is over thirty feet tall, so it provides a serious adrenaline rush. If you're looking for something more sedate, you can go tubing on Turtle Creek. It's half a mile long and the stream is slow-moving, which gives you plenty of time to enjoy your day."

"Great. Thanks for the information."

"No problem. And if you have any more questions about the water park, there are several brochures in the kiosk across the lobby."

"Thanks again."

Jordan handed them their keys and gave them the directions to their room.

"I was going to ask Larry how you're doing with the guests, but I think I've seen the answer for myself." Tatum rolled her wheelchair across the lobby, Lincoln following closely behind. "You could have a future in the hospitality industry—or any other you set your mind to."

"Thanks."

Jordan hadn't seen or heard Tatum come into the lobby. She wondered how long Tatum had been watching her. And if Tatum liked what she saw.

"Granted, I haven't been in this business very long, but I've been in it long enough to know some people aren't going to be happy no matter what you do. Larry says you've managed to keep a pretty level head despite the curveballs a couple of guests have tried to throw at you. He thinks you're going to work out well for us and I'm inclined to agree." Tatum slowed the wheelchair's progress with her hands. "Have you had dinner yet?"

"No. Grandma Meredith made spaghetti last night. I have some leftovers in the break room. I was planning on nuking them in the microwave in a few minutes."

"Correction. You *had* leftovers in the break room."

"Do you know something I don't?"

"Hilda in accounting cleans out the refrigerator every Friday. The rule is, she's supposed to toss anything that's on the verge of becoming a science experiment, but she doesn't bother to check labels or expiration dates, so everything ends up in the trash."

"I thought Riley was kidding when she said Friday was takeout day."

Tatum tossed a pile of takeout menus on the counter. "Order whatever you like. Dinner's on me. Most of the offerings are pizza or subs, I'm afraid, so I hope you aren't counting carbs."

"I'm sure I can find something." Jordan gathered the scattered menus into a neat stack. "Would you care to join me?"

"Sure. Why not? It would save me from having to make a trip home to try and scrounge up something on my own."

Tatum came around the front desk. While Jordan busied herself petting Lincoln, Tatum pulled a pneumatic desk chair toward her and transferred herself into it. With the touch of a button, she raised the chair from its lowest setting to its highest. Her legs dangled uselessly in the air. As she carefully placed her feet on the chair's circular footrest, she looked at the bouquet of flowers Jordan had placed on the counter and unabashedly read the accompanying card resting on Jordan's keyboard. The card and flowers had added an unexpected bright spot to Jordan's otherwise down day. A local florist's logo was printed on the card, but Brittany's name was scrawled under the handwritten note, which read, *I never learned to agree to disagree very tactfully. Sorry for being an asshole. Friends?*

Jordan examined Tatum's face, trying to gauge her reaction to what she'd read, but Tatum didn't give her anything to go on.

"Who's Brittany?"

"My ex."

"Are you two planning on kissing and making up?" Tatum stared at one of the menus as if she had never seen anything so fascinating.

"No. We didn't pull any punches when we broke up. She's just trying to apologize for hurting my feelings. At least, I think that's what she's doing. I've given up on trying to figure her out. She gave up on me a while ago, it seems, but it took longer for me to get the message."

"I'm sorry."

"Don't be. Water under the bridge."

Tatum finally met her eye. Jordan couldn't get over the directness of her gaze. Was that why she felt so unsettled right now or was it something else? Every time she resolved one problem, another popped up to take its place.

"Are you okay?" Tatum asked.

"I'm not having the greatest of days." Learning a new job was always a challenge, but Jordan would rather deal with that headache than all the other ones in her life. Receiving the flowers from Brittany had put a smile on her face, but it had also reminded her how much disarray her life was in at the moment. She longed for the days when the hardest decisions she had to make were what outfits to wear to school and which parties she should hit on the weekend. She looked at the selection of sandwiches on one of the menus, then she slowly slid the menus across the counter. "I'm not very hungry tonight. A salad will be fine."

"Two dressings on the side?"

"How did you know?"

"I've dated women like you before."

Jordan plucked at the collar of her French blue Oxford shirt, which she had combined with a pair of crisp khaki pants to comply with the business casual dress code. "If I'd known this was a date, I would have worn something more revealing."

"I didn't mean—"

"I know what you meant," Jordan said with a smile, "but you're cute when you're flustered."

"Then I must be fucking gorgeous right now."

As a matter of fact, she was. The more time Jordan spent with Tatum at work, the more she wondered what it would be like to spend time with her after hours. Would Tatum be sweet and charming like she was now or defensive and angry like she'd been when they ran into each other in the parking lot of her apartment complex?

After she decided what she wanted to eat, Tatum phoned a nearby sandwich shop. The employee who took the order said the food would arrive in thirty minutes, but Jordan didn't expect to see the delivery van pull up for at least an hour. She and Tatum settled in to watch the Milwaukee Brewers play the Atlanta Braves at Turner Field. To Jordan's pleasant surprise, the food showed up during the bottom of the second inning.

"I wouldn't have guessed you were a baseball fan," Tatum said after they cleared some space on the counter, unpacked the oversized bag, and opened the containers.

Jordan opened one of the two bottled waters she had grabbed from the break room. "Some of the best conversations my father and I have ever had occurred in the stands while we were watching Brewers games. He probably feels more comfortable talking to me in a crowd because he doubts I'll say or do anything too outrageous in front of so many people. Then I came out to him during a playoff game and shot his theory all to hell." Jordan grinned. "Perhaps that's why he hasn't taken me to a game since."

"What about your mom?"

"You couldn't pay her to go to a game. She's the only member of the family who doesn't like sports. If she didn't look so much like Grandma Meredith, I'd swear she was adopted."

"I take it you aren't close?"

"No." Jordan faltered. "In fact, I feel like I'm a disappointment to her."

"Why do you say that?"

"We're like oil and water. We just don't mix. It must be a mother-daughter thing because her relationship with Grandma Meredith is just like the one she has with me. They love each other, but they don't know how to show it."

Jordan didn't want to be rude and ask Tatum to change the subject. Thankfully, Tatum did it on her own.

"You're getting really brown. Have you been spending a lot of time at the beach?"

Jordan looked at her hands. The tawny skin she had inherited from her father's side of the family was several shades darker than it had been when she had first arrived on the island.

"Grandma Meredith gets up at the crack of dawn each morning to do an hour of yoga. While she's doing that, I ride my bike to the beach, take a long walk, and get in a chill mood for the rest of the day. I could probably get into the same mindset if I did the yoga, but I'm not that flexible."

"Neither am I."

Tatum was obviously trying to make a joke, but Jordan didn't know whether to laugh or be offended on her behalf.

"What do you do for fun?" Jordan asked after she regained her equilibrium. "Do you like the beach?"

"I love it, but I haven't been able to go for a while."

"Why? Too busy with work?"

"I have a hard time maneuvering my chair through the soft sand. It's okay once I get to the hard-packed as long as I swap out my regular wheels for my wider ones."

"Sort of like switching from a road bike to a mountain bike. From Lance Armstrong to Missy Giove, to be exact."

"I never thought about it that way, but, yeah. It's funny you used that analogy because I used to be a bike racer."

"Do you miss it?"

"More than you know. I miss being in the saddle, feeling my lungs, calves, thighs, and glutes burn while I chase other riders or break away from the pack. During some of my physical therapy sessions, I ride a recumbent bike with my feet strapped to the pedals, but the sense of accomplishment I feel at the end of a run isn't the same. I feel some of the same pain, but none of the same high."

Jordan couldn't imagine no longer being able to do something that had once meant so much to her. Judging by the wounded expression on Tatum's face, Tatum could imagine it only too well.

"I bet Lincoln loves the water."

Lincoln's ears perked up at the mention of his name.

"Actually, he's never been," Tatum said with what sounded like genuine regret. "I do what I can to make sure he stays active and gets plenty of exercise. We take road trips to Savannah so he can roll in the grass in Forsyth Park, play fetch, or watch the college kids play Frisbee football, but we haven't been to the beach."

"But dogs are allowed, right?"

"Yes, on a leash or off-leash as long as they're well-trained and in the owner's control at all times." Tatum reached down and gave Lincoln a scratch. "I'd love to watch him play in the water and feel beach sand between his toes for the first time."

"Why do you drive all the way to Savannah when there's so much for you to do right here? I've been reading the brochures. There are handicapped accessible ramps to the beach near the St. Andrews picnic area and the Convention Center. If you need some extra muscle to get through the soft sand, I'm sure someone would be willing to help you."

"That's why I prefer to hang out in Savannah in my spare time. If I need help, I'd rather ask someone who doesn't know me rather than someone who does. I can handle pity from strangers, but not from family or friends."

Jordan remembered Tatum's initial unwillingness to accept her help on the day they had met. For someone as independent as Tatum seemed to be, it couldn't be easy for her to accept being dependent on other people.

"How was your first week?" Tatum asked, changing the subject yet again.

"It's a lot to learn, but I think I'm doing pretty well so far, if I say so myself."

"You don't have to. Larry sang your praises loud and clear."

"Tell him the check's in the mail."

Tatum wolfed down the first half of her sub, but made sure to toss Lincoln a bite or two of steak from time to time. Jordan, in contrast, barely picked at her food.

"How's your salad?"

"It's good." Jordan brought a forkful to her mouth and chewed without much pleasure, then went right back to pushing lettuce around her Styrofoam plate. "Like I said, I'm not very hungry tonight."

Tatum wiped mustard off her mouth with her napkin. Lincoln greedily eyed the other half of her sandwich. She made sure it was safely out of his reach. "Is there something on your mind?"

"Besides the whole apologetic ex-girlfriend, unfortunate new hookup drama, you mean?"

"There are worse problems to have."

Jordan speared some of her salad with her fork but didn't eat it. "Is it true Lt. Col. Daniels is dying?"

"Billie, you mean? She's a general now, but, yeah, I'm afraid so."

Jordan rested her fork on the side of the container and propped her chin on the heel of her upraised hand. "Grandma Meredith wants me to meet her, but I'm not sure I'm ready to."

"Why wouldn't you be? Billie's a wonderful person, even though she has no idea who she is most days."

"My point exactly. Papa George was out of his mind on morphine by the time he reached the end. I hated seeing him that way. I wish I could have known Billie as she was in Grandma Meredith's stories, not how she is now."

"So do I."

Jordan's hand crept to the dog tags around her neck. She absently fingered the upraised letters.

"As close as you and your grandfather seem to have been, losing him must have been hard for you."

Jordan nodded mutely and let her hand drop. "It was the toughest thing I've ever experienced. It sucks watching someone you love die."

"Yeah, I know what you mean." Jordan watched Tatum flash back to Afghanistan, where she'd undoubtedly seen too much blood, brains, and gore spilled on the sand. Tatum wrapped up the rest of her sandwich as if her appetite had abandoned her.

"Did I remind you of the war? I didn't mean to bring back unpleasant memories."

"It's okay."

"What was it like for you over there?"

"It wasn't a walk in the park, that's for sure. I think Charles Dickens said it best. It was the best of times and it was the worst of times. I made memories that will last a lifetime, not all of them pleasant. I made friends that were as close as family, but not all of them made it home."

"But I bet you'd do it all again if you could."

"I'd do it without thinking twice."

"Why?"

"Wouldn't you?"

Jordan's knitted her eyebrows in confusion. "I don't understand."

"Even though losing your grandfather was painful, wouldn't you go back and relive the good times if you could?"

"In an instant," Jordan said as tears clouded her vision.

"See?" Tatum said gently. "We have something in common."

"More than one thing, I hope." Jordan felt her interest in Tatum begin to grow. "Do you know how to shag?"

Tatum blushed. "That's a pretty loaded question, don't you think?"

"There are more connotations of shagging than Austin Powers movies would lead you to believe. I read somewhere that shagging is the kind of dancing you do to beach music."

"It's kind of like swing, except it's never gone out of style."

"Right."

"And you're asking me about it because?"

"The Beach Music Festival's coming up in a couple of months. I'd love to go, but I don't want to go by myself. If you're not doing anything, perhaps we could go down to the pier and check out one of the sessions." Tatum didn't answer right away, so Jordan kept talking to fill the silence. "If you don't want to go or you have other plans, that's okay. I could ask Larry if I could be his and his wife's plus one."

"August is two months from now. I don't know what I'll be doing two weeks from now, let alone two months. But I don't have any entries on my social calendar for the foreseeable future, so I'll be sure to pencil you in."

"Could you make that pen instead?"

"Anything to make you stop reading the brochures I see you poring through in the lobby. Otherwise, you'll want to try kiteboarding next."

In the new extreme sport that was steadily taking over the beach, kiteboarders harnessed the power of the wind to glide and flip over the water or jump the waves.

"I've already read that brochure. It sounds like a lot of fun. Are you sure you don't want to go?"

Jordan rested her hand on Tatum's leg, the one a Taliban sniper's bullet had left riddled with scars. Could Tatum feel the weight of Jordan's hand against her leg? Could she feel its warmth? Jordan felt the atrophied muscles in Tatum's thigh spasm. Tatum's right foot began to twitch, causing her knee to bang against the underside of the desk. The noise sounded like machine gun fire. Horrified, Jordan drew her hand away. "Did I do that?"

"No."

Tatum lowered the desk chair and slid into her wheelchair. She looked like she was having some kind of seizure. Jordan felt trapped. She didn't mean to stare, but she didn't know how to help. She just wanted whatever was happening to be over.

Tatum reached for her ankle, pulled her leg straight, then propped it on the bottom drawer of the desk.

"Whenever your body gets tired of sitting in the same position, you can get up and walk around to ease the tension," Tatum said. "I can't."

As Tatum kneaded the muscles in her leg, her foot flopped around in the junk drawer like a fish out of water. When the tremor finally—mercifully—stopped, Tatum put her hand under her knee and positioned her foot above the metal footrest attached to her wheelchair. Then she let her leg drop into place.

"There. That's better. Now what were you saying about the Beach Music Festival?"

"Um." Jordan looked across the lobby. The family of five she had checked in a few minutes ago was staring at her and Tatum with disgusted looks on their faces. From their vantage point, they hadn't been able to see everything that had gone on, but they'd apparently been able to see enough. And Jordan had seen too much. Hoping her expression didn't match the guests', she turned back to Tatum. "I'm sorry. What did you say?"

"The Beach Music Festival. Did you want to go?"

Jordan realized she had been fooling herself when she told Hayden and Willow she could date someone with a disability. There were so many things she didn't know about Tatum's condition. Things she needed to know if she planned to go out with her. Things she didn't know if she could handle.

"We should poll the employees and see how many would like to go as a group," she said, opting for safety in numbers. "We could treat it as a company outing. Instead of embarrassing trust exercises everyone hates, we could have a few drinks, listen to some good music, and get to know each other better."

"And you could hide in the crowd instead of being forced to deal with me or my issues on your own."

Tatum's voice was filled with disappointment. As if she had gotten her hopes up and been let down. Jordan hadn't expected Tatum to see through her explanation or call her on her BS. Tatum's familiarity with enhanced interrogation techniques probably allowed her to see through even the most well-crafted lies. The flimsy one she had come up with on the fly never stood a chance. "No, that's not what I meant at all."

"Right." Tatum wheeled around the desk. "I'm sorry I embarrassed you in front of the guests. I'll hide myself away in my office so I won't embarrass you any further. Lincoln, come."

Lincoln jumped to his feet and followed Tatum across the lobby. He looked back before he rounded the corner, his soulful eyes giving Jordan a silent rebuke that was just as devastating as Tatum's verbal one had been. He needn't have bothered. Jordan didn't think she could feel much worse.

She hadn't meant to hurt Tatum's feelings, but she had been thrown by both the episode and her reaction to it. An apology was in order, but for some transgressions, "I'm sorry" just wasn't good enough. And this one? This one definitely qualified.

CHAPTER THIRTEEN

Meredith tucked Natalie's copy of *To Kill a Mockingbird* under her arm as she and Jordan slowly walked up the hall of the Peaceful Manor nursing home.

"I'm thinking of changing my major," Jordan said.

"Again?" Meredith smiled at the amused exasperation she hadn't been able to keep out of her voice. "To what this time?"

"Hotel and restaurant management."

"Your job at the hotel must be working out well if you're thinking of turning it into a full-time occupation."

Jordan looked thoughtful—despite her I'm with Stupid T-shirt. "My other forays into the service industry drove me crazy after a few days, but this one's different. I'm working with a bunch of great people and the guests are really interesting. I know it's only been a few weeks, but I'm really having a good time."

"At work or in general?"

Jordan stopped walking. "I'll be honest. I wasn't having very much fun the first few days after we arrived. I'm sure I owe you an apology or three. I doubt I was a joy to be around."

"But then you met Hayden. Isn't that her name?"

"Get with the program, Gran. Hayden's old news."

"Good. Because I wasn't very fond of her. Are you seeing someone else now?"

"Not really. I've been hanging out with the people at work because there isn't anyone else to talk to during the wee hours of a late shift, but I'm not seeing any of them."

"What about Tatum, Natalie's niece? Have you been spending time with her, too?"

Jordan shifted her weight from one foot to the other as if the question made her uncomfortable. "We had dinner once. At work, I mean. She's quite a fascinating character. Gruff on the outside, but tender on the inside. A little flinty until you get to know her."

Meredith chuckled. "Sounds familiar. Must be a family trait."

"Did Natalie tell great stories, too?" Jordan asked wistfully. "The day we met, Tatum told some that made me want to listen to her all day."

"Natalie kept to herself as much as she could because she didn't want to lie about her sexuality, yet she couldn't be honest about it and expect to be allowed to stay in the military. Not in 1967. Unlike some other female service members who were in the closet back then, she didn't make up stories about an imaginary boyfriend waiting back home or serving at some remote outpost. She always craved respect rather than recognition. I've always admired her for that." Meredith had never told her so, but she intended to rectify the error as soon as she could. "Work kept us so busy we didn't have many opportunities to share stories about our personal lives or the loved ones we'd left back home. The few times we did, though, are moments I'll always treasure."

Jordan seemed solemn today. Meredith had initially attributed it to their surroundings, but now she thought something else might be to blame. Something Jordan either didn't want to talk about or didn't want to face.

"Has talking with Tatum changed your opinion of the war?"

"No, I still think most differences could be settled diplomatically rather than militarily. But between the two of you, you've given me newfound respect for the people who have chosen to wear the uniform. I used to think of military service as a way to pay for college for those who couldn't afford it otherwise or an alternative to a jail sentence for delinquents who were running out of options, but it's more than that. It's patriotism at its highest level, and it requires a serious commitment I, for one, would never have the guts to make. But you did. So did Tatum. I've always suspected you were a real badass back in the day, but Tatum puts you to shame."

"No argument there."

"She's one of the strongest women I've ever met. I've never known anyone so dedicated to protecting others at the expense of herself. Even after everything that happened to her in Afghanistan, she'd re-up if she could. Can you believe that?"

"You sound smitten."

Jordan didn't receive the jibe with the humor Meredith had intended.

"It isn't like that," Jordan said testily. "Like I said, she and I are just friends. At least, we used to be. Now, I'm not so sure."

"What happened?"

Tatum leaned against the wall and blew out a breath. "When Hayden and Willow asked me if I'd ever date someone with a disability, I said, 'Sure. No problem.' But the night Tatum and I had dinner, she had some kind of spasm in her leg and it freaked me out. If I can't handle a freaking muscle spasm, how am I supposed to handle the more serious stuff?"

"Like what?"

"Urine catheters or colostomy bags or—"

"But Tatum might not have either."

"I know. I was using those as an example. But you get the point, right?"

"I do, but the real question is, do you?"

"I have a three point seven GPA, Gran. I'm not an idiot. I know the wheelchair is part of the package." Jordan put her hands in her hair and drew it away from her face. "I thought I'd be able to handle it, but I can't."

"When you look at her, I'm sure she wishes you'd see her, not the chair."

"I do. That's why I'm kicking myself right now. Because I see her and I like her, but I'm not ready to tackle anything that life-changing. I'm on vacation. I came down here looking for a good time for the summer. Nothing serious and nothing long-term. Tatum deserves more than that. She deserves someone who's going to be in her life for the rest of her life. That isn't me. I'm only going to be in town for two more months. Then I'm out of here. I don't want to start something with her knowing it's going to end badly, but I guess I already did."

Meredith smoothed the front of Jordan's shirt. She wished Jordan's ruffled feathers could be tended to just as easily. "How can you possibly know how your relationship with her will end when you've barely begun?"

Jordan rolled her eyes and tried to defuse the seriousness of the situation with humor. "Stop being so logical, will you? I'm trying to be noble and you're poking holes in my balloon."

Meredith took Jordan's face in her hands and forced her to look her in the eye. "Put the jokes aside and tell me what you're really thinking, sweetie."

Jordan was a few inches shy of six feet tall. At the moment, though, she seemed much smaller.

"I love spending time with Tatum, but I never imagined myself getting involved with someone who has a disability."

Meredith suspected Jordan had never said the words out loud before. The confession seemed to take something out of her. Like the balloon she had just mentioned had started to deflate. Jordan's chin trembled as she tried not to cry.

"I don't know if I'm cut out to play nursemaid."

"You never know what you can do until you're asked to do it."

"Maybe. But you're forgetting one thing, Gran. I'm not you."

"You're forgetting something, too. You don't have to be."

Meredith gave Jordan a hug and waited for her to regain her composure before they resumed their journey.

Meredith knocked on the door of Billie's room and poked her head inside. She had been coming to see Billie every day for the past week. If Billie was having a good day, they would talk for a while and Meredith would read to her until Billie fell asleep. If she was having a bad day, the only thing Meredith could do was be there for her and wonder how long it would be before her suffering came to an end.

How, Meredith wondered, would Billie react to having Jordan's unfamiliar presence added to their now-familiar routine? Billie didn't always respond favorably to change, but perhaps having Meredith in the room would help matters.

"Billie, this is my granddaughter, Jordan. I told you about her, remember? You said you wanted to meet her."

Billie screwed up her face in concentration as if she were trying to see through the thick fog shrouding her brain. Then her features relaxed and she flashed a relieved smile. "Of course I remember. Come closer, Jordan. My eyes aren't as good as they used to be. Then again, neither is the rest of me."

Jordan stood next to Billie's bed. "It's an honor to meet you, ma'am. Grandma Meredith has told me so much about you, I feel like I already know you."

Billie slowly shook her head, her thinning hair fanned around it like a silver halo. "You remind me so much of your grandfather. You're a lot prettier than he was, but you have his mannerisms."

Jordan rubbed the back of her neck like George used to whenever he was flustered or, as in this case, received a compliment he didn't know how to take. Meredith's heart filled with love as her past and present collided.

After Jordan found a seat on the far side of the room, Meredith sat in the chair next to the bed and made small talk with Billie for a while before she opened the book and picked up where she had left off during her previous visit. She was only a few pages into the chapter about Scout Finch getting into a fight at school when Billie became confused.

"Who are you," Billie shouted, "and what are you doing in my room?"

"Billie, what's wrong?"

"You're trying to steal from me, aren't you?"

Meredith closed the book and followed Billie's line of sight. Across the room, Jordan was holding a moldy dinner roll over a plastic wastebasket. "Honey, stop."

"But this drawer smells putrid. It's crammed with food and most of it's spoiled."

"I understand, honey, but I need you to stop, okay? Right now."

"If you say so." Jordan let the moldy bread fall into the trash and raised her hands in surrender.

"I'm not going to let you take what's mine." Billie's arms trembled as she tried to push herself into an upright position.

"Billie, it's okay. Jordan was simply trying to do a little spring cleaning for you, but she's stopped now."

Meredith tried to keep her voice calm, but Billie grew increasingly agitated. Billie grabbed a glass-encased silver dollar off the nightstand, drew her arm back, and threw it as hard as she could. Meredith instinctively raised her hands, but she didn't move fast enough. She felt a thud, followed by a blinding flash of pain as the paperweight struck her in the head.

Despite the ringing in her ears, Meredith heard Jordan snatch the door open, run into the hall, and yell, "Someone please help. My grandmother's bleeding. Here. In here."

Meredith heard heavy footsteps running down the hall. She needed to get a handle on the situation before it spiraled out of control. As Billie continued to hurl whatever she could get her hands on, Meredith staggered out of the room with her hand pressed to her forehead. "No need to call the cavalry just yet," she said, even though she felt blood seeping through her fingers.

"But, Gran, you're hurt."

Meredith motioned for Jordan to calm down. "It's just a cut, honey. And not a deep one at that. Trust me. I've seen worse."

"You may have, but I haven't." Jordan wrapped her arms around Meredith's waist as if to hold her up, but Meredith felt her head begin to clear.

Two attendants ran into Billie's room. Another sat Meredith in a nearby wheelchair and examined the cut on her head. Natalie peeked into Billie's room, where the attendants were attempting to calm her without having to restrain her.

"What happened in there?" Natalie asked. "Did she get confused?"

Meredith looked up at Natalie while an attendant disinfected the cut on her forehead prior to affixing butterfly bandages over the wound. "Yes." She shook her head disconsolately, prompting a gentle admonishment to hold still. "It's unfortunate. We were having such a nice visit. I brought Jordan by to meet her because I wanted them to get to know each other while there's still time. I was reading to her when she flew into a rage."

"I think the whole thing was my fault," Jordan said shakily. "I smelled something bad, so I opened one of the drawers to see what it was. The drawer was stuffed with congealed packages of butter, old dinner rolls, some fuzzy bananas, and all kinds of junk food. I got rid of the bananas first, then I trashed the rolls because they were starting to turn green. Instead of thanking me, Billie got this strange look on her face and accused me of trying to steal from her. Then she started yelling and throwing things. If I had known she was so attached to that stuff, I would have left it where it was."

Natalie nodded knowingly. "Alzheimer's patients go through phases where they collect things. They burn through their savings buying everything they see on the Home Shopping Network until a family member discovers what's going on and takes away their credit cards. If they're in institutions like this one, they hoard food because they think someone will forget to come by to feed them. Once every couple of weeks, we get someone to distract Billie while we throw out the perishable items in her stash before it goes bad. If she sees us doing it, it tends to upset her and we have outbursts like the one you witnessed today."

"I didn't mean to piss her off," Jordan said.

"It's okay," Meredith said as the attendant handed her two aspirin and a cup of water. "You didn't know."

"I'll know better next time."

"Do you want there to be a next time? I thought what happened today might put you off future visits."

Jordan shrugged like George used to whenever he made an honorable gesture he preferred to have go unrecognized. "I don't want today to be my last impression of Billie, and I want a chance to try to make a better one on her."

"I am so happy to hear that," Meredith said. "The way you ran out of the room, I was afraid you might be scarred for life."

Jordan ran a finger over the bandages on Meredith's forehead. "You're the one who's going to come out of this with a scar, Gran, not me."

Natalie stepped into Billie's room and came back a few minutes later with an update. "The attendants have managed to clean up the mess and get Billie back in bed without having to restrain her hands and feet, which is good because she hates being restrained even more than I dislike seeing her that way. She'll be okay in a little while if you'd like to resume your visit."

Jordan checked her watch. "We can't stay much longer, I'm afraid. We have to get back so I can get some sleep before my shift."

"I forgot we were operating under a time limit this afternoon." Meredith looked at the book in her hands. "I didn't reach the end of a chapter today, but I suppose I can make up for it next time."

Jordan offered her hand to help Meredith out of the wheelchair and Meredith prepared to leave, but Natalie stepped into her path.

"My shift ends at five. I could drive you home if you'd like to stay a while longer."

Meredith felt stunned, though she couldn't tell if the blow to the head or Natalie's magnanimous gesture was to blame. "Yes, I'd like that very much. Thank you." She handed Jordan the keys to her car. "Have a good day at work, dear. I'll see you tonight."

Jordan looked at Natalie as she pocketed the keys. "Keep an eye on her, okay? She's been through enough for one day."

"I won't leave her side. You have my word on that."

After Jordan left, Natalie led Meredith to the courtyard, where a few visitors were sitting with their loved ones and several residents were slowly making their way around the grounds, alone or in groups.

"I thought we could get some fresh air while we wait for Billie to find herself again."

"That sounds like a lovely idea." The aspirin must have started to take effect because Meredith could feel her throbbing headache begin to abate.

"Is Jordan going to be okay?" Natalie asked as she and Meredith took a seat on a nearby bench. "She looked pretty shaken up."

"I'm sure she'll be fine."

Natalie shoved her hands in the pockets of her uniform smock as if she didn't know what to do with them. "At the potluck, were you telling the truth when you said you had slept with a woman, or did you make that up to impress your audience?"

"Did that bit of news come as a shock to you or a pleasant surprise?"

"Both. But it also made me a little bit jealous."

"I can't say that makes me unhappy because it doesn't." Meredith edged closer until their knees were touching. Her body reacted to the contact, making it difficult for her to concentrate on what she wanted to say next. "Since we're being honest with each other, I have to admit I wasn't completely forthcoming that night. Though the story was true, I purposely omitted the part about how the experience made me feel."

"How did it make you feel?"

"Being with Evelyn helped me accept who I was—who I am—but it also made me realize what I was missing. Being with her made me want to be with you. I wanted her to be you."

"Then why didn't you try to find me?"

Meredith looked away. "I'm here now. Isn't that enough?"

"No," Natalie said, restoring the distance between them. "I wish it was, but it isn't. I need to know where you're coming from and where you want to go. I can't know either of those things until you're able to tell me. I know the reason you walked away from me when we were in Vietnam. You wanted a family and I couldn't give you one. But after you made the family you'd longed for and you were free to be yourself, why didn't you take the chance when it was presented to you? If you didn't want to upset the status quo, say so. But don't come to me after all this time saying you're willing to embrace a life you once refused and expect me to believe you unconditionally."

Meredith looked deep into her eyes. "If I tell you what I was afraid of then, will you tell me what you're afraid of now?"

"Like you, the only thing I can do is try."

"Is tonight too soon? Jordan worked overnights last week, and she's working until eleven every night this week. I'm a little tired of having dinner alone."

"No," Natalie said, "tonight sounds perfect."

❖

Jordan rang the doorbell. She didn't expect to be welcomed with open arms, but she didn't know where else to go.

"This is a surprise," Tatum said after she opened the door.

"A pleasant one, I hope."

Tatum rolled backward, but Jordan leaned in the open doorway instead of following her inside. "Are you in the middle of something or can I borrow you for the next hour or so?"

Tatum turned and examined Jordan's face. "Is something wrong?"

Jordan didn't want to think about this afternoon. She wanted to put it behind her as soon as she could. How could she have been so stupid? Grandma Meredith had told her Billie didn't react well to change and she, like an idiot, had done something to set her off. Like her parents had once told her during a particularly withering lecture, sometimes she had plenty of book sense but zero common sense. And today was one of those times.

"Later, okay? Right now, I need you to drive me somewhere."

Tatum's eyes flicked toward Grandma Meredith's SUV. "You drove yourself this far, but you can't manage it the rest of the way? What's going on, Jordan?"

Jordan felt an odd mix of sadness and exhilaration. "Just trust me, okay?"

Tatum grabbed her keys and Lincoln's leash and locked her condo door behind her. "Where would you like to go?"

Jordan moved aside and allowed Tatum to pass. "I'll tell you on the way."

In the parking lot, Tatum slid behind the wheel of her car. Jordan sat in the passenger's seat and Lincoln hopped in the back, squeezing in next to Tatum's wheelchair. Jordan called out the turns while Tatum drove.

"We're here," Tatum said after she parked in front of a beachside restaurant. "Now what?"

"Now *I* drive."

Jordan hopped out of the car and waved at Dusty Spradlin, the owner of a nearby business specializing in kiteboard and kite buggy rentals.

Tatum set her wheelchair on the ground and transferred into it. As soon as she clipped Lincoln's leash to his collar, he began straining at the lead.

"Thanks for all the business you two have been sending my way. Your guests have been keeping me hopping." Dusty held his hand under Lincoln's nose and waited until he passed the sniff test before he extended the same hand to Jordan and Tatum. "I was wondering when I was going to see you out here, too."

"Are we all set?" Jordan asked.

"Ready whenever you are."

"Ready for what?" Tatum asked apprehensively.

Jordan shot her a quick look. "Give us a few minutes, okay, Dusty?"

"Sure thing."

"What are you trying to prove, Jordan?" Tatum asked after Dusty left to wait on another customer.

"Nothing."

"Then why are we here?"

"I'm trying to help you make one of your dreams come true. You said Lincoln had never been to the beach before. I wanted to watch him play in the water and I wanted to watch your face while he did it. No ulterior motives. No hidden agendas. I promise. I just want something to go right today."

"What about those? What are they for?"

Tatum pointed to the row of tiny buggies with large, foil-shaped kites attached to them. Most of the buggies were designed to carry only one person. One, however, was slightly oversized with enough room for two adults and a child—or, in this case, one very excited German shepherd.

"Those will allow me to watch you soar. All you have to do is trust me. Are you game?"

"You've gone to so much trouble, I can't exactly say no, can I?"

"Cool."

They crossed the paved parking lot and headed for the rental stall.

"Need some help?" Dusty asked, offering to push Tatum's chair through the sand.

"No," Tatum said, even as her wheels began to bog down.

"If you say so. Call me if you need me." He knelt next to the large buggy and inspected the riggings.

Jordan watched Tatum struggle to keep pace. She wanted to lend a hand, but she convinced herself to wait for Tatum to ask for help.

"Can you take Lincoln for me?" Tatum asked a few minutes later. "I'll watch you from here."

"Okay. Sure."

Jordan took Lincoln's leash and allowed him to lead her to the water. Lincoln braced his front legs and barked at the crashing waves, then pinned his ears back and ran headlong into them. Jordan let him go far enough out to test his sea legs before she urged him back to shore. Lincoln sprinted across the sand, his tongue flapping wildly in the breeze. Running alongside him, Jordan had never felt so happy or so free. She knew reality would set in eventually. For the moment, though, she had found the escape she longed for. When she returned to shore, Dusty went over the safety rules and operating procedures.

"If the wind hits your kite just right, you can get up to twenty-five MPHs out of your buggy. The two-line kites are smaller and not as easy to maneuver as the four-line kite attached to this baby. With two lines, you get a serious upper body workout trying to get where you're going, and driving is a bit of a challenge. With four lines, the driver has complete control."

He gave a quick but informative lesson on how to operate the buggy, demonstrating how to produce power and lift, steer, stop, and back up.

"If you tack back against the wind like this, you can ride rather than walk back to your starting point."

He didn't seem to realize the impossibility of what he had just said. If they ran out of wind, Tatum would be as helpless as the stranded buggy. But Jordan chose to ignore rather than correct his error.

"Did you two have fun?" Tatum asked after she strapped herself into the buggy.

Lincoln barked once and shook seawater out of his thick fur.

"I'll take that as a yes."

Lincoln jumped into the buggy after Tatum patted the spot next to her. Jordan tossed her a helmet and slid behind the wheel. Then Dusty gave them a push to get them going. Once the wind hit the kite, they were off. The buggy's wheels kicked up sand as they zipped across the beach. Lincoln barked his approval after Jordan let out a rebel yell.

Tatum seemed nervous at first, but she soon began to relax. "Faster!" she yelled as the wind whipped her face. "Go faster."

Jordan looked over at her, feeling the same sense of freedom she had experienced while running on the beach with Lincoln. "I'd love to, but there's no gas pedal."

After Jordan steered toward the water, Tatum ran her fingers through the spray. Then she brought her fingers to her mouth and licked the salty residue from her skin. Next to her, Lincoln could barely sit still. If he hadn't been strapped into his seat, Jordan thought he might sprout wings and fly. Tatum's laughter floated on the wind. The sound was more melodic than any music Jordan had ever heard.

Much too soon, their allotted time expired and they had to return the buggy. Using the techniques Dusty had demonstrated, Jordan tacked back against the wind. The move saved them from having to find an alternate mode of transportation back to the shop, where Dusty waited with his hands on his hips and an amiable grin on his face.

"How was it?" he asked.

"Awesome," Tatum said as Lincoln rolled in the sand.

"I think someone wants to go again," Jordan said after Lincoln leaped to his feet and shook himself off.

"I'm here seven days a week," Dusty said, protecting his eyes from flying sand. "Come back and see me any time."

"We will. Thanks," Tatum said. "But this big guy needs a shower first."

"I'll take him." Jordan braced her feet against the wheels of Tatum's chair to keep it from moving as she transferred into it from the buggy. "Are you going to be okay?"

"Yeah, I'm fine. Go."

"Come on, boy."

Jordan jogged toward one of the outdoor showers. She carefully rinsed salt and sand out of Lincoln's fur, only to get soaked when he shook off the excess water before she could dry him off with a towel from her beach bag.

Standing on his hind legs, Lincoln put his front paws on Jordan's stomach and stretched his neck forward as he tried to kiss her face. She leaned down so he could lick her cheek.

"You're welcome. We'll do it again soon, okay? I promise."

He barked once as if to let her know he intended to make sure she kept her word.

"Did you have fun?" Jordan asked after she met up with Tatum on the sidewalk.

"My adrenaline's still pumping even now. That was incredible, Jordan. I can't thank you enough for this."

"You don't have to thank me. Seeing you this excited about something is enough." Jordan knelt in front of Lincoln. "I already know what you think. You had fun, too, right?" He put his paws on her shoulders and gave her face another enthusiastic lick. "Glad to hear it," she said, drying her cheeks with the back of her hand.

"If I buy you an ice cream cone, will you tell me what happened today?"

Jordan felt her smile begin to fade. "Are you trying to bribe me?"

"Whatever works." Tatum drove to an ice cream shop near the north end of the beach and paid for their order. "Okay," she said between licks of her rapidly melting scoop of butter pecan. "Spill."

Jordan dipped her spoon into her cup of French vanilla. "I met Billie today. To say it didn't go well would be an understatement. Grandma Meredith was cool about it—your aunt was, too—but I feel like I let them down."

"Dang. You're harder on yourself than I am. Today couldn't have been that bad."

Jordan nodded emphatically. "Yes, it could. I was trying to help and I ended up making things worse."

"I doubt that. Just tell me what happened."

Jordan took a deep, calming breath. "After I tossed some things in one of Billie's dresser drawers in the trash, she went ballistic and clocked Grandma Meredith in the head with a paperweight. I thought Gran was going to need stitches, but one of the nurses bandaged her up and stopped the bleeding. I still think she's going to end up with a scar, though."

"Let me guess. You raided Billie's stash."

Jordan did a double take. "How did you know?"

"See this?" Tatum showed her a faded scar on the back of her left arm. "When I made the mistake of touching something in that drawer, she stuck a plastic fork in my arm."

"Ouch." Jordan had assumed the wound was war-related, not inflicted by a supposedly helpless old woman.

"It's happened to all of us at least once. Welcome to the sorority."

"Thanks." Jordan laughed for the first time since they'd left the beach. "I don't feel so bad now that I know I'm not the only member."

"You were hesitant to see Billie because you didn't want the real version to be different from the one you'd imagined. Paperweight tossing aside, how was the rest of your visit?"

Jordan thought for a moment. "It was good. I'm glad I went. Even though she's a shell of the woman she once was, I could see why Grandma Meredith raved about her as a leader. Billie would lay her life on the line for the women who reported to her. Her only goal wasn't to make herself look good, but to make them better at their jobs. I can understand why Gran's so upset at the prospect of losing her as a friend. Seeing them together made me envious."

"Why?"

"Because I don't have any friends like that."

Tatum reached across the wrought iron table and grasped Jordan's hand. "You do now." After Jordan laced her fingers around hers, Lincoln reached up and placed a paw on top of their clasped hands, prompting Tatum to amend her statement. "Make that two of them."

CHAPTER FOURTEEN

Meredith sat on the front porch of her rented house and sipped from a glass of sweet tea while Frances Turtledove watered her teeming flower beds in the frontyard of the bungalow next door. Frances's gaudy garden hat looked like a fruit salad on steroids, but it certainly provided ample coverage to protect her pale skin from the sun.

"Your bougainvilleas are gorgeous, Frances. What's your secret?"

"I talk to them every day, water them religiously, and make sure they have plenty of fertilizer."

"Whatever you're doing seems to be doing the trick."

Frances beamed. "Don't say anything to Aaron and Erma, Meredith, but I think I like living next door to you better than I do living next to them. Even if you are a Yankee." She jerked on the garden hose to clear a kink that had slowed the flow of water to a trickle. "Aaron's ears are so big he can hear a dog fart from a mile away. Half the time, Erma acts like butter wouldn't melt in her mouth. And if I have to hear another word about how much money their son the doctor makes or how many houses he owns, I swear I will lose what's left of my mind."

Meredith covered her mouth with her hand to stifle the laughter that threatened to escape. She was sure Aaron and Erma could probably say the same thing about Frances's daughter the lawyer—if they hadn't already.

"Like they say, good fences make good neighbors. What's Marion up to tonight?"

Like Beverly's partner, Mary, Marion Turtledove didn't say much, preferring to let his wife do all the talking.

"That man. Sometimes he makes me want to knock him naked and hide his clothes." Frances jerked the hose again. Out of frustration rather than necessity since, as far as Meredith could tell, the water was flowing just fine. "He grouses so much I'm tempted to book him a room at the Peaceful Manor. If I did, then you could tell him hello for me the next time you pay Billie Daniels a visit."

This time, Meredith let her laughter out instead of trying to keep it inside. When her glass of tea was empty, she rose from her rocking chair. "I'd better check on dinner before I burn the house down. Take care, Frances."

"You, too." Frances waved so enthusiastically one of her floppy garden gloves nearly flew off her hand.

Before Meredith made it to the front door, she saw Natalie's Bronco making its way down the street. She paused to wait for her. "What's in the bag?" she asked after Natalie parked the car and began to walk toward the house.

Natalie held out the package she was carrying. "I was going to bring a bottle of wine, but after the story you told at the potluck about the effect wine has on you, I decided to bring two."

Meredith's cheeks warmed. When she saw what looked like desire in Natalie's eyes, the rest of her body heated up, too. "If I had a dime for every time I heard that, I'd have ten cents."

"At least I'm original."

"You are that." Meredith took the bag out of Natalie's hands. A bottle of red wine and a bottle of white rested inside. "Have a seat while I open one of these and pour us a glass."

"Is there anything I can help you with?"

"Don't even think about it. Dinner's almost ready. Make yourself comfortable. I'll be back in a jiffy."

When Meredith came out of the kitchen with a glass of wine in each hand, Natalie had taken a seat on the slipcovered couch. Despite the chair's comfort, Natalie looked like she felt out of place. She looked like Meredith felt the night she walked into Suzy's. She looked like she wanted to leave. She looked like she wanted to stay. She looked like she wanted to revisit the past. She looked like she wanted to let it lie fallow.

Meredith handed her a glass of white wine and sat across from her. Natalie lifted her glass and downed half its contents in one long swallow. In Vietnam, Natalie had faced machine gun fire and mortar rounds with aplomb, but here, in this setting, she looked scared to death.

Meredith had hoped rekindling their relationship would be easy. Now she realized how difficult a task she faced. Natalie was settled in her life. Settled in her ways. Meredith's visit had obviously prompted Natalie to re-examine both. She didn't look comfortable with the process. Was she willing to take another chance on an idea Meredith had asked her to abandon long ago or had their years apart convinced her that they weren't meant to be?

"Something smells good," Natalie said. "What are we having?"

"Baked salmon, roasted asparagus, and rice pilaf. If we have room left, there's rhubarb pie for dessert."

"You must have gone back to the Bread and Butter. Beverly serves rhubarb pie every Thursday like clockwork."

"I know. I've been there almost daily since the afternoon you introduced me to the place." Meredith patted her middle. "Does it show?"

"Hardly." Natalie's eyes slowly traveled over Meredith's body.

Meredith was wearing yellow Capri pants and a matching sleeveless top. The way Natalie was looking at her, though, she wished she had chosen something more revealing.

"You look as fit and trim in that outfit as you did when all your clothes were Army-issue green. What's your secret?"

"I do an hour of yoga every morning and thirty minutes of Pilates each night. In between, I walk more than I drive and stay as active as I can. I try to eat right, but when I find places like Beverly's where everything on the menu looks good to me but might not be good for me, I occasionally give in to the urge to have one of everything and worry about the consequences later." She looked Natalie up and down, treating her to as thorough as inspection as Natalie had just given her. "The years have been kind to you as well. You used to run laps around us on the base. You look like you could still clock a five-minute mile."

Natalie snorted laughter. "I'm too creaky for that now. Even in my dreams."

"That's funny. In my dreams, you're still eight feet tall and bulletproof. You're still the woman who runs toward danger instead of away from it. You're still my knight in shining armor."

Natalie's gaze was challenging but transparent. Meredith could clearly see the questions in her eyes. If she had been Meredith's knight in shining armor, why hadn't Meredith allowed her to fill the role? Why had she cast George in the part instead? If Natalie had fought harder for Meredith's affections, would it have made a difference? Would Meredith have chosen to follow her heart instead of bowing to the demands of societal pressure? Now that they had a second chance, would the outcome be different this time around?

But Natalie's questions went unasked and, for the moment, remained unanswered.

"One thing you have never been is a damsel in distress," Natalie said. "And I hardly think a confused woman wielding a paperweight constitutes an invading army."

The reminder of the afternoon's events prompted Meredith to stare into the depths of her wine glass as if she were a fortune-teller perusing a set of tea leaves. But she didn't need to be able to predict the future to know what Billie's held.

"She seems weaker to me. When I went back in to see her today, she slept through the rest of my visit. Her outburst this morning felt like a last-ditch effort to win a battle that's all but lost. She's raging against the dying of the light. It's only a matter of time now, isn't it?"

"Unfortunately, yes."

Meredith took a sip of wine for fortification. "I want to be there when it happens. Will you call me when her time draws near? I want to be there for her the way she was for me. For all of us."

"I'll make sure you're notified when she makes the inevitable turn for the worse." Natalie's voice was clinical. As if she'd had entirely too much practice delivering the line to bereaved family members. Then her tone softened. "As a matter of fact, I'll call you myself."

"Day or night?"

"Day or night."

"Thank you."

Meredith was quiet for a moment as she tried to absorb the enormity of the events to come. Events that were bound to take place much sooner than either she or Natalie desired.

"Do you remember when Billie was wounded in Xom Que and she chose to stay with her team rather than cashing in a guaranteed ticket home?" Natalie asked. "She wanted to finish the job she started. Now it's my job to make sure she does it with dignity."

"No," Meredith said, "it's ours. Has she told you what kind of service she would like?"

"She wants to have a small memorial service in Savannah for friends and family. Then she would eventually like to have her ashes scattered at the base of the Wall in DC. She says she left a lot of friends behind when she left Vietnam and she wants to be reunited with them, if only in spirit."

"A fitting final tribute. How would you like to be remembered when it's your time?"

Natalie frowned as if she found the subject distasteful. "That's a rather morbid question, don't you think?"

"It's the kind of question the soldiers used to discuss on an almost daily basis but you never would answer. Why?"

"For the same reason I refused to write my own obituary during a high school English assignment. I was afraid what I said or wrote would actually come to pass. I wanted my life to be beyond the scope of my imagination, not bound by what my fourteen-year-old mind managed to put on paper."

"Has it?"

"Yes. Because when we left Vũng Tàu, I didn't think I'd ever find myself sitting across from you again."

Meredith's heart stopped for a moment. Time seemed to stand still. She was transported back to Vietnam. Back to Vũng Tàu. She could feel Natalie's lips on hers. Caressing. Exploring. Kissing her hello. Kissing her good-bye.

"*I want to be with you,*" Meredith had said that night, "*but I can't. I just can't.*"

She had wanted a family. She had wanted to live a "normal" life without the glare of accusing eyes questioning her choices. And Natalie had let her go. Now Meredith wanted—needed—Natalie to take her back. She didn't know how much time she had left in this life, but she didn't want to waste any more of it playing *what if.* She was ready now. Ready to stop existing and live—truly live for the first time.

A bell dinged in the kitchen, breaking the grip Natalie's eyes held on her.

"Dinner's ready," Meredith said reluctantly. "I hope you're hungry."

Natalie followed her into the kitchen, where they fixed their plates. After they sat at the dining room table, Natalie unfolded her napkin and spread it in her lap. Meredith reached for her hand. They bowed their heads as Meredith asked the blessing.

"Lord, thank you for the food we are about to receive. Thank you for family. And thank you for friends long lost but newly found. For all these things, we pray in your name. Amen."

"Amen," Natalie whispered in a voice choked with emotion. She took a moment to gather herself before she attempted to say anything else. Smoothing her napkin with one hand, she lifted her fork with the other. "I've heard you talk about your granddaughter several times, but you've mentioned your daughter only in passing. Is there a reason for that?"

"Diana and I aren't especially close. We never have been."

"Are you estranged?"

"I wouldn't say that. Our relationship is…complex. We're like opponents in a political debate, saying how much we respect each other on one hand while refuting each other's arguments on the other. The sad part is, no one wins."

"Just like in an actual debate. Has it always been this way?"

"When Diana was born, the nurse placed her in my arms, I looked down at her, and I felt like I was meeting my best friend for the first time. As she began to grow up, it quickly became clear we were more like acquaintances. She was, without doubt, daddy's little girl. She went to George for everything—approval, comfort, reassurance.

I felt extraneous. The more I tried to build a relationship with her, the more she pushed me away."

"Why?"

Meredith pushed what was left of her meal around her plate. "Because she realized very early on I was a fraud."

Natalie arched her eyebrows, wordlessly inviting Meredith to explain what she meant by such a provocative statement.

"When I was younger, all I wanted to be when I grew up was a wife and a mother. You heard me say it more times than either of us could count. I eventually added more goals to the list, but getting married and starting a family seemed like the keys to my happiness. The keys that would lock the door on all the discontent I'd felt ever since I began to suspect I had feelings for other girls. When Diana was born, I had everything I thought I wanted, but it wasn't enough. I didn't want the life most people described as their ideal. I wanted the one I imagined when I danced with you one night in Saigon. I wanted the one you described to me one night in Long Binh. And I wanted to live my life with you. But how was I supposed to do that without hurting George or making Diana feel like she was a mistake?"

"The most admirable quality of a mother's love," Natalie said after a brief pause, "is her willingness to sacrifice anything for her child. In your case, you sacrificed your own happiness to make sure your daughter maintained hers. I always felt like I wasn't enough for you. The way we left things in Vũng Tàu and the fact you didn't reach out to me over the years seemed to confirm that notion. Now I realize you didn't stay away because you didn't want to be with me. You stayed away because you did."

When Natalie took Meredith's hand in hers, Meredith felt the distance between them begin to erode.

"When Jordan was born, I felt like I'd been granted a second chance. We immediately bonded in a way Diana and I never had. Then, when she came out to me and the rest of the family, I was overjoyed. Aside from being happy she had effortlessly come to terms with who she was and what she wanted, I suppose I saw the occasion as an opportunity to live my life vicariously through her. I might not have been able to have the life I wanted, but she could. So far, she's doing just that. She's had a few stumbles and made a few wrong turns along the way, but I think she's learning from her mistakes."

"What about you?" Natalie topped off their glasses of wine without releasing her grip on Meredith's hand. "Have you learned from your mistakes?"

"Which ones?" Meredith spun her glass by its stem. The swirling contents caught the flickering light from the candles lining the table. "There have been so many, I've lost count."

"It sounds like you've been down on yourself all these years because you were afraid you didn't love your daughter enough when the truth is you love her too much."

Meredith grew so still she barely remembered to breathe.

"You're not a terrible mother, Meredith," Natalie said, giving voice to Meredith's greatest fear. "You're the best. Selfless, kind, and generous to a fault."

"How do you know?" Meredith asked tremulously.

"Because I know you."

Meredith's resolve melted. She covered her face with her napkin as heavy sobs wracked her body.

"You've always put everyone else's needs ahead of yours," Natalie said gently. "Isn't it time you came first?"

"I keep telling myself I'm ready to do that. But every time I think about moving forward with my life, I wonder how my family will respond. At first, it was my parents' reaction I was worried about. Then it was my siblings'. Now it's my daughter's. If Jordan didn't respond favorably to hearing I have feelings for you, how do you think Diana will? She always took her father's side on everything. Why would she switch to mine now?"

"Because she loves you. As for Jordan, she loves her grandfather so much, I think she'd have a problem with anyone you said you were interested in—male or female. I just happened to be the lucky one to face her wrath this time."

"This time?" Meredith asked with a disbelieving laugh. "You make it seem like I have a string of persistent suitors lined up outside my door."

"I'm sure you're the hit of the senior center back in Wisconsin."

Meredith dried her eyes with her napkin. "Except for that one night with Evelyn, there hasn't been anyone in my life or my bed since George died."

"By choice or lack thereof?"

"More like lack of interest. I'm not attracted to anyone in my circle of friends, and I'm not willing to set up an online dating profile or whatever it is people are doing these days to meet people. Life's too short to spend it lying about my age, weight, or natural hair color to someone who's probably doing the same to me. What about you? How long has it been for you?"

"I've had my share of experiences over the years, but I haven't been in a relationship, serious or otherwise, in years."

"Why?"

"It's difficult to explain."

"Try."

Even though Meredith was glad Natalie was single, she wanted to know why she had chosen to remain that way.

"During the war, I felt sorry for the expectants because they had to face death without their families by their sides. I couldn't imagine a worse fate and I didn't want it to befall me."

Meredith remembered the soldiers' anguished expressions, their sorrowful cries for the mothers, fathers, brothers, sisters, wives, and children they were leaving behind as they reluctantly made their way out of this world and moved on to the next.

"At some point, I stopped planning for the future and started living for the moment. I wrestle with the fear of ending up old and alone, dependent upon the kindness of strangers to see me through to the end, but I don't want to be a burden on someone I care for. Having a lover watch me suffer would only make my suffering worse. I don't want to see my pain reflected in her eyes." Natalie flinched as if she had just remembered Meredith had lived through the nightmare scenario she had just described. "I'm sorry. George's passing had to have been painful—physically for him and emotionally for you."

"Yes, it was. I wouldn't wish it on anyone. Instead of being weakened by the ordeal, though, I feel strengthened by it. I'm not glad I had to go through it, but I'm glad I made it through. Would you rather miss out on love in order to avoid the hurt?"

"It's a compromise I thought I was willing to make."

"Until?"

"Until there was you. In Saigon, in Long Binh, in Vũng Tàu, and now here. No matter which road I take, it always ends up leading back to you."

Natalie reached across the table with both hands. Meredith reached for her, too. Reached back into the past. Reached toward the future. "Where do you think this road will take us?"

"We could go just around the bend or we could end up driving a country mile. Who knows?" Natalie smiled. The crow's feet around her eyes accentuated their beauty. "Why don't we decide when we get there?"

Meredith brought Natalie's hands to her lips and kissed her fingertips. "Sounds good to me."

CHAPTER FIFTEEN

Jordan was envious. Grandma Meredith and Natalie had had dinner together every night this week. They'd spent their afternoons together, too, sitting with Billie and reading to her from her favorite book.

Grandma Meredith and Papa George had gotten together long before Jordan was born, so she hadn't been able to watch Grandma Meredith fall in love. This time, however, she had a front-row seat. Except she didn't want to be in the audience. She wanted to be on the stage.

She and Brittany were over. She and Hayden had never really gotten started. She was ready to move on. To put herself out there and see what happened. And she wanted to do it with Tatum.

Tatum was smart, funny, honest, and brave. All the qualities Jordan could ask for in a girlfriend. But even though Grandma Meredith tried to convince her that Tatum's paralysis was an obstacle she could overcome, Jordan couldn't see her way around it, past it, or over it.

She could be friends with Tatum. She could sit with her during her dinner breaks at work or stop by her place to help her walk Lincoln when time allowed, but she didn't think they were capable of more.

Sex wasn't the be-all and end-all for her that Brittany had made it out to be, but Jordan couldn't deny its importance. How much mobility did Tatum have? How much sensation? Had she been with anyone since she lost the use of her legs, or was physical intimacy now an impossibility for her?

But she didn't know how to ask those questions without offending Tatum or, even worse, getting her hopes up for something that might not come to pass. Because the fact remained that as much as she enjoyed being with Tatum, she didn't enjoy being seen with her. She hated the looks and stares they received—and she hated herself for letting the looks and stares get to her instead of ignoring them.

Was this how Grandma Meredith felt when she was fighting her feelings for Natalie back in Vietnam? Wanting something—someone—so much but unable to deal with the stigma of being associated with her?

Grandma Meredith had gotten over her fears. Jordan hoped it wouldn't take her forty-seven years to do the same.

She stuck her head in Tatum's office door but backed away when she saw Natalie sitting in front of Tatum's desk. "Sorry. I didn't mean to interrupt."

"Nonsense." Natalie rose from her chair. "I should thank you for preventing me from wearing out my welcome." She turned back to Tatum. "We'll talk later, okay, Tater?"

"Sure thing."

Natalie took a long look at Jordan's outfit and the corners of her mouth lifted into a smile. "How many wishes do I get?"

When Jordan had suggested the employees wear costumes to match the themed rooms, she hadn't planned on getting stuck playing Barbara Eden in *I Dream of Jeannie*.

"Three. And the first two don't count."

"That's okay. I already got the one I wanted. See you later, kid."

"What's up, Jordan?" Tatum asked after Natalie closed the door behind her with a soft click.

"It's almost time for dinner and I need to borrow your menus."

Tatum pulled the dog-eared documents out of her desk and handed them over. "You should make copies so you don't have to ask me for them each time you want to place an order."

"And lose my excuse to see what you're up to in here? Where's the fun in that? I'm in the mood for pizza. How about you?"

"I can't tonight." Lincoln, who had lifted his head at the sound of the "P" word, rested his chin on his paws after he realized he wouldn't be receiving pepperoni samples in thirty minutes or less. "I have a ton of paperwork to get through before the end of my shift." Tatum shuffled the reports on her desk for emphasis. "Maybe next time."

"You said that last night. And the night before that. And the night before that. As a matter of fact," Jordan realized with a start, "you've been saying it for a week now. Are we okay?"

Tatum's smile didn't reach her eyes. "Of course we're okay. Why wouldn't we be?"

"You haven't said more than two words to me today until now. Did I do or say something to piss you off?"

"Why would you think that?"

Jordan felt like an enemy combatant being subjected to interrogation. "How much longer do you intend on answering a question with a question?"

"I'm sorry if you think I'm being a dick, but I don't know what you want me to say."

"Just tell me the truth. It just seems like—I don't know. It seems like you've been holding me at arm's length lately. I miss having dinner with you. I miss spending time with you."

"I miss you, too." The admission seemed to come at a cost. "But I can't do this anymore."

"Do what?" For a brief, absurd moment, Jordan thought she was being fired. But the reality was much, much worse.

"Spend time with you and pretend I don't want to be with you. Look at you and pretend I don't want you. Have you look at me and pretend you see me instead of someone in a wheelchair. Go out in public with you and pretend you don't care what people think when they see us together. Take you to the Beach Music Festival and dance with you, even though I never learned how to shag."

Lincoln came over and butted his head against Jordan's hand. She reached down and gave him the attention he sought, but she never took her eyes off Tatum's face.

"I may be in a wheelchair, but I'm not dead, Jordan. I have feelings. I have emotions. I have desires. I don't know if you're hanging out with me because you like me or because you think you'll get bonus points in heaven for being nice to a cripple."

"That's not what I'm—"

"Wait. Let me finish."

Tatum's voice trembled with rage. Lincoln let out a high-pitched whine and left Jordan's side to stand next to Tatum's. He leaned against her leg, trying to ease her obvious distress. Tatum's hand trembled as she buried her fingers in his thick pelt.

"I was fine until I met you. I had learned to accept all the things I couldn't do and rejoice in the things I could. The moment I saw you, I felt like I was back at square one."

"Tatum—"

"You asked me once if I would do it all again. If I would sacrifice my body for a cause you obviously don't believe in. I would take a thousand bullets for my country, but none of them would hurt even a fraction as much as not being able to do the things I want to do with you. All the things I can't do because this chair—this body—won't let me."

Tatum pounded her fists against her legs in frustration. She might not have been able to feel the blow, but she didn't have to. Jordan felt it for her.

"Stop," Jordan said plaintively. "You're going to hurt yourself."

But Tatum didn't stop. Instead, she struck harder.

"Tatum." Jordan went to her and grabbed her hands. "Please stop."

Tatum struggled to break free, but Jordan held fast, panting from the effort. She used her superior leverage to wrestle Tatum's arms down while Lincoln whined with concern.

"Are you done?" Jordan loosened her grip on Tatum's wrists and knelt in front of her wheelchair. "If you are, it's my turn to talk." She reached up to tuck a stray lock of hair behind Tatum's ear. Tatum tried to lean away from the pressure, but Jordan used both hands to gently but firmly hold her head in place. "Look at me."

Tatum resisted but finally managed to look Jordan in the eye.

"The last thing I would ever want to do is hurt you," Jordan said. "I meant it when I said I miss you, Tatum. I've never had a friend like you. Aside from Grandma Meredith, you're the only person I can talk to about any subject that comes to mind, whether it's silly or serious. I don't want to lose that. I don't want to lose you. Tell me I haven't. Tell me it's not too late."

Jordan didn't know if she instigated the kiss or Tatum did, but the next thing she knew, their lips were pressed together with no space for even a breath between them. Tatum's mouth was tense at first, as if she had been taken by surprise. Then her lips relaxed and melted into Jordan's, searing her with their heat.

Jordan tentatively parted her own lips and traced Tatum's with the tip of her tongue. Tatum groaned deep in her throat. Her tongue darted out and slid across Jordan's. She tasted like strawberries and mint. She tasted like heaven.

As the kiss continued, Tatum slid her hand up the back of Jordan's neck. Her fingers toyed with the loose tendrils of her upswept hair. Jordan shuddered and pulled away long enough to whisper, "Don't stop."

Their lips met again. Jordan felt herself getting lost in the kiss. Getting lost in Tatum. No, that was wrong. She wasn't lost. She had been found. And Tatum had made the discovery.

A quick rap on the door forced them to part. Bud entered the room before Jordan could rise from her knees.

"What's going on in here?" he asked, surveying the scene.

Tatum wiped traces of Jordan's lipstick off her mouth with her thumb while she surreptitiously knocked her pen off her desk with her elbow. "I dropped something and Jordan was helping me find it."

Jordan ducked under the desk. Tatum watched out of the corner of her eye as Jordan hurriedly scrubbed off her smeared lipstick with the heel of her hand.

"What's the matter?" Bud asked. "Doesn't that dog of yours know how to fetch?"

Lincoln barked indignantly at the insult.

"Found it." Jordan brandished the pen and scrambled to her feet. "You should be more careful," she said with a wink. "I might not be around to rescue you next time."

"I will. Thanks."

"I'd better get back to work. I'll leave you to it." Jordan hustled for the door.

"Not so fast," Bud said before she could turn the knob.

Jordan swallowed hard, wondering how much Bud had seen. There weren't any rules banning employees from dating each other.

Otherwise, his and Riley's relationship would be even more illicit than it already was. Despite the dubious precedent Bud had set, she didn't want to lose the respect of her fellow employees by becoming the subject of office gossip.

"How may I help you, Bud?" Tatum asked.

"I didn't come to see you. I came to see her." He spun toward Jordan. "Larry told me I could find you in here. Are you free for dinner? There are some things we need to discuss."

"Such as?"

"I've been talking to some of the guests and they love the new costumes. The staff seems to like them, too. I want to hear what other ideas you have in mind for this place. Let me take you to The Reef. Best seafood on the island. And I'm not just saying that because I have a minor ownership stake in the place. Okay, maybe I am. Either way, dinner's on me. What do you say?"

"Give me a couple minutes to change and I'll meet you in the lobby."

Bud looked disappointed. "If you insist, but what you're wearing looks fine to me."

"Thank you, but this outfit doesn't scream business meeting. That is what you had in mind, right? A business meeting?"

"Yes, of course. Believe me, I already have enough women in my life."

Jordan suspected his wife would say he had one too many. She turned to Tatum. "Larry's scheduled to clock out in a few minutes. Are you going to be okay by yourself?"

"Don't worry about her," Bud said. "She's used to holding down the fort. Aren't you, Tatum?"

"That's me. The last line of defense."

"See? I told you. Let's go."

He tried to steer Jordan toward the door, but she refused to be herded.

"I almost forgot. What kind of beer should I bring tomorrow night?"

"Tomorrow night?" Tatum asked.

"We're still on for dinner, aren't we?"

Tatum frowned. Jordan could practically read her mind. For one thing, they weren't allowed to drink on the job. For another, they were both scheduled to be off tomorrow. Jordan hoped Tatum could guess what she was getting at without forcing her to spell it out for her in front of Bud.

"I'll supply the beer if you man the grill," Jordan said.

"How does eight o'clock sound?"

"Why don't we make it six? We can watch a movie while we wait for the beer to chill. Now tell me. What kind of beer would you like?"

"I don't care as long as it's wet."

"I think I can manage that. See you at six?"

Tatum grinned as she grabbed a Stetson to complete her J.R. Ewing outfit. "It's a date."

CHAPTER SIXTEEN

G ran, will you drop me off at work before you head over to Natalie's?"

"Of course, honey. I'd be happy to."

It was Natalie's turn to make dinner. Meredith checked her makeup in the bathroom mirror before she prepared to go out. Jordan watched her from the open doorway.

"So have you kissed her yet?"

Meredith was so surprised by the question she nearly stabbed herself in the eye with her eyelash curler. "No."

"What are you waiting for? An engraved invitation? The perfect moment? Neither's going to take place without a little help."

When it happened, Meredith wanted it to feel natural. Unhurried. She didn't want to overthink it. But now that Jordan had brought it up, kissing Natalie was all she could think about. She wanted to put their last kiss behind them. Erase the stigma and start fresh.

"I should just do it. Plant one on her as soon as she answers the door tonight. But where's the romance in that?"

She laughed to herself. At herself. Who would have thought she'd be thinking about romance at her age?

Jordan ruffled Meredith's hair. "There may be snow on the roof, but there's still fire in the furnace."

And Meredith's fire was getting hotter every day. She hadn't realized dying embers could hold so much heat.

"If you want some action tonight," Jordan said, "you should undo a few more buttons on your blouse and hike up your skirt at least two more inches. Just my suggestion, but you don't have to listen to me."

"I'm seventy, honey, not seventeen."

But as soon as Jordan's back was turned, Meredith followed her suggestions to the letter. Jordan broke into a grin as soon as she saw her.

"Looking good, Gran. Don't do anything I wouldn't do."

"I'm afraid you're a good thirty or forty years too late for that." As she locked the front door, Meredith noticed Frances and Marion Turtledove sitting on their front porch having their nightly bourbons and branch. "Evening, you two. How goes it?"

Marion raised his drink in greeting. "Evening, Meredith."

Frances leaned forward in her rocking chair. "Going somewhere?"

"I thought I might." Meredith answered the question without giving away too much. She had never sought to publicize her private life, and she wasn't about to start now, no matter how much she wanted to crow about how happy she was. For the past week, her head had been in the clouds and her feet barely touched the ground.

"Nice night for it, whatever you have in mind," Marion said. "Enjoy yourself."

"I intend to." Before she could make it to her car, Natalie showed up in hers. "I thought I was meeting you at your place," she said as Natalie joined her and Jordan in the yard.

"I have something better in mind."

"Such as?"

"I thought we could have a picnic on the beach and watch the sun set. How does that sound?"

"Like I need to change my shoes."

Meredith pointed to her loafer-clad feet. The shoes' leather was so bright it was nearly as blinding as the copper pennies gleaming in the eyelets.

"Yeah, that might be a good idea," Natalie said.

"Here, honey, you take the car."

Meredith gave Jordan the car keys, dashed inside the house, and grabbed a pair of sandals. When she got back outside, Jordan had driven away, but Natalie was waiting for her on the porch.

"Ready to go?" Natalie reached for Meredith's free hand.

"I think we have an audience." Meredith shied away.

Natalie followed her line of sight. Marion and Frances were watching them intently.

"In that case, why don't we give them a show?"

Natalie pulled Meredith into her arms and kissed her. Meredith kissed her back. Kissed her without thinking. Kissed her without remorse. Kissed her without regret. Kissed her without regard for who might be watching.

"Oh, my," she said breathlessly after Natalie let her go. "That was certainly worth the wait. You know what would be even better than a picnic on the beach?"

"No. What?"

"A picnic on the living room floor. We might miss the sunset, but perhaps we could watch the sun rise. How does that sound?"

"Like I need to shut off my truck."

The Bronco's engine was idling, but Meredith's was starting to rev. She felt herself grow wet as she watched desire bloom in Natalie's eyes. Natalie practically ran up the walkway. She switched off the Bronco, grabbed a picnic basket out of the backseat, and rejoined Meredith on the porch.

"Shall we?" Meredith asked.

She offered her hand, inviting Natalie inside. Natalie eagerly heeded her call. Meredith hadn't planned on this. She hadn't planned on any of it. But what was happening was so much better than anything she might have come up with herself.

She heard a loud smack when Frances slapped Marion on his arm. "Why can't you be spontaneous like that?"

"Give me a reason to and I might," Marion said dryly.

Meredith closed the door, shutting out the world and everyone in it. No one else mattered. Nothing else mattered. Nothing except the woman with her and the act of love they were about to perform.

Natalie placed the wicker basket on the coffee table and turned to face her. Meredith regarded the woman who had piqued her interest from the moment they boarded a transport plane bound for Vietnam and who now commanded her full attention.

"Are you nervous?" Natalie asked.

"I'd be lying if I said I wasn't."

Natalie cupped Meredith's face in her hands. "Relax. I don't bite."

"No?" Meredith placed her hands over Natalie's. "Because I'm sure I read on page thirty-seven of the official lesbian how-to manual that you're supposed to."

"You must own the revised version of the manual. Page thirty-seven of my copy says I'm supposed to do this."

She drew her thumb across Meredith's lips, eliciting a gasp. Then she pulled Meredith into her arms and began to hum the Patsy Cline song they had danced to so long ago.

Meredith's eyes misted with tears.

"What's wrong?" Natalie asked, holding her at arm's length.

Meredith shook her head to assure Natalie that everything was all right. "I've never been able to listen to that song without thinking of you. In my heart, it's always been our song."

"And in my heart, you've always belonged to me."

"Care to make it official?"

Natalie placed her fingers under Meredith's chin and tilted her face upward so she could kiss her forehead, her cheeks, and her lips.

"I thought you'd never ask."

CHAPTER SEVENTEEN

These are mine. You'll have to fend for yourself." Jordan held up a six-pack of beer. Each slot in the cardboard container was filled with a different brand, half of them domestic and the other half imported. "I need to drink as much as I possibly can today because I think Grandma Meredith had sex last night."

Tatum backed away from the door. "That is so not what I was expecting to hear you say when you rang the bell."

Jordan went inside and closed the door behind her. "I'm sorry," she said, dropping a bag of DVDs on the coffee table. "Would you like me to try again?"

"Please."

Tatum wheeled to the kitchen to check on the steak and vegetables that were marinating in a plastic container on the counter.

"Okay. Take two." Jordan placed the six-pack on the kitchen counter, twisted the cap off one of the bottles, and took a long swallow. Sweat dampened the fabric of her Wonder Woman T-shirt as if she'd run the two miles from her place instead of driving. Lincoln leaned against her legs, waiting for her to say hello. She reached down and gave him a pat but addressed her comment to Tatum. "I think your aunt deflowered my grandmother."

"Yeah, that's way better." Tatum selected a beer from the container, deposited the rest in the refrigerator, and placed several bamboo skewers in a bowl of water to soak. "How did you come by your information?"

"Let's just say I witnessed the afterglow."

"Meaning?"

"When I got home after my shift, Natalie and Grandma Meredith were eating potato salad and fried chicken. For breakfast."

"People have breakfast for dinner all the time. Maybe Meredith and Aunt Natalie decided to flip the script."

Jordan pursed her lips. "Gran was wearing your aunt's shirt, a great big smile, and not much else."

Her bottle of beer tucked between her thighs, Tatum headed to the living room. "Admittedly, it's been a while, but that definitely sounds like afterglow to me."

"I told you so." Jordan sat on the couch and Lincoln draped himself across her legs like the lap dog he evidently thought he was. His wagging tail thumped against the seat cushion as she scratched him between his ears.

Tatum placed her bottle of beer on a coaster, reached into the bag of DVDs, and took a look at the titles. Jordan had brought a little bit of everything. The movies ranged from a documentary to a romantic comedy to a foreign language art film to an action-heavy Hollywood blockbuster.

"How do you feel about the scene you walked in on this morning?"

"I feel skeevy thinking about Grandma Meredith getting busy with someone. She's seventy, for God's sake. On the other hand, I've never seen her look so happy." Jordan slowly lifted her shoulders in a shrug. "If she's happy, I'm happy."

"Did you tell her that?"

Jordan rolled her eyes. "Uh, no. I figured she and Natalie wanted to be alone, so I went for a walk on the beach. When I got back, they were gone."

"That's right. It's Saturday. Aunt Natalie had to work today."

"And I'm sure Grandma Meredith went with her. They've been like a pair of newlyweds for a week now—joined at the hip and never too far from each other's sight. If they reserve a room at the Remember When to spice things up when their relationship gets stale, you're checking them in, not me."

"I don't see any chance of that happening. I think they prefer to do whatever they're doing in the privacy of their own homes."

"A few months ago, I might have said the same thing. I thought Grandma Meredith was a bit of a prude. Now I wouldn't put it past her to have a sex tape on the market by the end of the year."

"Do you practice the one-liners you come up with or do they happen naturally? Let me check the fridge. I may have some cheese to go with your whine."

"Very funny."

"I thought so, too." Tatum flipped over one of the DVDs to read the synopsis on the back of the box. "I've been meaning to ask. How did your meeting with Bud go?"

"It was interesting."

"How so?"

"He offered me a permanent position."

"Really? Are you going to take it?"

"I told him I'd think about it. I have another year left of school. If I changed my major, that one year could turn into two. I don't know if he'd be willing to wait that long."

"What about you? Could you see yourself living here?"

"For the summer, yes. For the rest of my life? I don't know. Berkeley has me spoiled. I like the hustle and bustle of the big city. The convenience of being able to get whatever I want at any time of the day or night. Being here is like being back in Kenosha. Everyone knows everyone and everything closes at ten o'clock. If I were to move this far south, I'd want to live in Atlanta or Miami."

"What about Savannah? It has big-city appeal in a small-town package. It's a college town, so there's a young, hip vibe, but it's one of the oldest cities in the South so there's history on almost every corner. And hotels are popping up all over to handle the steady stream of tourists."

"I should hire you to be my tour guide. Either that or my guidance counselor." Jordan leaned forward to take a closer look at the DVDs. "What are you in the mood for?"

"This one looks interesting, but it's subtitled and we might wear out the Pause button if I leave to check on something in the kitchen or on the grill."

"What about this one? Have you seen it?"

Jordan picked up the documentary, a film about a group of quadriplegic athletes who played full-contact wheelchair rugby for the US national team. The featured jocks were a bunch of tattooed badasses who played hard on and off the court. Tatum was impaired in only two of her limbs. The guys on the video had issues with all four, but they hadn't let that hold them back.

"I saw it when I was in rehab after my first round of surgery. The doctors and nurses thought it would inspire me. I was supposed to watch it and realize I could still party, have a good time, and live a well-rounded life even though I was in a wheelchair."

"Did it work?"

"I wasn't in the right head space. At the time, I didn't want to sit through anything designed to make me feel better. I didn't want to be inspired. I just wanted to be left alone to brood. Fortunately, the personnel treating me didn't let me have my way. If they had, I would have missed out on a great movie and I'd be even more antisocial than I am now."

"That's a scary thought," Jordan said with a smile. She put down the documentary and picked up another DVD. "What about this one?"

Tatum looked at the cover. The box contained the first season of a cable reality series revolving around four wheelchair-bound women trying to navigate the rocky road of romantic and familial relationships in image-conscious Los Angeles.

"I watched the first episode out of curiosity because I'd read somewhere that one of the women in it had a girlfriend. I watched the rest of the episodes because, even though the woman and her girlfriend broke up a few weeks into the season, the producers managed to get everything right. The frustration, the stares, the pitying looks, the sense of betrayal brought on by a body that can't do all the things it once could. All the bullshit I have to deal with every day was right there on the screen each week. The women on TV have an air of glamour and sophistication I could never hope to achieve, but their struggles were the same as mine." She paused. "I'm sensing a theme here."

"Yeah, I probably couldn't have been more obvious if I'd brought over a bagful of afterschool specials. No life lessons or very special episodes. Got it." Jordan laughed amiably and tossed Tatum another DVD. "Is that more to your liking?"

Tatum looked at the box in her hands. The movie, a romantic comedy, was a funny but touching tale of a woman who falls in love with her female florist as she's walking down the aisle on her wedding day. Jordan had seen it so often she had the dialogue memorized, but the story sucked her in every time.

"Good choice."

Tatum put the DVD in the player and queued up the movie. Jordan moved closer to her after she transferred from her chair to the sofa. Lincoln jumped down to make room. He circled three times and lay at Tatum's feet.

Jordan could feel the heat from Tatum's leg where her thigh pressed against hers. She wished Tatum had worn shorts so she could feel the sensation of skin on skin, but she figured Tatum didn't want her to see her ravaged legs, the withered limbs crisscrossed with scars.

"This is nice."

When the summer began, Jordan didn't have any idea it would play out this way. Now she wondered how it would end. Would she and Tatum get even closer or would her lingering doubts keep them apart?

Tatum draped her arm across the back of the couch as the movie's opening sequence began. Jordan curled into the crook of Tatum's arm and rested her hand on her leg as if it belonged there. As if she belonged here.

"Can I get you another beer?" Tatum asked after the movie ended to the strains of the extremely hummable title track.

Jordan followed her into the kitchen. "No worries. I can get it myself."

"Put the brownies in the oven while you're at it. I thought we could have some for dessert."

"Cool. If you have ice cream, I think I might kiss you."

"Don't say that too loud. I might hold you to it."

The thought made Jordan's stomach do a funny little flip as she tossed their empty beer bottles into the recycle bin. "What temperature should I set the oven for?" Tatum told her and handed her the batter-filled baking dish she had prepared earlier. Jordan set the dish on the counter and pressed some buttons on the control panel to let the oven preheat.

Tatum grabbed the containers she needed, balanced them on her lap, and rolled to the patio to light the grill. After the oven beeped to announce it had reached the desired temperature, Jordan put the brownies in to bake, plucked two bottles of beer out of the refrigerator, and joined her outside.

"Are we going to talk about what happened yesterday," Jordan asked, setting their beers on the patio table, "or are we going to pretend it never happened?" She raised the umbrella over the table and took a seat in one of the well-padded chairs. "I've got news for you: I'm no good at pretending. Especially with you."

"That's good to hear because neither am I." Tatum held a hand over the grill to check the heat. Then she began threading the marinated meat and vegetables onto skewers. "I will readily admit I am attracted to you, but I sometimes doubt the feeling is mutual."

"Whoa." Jordan came halfway out of her chair before settling back into it. "Let me correct that false assumption right now. If you couldn't tell by the way I responded to your kiss yesterday, let me say it loud and clear: I think you're fucking hot."

"But?"

"No buts. I think you're fucking hot." She poked her finger against the table for emphasis.

Tatum placed the prepared skewers on the grill and wiped her hands on the dish towel draped over her shoulder as the meat and vegetables began to sizzle. "Thank you for saying so, but there must be something holding you back. Because if I'm as fucking hot as you say I am, I think you would have tried to jump my bones by now."

Heat rose to Jordan's face, letting Tatum know she had hit on the truth.

"Now do you care to fill in the blank? You're attracted to me, but what?"

Jordan decided to be honest. With Tatum and herself.

"I am attracted to you, but I wonder how far we can go." Jordan paused between each word, unsure if she should keep talking or shut the hell up. Her eyes dropped to Tatum's crotch. "If we were intimate and I touched you there, would you be able to feel it?"

"I've touched myself enough times in the dark of night to know the correct answer's yes. As for the questions you didn't ask, those are trickier to answer. When the time comes—*if* the time comes—would I be able to maneuver my body the way I need to in order to please you? Would there be awkward pauses as I struggle to get my limbs into position? Would I be able to give you an orgasm? And would I be able to feel comfortable enough with myself and the situation to allow you to give me one? Is that what you want to know?"

Jordan tried to speak but couldn't. All she could do was nod. All she could do was feel. Confusion. Curiosity. Desire.

"Since you're asking, yes, I have full sensation in that particular area." Tatum took Jordan's hand in hers and laid it over her heart. "But no matter where you touched me, I'd feel it here. Where it counts."

Jordan looked at her, still at a loss for words. Her lips moved, but no sound came out. How much was she willing to give up in exchange for being in a relationship with Tatum? How much was she willing to miss out on by being with a partner who was disabled? Could she live without shared walks on the beach, bicycles built for two, or slow dances under the stars? Could she live with stares, handicapped stickers, and special accommodations?

She didn't know if she could live with any of those things, but one thing was becoming increasingly clear: she couldn't live without Tatum.

CHAPTER EIGHTEEN

Meredith's skin was warm from the rays of the morning sun streaming through the bedroom window. Natalie propped her head on her upraised right hand and ran the fingertips of her left along the length of Meredith's bare back, exploring the plateaus, rises, and falls of every plain and valley.

A distinct musky perfume hung heavy in the air. The room smelled like sex. Meredith changed positions to get out of the wet spot. How had this happened and why? The how didn't matter. Neither did the why. She hadn't been so in thrall to her hormones since she was a horny teenager. And she was loving every minute of it.

Natalie tossed the top sheet aside and moved her hand lower so she could trace the curve of Meredith's hips. Meredith squirmed and turned to look at her.

"What you're doing is not distracting in the slightest."

Smiling, Natalie kissed the dimples in the small of Meredith's back and covered her with the sheet. She bunched her pillow and stuffed it beneath her to ease the strain on her back as she lay on her stomach.

Meredith's side of the bed—yes, she already thought of it that way—was littered with dozens of old photographs, some in color but most in black-and-white. Helen Cummings had taken them while she covered the war. Though Helen had started out attempting to record the conflict in words, her photographs had eventually become more famous than her dispatches from the front lines. When she had finally retired, she was known more as a photographer than a journalist.

Meredith sifted through the arresting images of soldiers, civilians, and bombed-out towns and villages. Natalie pored through them with her.

"We haven't talked about what might happen when the summer ends, but we could have everything we've ever wanted. And we could have it together. Meredith, will—"

Natalie's cell phone rang, instantly filling Meredith with dread. The phone was Natalie's work number and was meant to be used only in case of an emergency. Natalie reached for it and turned on the speaker.

"Nat, it's Debbie," one of Natalie's co-workers said.

Meredith could hear the fear Debbie was trying to hide.

"What's wrong?"

"It's Billie. When I went in to check on her this morning, she was already awake."

"That's nothing unusual. She's always been an early riser."

"She asked if you were on duty. When I said you weren't, she told me to find you and let you know she was ready. Those were her exact words. 'Tell her I'm ready.' Shortly afterward, she lapsed into a coma. She's been unresponsive ever since. I think you need to get here as soon as you can."

"I'm on my way."

After Natalie ended the call, Meredith climbed out of bed and reached for her clothes.

It was time.

❖

Natalie's voice was giving out. She and Meredith had been taking turns reading to Billie for hours, trying to reach the end of her favorite book before she reached the end of her life.

"Here. Drink this." Meredith handed Natalie a can of lemon-flavored sweet tea from the vending machine in the hall. "I'll take over for a while."

"Thank you," Natalie said gratefully. "I need to walk around for a while. My legs are stiff."

Meredith helped her out of her chair. Natalie moved gingerly as she tried to restore circulation.

"I'll call you if anything changes," Debbie said.

They had been holding vigil since this morning. One by one, all of Billie's friends who lived close by had come by to pay their respects. Billie wasn't from the immediate area—Savannah, her hometown, was nearly a two-hour drive away—but for two years, she had been part of the fabric of the community. She wasn't related by blood, but she was part of the extended family. Tellingly, none of the members of her biological family had deigned to make an appearance. Meredith was glad she could be here in their absence. For Billie's sake as well as her own.

Meredith moved her chair closer to the bed, opened the book to the marked page, and picked up where Natalie had left off.

"Chapter Twenty-six."

She read about Scout Finch, her brother Jem, and their adventures growing up in the fictional sleepy southern town of Maycomb.

"Chapter Twenty-seven."

Natalie came back in the room looking slightly refreshed but still weary. "Did I miss anything?" she asked anxiously as she resumed her seat on the opposite side of the bed.

"No," Debbie said quietly, "she's still here."

"Chapter Twenty-eight."

Meredith took a sip of water before she read about Scout and Jem's fateful encounter with Bob Ewell in the woods on a dark October night.

"Chapter Twenty-nine."

Billie's breathing grew shallow. Meredith could feel herself starting to falter—her voice broke as she read about Scout's first meeting with the reclusive Boo Radley—but she couldn't stop. Not now.

"Chapter Thirty."

Meredith felt tears wet her cheeks as Atticus Finch thanked the shy, misunderstood man who had saved his children's lives. As Natalie began to cry, too, Debbie checked to see if Billie was still breathing.

Meredith looked at the bed. Billie looked peaceful and free from care. She even seemed to have a smile on her face. Natalie came around the bed and stood behind Meredith's chair. She rested her hands on the back of Meredith's neck, kneading the tense, tired muscles.

"Chapter Thirty-one."

When Meredith reached the final page, she couldn't read the last few lines. They had made her cry the first time she'd read the book, they always made her cry whenever she watched the movie, and it was no different now.

"He turned—"

She stopped, unable to go on.

Natalie gently pulled the book from her hands. As Debbie placed her fingers on Billie's wrist to take her pulse, Natalie read about Atticus turning out the light and going into Jem's room, where he would remain all night, and where he would still be when Jem woke up the next morning.

But Billie would never wake again. Because as soon as Natalie read the final words, Debbie nodded solemnly and said, "She's gone."

Meredith placed her hand over Billie's, still warm but much too still. "Rest in peace, my friend. Your war is over now."

CHAPTER NINETEEN

Natalie sat on her back porch staring into space. Dealing with the constant stream of well-wishers had grown tiresome and she needed some time to herself, even if it meant doing absolutely nothing with that time. Jordan couldn't blame her. She'd been the same way when Papa George died. She'd just wanted to be alone. Far away from all the well-meaning visitors asking if she was okay when it was plain to see she was far from it.

Natalie closed her eyes and tilted her face toward the sky, enjoying the warmth of the sun's rays on her skin. Not wanting to startle her, Jordan cleared her throat to announce her presence. "I have something for you."

Natalie opened her eyes and turned to face her. "What?"

Jordan peeked inside the foil-covered dish in her hands. "Looks like turkey tetrazzini. Smells like it, too. A lady with blue hair brought it by."

Natalie reached for the cup of coffee steaming on the side table next to her chair. "That could be anybody."

"What do you want me to do with it?"

With food being the common currency of grief, Natalie and Grandma Meredith were richer than anyone could ever hope to be. Cakes, pies, casseroles, soups, salads, and several barnyards' worth of chicken lined Natalie's kitchen counters. Just as many were piling up at Grandma Meredith's rented house, too.

"I would tell you to stick it in the refrigerator," Natalie said, "but I think the fridge is slap full. I'm going to have to freeze some of this stuff or start giving it away. Otherwise, it's going to spoil."

"You should take some to work with you. I'm sure both the residents and the employees would appreciate it. The rest, you could donate to a homeless shelter. I'll help you pack it up, if you like. Just let me know when you're ready."

"Sounds like a plan to me."

"Cool." Jordan went into the kitchen and returned a few minutes later, minus the turkey tetrazzini. "Where's Gran?"

"Lying down."

"Is she okay?"

"She's fine. Just tired. The past few days have been hard on her. On both of us, really. I'll wake her in plenty of time to get ready for the service."

"Would you like some company?"

Natalie seemed surprised by the request. Jordan couldn't blame her. They had never spent any time together without Grandma Meredith around to act as a buffer.

Natalie removed the remains of the morning paper out of the chair next to hers. "Have a seat."

Jordan settled into the chair and folded her legs underneath her.

"That makes my knees hurt just looking at you. Oh, to be young and flexible. Some days, just being flexible would do." Natalie looked over her shoulder. "Is Tatum with you?"

"No, she said she had some things she needed to take care of before this afternoon. I'll meet up with her later. We're riding to the service together."

"I figured as much." Natalie took another sip of her coffee. "Tatum doesn't take to many people. Neither does Lincoln. Yet they both seem to like you. There's something to be said for that, don't you think?"

"I wouldn't go that far."

"I would. You've been good for her."

"No, she's been good for me."

"Do you love her?"

"What?"

Natalie flashed a lopsided grin. Jordan caught a brief glimpse of the young woman Grandma Meredith had fallen for long ago. "You heard me."

Jordan shifted in her seat. "I like her. A lot."

"That's good to know, but if you do love her, make sure you tell her."

"Yes, ma'am."

Natalie smiled at the example of Southern politesse Jordan had picked up, almost without realizing it. Jordan wondered if she had acquired the accent, too. If she had, her friends at Berkeley—and the ones in Kenosha, for that matter—would never let her hear the end of it.

"Are you hungry? Gran says you haven't been eating. Let me make you a plate."

"That's not necessary."

"Yes, it is. I know you don't feel like eating, but you have to force yourself. When Papa George died, I felt like my world had ended. I didn't eat for three days. My parents cooked all my favorite meals, but nothing appealed to me, not even my dad's world famous spicy pork and egg stew. Normally, I could eat an entire pot of the stuff by myself, but I just pushed it away and asked to be excused. Then I went up to my room and cried."

Natalie looked out into space again. "I've cried so much this week I keep thinking I'll run out of tears at some point. But they just keep coming. I knew this day was coming. I've known it for years. I don't know why I'm taking it quite so hard."

"Instead of mourning solely for someone you've already lost, perhaps you're mourning for someone you hope not to lose again."

"How old are you again?"

A lot older than she was at the start of the summer. That was for sure.

"One day," Jordan said, resuming her story, "Grandma Meredith made a chicken salad sandwich and split it with me. Sitting with her, I knew everything was going to be okay. And it has been. To this day, a chicken salad sandwich is still my favorite comfort food. Would you like one? I'll split it with you."

Natalie reached over and took her hand. "When I met you, I thought you were a moody little brat. But that girl's gone now. A mature, level-headed young woman sits here in her place. You still say some things that make me shake my head in exasperation from time to time, then you turn right around and tie a ribbon around my heart like you're doing now."

Now it was Jordan's turn to cry. She leaned over and kissed Natalie's cheek.

"What was that for?" Natalie asked.

"For making Gran's life complete. None of us realized it, but she was missing something until you came back into her life. Thank you for helping her find it. Thank you for helping her find herself."

Jordan wrapped her arms around Natalie's neck. Natalie returned her hug. "The pleasure was mine."

Grandma Meredith came on the porch rubbing her sleep-reddened eyes. "Am I interrupting something?"

"I was trying to steal Natalie from you, but she's proving resistant to my charms."

"Don't pay any attention to her. You know this younger generation can be trusted only as far as you can throw them."

Jordan gave Natalie another peck on the cheek. Natalie pulled Grandma Meredith into her lap as Jordan made her way to the kitchen.

Unlike Grandma Meredith, Jordan didn't believe in fate or destiny. She believed people made their own luck. Yet she couldn't deny something was at work here. She and Grandma Meredith were meant to be here. Here. Now. For Billie. For Natalie. For Tatum. For each other.

Natalie and Grandma Meredith's voices carried through the screen door. Jordan listened to them talk as she prepared the sandwich.

"What are you doing up?" Natalie asked. "I wasn't planning to wake you for at least another hour."

"I'm afraid Diana beat you to it."

"How?"

"She and Frank are in Savannah."

"They've come all the way from Wisconsin?"

"After Jordan called to tell them Billie passed away, they decided to fly in and show their support. They checked into a hotel near River Street about fifteen minutes ago."

"Wait. Mom and Dad actually came?" Jordan licked mayonnaise off her fingers as she pushed the screen door open with her butt. She handed Natalie a plate containing a sandwich and a handful of carrot sticks. "Whose idea was it, Mom's or Dad's?"

"What does it matter?" Natalie asked. "Their wanting to be here is a good thing, isn't it?"

Jordan frowned. "You don't know my mother. When she wants to, she can be a real—"

"Tough person to live with," Grandma Meredith said quickly.

Jordan reached for her half of the sandwich. "That's one way of putting it."

"Why don't you and your mother get along?" Natalie asked.

"My dad says we're too much alike."

"You don't agree?"

"I think we couldn't be more different. All I know is, nothing I do is ever good enough for her. My clothes, my grades, my friends, and my 'cause of the week.'" Jordan drew air quotes around the hated expression that seemed to come up every time she and her mother had a serious conversation. "She says I flit from cause to cause and person to person like a butterfly looking for the prettiest, most interesting flower."

"Do you?"

"No, I—" Jordan paused to give the question serious thought instead of reflexively responding with her standard denial. "Maybe at one time, but not anymore. I'm more mature now."

"Don't tell me," Natalie said. "Tell her."

Natalie made it sound so much easier than it really was. Every time Jordan tried to refute her mother's arguments, the words got stuck in her throat. "Grandma Meredith, are you going to come out to Mom?" she asked around a mouthful of chicken salad on wheat.

"How's that see-food diet working out for you?" Natalie asked.

Jordan stuck her tongue out at her. Okay, maybe she still had some work to do in the maturity department. But she dutifully swallowed the food in her mouth before she asked Grandma Meredith her next question. "Do you plan to tell her before or after the service?"

"It's a conversation she and I need to have sooner rather than later."

"Whenever you're ready," Natalie said, "I'll be there for you."

"I know." Grandma Meredith grasped Natalie's hand. "You always have been."

"And I always will be."

"I'll be there, too," Jordan said, crunching on a carrot stick. "Because if I know Mom, you're going to need reinforcements. I wonder if Lincoln's available for backup."

❖

Jordan's mouth fell open when she opened the door and saw Tatum wearing her dress blues.

"What do you think?" Tatum asked. "Do I look good enough to pass muster?"

Tatum's black leather shoes were shined to a high polish, her dark uniform coat accentuated her broad shoulders, and the colorful conglomeration of pins and medals on her chest offered tangible evidence of her past achievements. Her hair was drawn into a bun, high enough to remain off her collar but low enough to allow her white cap to sit on her head at the proper angle. Matching white gloves covered her hands. Wheelchair or not, she looked like she belonged on a recruitment poster.

"Damn. It is true what they say about a woman in uniform."

"Hoo rah," Tatum said with a broad grin. "Did Meredith and Aunt Natalie already leave?"

Jordan locked the door and followed Tatum to her car. "Yeah, they left hours ago. They had to take care of some last-minute details and make sure the chapel is set up exactly the way Billie wanted." She tossed her bag in the backseat. When she turned around, Tatum was staring at her. "What?"

"You clean up good."

Jordan had paired heels with a simple black dress. She wore no jewelry except for Papa George's dog tags. When she had looked in the mirror as she was getting dressed, she had noticed the drape of the tags' silver chain over her collarbones perfectly mimicked the waves in her hair.

"Thanks. I could say the same to you." Jordan lingered on the exposed expanse of skin from Tatum's knees to her ankles. She didn't know what she had expected to feel the first time she got a good, long look at Tatum's legs, but she knew it wasn't this. "You look…"

Jordan's hand hovered between them. She longed to touch Tatum—to feel the nap of her uniform and slide her hand under her skirt to feel the heat at the apex of her thighs.

"Different?" Tatum asked.

"I was going to say beautiful."

Tatum shook her head in a gentle admonition. "Marines aren't beautiful. They're—"

"Noble, brave, and strong. I know. You're all those things and more, Tatum Robinson. Because you're also—"

"Fucking hot?"

Jordan grinned. "I couldn't have said it better myself. Wait. I did say it, didn't I?"

"I don't know. You talk so much, it's hard to keep track of everything that comes out of your mouth."

"I would be offended by that if it weren't true. Where's Lincoln?"

"He's having a play date with Boz, the English bulldog who lives on the other side of the complex. Boz's owners always offer to doggysit whenever I have plans. I do the same for them. I see more of Boz than they do of Lincoln, but the arrangement works out well for us. Lincoln pouted when he realized he wasn't going with me today."

"Aw." Jordan pouted, too, when she pictured Lincoln's sad eyes watching Tatum drive off without him.

"Don't worry. By the time I dropped him off at Casey and Mahesh's place, he had forgotten all about me. It's for the best. Chances are he would have gotten restless during the drive. If not there, then definitely at the service."

"You booked a hotel room in town, didn't you? Would you mind if I stayed with you tonight? Natalie and Grandma Meredith are still on their honeymoon. I don't want to horn in on them."

"I don't mind, but you might. Your parents booked a suite. You'd probably be better off staying with them. Doubling with me would be a tight fit. I booked a room with a standard bed. One with a queen or king would have been twice the price."

"I don't mind the close quarters."

In fact, she was kind of looking forward to them.

❖

The service was supposed to be small, but the vestibule was crowded when Jordan and Tatum arrived at the funeral home. Natalie and Grandma Meredith waved to them over the heads of the crowd.

Jordan had hoped a few of Billie's family members would be in attendance, but none seemed to have shown up, even though Billie's obituary in the *Morning News* had clearly stated the date, time, and location of today's memorial service. They hadn't bothered to send flowers, either, but the countless arrangements signed by the many women who had reported to her over the years more than made up for the slight. Even Kerry, who hadn't been able to make the trip from Australia, had made a donation to Billie's favorite charity and forwarded Natalie and Grandma Meredith a touching message that made them alternately hold their sides from laughter and reach for tissues to dry their tears.

Jordan and Tatum moved closer to them. Jordan squeezed Grandma Meredith's arm as she spotted a couple who looked vaguely familiar. "Is that Alice Poythress and Hector Ortiz?" Grandma Meredith's descriptions of them still seemed to fit.

"Yes, it is. They got married some time ago."

"Alice and Hector?" Natalie asked.

"Yes. Didn't you know?"

"How would I? I haven't seen them since Ho Chi Minh City was still known as Saigon."

Hector stood straight and tall, but Alice leaned heavily on an ornately-carved wooden cane that had "Bowed But Not Broken" engraved along its shaft, the phrase an obvious allusion to the life-threatening injuries she had suffered during the war.

Jordan looked around the room. Dozens of the women Natalie and Grandma Meredith had served with and who had served for Billie had turned up to say their final good-byes. She hadn't expected so many to make the trip. One or two, yes. Five at the most. By her count, however, nearly twenty former nurses—each wearing a single white rose in solidarity—had felt the need to be present on this solemn day.

"Thank you for coming," Natalie and Grandma Meredith said to each one they encountered. "Thank you for being here."

When the chapel doors opened, people began to take their seats. Jordan glanced inside as uniformed soldiers from nearby Hunter Army Airfield escorted female mourners down the aisles. A large framed photo of Billie at the start of her career sat on a gold easel on one side of the room. Another photo sat on the other side. The second picture must have been taken shortly before Billie retired, the dark hair in the first photo painted with a liberal smattering of gray. Billie's urn sat between the pictures.

The beginning, the middle, and the end.

One day soon, Natalie and Grandma Meredith would leave the contents of the urn at the base of the Vietnam Memorial. But not today.

Jordan anxiously scanned the sea of faces waiting to stream inside.

"Do you see your parents anywhere?" Tatum asked.

"Not yet." Jordan's breath caught when she saw her mother and father wading through the thinning crowd. "Wait. There they are. Hi, Mom. Hey, Dad," she said, giving each of them a hug. "I'm glad you could make it."

"Well, you didn't give us much choice." Her mother's eyes twinkled as she pinched Jordan's cheek. "You can be rather persuasive when you want to be." She glanced at Tatum, then turned back to Jordan. "Who's this?"

"Mom, Dad, I'd like you to meet Lt. Tatum Robinson. Tatum, my parents, Diana and Frank Gonzalez."

Tatum extended her hand to each in turn. "A pleasure, ma'am. Sir."

"Are you still serving, Tatum?" Jordan's mother asked.

"No, ma'am, I've been medically retired for several years now. Jordan and I work together at the Remember When Inn."

"You're *that* Tatum?" Jordan's mother asked. "Forgive me. I thought you were one of the escorts."

"She is," Jordan said. "She's escorting me."

Jordan steeled herself for the inevitable challenge, but the challenge didn't come. Her mother arched her eyebrows but didn't say anything. Jordan figured she was biding her time. Waiting for the right moment so her words would achieve the maximum effect.

"How long were you in the Marines?" her father asked.

"Five years, sir. I've been retired for three."

"Thank you for your service."

"You're welcome, sir."

"Are you always this polite?" Jordan's mother asked.

"It comes with the uniform, ma'am."

"Are you two…dating?"

Tatum deferred to Jordan. "Yes, we are," Jordan said without hesitation.

Her mother shook her head. "Based on your past history, I never thought you would date a—a—" Jordan stiffened, afraid to hear how her mother planned to finished her sentence. "A Marine."

Jordan nearly laughed with relief. "Me neither." She took her mother's arm as her father and Tatum made small talk. "Come on. I'll take you to Grandma Meredith."

Her mother looked at her as if seeing her for the first time. "All right."

"Grandma Meredith, look who I found."

"Honey, you made it. I'm so glad." Grandma Meredith took Jordan's mother's hand and pulled her closer as she turned back to the quartet of nurses she and Natalie had been talking to. "Ladies, this is my daughter, Diana. Isn't she beautiful?" Grandma Meredith beamed with pride after they murmured their assent.

Jordan's mother's free hand fluttered over her heart. "Jordan, you look so grown up. And, Mother, you look so…happy." She looked back and forth between them. "What have you two been doing this summer?"

Jordan looked at Grandma Meredith and smiled. "We've been making a family."

Grandma Meredith gave Jordan's arm a quick squeeze and beckoned Natalie forward. "Diana, I'd like you to meet someone." She wrapped her arm around Natalie's, laying claim to her for all to see. "This is my friend, Natalie Robinson. Natalie and I served together in Vietnam. Billie was our commanding officer."

Jordan thought she saw a glimmer of recognition in her mother's eyes. "I'm pleased to meet you, Natalie, though it's a pity it had to be under such unfortunate circumstances. My father spoke very fondly of you."

"George talked to you about me?"

"Once or twice near the end."

Jordan's family had held a vigil over Papa George the same way Natalie and Grandma Meredith had done for Billie. Jordan's mother had barely left Papa George's side. Jordan hadn't been fully able to appreciate her mother's devotion. Until now. Now she wondered if her mother's love for Papa George would keep her from being able to accept Grandma Meredith's love for Natalie.

Grandma Meredith's hand crept to the dog tags around her neck. "What did George say?"

"He said Natalie was the best friend he had ever had. Aside from you, of course, Mom. He also said she was the bravest woman he'd ever met. He once said he stole you from her, but I thought it was the morphine talking. I thought he was out of his head. Now I know he was speaking from his heart."

Jordan's mother was already holding Grandma Meredith's hand. She reached for Natalie's too, completing the circle. That's when Jordan saw it. The light in her mother's eyes Grandma Meredith said would appear if Jordan were patient enough to wait for it to happen.

"Dad said you did one of the most courageous things he had ever seen, Natalie. He said you loved my mother enough to let her go, not knowing if she would ever come back. I'm glad she found you. I'm glad you found each other."

"Oh, honey." Grandma Meredith hugged Jordan's mother so hard her mom's eyes bugged out. "I love you, sweetie."

"I love you, too, Mom."

"Did we miss something?" Jordan's father asked as he and Tatum joined the group.

Grandma Meredith and Jordan's mother were too broken up to talk, so Jordan stepped up. "I was just about to invite you and Mom to join us for dinner after the service. My treat. What do you say?"

Her father put his arm around her shoulder and kissed her on the forehead. "You're feeling awfully generous today."

And incredibly loved.

An army officer offered Jordan his arm. "Would you like an escort, ma'am?"

"No, thanks." She rested her hand on the back of Tatum's chair as they made their way inside. "I already have one."

❖

The honor guard assembled outside the open doorway and raised their rifles into position.

"Present arms."

Tatum turned to one of the photos of Billie and lifted her arm to salute.

"Ready. Aim. Fire."

Jordan, her hands wrapped around Tatum's left forearm, flinched as the twenty-one gun salute rang out. Tatum was used to the sound—and the smell of cordite in the air—but she was unaccustomed to both.

"Semper fi," Tatum whispered. Billie wasn't a Marine, but if anyone embodied the phrase "always faithful," she certainly had.

Jordan rested her head on Tatum's shoulder.

"Are you okay?" Tatum asked.

People were starting to leave, but Jordan wasn't ready to go.

"I'm fine." Jordan wiped away a tear. "I just hate funerals. If I had a choice, the only one I'd ever attend is my own."

"Hopefully, that won't happen any time soon." Tatum touched Jordan's cheek, then knuckled away her tears.

"Is this a private party or can anyone join?" Jordan's mother asked. Jordan patted the spot next to her and her mother took a seat. "That was a lovely service."

"Natalie and Grandma Meredith will be happy to hear you say that. They were in charge of the arrangements." Jordan watched them converse with the minister who had presided over the service. "Where would you and Dad like to go for dinner?"

"Someplace that epitomizes Savannah but isn't too touristy and won't cost you a week's salary."

"That certainly narrows down the list," Tatum said. "I'm sure Aunt Natalie can recommend a good local haunt. I'm more of a TV dinner kind of girl myself."

"That's not true," Jordan said. "You can work a pretty mean grill when you set your mind to it." She bumped Tatum's shoulder with her own. "That night was fun. We should do it again sometime. How about next weekend?"

"I think that can be arranged. As long as you let me pick the movies this time."

"Oh, that should be interesting. I feel a John Wayne marathon coming on."

"My dad's the Duke fan. I prefer my action heroes to look more like Angelina Jolie."

"In that case, I cast my vote for *Tomb Raider*. In the tank top and short shorts Angelina wears in that movie, she could give you a run for your money."

"I beg to differ with you, honey," Jordan's mother said. "In that uniform, Tatum beats Angelina hands down." Jordan turned to look at her. "What? You disagree?"

"No." Jordan felt the antipathy from their past battles begin to fade away. Instead of telling her mother how much she had matured, perhaps all she needed to do was show her instead.

Jordan's mother leaned back to take a good, long look at her. Her smile was filled with even more pride than Grandma Meredith's had been when she had introduced Jordan's family to her old Army buddies. "I think I like the new you," her mother said.

"Me, too, Mom. Me, too."

❖

As she dried off after her shower, Jordan was filled with questions about the future. Not her own but Natalie's and Grandma Meredith's. Now that her mother had given them her approval, nothing stood in their way.

"Do you think they'll move in together?" she asked as she got dressed. "I can't picture Natalie living anywhere but the South, which means Gran would have to sell her house and move down here. They could live in Natalie's place or, better yet, pool their resources and buy a house near the water. A big one with plenty of room for guests. Namely me."

"Slow down," Tatum said from the other room. "They just got together and you're already trying to turn them into the Waltons."

Jordan stuck her head out the bathroom door. Tatum was lying in bed with the covers pulled up to her waist and her hands folded behind her head.

"Slow down, did you say? Because they've obviously been moving way too fast all these years. Remind me again. It took them how long to get to this point? Forty-seven years? Yeah, they need to wait another forty-seven before they take the next step."

"Smartass." Tatum took one of the extra pillows off the bed and threw it in Jordan's direction. Jordan let out a yelp and ducked her head inside the bathroom a fraction of a second before the pillow hit the door.

"So that's how you want to play it, huh?"

Jordan dropped the towel she was using to hand-dry her hair, picked up the pillow, and charged the bed. Tatum barely managed to drag herself into a sitting position before Jordan completed her swing. The blow bounced harmlessly off Tatum's shoulder and arm. As did all the others that followed. And there were many before Tatum got a chance to grab a weapon of her own.

Jordan's giggles grew higher in pitch when Tatum finally joined the fray. Tatum started laughing, too, as the emotions of the day left their bodies in a delirious rush. Jordan hadn't been in a good pillow fight in ages. Tatum was a worthy opponent, and her superior upper body strength gradually began to give her the upper hand.

Jordan straddled Tatum's legs and held up an arm to ward off another blow. "Okay, okay," she said, out of breath from laughter and the aftereffects of the pitched battle. "I give."

Tatum lay back, looking as spent as Jordan felt. The sheet and comforter had slid down to Tatum's shins, but they were pinned under Jordan's feet. Displaying none of the self-consciousness Jordan had witnessed when they'd met, Tatum left her legs exposed instead of trying to cover them.

In contrast to Jordan's tight tank top and boy shorts, Tatum was wearing a T-shirt and loose-fitting boxers. She rested her hands on the tops of Jordan's thighs after Jordan settled into her lap.

"Am I hurting you?" Jordan asked.

"No."

"But you can feel this, can't you?"

Jordan pushed Tatum's T-shirt up a few inches and grazed her fingertips over Tatum's washboard stomach.

"Yes, I can feel you."

"What about this?"

Jordan trailed her fingers up Tatum's arms, pausing to trace the scar marking the exit wound on Tatum's shoulder before she reversed her course.

"Yes," Tatum hissed as her nipples tented the fabric of her T-shirt, "I can feel you. Can you feel me?"

Jordan nodded as Tatum's thumbs slid along her inner thighs. She leaned forward, her still-wet hair dripping in Tatum's face. Tatum blinked as raspberry-scented water droplets splashed on her cheeks.

"Is that your cunning plan," Tatum asked hoarsely, "to call a truce, then subject me to the Chinese water torture?"

"No. I don't want to torture you. I want to—" Jordan pushed Tatum's hair out of her eyes. She needed to be honest with Tatum. She needed to be honest with herself. "I think I'm a little bit in love with you, Tatum."

"Just a little bit?"

Jordan's heart jackhammered in her chest. She had never felt so uncertain about what she was doing but so sure about what she wanted. "Okay, maybe a lot."

"Good. I was beginning to think it was just me."

"So you're in love with you, too?"

"No, smartass, I'm in love with you." Tatum cupped her palm against Jordan's cheek. "The question is, what do we do about it? You're leaving in a few weeks, aren't you?"

"Yes, but today's not that day. And just because I'm leaving doesn't mean I won't be coming back. So why don't we start by doing this?"

Jordan slowly pulled her tank top over her head and dropped it on the floor. Then she took Tatum's hands in hers and placed them against her belly. Tatum grazed the back of her hand against Jordan's stomach. The sensation was exquisite. Rough and smooth at the same time. Jordan gasped as her muscles began to contract. Tatum looked up, seemingly enthralled by Jordan's reaction to her touch.

"Are you sure you want to do this?" Tatum asked.

Jordan's response wasn't verbal but physical. She kissed Tatum so soundly she felt the heat permeate her entire body. She slid her tongue into Tatum's mouth at the same time she slipped her hands under Tatum's T-shirt. Tatum arched her back as Jordan's hands moved higher. Jordan's hands found Tatum's breasts, her fingers teasing the hard points of her nipples. Tatum groaned into her mouth.

When Jordan finally pulled away, Tatum's eyes were wide, wild with desire. Jordan felt the same emotion building inside her as Tatum gazed up at her.

"What do you want, Jordan? A summer fling or—"

Jordan silenced her by placing her fingers over her lips. "I want you, Tatum. I want to work with you. I want to come home to you. I want to make a life with you." She placed her hand over Tatum's heart. "And I want to touch you where it counts."

Tatum pulled Jordan to her and cradled her in her arms. Arms Jordan never planned to leave.

"Baby, you already have."

EPILOGUE

The Beach Music Festival was well underway. The music provided by the colorfully attired band competed with the sound of the crashing waves, but none of the festivalgoers seemed to care. Meredith sure didn't. Natalie didn't seem to, either. Natalie spun Meredith in a circle and drew her into her arms. The last time—the only time—they had danced together was in a bar in Saigon nearly half a lifetime ago. Then they had been hidden away from the world. Now their love was on display for all the world to see. Instead of shrinking from the attention, Meredith basked in it.

When the up-tempo song ended, the band switched to something slower. "For all the lovers in the house," the lead singer said.

"I think he means us," Meredith said with a wink.

"I think so, too." Natalie rested her hands on Meredith's waist while Meredith locked her arms around her neck. "What's with the big smile? You look like the Cheshire Cat."

Meredith nodded toward the edge of the crowded dance floor, where Tatum and Jordan were talking with Diana and several employees from the hotel while Frank played fetch with Lincoln. Smiles, laughter, and happy barks abounded.

Meredith didn't know what the future held for Jordan and Tatum, but, in her heart, she knew they would face it together. They all would.

She took in the faces of her expanded family. Her family of blood. Her family of choice. All bound by love.

"We have a beautiful brood, don't we?"

"Yes, we do," Natalie said.

Meredith kissed her in the rosy glow of the setting sun, content in the knowledge that this kiss wouldn't be the last.

"I love you, my darling," Meredith said.

"I love you, too." Natalie held her tight. "Thank you for making this worth the wait."

About the Author

Yolanda Wallace is not a professional writer, but she plays one in her spare time. Her love of travel and adventure has helped her pen the globe-spanning novels *In Medias Res*, *Rum Spring*, *Lucky Loser*, the Lambda Award-winning *Month of Sundays*, and *Murphy's Law*. Her short stories have appeared in multiple anthologies including *Romantic Interludes 2: Secrets* and *Women of the Dark Streets*. She and her partner live in beautiful coastal Georgia, where they are parents to four children of the four-legged variety—a boxer and three cats.

Books Available From Bold Strokes Books

Kiss The Girl by Melissa Brayden. Sleeping with the enemy has never been so complicated. Brooklyn Campbell and Jessica Lennox face off in love and advertising in fast-paced New York City. (978-1-62639-071-3)

Taking Fire: A First Responders Novel by Radclyffe. Hunted by extremists and under siege by nature's most virulent weapons, Navy medic Max de Milles and Red Cross worker Rachel Winslow join forces to survive and discover something far more lasting. (978-1-62639-072-0)

First Tango in Paris by Shelley Thrasher. When French law student Eva Laroche meets American call girl Brigitte Green in 1970s Paris, they have no idea how their pasts and futures will intersect. (978-1-62639-073-7)

The War Within by Yolanda Wallace. Army nurse Meredith Moser went to Vietnam in 1967 looking to help those in need; she didn't expect to meet the love of her life along the way. (978-1-62639-074-4)

Escapades by MJ Williamz. Two women, afraid to love again, must overcome their fears to find the happiness that awaits them. (978-1-62639-182-6)

Desire at Dawn by Fiona Zedde. For Kylie, love had always come armed with sharp teeth and claws. But with the human, Olivia, she bares her vampire heart for the very first time, sharing passion, lust, and a tenderness she'd never dared dream of before. (978-1-62639-064-5)

Visions by Larkin Rose. Sometimes the mysteries of love reveal themselves when you least expect it. Other times they hide behind a black satin mask. Can Paige unveil her masked stranger this time? (978-1-62639-065-2)

All In by Nell Stark. Internet poker champion Annie Navarro loses everything when the Feds shut down online gambling, and she turns to experienced casino host Vesper Blake for advice—but can Nova convince Vesper to take a gamble on romance? (978-1-62639-066-9)

Vermilion Justice by Sheri Lewis Wohl. What's a vampire to do when Dracula is no longer just a character in a novel? (978-1-62639-067-6)

Switchblade by Carsen Taite. Lines were meant to be crossed. Third in the Luca Bennett Bounty Hunter Series. (978-1-62639-058-4)

Nightingale by Andrea Bramhall. Culture, faith, and duty conspire to tear two young lovers apart, yet fate seems to have different plans for them both. (978-1-62639-059-1)

No Boundaries by Donna K. Ford. A chance meeting and a nightmare from the past threaten more than Andi Massey's solitude as she and Gwen Palmer struggle to understand the complexity of love without boundaries. (978-1-62639-060-7)

Timeless by Rachel Spangler. When Stevie Geller returns to her hometown, will she do things differently the second time around or will she be in such a hurry to leave her past that she misses out on a better future? (978-1-62639-050-8)

Second to None by L.T. Marie. Can a physical therapist and a custom motorcycle designer conquer their pasts and build a future with one another? (978-1-62639-051-5)

Seneca Falls by Jesse Thoma. Together, two women discover love truly can conquer all evil. (978-1-62639-052-2)

A Kingdom Lost by Barbara Ann Wright. Without knowing each other's fates, Princess Katya and her consort Starbride seek to reclaim their kingdom from the magic-wielding madman who seized the throne and is murdering their people. (978-1-62639-053-9)

Season of the Wolf by Robin Summers. Two women running from their pasts are thrust together by an unimaginable evil. Can they overcome the horrors that haunt them in time to save each other? (978-1-62639-043-0)

The Heat of Angels by Lisa Girolami. Fires burn in more than one place in Los Angeles. (978-1-62639-042-3)

Desperate Measures by P. J. Trebelhorn. Homicide detective Kay Griffith and contractor Brenda Jansen meet amidst turmoil neither of them is aware of until murder suspect Tommy Rayne makes his move to exact revenge on Kay. (978-1-62639-044-7)

The Magic Hunt by L.L. Raand. With her Pack being hunted by human extremists and beset by enemies masquerading as friends, can Sylvan protect them and her mate, or will she succumb to the feral rage that threatens to turn her rogue, destroying them all? A Midnight Hunters novel. (978-1-62639-045-4)

Wingspan by Karis Walsh. Wildlife biologist Bailey Chase is content to live at the wild bird sanctuary she has created on Washington's Olympic Peninsula until she is lured beyond the safety of isolation by architect Kendall Pearson. (978-1-60282-983-1)

Windigo Thrall by Cate Culpepper. Six women trapped in a mountain cabin by a blizzard, stalked by an ancient cannibal demon bent on stealing their sanity—and their lives. (978-1-60282-950-3)

The Blush Factor by Gun Brooke. Ice-cold business tycoon Eleanor Ashcroft only cares about the three Ps—Power, Profit, and Prosperity—until young Addison Garr makes her doubt both that and the state of her frostbitten heart. (978-1-60282-985-5)

Slash and Burn by Valerie Bronwen. The murder of a roundly despised author at an LGBT writers' conference in New Orleans turns Winter Lovelace's relaxing weekend hobnobbing with her peers into a nightmare of suspense—especially when her ex turns up. (978-1-60282-986-2)

The Quickening: A Sisters of Spirits novel by Yvonne Heidt. Ghosts, visions, and demons are all in a day's work for Tiffany. But when Kat asks for help on a serial killer case, life takes on another dimension altogether. (978-1-60282-975-6)

Smoke and Fire by Julie Cannon. Oil and water, passion and desire, a combustible combination. Can two women fight the fire that draws them together and threatens to keep them apart? (978-1-60282-977-0)

Love and Devotion by Jove Belle. KC Hall trips her way through life, stumbling into an affair with a married bombshell twice her age. Thankfully, her best friend, Emma Reynolds, is there to show her the true meaning of Love and Devotion. (978-1-60282-965-7)

The Shoal of Time by J.M. Redmann. It sounded too easy. Micky Knight is reluctant to take the case because the easy ones often turn into the hard ones, and the hard ones turn into the dangerous ones. In this one, easy turns hard without warning. (978-1-60282-967-1)

In Between by Jane Hoppen. At the age of fourteen, Sophie Schmidt discovers that she was born an intersexual baby and sets off on a journey to find her place in a world that denies her true existence. (978-1-60282-968-8)

Under Her Spell by Maggie Morton. The magic of love brought Terra and Athene together, but now a magical quest stands between them—a quest for Athene's hand in marriage. Will their passion keep them together, or will stronger magic tear them apart? (978-1-60282-973-2)

Rush by Carsen Taite. Murder, secrets, and romance combine to create the ultimate rush. (978-1-60282-966-4)

Homestead by Radclyffe. R. Clayton Sutter figures getting NorthAm Fuel's newest refinery operational on a rolling tract of land in upstate New York should take a month or two, but then, she hadn't counted on local resistance in the form of vandalism, petitions, and one furious farmer named Tess Rogers. (978-1-60282-956-5)

Battle of Forces: Sera Toujours by Ali Vali. Kendal and Piper return to New Orleans to start the rest of eternity together, but the return of an old enemy makes their peaceful reunion short-lived, especially when they join forces with the new queen of the vampires. (978-1-60282-957-2)

How Sweet It Is by Melissa Brayden. Some things are better than chocolate. Molly O'Brien enjoys her quiet life running the bakeshop in a small town. When the beautiful Jordan Tuscana returns home, Molly can't deny the attraction—or the stirrings of something more. (978-1-60282-958-9)